P9-BBO-699

THE
DISPLACEMENTS

ALSO BY BRUCE HOLSINGER

The Gifted School
The Invention of Fire
A Burnable Book

THE DISPLACEMENTS

BRUCE
HOLSINGER

RIVERHEAD BOOKS

NEW YORK

2022

RIVERHEAD BOOKS
An imprint of Penguin Random House LLC
penguinrandomhouse.com

Copyright © 2022 by Bruce Holsinger
Penguin Random House supports copyright. Copyright fuels creativity,
encourages diverse voices, promotes free speech, and creates a vibrant culture.
Thank you for buying an authorized edition of this book and for complying with
copyright laws by not reproducing, scanning, or distributing any part of it in any
form without permission. You are supporting writers and allowing Penguin
Random House to continue to publish books for every reader.

Riverhead and the R colophon are registered trademarks of Penguin Random House LLC.

LIBRARY OF CONGRESS CATALOGING-IN-PUBLICATION DATA
Names: Holsinger, Bruce W., author.
Title: The Displacements / Bruce Holsinger.
Description: New York : Riverhead Books, 2022.
Identifiers: LCCN 2022008958 (print) | LCCN 2022008959 (ebook) | ISBN 9780593189719
(hardcover) | ISBN 9780593542170 (international edition) | ISBN 9780593189733 (ebook)
Classification: LCC PS3608.O49435658 D57 2022 (print) | LCC PS3608.O49435658 (ebook) |
DDC 813/.6–dc23
LC record available at https://lccn.loc.gov/2022008958
LC ebook record available at https://lccn.loc.gov/2022008959

Printed in the United States of America
1st Printing

BOOK DESIGN BY LUCIA BERNARD
Maps by Jeffrey Ward

This is a work of fiction. Names, characters, places, and incidents either are the product
of the author's imagination or are used fictitiously, and any resemblance to actual persons,
living or dead, businesses, companies, events, or locales is entirely coincidental.

For Campbell and Malcolm

And sometimes a dust storm would stand off in the desert, towering so high it was like another city—a terrifying new era approaching, blurring our dreams.

—Denis Johnson, "Beverly Home"

THE
DISPLACEMENTS

Hamid has a flashlight. Mia doesn't, so she pounds along after him, panting up Avenue Q2 and dodging left as her squad gathers for the next attack. The new tents have gone up over the last four days. Hundreds, maybe a thousand. Dozens of new streets named in fluorescent signs at the crossings. Perfect for the game.

Mia lost her flashlight last week so now she can't be a leaper, because you have to have a flashlight to be a leaper and you have to be a leaper before you can be a guide. Mia isn't fast enough to be a guide and besides she doesn't like to fight. But she's quick, slippery, smart, knows the cleverest tricks, the best places to hide.

Plus she's okay with being a scout. Even noobs can be Demigod someday, and you don't have to be a leaper or even a guide to be Demigod. The rules say you can elevate straight from noob if you find the Link—which no one, not even a guide, ever has.

The game is Range. They play it every night when the sun goes down. Ask any of the eight thousandish grown-ups in Tooley Farm about the rules of Range and you'll get rolled eyes and snorts, worried frowns from the parents who disapprove, like that lady Barb who stood at open mic last week and barked through a whiny speaker: "So I'm asking FEMA or the Red Cross or whoever runs this place to stop this Range silliness. I mean, have you watched them? Has anyone really really *watched* them? It's like *Lord of the Flies* out there. Who even knows what the *rules* are, for Pete's sake?"

The kids. The kids know the rules.

You learn about Range within your first hours off the bus, whispers from boys in the pavilions or girls in the potty lines. After fourth dinner shift, as dusk comes on, the kids start bugging their parents for permission to go play Range. The parents are too tired or drunk or suicidal to say no, or even ask questions. If you're a new kid, you get a quick orientation in the quadrant HQ, then your ritual, then you're in.

Mia remembers her first Range like it was yesterday, slashing with Luz through the outer reaches of the shelter, wild order in the night, friended like she's never been.

She would do anything for Crow Squad.

They squat between tents, huddled on the mulch. Bear Squad has the next street. Their guide is Louanne, a tall girl with a buzz cut because of lice and skin the color of instant camp milk. She's sending her noobs and scouts out like ants to colonize the surrounding streets. It's up to the Crows to keep them from spreading too far.

The squad peer down onto the next row of tents when they see their target: a noob from Bear, small and brown skinned and wearing a Miami Dolphins jersey that goes down to his feet. He can't be more than five, Mia guesses, but he's strutting along with his shoulders back and his tummy out like he's already a leaper or something. He risks a few steps into the gap between the tents, scoping out the enemy.

"Brave little dude," someone whispers.

"Shut up," Hamid hisses.

Moonlight shears through a cloud and casts the boy's shadow across the middle of Avenue Q3. He reaches up and grabs a tent flap and shakes until the plastic shimmers like a sheet of aluminum foil. He giggles, clueless.

Hamid spreads his fingers. Mia's muscles tense. Luz grasps her right arm. Mia grabs back, pressing the damp heat of her friend's skin.

Five . . . four . . . three . . .

She leans forward on the balls of her feet, tugging at her IDP bracelet.

. . . two . . .

SQUEEEEEEEEEE

From the barn a megaphone wails: "Hey, kids! The popsicles are here!"

The target skips off, clapping. Dozens of kids swarm out from between the tents.

"Screw it." Hamid frowns in the red of a flashlight cone. A new kid asks what flavors they have; another asks if there's ever ice cream. Whoops and hollers from the sprinting squads. The Crows wait a few more seconds until finally Hamid clicks off his flashlight. "Fine," he says, sounding like Mia's little brother Oliver, a scout in Elephant Squad.

Down by Pav4, a pickup truck idles with two coolers on its open tailgate. A FEMA lady distributes popsicles one by one. The line snakes all the way up to Idaho Street.

Oliver walks by and sticks out his tongue at Mia. Her shoulders sag when she sees what's in his hand: a cheap non–Whole Foods kind of popsicle, fifty to a box. She chooses lime green, Luz chooses red, and they suck on their spikes of frozen high-fructose corn syrup while everybody stands around waiting to hear if tonight's game will keep going or not. The guides are about to make a decision when headlights flash from above the Square.

Vehicles come and go during the day though usually not at night. Plus it's not a car or a truck coming through Main Gate but a bus, with another right behind it, and another—

"Whoa," Luz says, turning to face the caravan.

A kid nearby starts to count. "One . . . two . . . three . . ."

Others join him.

"Four . . . five . . . six . . . seven . . ."

Soon every Range player is counting buses.

"Fourteen . . . fifteen . . . sixteen . . . seventeen . . . eighteen . . . nineteen . . . twenty."

Twenty buses.

Mia does a quick calculation. The coach her family took from Florida had fifty-five passengers. Fifty-five times twenty equals 1,100. Which means over a thousand new IDPs in a single night. Which also means more meal shifts. Longer lines for absolutely everything. The toilets fuller and more disgusting.

"So much for Range," someone murmurs.

What?

The notion spreads in whispers and groans and swear words. Mia gets a wrenching pain around her heart. For days the new tents have stood empty and now it's impossible to imagine Range without those rows and columns of empty dwellings. Crow Squad has a whole head-quarters set up in a tent on Arizona Street and the thought of some new family taking it over is just—

"Where are they even from?" Luz wants to know.

"Houston, I bet," Hamid says, his voice thick with loss and hate. Mia feels it, too, a throb of enmity toward these outsiders, these thieves, these new ones already ruining it all.

PART
ONE

1.

Shortly after sunrise, a squall off the Gambian coast joins a rank of thunderheads crowning miles into the stratosphere. Dueling systems, two storms converging where the Canary Current dips to meet the Atlantic North Equatorial. A play of lightning and sheeting rain roils the ocean waters. Whitecaps foam the crests of waves.

Late the same morning, from the south and the scattered islands of the Bijagós archipelago, another storm edges in. Lower, more tempestuous in its churnings. The third system carries warmer waters beneath its front. The storms mingle and convect, a cycling dance of sea, sky, and rain.

Hundreds of miles to the south-southeast, the father-son crew of a fishing charter off Cape Verde help a banker from Lisbon struggle a blue marlin to the deck. Once the fish is stowed in ice below, the three clients arrange themselves along the gunwales, swilling coffee from foam cups while the craft rides the swells.

Without warning, a heavy gust sweeps the deck, whisking cups into the sea, slamming one of the men against the superstructure. The other two clients share a good laugh at their companion's expense.

The captain and his son trade looks. A subtle wag of the father's beard. When you've fished the countercurrents for going on thirty years you know a thing when you smell it. The pressure rises in your bones and bends the invisible air. Even the son knows what this new sea means.

Another hour, two at most, then it's all out for São Vicente. The Lisboans will not be pleased.

The gathering storms fuse and collide. For hours the system remains loose, a disturbance in the Atlantic weather pattern.

Deep within a high cloud there is a shift in the convection flow and a modification in vertical temperature variation. The system organizes the warms, rallies the winds, until, as one, the three storms accelerate and spin.

A slow cyclonic spiral 108 nautical miles north of the equator. The rotation is counterclockwise. By 4:00 p.m. Gambian time, the satellites have captured enough data to effect a change in status. The system upgrades to a tropical depression, drawing more eyes to weather screens in the Caribbean islands, along the eastern seaboards of the Americas.

Five hours later, the depression has matured into a tropical storm. She spins and strengthens until she is hale enough to earn a name.

She is Luna.

2.

She spins and pedals and turns the clay mound until a cylinder rises in her hands. With four fingers in the mouth and a sponge on the shoulder she lightens the walls, creating form. The glaze will be an aquamarine, one of twelve shades Daphne and her Key West client have selected for the installation, a spectrum of blue-green hues inspired by the client's love of the Caribbean Sea. Six finished vessels already line a shelf and gather the sunlight brimming off the lagoon. Today Daphne has been working on the seventh, but each time she pulls, something goes wrong. Too much water, a flinch of the hand. Some unseen flaw in the clay.

She pinches along the neck ring so the mouth floats above the body, creating a slight pressure with only her pinkie engaged, to the edge of what the thickness can withstand. The wall thins, goes thinner still—

Too much, and the neck collapses into the base. She rams the sponge down through the upper walls until a shapeless lump sits on the bat. She pulls it off and slams it into the reclaim bin.

Cricket, alarmed, cranes up from her bed. "It's okay, girl." The beagle mutt lowers her patchy head, brown eyes moist with concern.

Daphne stretches on her stool and breathes in the earthy air of her studio, a high-ceilinged room flooded with light from windows on two sides, so different from the old converted garage back in Ann Arbor, where she belonged to a co-op and relied on a collective kiln. Here she has her own high-end Paragon, a guilt gift from Brantley after the move. Built-in shelves along the walls display her work, over a hundred figures in ceramic and porcelain, many shipped from Michigan, others crafted here in Miami. *Sentinel* stands at the highest point with her floating tendrils and her many eyes, looking down on it all.

There are years of labor in this studio, countless hours at wheel and workbench. Daphne could sell every piece if she wanted to. But Pilar Guerra, the Miami Beach gallerist who represents her, likes to hold back stock to keep potential buyers hungry. Daphne's most important pieces are already out at Gallery 25 on South Beach, installed in advance of next week's opening. Hybrid beasts of sea and air, delicate fantastical creatures that make even her newest vessels appear weighty and dense. For two years her art has been building toward this moment—which makes this sudden dry spell all the more jarring. There have been other stale periods, though nothing like this summer.

No mystery why. Bedsprings creak from upstairs, plucking her nerves as if connected by some invisible filament to the tendons in her neck. Now a parade of stomps into the bathroom where her stepson pees a stallion-worthy bucketful, slams the lid, and thumps back into his lair to collapse on his bed. His bass amp powers on and the thudding reverb rattles Daphne's sculptures like the percussive ring of a bomb.

The suite on the second floor was supposed to stay unoccupied, reserved for occasional visitors. Instead, Gavin has colonized the space since moving back home in March, nested like a buzzard up there. She imagines him rolling over to check his phone, fast-forwarding through stale episodes of *Survivor*.

A puff of plaster dust loosens from the acre of drywall. A five-thousand-square-foot house and yet every thump of the kids' feet pounds through the floors, every flushworth of waste rattles the drainpipes. You'd think the architect might have anticipated a soundproofing issue, that Brantley might have lavished as much attention on noise-reduction technology as he did on the Miele convection range in the kitchen, or the LG Signature washer-dryer sets in both laundry rooms, or the "tropical landscape package" installed around the yard.

The wall clock reads 3:12. Oliver's eighth birthday party starts in less than two hours. After a few minutes cleaning her equipment, Daphne hangs her smock and trudges into the kitchen, where the party list sits on the counter, staring her down.

"Alexa, start the Odyssey," she says, so the minivan will be cool when she leaves. The AI burbles and chimes.

The X factor is the cake. She glances again at the ceiling, trying to decide whether her immediate need is worth another skirmish. Bracing herself, she climbs the stairs and knocks.

"Yeah?" No hitch in the bass rhythm.

The door opens to a waft of late adolescence. Stale laundry, old pizza, open luggage half-unpacked, and, in the middle of it all, Gavin, huddled against a bed pillow two-fingering his bass, with an open laptop and an iPad at his feet, phone by his knee. Behind him rises a floor-to-ceiling bookcase stuffed with volumes he once devoured at the rate of three or four a week. These days her stepson reads on his phone, if he reads at all.

"Hi, sweetie," she says brightly.

"Heya." Two flat syllables from behind the curtain of hair. Cricket noses in, jumps on the bed.

"You busy right now?"

He looks around blankly as the dog nudges at his free hand.

"I need you to run to Beachery Bakes and pick up the birthday cake. Make sure they've put Oliver's name on it with the soccer decorations. Can you do all that?"

Wrong question. She winces.

"I don't know, Daphne." Sarcasm thickens his voice. "I mean, I'm a Stanford dropout and this task sounds almost Byzantine in its complexity."

"I'm sorry, I meant—"

"I'll take care of it. Anything else?"

"Actually . . ." She glances at her phone. "Would you mind grabbing Mia from gymnastics?"

"I can manage that."

"Thanks so much, Gavin, I really appreciate—" He thwacks the strings, ending it.

Once in the Odyssey she lets herself sit for a moment in the frigid air. As her fingers trace circles on her temples she orders the van to drive to Whole Foods, the sound system to play NPR. The minivan floats through the winding streets of Pineapple Isles, these man-made inlets on the western shore of Biscayne Bay.

. . . a third intifada made more likely by the day . . .

. . . that the unemployment rate may remain above 8 percent, signaling a deepening of the recession . . .

. . . which formed late Thursday night off the western coast of Africa, and is now tracking west-northwest toward . . .

Too much. She touches off the sound. The bay a shimmering flatness, knife-stripe of sun across a perfect blue. Daphne lets the silence carry her on, and remind her how to breathe.

3.

Cricket rolls onto her back with her paws in the air, pleading.

"Okay, girl, you can come along."

Gavin rubs her belly and she scrambles to her feet and trots around him to the Volvo. Once out of the driveway he rolls the windows down. His dad and stepmom keep everything sealed up because they're afraid the dog will jump out to chase a squirrel. But Gavin lets her ride the way she likes, tongue flapping in the humid breeze. Cricket is smarter than they think. Rolling down Old Cutler Road, he texts Mia:

THERE IN 20 B READY LOOZR

Two lights later his half sister's reply blips up.

ready when u r sphinctercountenance

He texts back, launching them into their game.

stool 4 brains

kitten stomper

tick eater

effluent guzzler

He snorts, chucks his phone onto the passenger seat and merges into the freeway lane. The rule: when the other one makes you actually laugh, you lose. Mia's only eleven but she's getting good, largely because Gavin has made it his personal mission to teach her the fine art of euphemism. F-word, s-word, a-word, c-word: too vulgar, too direct. We're better than that, he advises his little sister, and so far she's been an excellent pupil.

Twenty minutes later the cake sits on the back seat and Mia in front with Cricket puddled in her lap. Gavin cruises along the boulevard, picturing the insufferable party to come, Oliver getting showered with parental approval while Gavin lurks around enduring all the waxed frowns from his stepmom and his equally oblivious grandmother.

"Let's go to Kennedy for soft serve," he suggests. "My treat."

Mia gives him a suspicious look. "Aren't you supposed to take me straight home?"

"Daphne'll be psyched we're out of her hair while she's setting up," Gavin says. "Plus Cricket didn't get a walk today. Mea schtoopin' culpa."

"Are you *sure*? I don't want to get in trouble."

"Nazi."

"Bite me."

"It's not like it's a surprise party. Nobody'll care if we're a little late."

"Fine." Mia folds her arms over Cricket's head.

Last year Oliver screamed in the middle of the foyer when everybody sprang out for his surprise. He made them promise not to do it again, and he's been saying ever since how much he hates surprises. I do, too, sweetie, Daphne likes to reassure him, patting his messy head. The next day a magnet showed up on the refrigerator with a quote from Jane Austen. *Surprises are foolish things. The pleasure is not enhanced, and the inconvenience is often considerable.* Clever, Gavin thought at the time, and everybody laughed.

And so the Larsen-Halls are keeping all the surprises at bay, for now.

His sister follows Cricket toward the dog run while Gavin makes for the ice cream stand. Halfway there he pats his hip pockets for his phone. He jogs back, grabs it from the console, and goes to shut the driver's side door when his eyes light on the cake baking in the back seat. He hesitates with his hand on the rubber molding and stares at the Beachery Bakes sticker affixed to the box.

Keep chilled until serving.

He imagines sweat breaking out on the neat filigrees of salted cara-
mel frosting. The liquification of the cold custard separating the layers,
the slop of all that melt. What delightful havoc the August sun will play
with the cake's firm glaciated structure, with the neat cursive inscrip-
tion of his half brother's name.

Gavin looks up over the Volvo's roof toward the bay and his hand
seems to close the door of its own accord as that great Donna Summer
ballad fills his head, the one his mother used to sing. What was it again?
Something about a cake left out in the rain, sweet green icing flowing
down. Not much of a bass line, but still. He saunters toward the ice
cream stand, away from the oven of his car.

4.

Daphne, home from the store, stares through the windshield at the fans of water jetting up from the sprinkler system, going full-bore despite the daily rains. In their old neighborhood back in Ann Arbor you could stroll the streets with a cocktail, follow your free-range kids while chatting with the neighbors. Here Brantley aspired to something different, a gated neighborhood with houses spaced luxuriously, a sprawling home, a cove by the water.

What he meant: a place befitting a successful surgeon and his family.

Daphne has met only a handful of their neighbors in Pineapple Isles, a subdivision filled with leather-skinned residents zipping around in golf carts. Nor has she made a single real friend in Coral Gables, and she misses the adjunct classes in studio art she taught at the University of Michigan. Brantley convinced her to wait until they were settled before looking for teaching work here. A few months turned into a year, now nearly two.

On the way inside, she empties the mailbox and adds a handful of bills to the sprawl on Brantley's desk. In the kitchen she pours herself a glass of pinot gris and texts Gavin: You guys close? The grill is sizzling when the first guests arrive, three of Oliver's teammates and an older sister Daphne has hired to lifeguard. Soon her mother-in-law breezes in with Oliver, back from a birthday trip to Best Buy.

"That place is a jungle." Flo waves off Daphne's offer of wine. "Should have brought a machete."

Oliver joins his teammates and leads them around the pool deck to organize a game, issuing orders left and right.

Flo wipes a lone potato chip crumb off the table. "And where's the man of the house?" The question worshipful, Flo a mother still besotted with her son. Daphne, like Brantley, is an only child, though without living parents to dote on her and the kids. One of the results: lots of time with the mother-in-law.

"Surgery," she says.

"He works so hard, doesn't he."

"He does."

"And you, too, dear. This all looks just *wonderful*." Flo's quick eyes sweep appraisingly over the spread. Buns, condiment containers, chips still in the bag, store-bought potato salad. Daphne, longing for an Ativan, sips at her wine.

"By the way, where are my other grandchildren?"

"Good question."

More teammates float in, and soon the back deck and pool teem with boy energy. She texts Brantley: You heard from Gavin? Three dots dance on the screen. Nope. Doing paperwork, home in thirty. Most of that half hour passes before the Volvo turns into the drive. Daphne stalks outside. Her stepson is lifting a cake box from the back seat.

"Gavin, where have you been?"

He bumps the door shut. "Just went for ice cream."

"At Kennedy Park," Mia adds. "Gavin said you wouldn't care."

"Mia, go inside."

Her daughter scurries into the house. Gavin leans back against the car, cake box pressing his midsection.

"Why didn't you text?"

"Phone died."

"There's a charger in the car."

A sullen shrug.

"You should have been home an hour ago. Besides, we already have ice cream here, for the cake."

"Yeah, about that."

"What?"

"It kinda melted. All sixty-eight dollars' worth."

"You're not serious."

"We stopped for a replacement."

He tilts the oblong box, stamped with the orange Walmart star. A sheet cake, blank, industrial, unadorned. Daphne stares at the box. Gavin clearly wants to see her lose it.

"The original one was pretty fancy for an eight-year-old," he says. "Frankly I'm surprised my dad approved the expense."

They face off in the driveway until Brantley's Jaguar glides in. Her husband takes his time getting out.

"Hey, you two."

"Hey, yourself, Dad!" Gavin mock enthused. "How's our surgeon general? Good day at the hospital?"

Brantley works his jaw. "Sure was."

"Great. See you both inside. Birthday cake to deliver." He pushes past Daphne toward the house.

Brantley approaches slowly. "What was that about?"

She shakes her head as he pulls her in. "More of his garbage," she says, missing the old Gavin: that shy, broken teen who came to shelter with them during those unimaginable months when his mother died in a car accident just as his classes were going online again. Once he moved in with them, Daphne was afraid Gavin would shrink further beneath his protective shell, especially after another displacement to Miami and his third school in four years.

Yet through it all the teen maintained a stoic sweetness, curious and bighearted, always more likely to bury his nose in a novel than scroll on his phone. For Daphne he became a pet project of sorts, a difficult form she tried to shape with the same light touch she brought to her work, though always aware of those places where Gavin's clay wouldn't give.

Yes, he could be something of an automaton at times, turning inward as he navigated an intense new school and did everything he could to please his father. He even won a statewide writing award, a distinction that helped him get into Stanford off the wait list.

Now that resilient young man is gone, vanished in a puff of California smoke. From high school valedictorian to college dropout, with all that bottled-up anger primed like a boil just beneath the family skin.

Brantley's arms circle her waist. "Look." He kisses the top of her head. "He's mad at the situation. He doesn't hate you any more than he does the rest of us."

Though this isn't quite right. Gavin's jabs these days are oddly pointed, keen little darts aimed at Daphne's most vulnerable places. Brantley makes the big money while you make pots. Brantley handles the finances, including yours. Brantley buys the cars.

And Brantley is currently the only parent Gavin will talk to, long, murmured conversations in his room at night. He just needs time to decompress, readjust, Brantley claims. I've got the situation under control.

"I know you've got a lot on your plate, with the opening and all."

He squeezes her shoulders, the hardness there. She gives in against the insistent pressure of his thumbs, grateful for his reason in the face of her catastrophizing.

"Mm-hmm." She sighs. "Though Pilar's confident she'll sell out the show. Apparently some big collectors are coming."

"That's great, Daph." His thumbs pause. "By the way, Bettina will be there."

"Seriously?"

"And possibly the dean."

"Oh."

"Hey, surgeons buy a lot of art."

"Will they really want to gawk at a bunch of ceramic?"

"You kidding? Cocktails at a Miami Beach gallery, a chance for the stuffed-shirt hospital admins to slum it with the artsy crowd? They'll eat it up."

Though she wishes he had asked. If she called him on it now he would claim to have issued the invitations as a gesture of support for her work rather than another chance to schmooze with the UMed overlords. Lately Brantley has had his eyes on a promotion. More stress, more money—and for what?

She lets him turn her around so they can take in their sliver of Biscayne Bay. An impossible blue, going to violet as dusk creeps up. A last glint of sunlight catches a studio window and sets her vases ablaze.

"Never gets old," Brantley observes, as he has observed a dozen times standing in this spot. Daphne gazes out with her husband at the darkening bay.

5.

What assaults Lorraine Holton at every turn, always, is the stench. Severed sewer lines, dead dogs, a foul stew of baking waste. Twenty hours have passed since the line of twisters swept east from the Rockies into Kansas, but already the town of Cold Spring is mostly a memory. Dazed residents pick through the F4's devastation with soaked cloths pressed to their mouths, searching for anything worth keeping, and for signs of the dead. All but one of the missing persons, a young boy, have been accounted for, the twenty-two deceased processed through the DMORT units. The county coroner can handle only two.

This is—was—the poorer part of town, wedged between a Sam's Club and the freight tracks, the Topeka line that parallels the highway. The topography scoops the neighborhood into a shallow bowl. Here the funnel acted like an electric mixer, churning dough.

The biggest twisters tend to choose the most vulnerable folks. Favor mobile homes over mansions, public housing over split-level suburban developments. The meteorologists claim it's about structural integrity, building codes, basic engineering. Of course a double-wide's going to blow down more easily than a show home. But the worst tornadoes know what they're doing, a superstitious part of Rain believes. They choose the poor. It's a deliberate thing.

A church still stands, nearly untouched with its steeple and clapboard siding intact, repurposed into a shelter for survivors. Staff at a Red

Cross tent nearby treat injuries, administer tetanus shots and antibiotics. Volunteers distribute clean water, sunscreen, bug spray.

Rain looks around, enervated by the operation's new phase. Recovery is her least favorite part of these assignments and has been since she retired from the army twelve years ago to become a disaster assistance engineer for FEMA, rising steadily through the ranks. But she never sits back to give orders when she can keep her hands busy. Some days she'll blow eight hours helping her crew hand out water bottles and blankets, others she'll spend in a crawl space assessing structural damage to a high-rise. Three times she's been offered a transfer to the Region IV office to run operations across six states; three times she's politely declined. Because white-picket-fence stability doesn't go with living out of your car, nights in and out of her back seat with the stray snatch of sleep, startling awake when the radio chirps. In winter, months can go by with little to do. Then the Missouri River crests out and she's flying to Omaha to coordinate response on yet another thousand-year flood.

You're too old for this shit, her daughter observes on their weekly FaceTimes. But Vanessa knows it will never change. Vani knows because she grew up as the child of a dual military couple, shuttled from base to base when she was little, losing her father at eleven to a roadside IED half a world away. Rain's daughter is now a doctoral student at UC Santa Cruz, where she thinks she can avoid uncertainty by studying it.

A colleague waves her over. Butch Jansen is a barrel-chested white guy who likes to gather first responders in prayer circles but swears like a sailor and has no issue with a demanding black woman as his boss, even though Rain's a former army puke and he's ex-Marine.

"That's a big fuckin' cone."

Hurricane Luna dances on his weather app.

"Damn," she says, drawing it out. The storm's track has been erratic. Luna could make landfall anywhere from Montserrat to Charleston.

"With that warm blob off the coast, the sumbitch could really explode," Butch says. "Imagine we'll all be heading there next week."

"I can't think about it." By this point even Rain's eyeballs feel exhausted. Her handset double-clicks. "Go ahead."

"Got a live one. Basement."

"Where?"

"Oak and Eighth. Northeast corner."

Three blocks over. She points to Butch's Chevy truck. "Let's go."

They climb in and Butch squeals off the curb. "Gotta be that boy," he mutters.

"Darby."

"Yep."

"How in hell did the dogs miss him?"

The truck pulls up. A deputy waits for them on the porch. "We heard his voice coming out the vent," he explains. "Best guess is he came over here to his friend's house before it hit."

They enter the sagging house. The way it looks now, the deputy says, Darby Wilkins must have found the place empty but was still here when the tornado struck. The kid sought shelter in the basement.

The stairs have been replaced by a police ladder extending from a ragged hole in the dining room floor. Rain climbs down and assesses the situation. Darby is trapped in the collapsed half of the basement beneath the kitchen, tucked inside a crawl space for a foundation vent. They can't reach him from the outside without jackhammering through unstable concrete. But lifting the floor joists risks collapsing the entire wall. Final option is to chainsaw through the chaos—risky, given the bearing loads on everything around them.

Rain peers across the wreckage and sees the boy, the back of his head just visible across a scatter of twisted lumber.

"Darby, we're going to get you out of there, okay?" She sees him nod against the block. "You're being a brave young man."

The team confers in low voices, weighing risks. Finally Rain decides they have to lift the floor joists, despite the danger. Darby can't be in great shape, and she sees no other feasible option. Two crew members hustle out for ceiling jacks while Rain works with the others to clear a path through the weakened lumber, alive to the peril. With the jacks in place, eight crew members get as close as they can to Darby's location.

Soon the damaged joists start to rise, inch by perilous inch. Smooth, no wasted effort. The jacks doing their job. Two-by-tens, plywood, and galvanized joist brackets elevating in unison.

Rain keeps up the chatter. Describes the sunshine on the grass outside, the food Darby will eat once he's out.

The beams reach head height when something cracks.

"Stop," she orders into silence. A groan from deep inside a joist, the house giving off a primordial moan. Lumber buckles. Darby whimpers against the block. A dusty rain starts to fall. The groan turns into a splitting sound, then a deep *crack* as a floor joist snaps. The structure shudders above.

"Away!" she screams. "Everybody away!" and the crew of eight crowds out of the danger zone to the undamaged half of the basement.

It happens in a kind of awful slow motion. There is a tilting sensation as the jacks give way, until finally, with a massive *whoosh*, the kitchen floor collapses into the basement like an elevator plunging to the bottom of a shaft. Stove, refrigerator, dishwasher: all eight feet lower than they were just seconds ago. A choking powder shrouds the ruin.

They find Darby crushed beneath a joist. Rain puts two fingers on his neck.

"Call DMORT." Nothing in her voice. A mercy his parents are dead, too, and his sisters. She climbs out of the basement and wades through the destruction on the upper level out to the porch and the relentless Kansas sun. She walks down and sits on the curb. Later Butch finds her there.

"It was the right call," he says gruffly as he settles his big body. "That grate? No way we could have gone in that way. Chain saws would have brought it all down." His left hand rests on her shoulder. "It's not your goddamn fault."

Rain spits a mouthful of dust into the gutter, hating the taste.

6.

In the gallery Daphne's art comes alive. *Sentinel II*, spotlighted from above, is the most ogled. Twenty porcelain tendrils splotched with oil struggle against an invisible wind. Pilar has placed the piece in the atrium between the pedestal and the ocean-facing windows so the guests will have to crowd in and make an effort to see it from the front. Other works cling to wall sconces or repose on stepped shelves placed to draw the eye. Recessed lighting softens the interior. A slate floor absorbs excessive noise. The sloped roof of the atrium sparkles with tiny bulbs that create a colored mist over a carpet of shimmering glass.

"We've sold everything," Pilar whispers. "And see that lion king over there?"

Pilar nods toward an older man looking at *Sentinel II*, silver mane over a linen suit. "Jeremy Stoneham, down from Manhattan. Huge collector." Pilar tells her what Stoneham has in mind: a lobby installation on the Upper East Side. "It's a big commission, Daphne. This could really open some doors for you up there, and with his connections . . ." She rattles off a few names, well-known curators of major shows at MoMA, the Whitney. Daphne has never had a piece acquired by such a venue, though Pilar assures her it's only a matter of time.

Pilar walks her over. For the next ten minutes Daphne speaks with her potential new patron about the art scene in New York. At one point she glances over his shoulder and sees Brantley with his back to her. Her husband shifts slightly and she glimpses Pilar, arms folded, arguing with him—over what, she can't imagine. He makes an angry grimace before Pilar walks away. Daphne watches him stalk up to an empty spot along the atrium wall and stare out at the beach.

She detaches herself gently from Stoneham and is heading over for an explanation when several of Brantley's colleagues walk up.

"So how is Gavin liking Stanford?" Bettina Duggan asks.

The question is jovial, and slightly off. But maybe Daphne's just being defensive. Duggan, division chief of surgical oncology and Brantley's immediate supervisor, peers over her champagne flute as the others await a response. In a flash of a moment Daphne has to decide between bravado and vulnerability. Show the belly or circle the family wagons?

Brantley, appearing at her elbow, decides for both of them. "We let him take the spring quarter off. The kid deserves a gap period after working so hard."

Let him? It's not as if he asked.

"Oh, poor guy." Bettina squeezes Daphne's arm. "All that pressure."

"I'll say." Eamon, Bettina's husband, a prominent Miami novelist. "But any kid who gets into Stanford is going to be fine."

"We hope so," Daphne says. If only things were so simple.

"Our middle one's starting that whole process now," Eamon says. "A dozen APs, all the test prep. Don't know how they survive."

The talk turns to the hurricane. The cone, the potential for landfall in Florida.

"So what happens if Luna hits Miami?" asks a woman Daphne doesn't know. "Would the hospital have to evacuate?"

"It's happened," Bettina says. "During Katrina, one of the major New Orleans hospitals was marooned. A lot of patients died. Ever since then, there's been a real focus on decision trees, ninety-six-hour windows."

"Are there evacuation protocols you have to follow?"

"Actually yes," Brantley says, and his head dips. "In fact, I'm designated as incident commander in the event of an evac. We coordinate with local liaison officers in emergency—"

"Wait. Is 'incident commander' actually a thing?" Eamon rocks on his heels, scare-quoting with a martini and two fingers. "Like, do you get to wear a hard hat and carry a walkie-talkie?"

Laughs, lighthearted, though at Brantley's expense. He flashes his charming smile but his jaw stiffens. Bettina looks away with a few slow blinks until her eyes settle on Daphne's.

"Your work is gorgeous," she says, pulling her slightly aside. Daphne listens as Bettina talks about her modest art collection and lets her know that she and Eamon purchased a piece tonight. She asks smart questions about Daphne's technique until Eamon interrupts and the couple leave for another event.

Brantley takes Daphne's elbow and guides her toward the hotel lobby outside the gallery, suggesting a stop by the bar. A caterer passes with the last of the canapés, something gorgeous on endive leaves.

"That Eamon's a funny guy," Brantley says, an edge in his voice.

"He was just teasing." Daphne signals to Pilar with a mock tequila shot and a nod toward the lobby. Pilar hesitates for a moment, an odd look crossing her face; but then she blows a kiss, giving her artist permission to take a break. "And I hate having to talk about Gavin and Stanford. I never know what to say when I don't understand the situation myself."

"Gavin's fine." Brantley curt as they weave through the exhibit. "In fact, we talked last night about enrolling him at the U this fall."

"You what?"

"He could stay on with us. And since I'm a faculty member the tuition would be free. It's a solid plan." Brantley keeps strolling.

"But . . ." Daphne senses things shifting, shards going askew. Another major life decision, taken out of her hands. She has an urge to hurl one of her pieces at her husband's back.

The real issue isn't Gavin leaving Stanford. She would understand if he burned out, or simply hated the place. The problem is that since coming home from California, her stepson has been a different person. Has changed somehow, grown bitter and small-minded, lost all the joy he once seemed to take in his hard work. The thought of the sullen guy buzzarding around above her studio for another year—

Is she being ungenerous? Yes. But sometimes, in her family these days, it feels as if she's been sealed off in a hidden room, thudding her head against the wall, waiting for someone to hear.

Brantley orders cognacs. Daphne downs hers in two gulps. Not a shot-friendly drink but she orders another. Brantley gives her a quizzical, somewhat lustful grin, mistaking her despondency for lack of inhibition.

"God, will you look at that," the bartender says to the television. Daphne stares glassy-eyed at the spiral on the screen. "Her cone's looking good for us now, though. Miami's on her top edge. She'll tickle us maybe, goose us in the ass."

Brantley gives Daphne's arm a pat intended to be reassuring.

"By tomorrow they'll have it passing south of the peninsula," the bartender continues. "The southern Keys might get a hit, but not us. After that she'll be out in the Gulf. Then she'll be—"

"Mexico's problem," Brantley finishes.

The men laugh together at the screen.

On the way home Daphne remembers to ask, "What were you and Pilar talking about? Were you guys arguing?"

He hesitates. "Not really."

"What then?"

She watches his face, that way he puckers his lower lip between his teeth as he conjures a response. An affair? Pilar is a hot little number,

Brantley a stress case lately. But the notion of her husband and her gallerist hooking up is ludicrous, if only because Brantley is too much of a
workaholic to find time for so much as a trip to the gym.

"Honestly, Daph, I'm a little worried we're getting fucked in
the ass."

Daphne feels her cheek flinch; there's a very specific combination of
vulgarity and resentment Brantley gets in his voice after certain social
events. It has become her job to navigate around his pique. "I'm sure
Pilar wouldn't do anything wrong," she says cautiously.

"The wire transfers aren't happening."

"Wait, what?"

"The piece you did for that prick up in Palm Beach—"

"Lou Walser."

"Six-thousand-dollar commission and we haven't seen a cent. Pilar
says the piece is, quote, still officially on loan, unquote."

"But that's true, Brantley."

"So she's loaning out your stuff?" He sounds enraged, as if Pilar has
been peeing on her work to mark ownership.

"It's standard practice in the art world," Daphne says, trying to
placate him. "A gallery owner wants to please her clients, keep them
coming back for more. The way you do that is with loans, sales, and
commissions. Let the buyer keep the piece for a while before commit-
ting. Lou Walser probably buys half a million a year from Pilar's galleries alone. I assume he settles his accounts every quarter. Besides, six
grand is pocket change for Walser."

And for us, she wants to add. Brantley makes over four hundred
thousand a year and he's suddenly quibbling over her art sales? No wonder Pilar gave her that strange look. Yes, Daphne's commissions are
picking up, and if what Pilar says is true, there may be bigger ones in
her near future. But her income is a drop in the bucket of their family

finances—which, to be fair, she knows next to nothing about. As Gavin is so fond of pointing out, his father handles the money.

On the causeway, Brantley retreats into a long silence. Daphne slumps against the passenger door, the elation of the show already fading. The Miami skyline blazes its splendor on the night. Height. Gleam. Glitz.

7.

Tate Bondurant flips a quarter along his knuckles as his coworkers' voices drift by with the cant of the trade. Uninsured motorist coverage, personal umbrellas, water backup riders. Today's the day; his Spidey sense tingles with it. Manager at the Rosedale branch, an escape from Houston West. Top lobster in a new tank, at last.

He pockets the quarter and heads out for his twelve thirty rendezvous.

"Hey, Tate." Norm Tanner leans out of his office. "Got a minute?"

"Mind if we do it around one?"

His boss shrugs. "I ain't going anywhere."

"Grab you some Wendy's?"

Norm smiles. "Anything to avoid my salad. Get me that bacon jalapeño. A double."

"Coke?

"That peach lemonade they got. Biggie fries."

"On it."

Tate hips open the door. A black heat rises from the asphalt and he slides into his BMW with everything clammy. By the time he reaches Sutland Street, the sedan's strong AC has chilled him nicely. He backs into a spot and keeps the engine running with the news on: all Luna, all the time. The insurance industry will be insane in the coming weeks.

He switches over to an in-progress episode of *Me Lads*, a podcast he discovered earlier this summer. The host, Jace Parkinson, is a Welsh ex-academic who got canceled last year for some bullshit reason Tate still doesn't understand. This latest episode: "Roast Your Albatross."

What's success, me lads? Not the outward stuff. Not perfect marks or the size a' your house. No, success is the strength to break free of our encumbrances. Taking that albatross off our necks. You feel it there, weighing you down? Now reach up and pull that big bird off your back.

A tap at the passenger window. Tate pauses the podcast as Liberty climbs in and starts rubbing her arms. Her skin a sickly pale, pink-rimmed eyes, and translucent ribbons of hair like those smeary plastic flaps fronting walk-in refrigerators.

Tate sells to Liberty directly, saving her a little something each week. With everyone else, he keeps layers between his product and its users. But he's maintained this one intimacy since those earliest days, even driving her to clinics a few times. He never gives her too much, never enough to sell. Liberty's more a pet than a customer.

He takes her bills, not bothering to count; she shorts him every time.

"And hey, listen, Liberty."

Her jaundiced eyes flicker at the baggie. He squeezes the birch stick of her forearm.

"Cut it, okay? Because this Bolivian shit I'm getting lately . . ."

Liberty wipes her ruddy nose with the side of a hand. For a moment their eyes meet and there is a glint of something hopeful that quickly dies.

"Okay. I mean—okay."

She climbs out. Tate hits Play.

Now snap it, lads. Snap that skinny neck over your knee and toss that dead albatross on the pebbledash. Now look at it lying there. What do you see? Your debts, all your burdens, the people pulling you down. That's what the albatross is, it's all our shite and troubles.

But me? When I look down at that dead albatross, you know what I see? One word, me lads.

Supper.

Tate looks up and there she is, his lovely mule sashaying across the lot, yoga mat tucked under her arm, guitar and knapsack slung over her shoulders. Jessamyn makes the run up to Saint Louis twice a month to get the package from the Russians. She isn't a user, like Liberty. All she wants is her cut to finance her guitar habit. Always a little spark when she's in the car, along with a whiff of patchouli.

A box emerges from her knapsack. Girl Scout cookies. Thin Mints. "What's this?"

"Russian humor." She pulls out a second box and shows him the black slash across a corner. "This one's real, just in case."

She gives him four more cookie boxes. Tate tucks all but the last into his gym bag. This one he opens. He dumps out the tight packets of pills, counts, and slips a wad of bills into Jessamyn's hand. She counts them in the tented bowl of her skirt.

"Same next week?" she asks.

"We'll see."

One of Houston's finest bumps up into the parking lot. Tate tracks the squad as it makes a leisurely arc toward the drive-through line.

"Come to our show tonight," Jessamyn says. "We're playing at the Rialto."

"Oh yeah?"

"We'll be on by ten. It's a benefit."

"For the band?"

"Food bank next door. They share the same building."

"Didn't know you had a charitable streak."

"There's a lot you don't know about me." Jessamyn hands him a flyer, a bright orange quarter sheet featuring the silhouette of a wild-haired girl shredding a Gibson Flying V, the band's name printed in a runic font.

"Galadriels?"

"We all look like elf queens. You should come."

Her face brightens, a bubbly enthusiasm, and this is the problem. A taut everything, a sweet, heart-shaped face, some fifteen years younger than Tate's forty-one years. But somehow the pieces don't fit. Maybe there's something in her youthful zeal that reminds him of Connor, how his son, even on his worst days, would prattle through the fog of a morphine drip about what he wanted for Christmas, and hell if Tate needs any shitty reminders of that particular albatross. But Jessamyn also has a wild side, a seditious edge, like she'd jack a bank if you only asked.

"I'll try," he says, but her face sags a little.

The patchouli lingers in the front seat once she's gone. He ponders again why he can't quite bring himself to bridge this gap, take this particular risk. Because for Tate, it's always about risk and reward. The risk of marrying too young versus the reward of having a kid. The risk of hooking up with a feral musician versus the reward of a statuesque Galadriel. Right now, the risk of getting busted after an opioid buy.

Tate had once planned a career pursuing the beautiful science of risk for Southerly Insurance. The firm was willing to pay for his actuarial exams, all the test prep. But then he failed Probability three times straight and took a consolation job as a sales agent. He's spent the last twelve years moving from branch to branch, skating along, as his ex-wife likes to say, on his mediocrity and charm.

Tate gets in line behind the cop, buys two combos, and heads back to the branch. After parking he shoulders his gym bag and gathers up the Wendy's. As he approaches the door a figure appears through the smoked glass.

Sunita Udin, gliding toward the exit. Despite the encumbrances Tate manages to open the door for her and makes a little bow as she passes, just to piss her off. Instead she laughs lightly. "Why thank you, good sir."

The exchange unbalances him. Sunita's hardly the type to joke about gender roles, especially since she got tapped as diversity liaison for the whole district. At the district can't-say-Christmas party last year, Sunita was making a point to a gal from the Galveston branch about scale adjustments, the urgent need for equity raises.

"Ah yes, the gender pay gap," Tate butted in.

Sunita looked at him. "What about it?"

"Total myth."

A few glares from the other ladies but Sunita was game. "It's seventy-seven cents to the dollar, Tate."

"That's only if you take the average of everyone working full-time. Once you control for differences of profession and part-time work, the genders come out basically even." A tap to his temple. "Stats major."

Jace Parkinson's podcast, actually, though they didn't need to know his source. More back-and-forth, a few ruffled feminazi feathers, and Sunita's given him the cold shoulder ever since.

Which is a Sunita problem, not a Tate problem. He can't stand people who use squishy sociological excuses for their own failure to get ahead when the numbers tell the real story. Take insurance. You enter the variables, then you either write the policy or you don't. You either cut the check or you don't. Insurance: color blind, gender blind, sexual-preference blind. Objectivity in action.

Once inside, Tate strolls back to Norm's office, collecting jealous looks from his fellow agents. The guys think Tate's an ass-kisser with the extra Wendy's and all, but it's his own ass that's about to get kissed, and they can shove the jealousy up theirs. Seriously, though. Tate's the only guy in the branch aside from Norm who wears a tie every day. *Dress for the job you want, not the job you have, me lads.*

Norm invites him to sit at the corner table. Tate adjusts himself on the vinyl cushion and looks around. Norm has managed Houston West for decades, his office wallpapered with framed certificates hailing by-gone contributions to the corporate ethos. South Texas Agent of the Month. Five-Star Branch Manager. A plaque over his head reads SOUTH-ERLY SOLID GOLD CITIZEN, AWARDED FOR EXCEPTIONAL, COOLHEADED SER-VICE DURING A CATASTROPHE. The award has been polished and cared for, the brass plate shined bright. A branch manager's pride in its even sheen.

Tate smells Lysol. The manager's office at Rosedale has an exterior window, so he's heard. They talk through their Wendy's about Luna, the likelihood of landfall on the coast. When the food is gone they ball up their trash and shoot a few hoops until Norm leans forward with his thick fingers interlaced.

"So Tate."

Here it comes.

"Yessir."

"They asked me to tell you. I'm sorry, buddy, but you're not getting Rosedale."

Outside Norm's office, through the glass walls, the work of the branch goes on. Tate can see his fellow agents out there chatting away at suckers present and future. No matter how big a life policy you buy, you're still going to kick it. No matter how solid your homeowner's, you only have it because someday a tree might fall and demolish your dining room. But meanwhile you flush your premiums down the toilet and most folks never see a cent.

"Who got it?"

Norm shifts in his seat. "That's confidential until the offer's ac-cepted."

"Let me guess."

Norm says nothing.

"It's Sunita." Her soft laugh at the door.

"Can't say."

Tate grits his teeth. A lighter clicks on in his neck. "The politically correct choice, I suppose."

"Hey now."

"Nothing I didn't expect." Tate crosses his arms. "Guys like us, Norm, we work twice as hard these days to get half as much."

"You think?"

"I mean, all this?" Tate gestures at the plaques and certificates on the walls. "You've won every award in the book and you're stuck at branch manager."

Norm stiffens. "That's by choice. You know that."

Mostly true. Norm has a wife with early onset dementia. And unlike Tate—who, as his ex is fond of reminding him, did a cut and run when serious illness grenaded his own family—Norm has taken care of Caroline over the years of her decline. Talk about a fucking albatross.

Tate swallows, tasting defeat on the back of his tongue. Clears his throat and cools the dragon, for now. "I'm sorry, man. Just that you're the real thing. Nobody ever gave you anything because of your gender or race or whatnot."

"No worries, buddy," says Norm, though Tate can tell he wants this conversation over. "And thanks for not going postal on me. Wasn't sure how you'd take the news. Besides, I need you here, given what's about to hit us. Luna's got everybody in the industry spooked. Hartford's freaking out, I mean there's half a million of our clients insured in Miami-Dade alone. And who the hell knows where she's headed next."

Tate gives him a lazy salute. "Private Bondurant reporting for hurricane duty, sir."

"Attaboy." Norm slaps his knees and looks about to rise when his eyes settle on the gym bag. "Say, are those Thin Mints?"

Tate follows his gaze.

"You holding out on me?" Norm leans forward to peer down at the boxes visible through the zipper, open an inch.

"Girl Scouts were selling outside the gym this morning," Tate says. "Couldn't resist."

"Always loved those dang things." Norm drums his fingers on the table.

Tate bends over and pulls out a box of cookies—the marked box, packed with actual Thin Mints rather than five hundred synthetic opioid capsules. He slides it across the table. "It's on me."

Without ceremony, Norm rips open the box and unsleeves a half dozen wafers. "You're a good man, Bondurant." Shrapnel flies from his lips.

8.

The pressure falls, and Luna feeds again.

Just west of a ledge several hundred miles off the coast of Florida, the subterranean floor drops with a precipitous sweep from three hundred feet to a frigid depth of four thousand. Far above, the surface waters have heated to eighty-four degrees Fahrenheit, their warmest in centuries. Wind shear is low, inviting the moist air on the sea to rise tens of thousands of feet, where it cools and condenses into a celestial rain that spirals around the strengthened core.

The eye. An immense cylinder of calm thirty-five miles in diameter. As it moves over the west Atlantic, the eye opens the storm to reveal the sea churning beneath. A weather plane passing through measures waves cresting at 130 feet. A record in this area; as is the eye wall, a ring of tornadic winds clocked at 180 miles per hour at their peak.

Yet even as the plane transmits the storm's brutal measurements to instruments ashore, a discernible shift occurs in Luna's wind environment. An eddy in the tropical ridge, a wobble in her unusual path. Her cone narrows, shifts several degrees north.

In Port-au-Prince, in Santo Domingo, in Kingston and Havana, there is relief, even cautious celebration, as observers begin to understand that their cities and homes may be spared the worst of her wrath.

In Miami, in Boca Raton and on Key Largo, there is dawning fear.

The great storm has turned.

In her middle, the winds quicken.

Along the coast, the waters warm.

Luna, now Florida bound, drinks.

9.

The rifle is a Sako TRG 42, a Finnish gun shooting a .338 Lapua cartridge and enhanced with a borrowed scope. Rain lies prone on a patch of Astroturf six hundred meters from the steel silhouette, centers the crosshairs, ticks right to account for the breeze.

Down breath. Squeeze.

The shot takes the head just behind the nose.

Rain gets off a dozen more rounds before heading inside for a cup of coffee, which she drinks alone on the shaded front porch. Once a month or so, when she's back home in Atlanta, she comes out to this ramshackle shooting range near Lake Lanier to blow off steam. The place has a no-bullshit feel, with a serious clientele and without an attached gun shop, which keeps out the weekend warriors. She'll get the occasional once-over from certain types but nothing overt, and as soon as they see her veteran's cap, their eyes soften and there's that ubiquitous white-guy chin toss, the flicker of grudging respect.

By ten minutes past five she's pulling into the parking lot of BougainVilla, her funky condo complex in the heart of Cabbagetown. Most of her fellow residents would be surprised to learn that the object inside the vinyl case over Rain's shoulder isn't a tennis racket or an alto sax but a broken-down sniper rifle, that this slim fortysomething woman huffing it up two flights of rickety wooden stairs has a grown daughter and two Purple Hearts to her name. But Rain appreciates the laissez-faire environment BougainVilla affords, the florid spectacle its residents make of the place. Ropes of pale yellow lights zigzag across the narrow courtyard, with residents adding individual touches on their private decks. The couple next door favors geometric patterns in lavender and white, another neighbor red chili pepper lights.

Rain's own tastes shade minimalist: a short string of white lights around a single rosemary bush and a modest array of outdoor plants she tends with the fussiness of a mother hen. Pots of wax begonias and hibiscus, twin Meyer lemon trees she's grown from seedlings, three basil plants, a planter of Roma tomatoes doing surprisingly well.

She plucks three tomatoes and a handful of basil. Two small globes of mozzarella and a splash of olive oil complete a caprese salad, which she eats along with a pan-fried chicken breast and leftover sweet potato fries.

When Vanessa calls, Rain props her phone against a flowerpot and listens to her daughter rave into her laptop about her summer seminar in urban sociology. The instructor has them visiting museums and writing blog posts. Not the typical fare for a doctoral program, but Vani seems enchanted and wants her mom to see what she's been up to.

During the first lull, Rain braces herself, dreading the question.

"So have you bought your tickets?" Vani asks.

Rain has promised to fly out to the Bay Area in a couple of weeks for a visit. It would be her first in nearly a year. But these last few work jags have gutted her.

"I'm thinking maybe October."

On the screen, Vanessa's face hardens. "You're doing this again?"

"Doing what, hon?"

"Canceling. Same as last spring."

"Vani, you were just here in May, and with hurricane season I can't justify that long flight, plus I've got—"

"Sure you can. You just don't want to."

Rain starts to reply when Leila edges in, dislodging Vani from the center of the screen. "Hey, Rain," Leila says with a big smile, a burst of sunshine through Vanessa's clouds. The pair have been together for nearly a year now, a relationship that has buffed Vanessa's keen edges, honed by cycles of teenage rage and rebellion after her father died, sharpened further by four years of activism at UC Santa Cruz. As far as Rain can tell, mostly what Vani's learned is how to judge her mother, though at least she knows how to pick a girlfriend.

They have movie tickets, Leila tells her after they catch up, bringing the conversation to a close. Rain watches the screen until the two young faces blip off.

In the shower, jets of water soften the iron in her shoulders as steam fills her lungs. It can take days to recover from site ops, weeks to dull the images jammed like glass shivs in her mind. Cold Spring was the worst in a while. Reminded her of Charikar, those days picking Afghan babies out of kindling.

Back in the living room she slides a canvas storage bin out from its shelf, the gray cube heavy with her latest finds. First, some recent issues of *Dwell*. The teaser on a cover promises a tour of "Affordable Style from Bozeman to Bratislava." She pages through from the back, pausing on a shot of an Auckland home crafted from a pair of nautical sheds. A lighting fixture catches her eye so she shoots it, crops and filters the pic, and posts it with a few comments on @rainsweethome, the Instagram feed she maintains in happy anonymity.

Eight issues and an hour go by. Less an obsession than a narcotic, this quiet hobby, always soothing to the nerves, like her grandmother's scrapbooking. Rain's magazine habit started the year after her honorable discharge, when she moved with Vani, just ten at the time, out of base housing at Fort Benning and into a series of rented apartments and houses. In that first place, they ate off Styrofoam plates for weeks because Rain couldn't bring herself to unpack moving boxes or suitcases when opening them would expose the absence of Gus's things.

Then one morning she looked around the kitchen and noticed the pizza boxes stacked on the fridge and the dingy olive paint on the walls and her little daughter picking Cheerios out of a paper bowl. That afternoon she went to Home Depot and came home with a roller and paint. After that it was warmer light bulbs, a few pieces of interesting furniture, and plants, plants, plants. She started picking up *House Beautiful* and its ilk in doctors' offices and soon had subscriptions of her own to a few of the more stylish alternatives. Vani teases her mother about the magazine habit but that's a small price to pay for the satisfaction Rain derives from her aesthetic routines, this ceaseless curation of dwellings near and far.

Home would always be a place of beauty, however sparse, however spare. A promise Rain has kept over the years, as a winding career path took her and her daughter to five states and three foreign countries before they finally settled here in Atlanta when Vani was in tenth grade. Home: good lighting, clean lines, only appealing objects on the surfaces. And home should always mean safety and security, so often missing from those suddenly shattered lives that her agency, at its best, helps piece back together.

Because, at its worst, FEMA can be a snake pit. The next morning, on her way to the gym, Rain sees her phone light up with a work alert from her boss, Joe Garrison, administrator for Region IV. No salutation, no how-you-holding-up check-in after that business in Kansas. Just two curt sentences: Need to talk, unless you're too busy with your photographer. Be by your phone at eleven sharp. JG

Garrison with that little dig. *Your photographer.* As if she seeks out the attention. As if circumstance and dumb luck were somehow her doing, her idea.

That photograph has been the curse of her career. The image, taken two years ago during another horrific flood season, depicts Rain emerging from the Alabama River with a cherubic baby cradled in her arms, his white cheeks smeared with blood, Rain's spattered with mud, the child's head resting in the crook of her elbow and his eyes wide in wonder. Didn't help that Rain looked like a goddess in that shot. Hair pulled back in a ponytail but several strands escaping to curl across her forehead, a ribbed FEMA tank plastered to her chest but tugged up from her waistline by the baby's grasping hand to expose the moist circumference of a sculpted stomach and abs. Her inked biceps surround the rescued baby like an ornate portrait frame.

The photo was splayed across the cover of *Time* magazine and enlisted in the most predictable of ways as a symbol of the color-blind integrity of disaster relief, of racial harmony in a badly fractured nation. The image inspired a corresponding flood of memes and GIFs, faux-Renaissance renditions of *Madonna and Child*, tongue-in-cheek imaginings of Black Savior Complex, an icon both heavily politicized and relentlessly riffed. The public affairs folks, seizing an opportunity, accepted all the invitations for Rain to appear on national talk shows to recount her experience of the flooding, to tout FEMA's recent successes, to amplify the call for disaster mitigation of every sort. Bastards even made her go on *Fox & Friends*.

Great PR for FEMA, maybe. For Rain the photo divided her life and career into a before and an after, throwing her into a monthslong maelstrom of unwanted notoriety. Once her sense of humor about the whole thing started to fade, she sheared her hair to the roots, turned down invitations to further fetings, and got back to the core of her work. Yet the unwanted celebrity still dogs her, at once a halo and a taint. Colleagues treat her differently, defer to her when they shouldn't. Her three big brothers ride her endlessly, and don't get her started on what the whole thing has done to her romantic life. Sure, there's the odd hookup, knees bumping in a darkened bar with no surnames needed. But anything more serious has been hopelessly compromised. When you google a prospect before a second date and see *all that* . . .

She pulls into a gas station in advance of the call, which is surely about Luna. She expects the customary bureaucratic probing, the disapproval and light condescension. Instead Garrison is hyped up and blunt.

"We need you on a plane tonight."

"Seriously?"

"You'll liaise with DHS, HHS, GSA, the Red Cross. We're looking at a direct hit, biggest thing we've ever seen. We're talking maybe a trillion dollars in damage, half of Miami-Dade rendered uninhabitable, the rest of it without power or clean water for months, if the place even gets rebuilt. It'll keep FEMA busy for years in the aftermath."

With plenty of opportunities for you to shine, Rain thinks.

"This is the one the climatologists have been warning us about for twenty years," he says, not bothering to hide his excitement, "slamming a major city in the hottest months of summer. The world's never seen anything like Luna."

Exhaustion crests somewhere behind her eyes. She remembers the prep and staging after Hurricane Zebulon, a cat 3 that bored through the Panhandle last year. "So where do you want me? We could station out of the airport, the medical center, the port."

"You're not going to Florida."

"Don't you need all hands down there?"

"We need you in Oklahoma."

"Say what?"

"It's a different kind of job. Not a lot of photo ops."

Rain thinks about the limits of her competence. A tingling creeps along her arms, raising the hairs. This is what she will remember from the call, the awful thrill of it. "Joe, what's going on? Don't we need everybody but everybody in Miami?"

"You're not getting it, Holton," he says. "The point is, after Tuesday there's not going to *be* a Miami."

10.

Daphne peels off her sleep mask and stares at the screaming alert on her phone.

Weather Emergency:

EXTREME

August 27, 6:47 A.M.

Mandatory Evacuation from Your Area Ordered by Governor

She scrolls through her news feed. This isn't what they were predicting, even as late as lunchtime yesterday. No one has packed, there's hardly any food in the house. And the gallery, her work—

"I need to get to the hospital." Brantley is stomping around in the walk-in. "I made some coffee already. And I'm—fuck. Just fuck."

"Leave it," she says. "I'll get your stuff together."

He palms his face from top to bottom. "Why don't you make sure they're up."

Daphne hustles down the hall. Devices clamor throughout the house, Gavin's cell from his suite, Mia's from down the hall, the iPad in Oliver's room. The kids grumble to life. Daphne pulls roller bags from closets and enjoins everyone to assemble what they'll need. Three days' worth of clothes, toothbrushes, books and phones and chargers, Mia's retainer. Last evacuation they all had their go bags standing by in the front hall. Not this time.

Downstairs she tunes the kitchen TV to local news, which is reassuring and horrifying at the same time. As long as they're on the move by the afternoon they'll be fine. But the images of Luna's coming menace are overwhelming.

Brantley walks into the kitchen and sets his bag on the counter.

"This can't be real," she says. "Does that say thirty feet?"

A map of the projected storm surge fills the screen. The entire Miami-Dade coastline is a spectrum of potential flood levels, color coded for severity. The darkest: Coral Gables, downtown Miami, the outer shores. Miami Beach is one jagged plum-colored strip.

Brantley fills a go-cup with coffee, turns the volume down, and leans back against the counter. "Listen, Daph. Before I take off, there are a few things I should tell you. Some arrangements."

"Okay."

"I've got guys coming by to board up the windows. They should be here by nine or so."

"Fine."

He shifts his weight.

"What else? I should get the kids moving."

His attention wanders to the screen. A reporter on the beach stands beneath a cloudless dawn sky, no breeze to lift her hair.

"Brantley."

"Sorry, what?" He rapid-shakes his head, seeming stunned by it all.

"What about your mother?"

"She'll be fine. The Willows has their own transport for these kinds of things."

"I'll give her a call later to check in."

"Great."

"Anything else I need to know?"

Her husband's spine straightens and his body seems to unfold against the lip of the counter, as if released from some unseen force. He cups her chin and kisses the tip of her nose. "See you in a few hours." With his bag and his go-cup, he is out the door.

Mia's bossy voice blasts from upstairs, followed by her little brother's croaky reply, the flush of Gavin's toilet. Daphne texts Pilar to ask if she should run out to the gallery. Too late, Pilar texts back. Quick call?

"The causeway is going in only one direction," Pilar tells her. "They closed the outbound lanes while I was coming over. I just made it."

"God, Pilar."

"Don't worry. Me and Zeb are already here with Lucia, we're crating everything, it'll all be in the loft by the time the storm hits."

The loft is a roomy area above the gallery where Pilar keeps art not currently on exhibit, including a dozen of Daphne's pieces that didn't make it into the show. But Gallery 25's high ceiling is a mere ten feet above sea level. If the storm surge reaches the predicted height, the whole space will be flooded, years of work ruined.

"You're a saint," Daphne says anyway.

"And you're a genius. Congrats again on selling out the show. I should be able to wire you the funds in the next couple of weeks."

"Are you kidding? Don't even think about that right now," she says, recalling Brantley's worries.

"Be safe."

"You, too, Pilar. And thank you for everything."

Drills scream from the neighbor's house. Daphne walks over. Two men on stepladders hang plywood over windows, a portable workbench and circular saw set up on the driveway. The ground floor is already half-done.

"Hi there!" she calls. "I think you guys are doing our house next." They exchange a look, shrug. "Mi casa?"

The older one shakes his head.

"No inglés?" she asks, feeling like an idiot.

Same response. Frustrated, she walks back to the house and finds Mia lugging her bags to the front door. The sight gives Daphne an idea. "Mia, will you go talk to those two men boarding windows next door? Your father said they're supposed to do our house next. A chance to use your Spanish."

Mia heads over to the neighbor's house and comes back with bad news. "Their English is good," she says. "But Daddy didn't pay them."

"He told me it was all taken care of."

"Maybe they're lying," Gavin says, coming downstairs with his bass. "Price gouging and all."

Daphne digs through her purse for cash. All she comes up with is a ten-dollar bill.

"You want me to tell them to forget it?" Mia says.

"I doubt they take credit cards."

Gavin snorts. "Call it a hunch."

Daphne surveys the expanses of glass on this floor alone. The bay window over the front lawn, the plate-glassed sunroom in back—the studio. She asks Gavin to follow her there and for the next fifteen minutes he helps move her pieces upstairs to his room. Before closing his door, Daphne takes one last look at the peculiar assemblage lining the floor, bookcases, dressers. Countless hours at wheel and workbench, years of coaxing the clay.

She reaches for the light switch and stops when she sees *Sentinel* on Gavin's dresser with seven other sculptures. She grasps it by two tendrils and lifts it carefully out of the array. In her room she wraps it in a T-shirt and bulwarks it with other clothing in her roller bag as she calls Flo.

Yes, the Willows has arranged evacuation for everyone, her mother-in-law tells her.

"Take care of yourself." Daphne flattens a fleece over the sculpture, thinking of cold hotel lobbies.

"Don't you worry about me. I'll be sipping a martini in Sarasota by sunset," Flo says.

Just before eleven Brantley calls. "The last transports should be here in a few, and we'll get the remaining patients loaded and out. Pick me up in, say, half an hour at the ER bay, okay? And if you—" The line goes dead.

Daphne grabs an oversize photo album from the den, then slips her iPad and keyboard into her purse along with her phone. She glances into Brantley's study, wondering whether she should throw a bunch of bills and files into a box, but she wouldn't know what to prioritize.

"Mia, will you grab my purse?" she calls on her way to the van. The kids have brought what looks like half the family's belongings outside to the driveway.

"Yep. And I've got mine, too," her daughter crows.

Mia struts down the front walk with Daphne's purse slung over one shoulder and her own pink number on the other. Daphne sets her roller bag down by the van and rushes back inside for a final sweep, locking doors, checking window latches, punching in the security code.

Outside, Gavin is efficiently transferring everything from the pile in the driveway to the back of the Odyssey. Daphne wants to intervene but forces herself to stay out of it. At the moment he's acting like his old self, cool and confident, teasing his siblings about their inferior spatial relations skills.

And she has her own essential task. Cricket rushes to the passenger side of the van, tail thumping Daphne's leg. A nervous rider, she always needs cuddling for the first stretch. As the tailgate descends and Gavin starts the ignition, the dog curls up in Daphne's lap.

Every radio station is screaming with hurricane coverage . . . *waters off the coast at record high temperatures, we're going to see the wind speeds build up . . . essentially a forty-mile-wide tornado cutting through the lower third of the Florida peninsula . . . explaining the delayed evacuation order.* She touches it off.

"They always weaken before they hit," Gavin says into the silence.

The van crawls up the ramp to I-95, the great north–south interstate that will soon deliver her family to safety somewhere up the peninsula. They will check into a hotel, wait out the storm, and return the day after tomorrow. Brantley will call someone to clear palm fronds off the yard. Across the gap in the elevated highway the southbound lanes stand nearly empty, the occasional emergency vehicle straddling the road, on the lookout for scofflaws.

At the downtown exit for the hospital, Gavin merges into the right lane—but the way is blocked by two police cars, lights flashing. Officers stand at the ramp's mouth clutching fluorescent batons.

"Take the exit," Daphne orders.

"It's blocked," Gavin says.

"Your dad's a doctor. Take it."

He obeys, but one of the cops waves them off with his batons.

Daphne lowers her window. "Officer, we have to get my husband. He's at—"

"Ma'am, you need to keep moving."

"He's a surgeon doing medevac. He's waiting for us."

The cop plants a forearm over her window and looks across at Gavin. "Son, technically you're breaking the law just by pointing your van at my squad. Now get back on the highway."

"Yes, Officer." Gavin reverses. The officer steps away.

In the back, Oliver wails: "Where's Daddy? I *want* him."

Daphne turns in her seat. Mia, too, is tearing up and the dog is panic-panting in her face. "Kids, chill out. We'll swing back at the next exit."

But that off-ramp, too, is blocked. Daphne pushes her back against the seat with her eyes squeezed shut.

"Listen," Gavin says, sounding like his father. "He'll be fine. He'll get on one of the evac buses from the hospital and meet us upstate."

He's right, of course, and Miami has weathered dozens of hurricanes over the decades. Donna, Charlie, Frances, Floyd, Jeanne, Katrina, Wilma, Ida, Andrew. That ridiculous list of names, each with its own associated floods and outages, disruptions and death tolls. Luna will be no different.

She looks around for her phone and remembers Mia carrying her purse out to the minivan. It's now in the back somewhere, wedged between their other possessions. She looks in the vanity mirror. "Mia, text your father." A task to calm them all down. "Tell him we can't get to the hospital. We'll text later to say where we end up."

Daphne watches her daughter's teary eyes slot down to her phone. A text whooshes off. Almost immediately the phone starts to chime. Mia's eyes go wide. "Hi, Daddy!"

"Hey, sweetie. How is everybody?"

Brantley's baritone fills the van over FaceTime. Daphne feels her whole body relax. She digs a nose into Cricket's ruff. The dog licks her chin.

"What's it like there?" Mia says.

"A little crazy, sweetie."

"Sorry we can't pick you up."

"Looks like I'll have to evac with the patients anyway. Tell your mom I'll be in touch once we have these folks resettled."

Garbled sounds, words Daphne can't make out. Mia's eyes are still fixed on the screen.

"Daddy?"

"Actually, Mia, can you give Mom the phone?"

Mia hands it over the seat. Brantley smiles up from the screen, a surgical mask plastered to his neck.

"Hey, love."

"Hey, yourself," Daphne says, sensing the chaos around him. "Wasn't everyone supposed to be out twenty minutes ago?" And aren't you incident commander?

"We're routing some critical patients to beds in Jacksonville."

"That far? In a helicopter?"

"We've got airborne ICUs, these jets that can take three or four patients at a time. Everything's under control. We're heading out to the airfield in a few. I'll probably be in Jacksonville before you guys even reach Orlando."

"Lucky you."

"Daddy gets to ride in a jet? That's not fair!" Oliver, somewhere between a plea and a whine.

"Did you hear that? Your son wants to come with you."

"I wish he could." Brantley looks over his shoulder and nods tightly at someone. "I should go. And listen. You'll be in the Orlando Hilton or whatever in a few hours, taking a bath, having some champagne."

She forces a smile. "Just be careful," she says.

"Will do."

Cricket finally wriggles out of Daphne's arms, scrambling between the front seats and settling on Oliver's lap.

Daphne looks over at Gavin. "Thank you for driving."

"No problem." His face serene as he guides the minivan along. Give Gavin a task, like packing or driving, and he usually responds like a pro (the cake fiasco being a notable exception). The observation plants a seed in her mind, ideas for getting him through the next few weeks once they're back home. A plan, a job, a purpose. It's the idleness that kills.

They cross the river and the I-395 interchange. Traffic quickens. At the edge of the city, Daphne looks east from the elevated interstate, toward the ocean and the bay. The sky is still a flawless topaz. But far off at the horizon stands what must be the leading edge of the storm. A puff of cloud, a ghostly tendril of the outermost band; beneath it, a dimness low on the sea.

11.

Mia looks down at the passing city and opens the screenshot she took of her father during the call, when he got mad at the nurse. For a second the nurse appeared on the wobbly screen. Daddy held the phone away so Mom wouldn't hear him, but Mia heard.

Doctor Hall, what should we—

Gomez, get back to the unit.

But—

Go, goddamnit.

The scary part was her father's face, how his lips pulled back when he yelled. And the way his hand sliced the air.

Last Saturday, Mia was lurking in the hallway by his study when she heard him on the phone. She slid up to the door and looked through the gap. He stood with his back to the hallway, right hand slicing and dicing. *Didn't we negotiate a—and now you're bringing me this bullshit?* He tugged on his hair. He started to turn around and Mia slipped away.

Her phone blips with a Snapchat notification. It's from Charlize, her best friend in Florida. The one girl at school who sits with her at lunch sometimes, and the only one she snaps with.

Another screenshot: a group chat with the Stone Cold Bitches, Gavin's nickname for a group of six popular girls at school. Charlize sends her the screenshots of their chats just to show Mia how mean they are about other girls, especially Mia, who isn't a SCB and thus gets to read about her fat knees and the neck rashes she gets when she's nervous. Gavin tells Mia she should ignore them but Charlize sends the snaps almost every day, so what choice does she have?

Mia swipes through today's screenshots and learns how she waddles when she walks, how bad her lunch smelled yesterday. She saves the pictures to her photos and opens the screenshot of her snarling father again. When she types a reply to Charlize she imagines Daddy's face lingering there, like a ghost on her screen.

ru evacuating?

ya, Charlize replies.

same

sorry for those chats ik there mean but figured u shd know

sokay

They RLY hate u!!!!

And they do, Mia can feel their hate surging from the low heat of her phone. She sets it screen-down on the seat.

"I hope the hotel has a pool," Oliver says with a yawn.

Mia slaps her forehead and almost starts to cry again. Her bathing suit, a new one-piece, her all-time favorite. She left it behind, flopped over the side of the bathtub.

Outside the window more of Florida goes by, signs and trees and parking lots. A girl's dim reflection gazes back from the glass. It wipes its piggy nose and runs fingers through its scraggly hair. It shows its big teeth to the minivan and the family evacuating north.

12.

For nearly a century they have graced the shore, nine square miles of art deco structures ranked sea to bay, fronted by ocean-facing hotels with sunshades fixed over windows; painted eyebrows, flirting with the waves. The exteriors flaunt a palette of pastels. Children imagine licking the buildings like soft serve or taffy; parents marvel at the decadent blend of hues.

The former Celino South Beach, a favored hangout of Gable, Bogart, Hayworth. The old post office, with its minimalist cream facade. And the nautical spire of the Hotel Breakwater, angled like a prow plying tides.

The Art Deco District occupies only a portion of the narrow strip of Miami Beach, dominated by high-rise hotels and condos. Some soar to forty stories of glass, concrete, and steel. More recent structures are designed to withstand sustained winds of up to 165 miles per hour, the maximum achieved by Hurricane Andrew back in 1992. Many are engineered to handle storm surges of fifteen to twenty feet. Andrew's crested at eighteen.

Luna first touches Miami Beach up in Bal Harbour, an outer band making a casual swat. For the better part of an hour, as she rotates in, this is Luna's rhythm, winds gusting and going, rains fleeting and weak. A patron at the Breakwater might be tempted to order another round, enjoy the incoming squall from beneath a canvas awning.

Awnings are among the first anchored objects to go. The mandatory evacuation takes Miami largely by surprise, leaving little time to secure movable properties. (The staff have families, too.) Many hotels have left their outside restaurants and lounges largely as they were before the hurricane's final wobble. Ten thousand glass doors stand unboarded, naked to the winds.

She approaches from the southeast. Her immense eye tracks through a great slot that extends from Old Rhodes Key north to Fort Lauderdale.

First, the surge.

Hours before landfall, Luna's cyclonic winds begin to push water before her like a snow shovel, mounding with the force of a tsunami. The enormous waves break first on Hollywood Beach, claiming a Häagen-Dazs and a souvenir stand along the boardwalk. Other structures follow—houses, stores, smaller motels. Luna carves her way along the edge of the state, slicing away millions of acres of sandy beach and toppling buildings into the frothing waters left in their place. Before her eye is within fifty miles of the Deco District, she has already inundated Biscayne Bay—a bay no longer but claimed as part of the ocean that Luna now commands as she submerges vast stretches of the coast. Destructive, corrosive, she gnaws highway and road, digs massive new channels through the land.

Second, the wind.

When she hits the vast metropolitan area, her eye wall clocks at 215 miles per hour, the power of the strongest tornadoes yet stretched over hundreds of square miles. She strikes Miami as if beating on some mountain-size drum, an invisible membrane that thrums along streets and alleys. She moves like a drunken butcher, flaying skyscrapers, eviscerating offices and conference rooms and lobbies. Tall buildings twist and buckle. The guts of civilization swarm and fly: desks, chairs, tables, carpets, lights, plants, computers, printers, books, and papers by the billions, landing in the rivered streets, pulped through the sewer channels, chewed by the winds.

Third, the rain.

In the first hours of Luna's tear across the peninsula, she drops twenty-two inches. As her eye nears Fort Myers and the Gulf Coast, she wheels on herself and stalls until her immense bands straddle all of South Florida and release unending torrents, less showers than ranked curtains whipping water as her clouds descend.

Lake Okeechobee, already swollen with the surge, bursts its southern levees to flood millions of acres, leveling wastewater plants and farms, wildlife preserves and parks. The great expanse of the Everglades fills with contaminated silt. Its mangrove forests, already scant from past storms, lie broken and uprooted beneath the deluge.

All along the southern coasts, Luna's unrelenting demolition of the lower peninsula leaves behind the detritus of her fury. Rain bombs leave endless shoreline whittled and gashed. Fragments of a thousand boats float in the remnants of bays and inlets. Her first assault leaves a great city shorn of its glory, its husks baking in the August gloom.

Here Luna pauses for a spell, poised above the ruin, weakened but biding her time.

THE GREAT DISPLACEMENT
A DIGITAL CHRONICLE OF THE LUNA MIGRATION

In the space of eleven days, Hurricane Luna, the world's first category 6 storm, swept across South Florida, strengthened again over the Gulf of Mexico, then surged through Galveston Bay and the Houston Ship Channel, destroying the hearts of two great American cities and permanently uprooting millions from their homes and communities. In the process, Luna generated a climate-induced diaspora that has reshaped the demographic and cultural contours of the nation in fundamental ways.

The Great Displacement, an ongoing collaborative project based at the University of California, chronicles this migration through the stories and struggles of internally displaced persons (IDPs) flowing through eighteen federally funded megashelters in the three months following Luna's landfall. Our team draws on a number of current tools and methods in the digital humanities to plot a range of approaches to Luna's aftermath while mapping the fluctuating populations of the megashelters and the paths of migration to and from federal facilities.

But this is also a project of countermapping, enabled by the powerful contributions of displaced populations to the reconstruction of their own itineraries through post-Luna America. While mining data from federal and state repositories, we have worked with affected populations to interrogate official accounts of displacement and their role in perpetuating environmental and economic injustice. Who owns the data of internal displacement? How is it generated, gathered, and deployed? Whose interests has it been made to serve, and how might these official uses be unsettled by the power of crowdsourced data, individual voices, and community activism? In this spirit, our multilayered maps of shelter and migration interface with small-scale itineraries, oral testimonials by the displaced (poor and rich alike), and works of environmental art created in the long wake of the storm. "Lunas," as the hurricane's internally displaced often call themselves, continue to remake American culture through their stories, their self-interpretations, and their art, showing the creative capacity of diaspora despite its often unfathomable challenges.

The Great Displacement was made possible through a Digital Humanities Innovation Seed Grant from DHNet, an intercampus research network funded by University of California Chancellor's Office; and a major collaborative grant from the Chase W. Morton Foundation.

THE GREAT DISPLACEMENT
A DIGITAL CHRONICLE OF THE LUNA MIGRATION

▶ **XAVIER T. TAMAYO, METEOROLOGIST**

The downtown studio was the last local news outfit to broadcast from Miami before the hurricane struck. From the weather desk, Xavier delivered a televised announcement of Luna's revised designation a mere twelve hours before the eye wall came ashore. Now employed at WSGA in Atlanta, Xavier was twenty-four years old at the time.

Play audio file:

Transcript:

It's how I got my fifteen minutes. Somebody turned it into
a meme and you'll see it now whenever something really bad
happens on the news.

My folks, they lived over near San Juan Bosco, little
neighborhood off Flagler. They'd packed up and left that
morning but they weren't too worried. You've got to
understand, most of the models predicted that Luna would
start an eye wall replacement cycle as she approached shore.
The European model still had her turning south-southwest. Or
she'd weaken to a cat 3, and yeah, it'd be bad, I mean,
everybody was still thinking about the condo collapse in '21
and those condemned hotels, all the porous limestone stacked
under Miami like swiss cheese. But nobody thought Luna would
do anything like what Dorian did to the Bahamas in '19.

Problem was, she didn't weaken. That heat blob west of Grand
Bahama warmed the ocean so much that the worst-case
scenarios were coming true right before our eyes. The
sudden intensification was insane. How do you message that
to the population? How do you get the governors and the
NGOs to model the requisite urgency? Because memories here
are short. Back in the 1830s, two hurricanes carved up Miami
Beach into separate islands when it used to be just one.
After Luna, it's a true archipelago.

So anyway, the night before she hit, word comes down to
NOAA from Rodriguez, secretary of commerce at the time. The
president has a question. And the question is, what can we
do to make people understand, to convince everybody, but
everybody, to clear the hell out? The director at the
National Hurricane Center—that was a political appointment—
he'd been pushing the new designation for over a year
already. The guy wanted a category 6 to add to his résumé, I
guess, and there was a lot of resistance from the senior
hurricane guys. Because a cat 5's already the highest
designation, totally open-ended. Plus some cat 2s do more
damage than any cat 4—all the old arguments.

But eventually the politicos win. They pretty much direct-
order the senior staff to force through a new designation.
These are conservative folks, not given to hysteria or
hyperbole, but they get the message. By dawn it's done. The
announcement goes out on emergency bulletins and emails,
including a post on the NHC Twitter feed.

That's where I saw it. You got to understand, I was three
years out of Florida State. I read that tweet on my phone,
just before going on air. You've seen the clip. Everybody's
seen the clip. Luna's on the screen bearing down on us and
I say, "It's official, folks. The National Hurricane Center
has created a new designation for Hurricane Luna."
They show that perfect spiral, then the camera's on me,
and that's when I say it: "That's right, Natalie. It's

absolutely beautiful. The world's first category 6
hurricane."

On live TV. "That's right, Natalie," with this goofy grin on
my face. "Absolutely beautiful," like I'm covering Calle Ocho
instead of a storm that's about to nuke my city.

It became the new "Okay, Boomer." The new "Bye, Felicia."
That's right, Natalie, it's absolutely beautiful, the Dow
Jones went down twenty thousand points in one week. That's
right, Natalie, it's absolutely beautiful, the last glacier has
melted in Wyoming kinda thing. They'll probably put it in my
obituary.

▶ **PENELOPE "PENNY" SAUNDERS, GOVERNOR OF FLORIDA
(RETIRED)**

The house sits on a low bluff overlooking the Apalachicola River, the governor on a white Adirondack chair sipping a Diet Pepsi. Her belated response
to Luna was seen by many as the main factor in thwarting a potential White
House run. Governor Saunders was forty-seven years old at the time.

Play audio file:

Transcript:

Look, you can judge me all you want to, you can second-guess
until the cows come home. But man oh man, the good people of
Florida were so sick of the National Weather Service by that
point, just *done* with Washington treating science like the
Bible. How many times had the predictions been wrong in the

past four, five years? Dorian wipes out Grand Bahama back in 2019 but just skims Florida. The next one swings in, Hurricane Harold. Huge expectations, supposedly Harold's the "Doomsday Storm." Abraham, same thing.

So by the time we get to Luna, everybody's gotten real cynical about all those geniuses at the National Weather Service telling Floridians to run for the hills five times a summer. That's why we delayed the order to evacuate. We had a voluntary advisory, but a full-on evacuation is a huge blow to tourism, the state's economy. And I'll be honest: The money down there? Before Luna, Miami was the most financially exposed urban center in the country in terms of real estate, investment properties, corporate headquarters, you name it. Indian Creek, Fisher Island, are you kidding me? Just gobs and gobs of wealth, all of it gone now. So as governor I had a lot of pressure from a lot of different directions.

Now, in hindsight, do I regret not giving the order sooner? Of course I do. Not a day goes by I don't think of those kids, those old folks who didn't make it out, all the illega— the farmworkers south of Lake Okeechobee. But I was working with the facts on the ground, and those facts told me we had more time.

Plus only a few of the models were predicting she'd blow up like she did. You never think you're going to get the worst-case scenario.

Until you do.

▶ **EMILIA GALARZA, PROFESSOR OF SOCIOLOGY**

She was a student at the University of Puerto Rico at Río Piedras when Hurricane Maria devastated the island nation and the campus. Emilia transferred to the University of Miami under the auspices of the Hurricane Maria Assistance Program (HMAP) but returned to Puerto Rico after Hurricane Luna. Twice displaced, she completed her PhD at UCLA and is now one of the leading figures in the interdisciplinary field of critical disaster studies.

Play audio file:

Transcript:

Hurricane Luna makes me think above all about scale. The official death toll from 9/11 was just around three thousand. Same with Hurricane Maria. Almost identical number of "official" deaths. But what about the aftermaths? What about post-traumatic stress, the contamination of water and soil? What about cancer clusters and infrastructure? That's what my work thinks about, that space between the moment of disaster and its long consequences. The comet and the tail.

After Maria, my father caught one of those paper towel rolls Trump tossed into the crowd at Calvary Chapel. You can see him in the footage, big gato in the back with a blue ball cap. That church was in one of the least affected neighborhoods in San Juan, and that's where el presidente holes up while trashing our mayor as a crazy witch, lying about the billions in nonexistent aid. Dry your tears with these paper towels, motherfuckers.

Because natural disasters are never natural. After Maria, large parts of Puerto Rico suffered the longest blackout in American history, an entire year without power. Even the reach of public utilities can be an intensely political and socioeconomic factor in governmental and corporate responses to disaster. So my own thinking on catastrophe and its aftermath is strongly intersectional, and here I'd go all the way back to 1977 and the work of the Combahee River Collective. The group recognized the interlocked systems of oppression, and how the synthesis of those oppressions creates webs of privilege and injustice that entangle us all.

There's a lot of sociological literature about the "therapeutic communities" that form after disasters. We call it the "solidarity and sisterhood" model. But there's a bleaker side to all of this. Hate crimes spike in the wake of catastrophes, that's just fact. You can't isolate one kind of inequality and assume you're getting the full picture. Economic disadvantage, environmental oppression, differences of sexuality and ability: catastrophe makes the collisions more shattering, more stratifying.

And that's how we have to look at the storm's aftermath. There you had this massive migration of differently bodied individuals from their communities into temporary emergency shelters. Schools, churches, shopping malls, motels. And when those filled up right away, into the megashelters, the stadiums and the open-air camps. A majority of the displaced were poor people of color, making the federal government's response all the more predictable.

Speaking of predictable. Doesn't surprise me that what finally focused the nation's attention on the megashelters was that spectacle in Oklahoma, what went down at Tooley Farm. There you had a perfect storm of climate change, displacement, extremism, and racial difference swirling around these white bodies at the center of it all, the big pale eye of the storm.

Call it the catastrophe of whiteness. You want the world to pay attention to your story, you make it all about white people in peril. Works every time.

PART
TWO

13.

The miles-long caravan sways away from the coast, northwest up the Florida Turnpike to Wildwood. Traffic moves at a clip swift enough for order, slow enough to display the vastness of the operation: four million Floridians decanted into the upper half of the peninsula in a single day. A rolling gas shortage forces the abandonment of cars along the route. White cloths dangle from windows. Belongings litter the shoulders. The radio blares with harrowing updates.

Twenty miles south of Gainesville, Gavin taps the dashboard. "Fuel light just flashed."

Daphne, shaken from a stupor, looks over with a frown. The hybrid so seldom needs fuel that she can't remember the last time she filled up. It's almost dinnertime, they've been driving for hours without a stop, eaten all the snacks. Her bladder is bursting and she needs her phone to start looking for a place to stay. "Do you see a station?"

"Everybody's out." Gavin points to an Exxon, a NO GAS sign scrawled on cardboard and tacked to a palm trunk.

"I'm hungry," Oliver announces.

"Shut up, whiny," Mia says.

"Don't call me that."

"Whiny heinie."

"Stop."

"Whiny white heinie that's ugly and spiny."

"Stop!"

"Hold it together, guys," Daphne says. "We'll find gas, we'll grab dinner and see if we can get in touch with your dad, okay?" They scan the side of the road. Daphne makes a game of it, telling them to count cars to find the shortest line.

"There!" Mia points out her window. Down a secondary road is a BP station, twelve cars in line.

"Good eye, sis." Gavin pulls the wheel to the right. They wait twenty minutes until the minivan slides up alongside a pump.

"Mia, hand me my purse," Daphne says.

Mia unclips her belt and climbs over the seat. Cricket starts to whine. Daphne gives the leash to Gavin and asks him to take the dog to a nearby patch of grass. She steps out and raises her arms, her spine snapping. The coming dusk will be warm but clear, up in the safe half of the state. According to the radio, even Luna's outermost tendrils will remain miles to the south. She opens the sliding door and sees Mia sprawled over the seat. An apologetic smile for the driver of the Mercedes coupe behind them. He waves it off, probably ecstatic just to be near the front of the line.

"I can't find it, Mom."

Daphne stoops to peer over the seat. The contents in back have shifted, roller bags tilted up against the tailgate. She walks around to the back as it lifts to expose their belongings. She pushes aside bags, Cricket's crate, Gavin's bass, looking for the brown leather hump. Her movements grow frantic, hurried. She starts to take the roller bags out when Oliver saves the day.

"Here it is, Mommy!" he crows. Daphne wants to kiss him; then—

Mia: "Wrong, heinie, that's Gavin's computer bag."

"Stop *calling* me that."

"Are you sure, Mia?"

"Of course I'm sure."

Her purse. Cash, credit cards, ID.

Phone.

iPad.

Ativan.

Everything.

"Gavin!" He comes shuffling toward the van. "Where'd you put my purse?"

"Mia has it."

"No, she doesn't."

His right eye tics. "Mia, where's Daphne's purse?"

"I gave it to you."

"No, you didn't."

"Did too."

"Don't fucking lie."

"I *tried* to put it in the back but you wouldn't let me."

"That's bullsh—"

"You said, quote, little girls don't have the spatial relations skills to handle an operation of this delicacy, unquote, and so you told me to just set it down by Cricket's crate."

Daphne stares, frozen by the specificity of the recollection. Mia's sunburned arms are folded tightly and her head tilted in her you-know-I'm-right pose. They see it when she tattles on Oliver for not feeding the dog. When she catches Brantley in a white lie about the fate of the last ice cream sandwich.

Mia, the moral outrage engine of their household—and right now, Daphne knows with a cold certainty, her daughter is telling the truth.

She turns on Gavin. "So where is it?"

"I—I mean . . ."

"Lady, you filling up or what?"

Mr. Mercedes stands with an elbow on his open door. A rank of twenty thirsty cars stretches down the street.

"Just a minute." She whirls back. "Where's your debit card?"

Gavin empties his card carrier. Driver's license, Stanford ID, a debit card.

"But it's cashed," he says in a quavering voice. "There's nothing in there."

"How much is in your Venmo or Zelle or whatever?"

"Nothing. And Dad canceled the credit card he used to transfer money."

"He did? But why—well, do you have—I mean . . ." She stares at her son's card holder, the reality of the situation sinking in. No cash, no credit cards, no phone; therefore no Apple Pay, no Venmo. No money for gas, for food, for a hotel—for anything.

"There's a line here." Mr. Mercedes again.

"Just a goddamn *minute*," she snaps. A car honks. Another.

First things first. Moving the Odyssey without buying gas will force them back to the end of the line. By then their last drops of fuel might run out. The station's tanks might be depleted. Then what would they do?

She takes three tentative steps toward the Mercedes. The driver has retaken his seat, his door still open. "Sir?" She stoops, a supplicant.

He frowns. "Yeah, what is it?"

"It seems my stepson left my purse in Miami." No question that Gavin can hear her but she doesn't care; she wants him to.

"And . . . ?"

"Would you mind loaning me enough to put some gas in the tank? I can take your number and—"

"You want me to buy you gas?"

"I'll pay you back as soon as I have my purse."

He gestures toward the pumps. "These tanks are almost empty. No way I'm risking it."

"You can't just loan me ten dollars?"

"Sorry, lady." Avoiding her gaze.

She stares at him, dumbfounded, trying to imagine herself showing such selfishness at a moment like this. Honks going in earnest now.

"Daphne," Gavin says, standing there with Cricket. "I'm sorry. It was an accident."

"Just keep walking her." Daphne can't look at him. "Mia, go with him. Oliver, stay in the car."

She pushes the gas cap shut, slams the passenger door, and walks around to the driver's seat.

"You mad?" Oliver asks in an excited voice as she climbs in.

"Mad doesn't begin to describe it." She guides the minivan over to a parking spot by the convenience store. "Go play with Cricket."

"I'm really hungry."

"Me, too. We'll figure this out, I promise. Now go."

She uses Mia's phone to call Brantley again. The network puts her through but the call goes straight to voice mail. She texts him.

PLEASE CALL ASAP!!!! Everyone ok but lost purse, no $$.
Where are you???????

She remembers their last conversation, Brantley's aside. *I'll probably be in Jacksonville before you guys even reach Orlando.* She searches for hospitals in Jacksonville and finds the most likely destination, one of the University of Florida hospital branches. She gets put through to an ICU nurse and asks about a medevac plane from Miami.

Daphne can hear the clicking of keys. "You know, I don't see anything here," the nurse says, "but that doesn't mean much. Entire state's a nightmare. We've got millions on the move, heart attacks, crashes on the highways. Best guess is they got rerouted to Atlanta, maybe Charleston or even Charlotte." Daphne leaves Mia's number in case the nurse hears anything.

She leans against a shaded corner of the convenience store. Out on the boulevard heat blurs off the pavement. So absurd, this moment, a preposterousness she wants to laugh off. She sees herself telling the story over cocktails with Pilar two weeks from now. Stuck in Central

Florida with three kids, one dog, a minivan out of gas, no cash, no purse, and then, out of nowhere—

What?

Out of nowhere, what?

The line of cars hasn't diminished. If anything the congestion has thickened. Two rows of pumps still work but the third has just given out. A man stands by his pickup truck slamming his fist on the glass. It helps a little, to see someone else losing it. But at least this man could pay for the gas he didn't get. He could go into the convenience store and buy an iced coffee, or endless water bottles. He could walk across the boulevard and check into that Motel 6. The world is his.

Back in her purse on the driveway in Coral Gables there are three working credit cards. Surely there must be a way to use them in an emergency. On Mia's browser she finds the number for National Bank of South Florida credit card services. After eight minutes on hold she speaks to an agent who asks her enough security questions to establish her legitimacy—but his only solution is to send new Visa cards to her home address. No, he can't give her number to a convenience store clerk. No, he can't help her pay for anything over the phone. She considers trying another bank but dusk is coming on, and her children look listless. She calls Gavin over.

"I can't get in touch with your father, and Mia doesn't have any of my contacts on her phone except yours and his. You got into Stanford. Help me fix this."

He swallows. "I heard some guys talking about FEMA shelters."

Daphne makes an effort to stay calm. "We don't need a shelter, Gavin. We need to figure out how to pay for our dinner. For gas."

"Wait." His eyes light up. "What's your Apple ID?"

She shakes her head. "I have no idea."

"It's probably your email. If your phone is backed up you can turn Mia's phone into yours."

"What do you mean?"

"You restore it with your ID," he explains. "It'll put everything of yours on Mia's phone. Your contacts, your apps, maybe even your credit card on Apple Pay."

A glimmer of hope. She hands him Mia's phone and he starts swiping. "What email do you use?"

"Probably just my Gmail."

He knows it already and quickly enters it. "Now your password."

"I don't remember ever logging on."

"Do you have a usual one?"

She takes the phone from him and enters a remembered password. When that doesn't work she tries another she's used, then a third. She gets a warning, tries an old password—

Too many attempts, the screen shouts.

"Dammit." She tears up. "I think I'm locked out."

From the edge of the parking lot she watches a perky blond woman swipe a credit card at a gas pump. The contours of Daphne's life ripple in the heat, these webs of connection that might be drawn upon at a moment like this. No parents, no siblings, and her phoneless mother-in-law is on a bus to God knows where. Brantley has a cousin in Idaho he's talked to maybe twice in ten years. Pilar and her husband are evacuating right now just like Daphne's family. The few other people she knows in Miami are all scattered to the winds, and why would they help her when they have their own families to attend to? Her life is built on her art, her routines, her credit cards, her iPhone contact list—on the stability of nuclear family and dependable technology. Now there is no one to call. No *way* to call.

And yet, in this moment, her children are hungry.

The blond woman strolls back toward the convenience store. An oval face smug with a full tank of gas. A working credit card. She has everything.

Daphne approaches her.

"Excuse me. Can I ask you something?"

"Of course," she says, returning Daphne's smile.

Daphne explains the situation: the evacuation, the abandoned purse. The woman's name is Shelley, from Fort Lauderdale. They're all heading up to her sister's place in Savannah to wait it out. The husband comes out with their two daughters, who veer off toward the car as he walks up and gives Daphne a once-over through his aviators.

"So, I guess what I'm asking," Daphne says, wincing, "is whether you can help us. I need to feed my kids and I was hoping you might give us . . . loan us some cash."

The husband crosses his arms. The convenience store bag dangles from his fingers. "I'm not comfortable with that."

Shelley elbows him. "Don't be an ass. Her husband is a surgeon at UMed."

"Oh." He still looks suspicious.

Shelley pulls out a wallet. "Take a twenty. Take two. Seriously, and don't even think of trying to pay us back. Just pay it forward to someone else." She pushes the bills into Daphne's hands.

"Thank you." Only forty dollars but her knees almost buckle. "Thank you so, so much."

"And good luck to you guys."

"Yeah, good luck," the husband says, already turning his wife away, and the couple walk together back to their fully gassed-up Subaru, where they hand out snacks and drinks to the two girls leaning against the hatchback playing on their phones.

"Why did you give that lady money, Mom?" one of them asks.

Shelley throws a chagrined smile back at Daphne. "We were just helping her family, sweetie. We all need help sometimes."

Daphne walks numbly back toward the kids. Mia, eyes closed, leans against a tree trunk with her head lolling to the side. Oliver draws lines with his toe in the dirt.

Only Gavin has witnessed the exchange. When she looks at him he smirks. "Daphne the beggar."

Something detonates in her skull. She steps up until her face is inches from her stepson's. "Don't you say a *word*." Slamming a finger into his bony chest. "You're the one who left my purse in the driveway. You're the reason we're in this whole goddamn situation in the first place. You are *so* ungrateful, Gavin. So *fucking* irresponsible."

An awful silence rings in her ears. Oliver gapes. Mia, awakened by her mother's volume, starts to cry. Gavin turns away, and the shame comes crashing in. She has never spoken to him like this, not even close. Customers stare over at her family from the pumps and from the entrance to the convenience store.

Shelley is just pulling out, windows open as the Subaru inches forward in the exit line. The husband has his elbow out. He looks right at Daphne and she glimpses herself as he goes by, her hungry family a distortion in his mirrored shades.

14.

After his stepmom's meltdown, Gavin throws a stick for Cricket and thinks back on Moral Philosophy, a class that blew his mind first quarter. A self-driving car has to swerve to avoid killing its driver. But the swerve will take out two toddlers on the sidewalk. How do you program a conundrum like that?

Or say you, your sister, and a stranger have been captured by a serial killer. The serial killer gives you a gun and points another gun at your head. Unless you shoot your sister yourself, the serial killer will shoot her plus the stranger. Can you bring yourself to kill your own sister to save someone else's life? What's the ethical thing to do?

Speaking of ethical. Gavin looks out over the stubbly grass and dirt, and he pictures Daphne's purse sitting there on the driveway. The particular delight in backing over the thing, how the van's suspension lifted slightly as a rear tire mangled the contents. That faint, gratifying, crunchy bump. Only Gavin noticed it, but the sensation filled him with an unfamiliar glee, the first pure thing he's felt in months.

Was it really his fault, though? Wasn't it Daphne's fault, for trusting her purse to an idiot like Mia? Or his dad's, for putting Gavin in a situation where he'd even contemplate doing something so psychotic? Or his mom's, for dying on her only child and forcing him to move in with a prefab family that still makes him feel like a slashed and deflated fifth wheel?

Because leaving Daphne's purse in the driveway during a hurricane evacuation was, indubitably, psycho. Nihilistic. Pointless, self-sabotaging. Gavin a new Raskolnikov, an ex-student murdering a couple of old ladies for the empty satisfaction of a few stolen trinkets. But hey, a college dropout with a dead mom and a dad like Gavin's must find such small pleasures wherever he can. He did it because he could. He did it to show his stepmother, finally, the truth, though so far Gavin's the only one seeing it.

He releashes Cricket and bends to rake his fingers through her ruff and smell her breath and let her nasty tongue baste his lips just so he can feel something. She responds in her unconditional way, already forgiving. Gavin hands her off to his half brother and turns away, so the brat won't see the wet rimming of his eyes.

That's what moral philosophy teaches you, he thinks as he shuffles inside to shoplift a Milky Way and take a leak. Collective responsibility. Distributed guilt. Blame to go around.

15.

They sleep in the Odyssey with the windows gapped and the seats tilted back and their guts working through a shared bucket of greasy KFC. Daphne half slumbers with the night air moist on her skin and awakens to Cricket's low growl. A hairy knuckle raps on the window.

"Ma'am."

She licks her pasty lips as Cricket climbs into her lap to protect her. A few moans from the kids. A guy wearing a British Petroleum shirt hunches outside the passenger door.

"Yes, what is it?" Daphne whispers through the gap.

"The Red Cross is telling people to go to the county fairgrounds," he whispers back. Cricket noses the gap. The clerk scratches her snout.

"Where's that?"

He tells her, and Daphne scribbles the address on an old receipt.

"They've got water, food, first aid. They're busing folks to hotels and whatnot."

Hotels. Comforts that already feel like things of a faintly remembered past. A soft bed, a hot shower.

His face softens. "Ma'am, there's an awful lot of folks in your boat. *Lot* of folks." His kindness is a needful sting. One night in a minivan and she's Scarlett O'Hara.

"Have you heard if they're letting everyone go back yet?"

"To Miami?" His lips purse. "Honestly, it'll be awhile. Plus nobody has gas."

Gavin and the kids sleep on. After taking Cricket out to do her business, Daphne ties her to a signpost and goes inside the station to pee. A small coffee costs $1.79 so she skips it. Instead she buys granola bars and milks for the kids for $10.28. After dinner last night, this leaves $5.27, which she can't use for gas because the station is dry.

Outside she calls Brantley but once again his line goes directly to voice mail. She looks at the news.

LUNA'S FURY UNABATED AS MONSTER STORM LINGERS

THOUSANDS MISSING, MILLIONS DISPLACED
IN WAKE OF FIRST CATEGORY 6

MIAMI BEACH, COASTAL AREAS "GONE," GOVERNOR SAYS

Luna is still dumping rain everywhere in South Florida, the first images of destruction already viral. A video of Miami Beach resembles the aftermath of a carpet bombing, with scarcely a single structure left intact. Luna has carved enormous channels across the width of the island, large swaths of which are now part of the ocean. There is nothing specifically about Coral Gables, though the damage downtown is catastrophic. Feet of standing water on the streets, every window shattered, upper floors of skyscrapers shorn like the tops of trees.

The kids greet the new day with sour-mouthed confusion. Daphne hands out milks and granola bars and tells them the plan. Drive to the fairgrounds, accept whatever help the Red Cross provides, and wait for their father to be in touch. Why Brantley hasn't been in touch already . . . the question charges the air between Daphne and her stepson. Gavin keeps checking his phone, his face a mask.

Daphne drives this time. The GPS takes them up a state highway to a narrower road lined with abandoned cars. Hundreds trudge north in a broken, straggling chain. The surface soon turns to gravel. Three miles short of the fairgrounds the fuel light begins an urgent blinking. In another mile, the engine coughs once, twice, and Daphne uses the last sputter of power to pull off. The Odyssey joins a scatter of dead vehicles on the shoulder.

Repacking involves a series of stark choices. They will take Daphne's toiletries but not the bulky photo album. Cricket's food bag but not her crate. Oliver's Rubik's Cube but not his action figures. When Gavin hefts his electric bass, Daphne doesn't have the energy to fight him, and they aren't saying goodbye to these things forever. The car will be here when they get back, perhaps towed somewhere else.

This is temporary. Temporary. Temporary.

The temperature has already spiked, the humidity an extra shirt as they leave the Odyssey behind and join the flow of foot traffic toward the fairgrounds. Red Cross and National Guard trucks and FEMA vans pass by in both directions, ferrying the elderly, the pregnant, the disabled, the obese. Water is not a problem, at least, bottles from huge pallets overseen by local volunteers and church groups cheerily doled out as the walkers go along. Dogs congregate to sniff and drink from bowls laid along the route. For Cricket, Mia observes, this is heaven.

Within the first half mile, though, Daphne begins to sense the darker sentiments among the trudgers. Many have been walking since yesterday, camping out in fields, beneath overpasses and bridges. She hears of sunstroke and blistered feet. Complaints of a deliberate delay by the governor in ordering the evacuation. Rumors of ten thousand residents of Miami-Dade trapped in a sports stadium with no working toilets ("Just like goddamn Katrina," someone says).

The road carves through treeless grassland, no breeze to cool the sweat, the whirr of insects a drone in the ear. Evacuees dodge off to relieve themselves with no shelter from shrubs.

"Fucking Bataan Death March," Gavin murmurs at one point, and Daphne doesn't bother to correct the hyperbole as she feels her own self-pity mounting with every step. *Twenty-four hours ago I was a wealthy surgeon's wife leaving my huge house with three kids and a dog in a hybrid SUV. Now I'm a sweating, penniless refugee dragging a wheelie bag up a rural road.* It all feels like a charade, though, a performance, a role Daphne's family has taken on in an unintentional and surreal show of solidarity with the truly unfortunate. A purse left behind, severed communication. A small swarm of inconvenient circumstance, soon, for her family at least, to dissolve.

And yet—

After her move to Florida, Daphne joined a book group at the local library. For the first meeting, the group happened to choose a non-fiction bestseller about the climate emergency, one of those apocalyptic tomes you read about in *The New Yorker* or hear about on *Weekend Edition*. What stood out at the time was the admonitions about the leveling effects of warming even in the short term, the author's sense— despite vast disparities between populations already experiencing its present-day effects, and despite the immense inequalities that will shape its future consequences—of how surprisingly *soon* the crisis would start to engulf even the privileged, the well sheltered, the smugly oblivious. Vintners in Napa Valley, owners of golf clubs in Palm Beach.

During the discussion, one of the book club members, a woman of retirement age, brought up the various states of mind provoked by the immensity of the problem. Such emotions, the author argued, conspire to keep our politicians and our industry leaders and our dutifully recycling selves from concrete and meaningful action. Compartmentalization, denial, automation bias, the bystander effect, illusion of control, fear of alarmism. The book tries to box out your denial, this woman said, to shatter your complacency. *But does it work?* she asked the group.

I don't know, Daphne remembers replying. *It all seems so—meta,* she said with a nervous laugh. The others agreed.

The fairgrounds at last. Low barns and pavilions rise above an enormous crowd with no discernible organization. Some stand in large packs, others wait in winding lines with no visible end or beginning.

She manages to locate a Red Cross worker who directs her to the far end of the fairgrounds, where an American flag and a Florida flag share a pole. Daphne rounds up the kids and finds the ends of four unmoving lines. Mia goes ahead to scout and comes back skipping. "They're getting everybody places to stay."

Daphne bites a lip, assessing. "Why don't you guys take the dog and all our stuff over there." She points to a fenced-off field or paddock where competing herds of sweaty kids play a game. *And put on sunscreen, all three of you,* she wants to call after them, before realizing they have none.

The line moves at shuffle pace as the kids come and go to check in. Gavin figures out where to get drinks and snacks. Finally Daphne reaches the head of the line, where four Red Cross workers sit at two adjoining tables pounding away on tablets and laptops.

"We're relocating folks out of state," her staffer gruffly says, tapping at his keyboard.

"We'd be happy to drive several hours," Daphne tells him. "Savannah, Atlanta, wherever. If we can just get a tank of gas and a few days' worth of food we'll be all set."

"Ma'am, we've got two million folks all-a-sudden homeless. The Red Cross is setting up some larger shelters. There's one in Oklahoma that'll be online day after tomorrow."

"*Oklahoma?* Aren't there other options? What about a hotel, or a nice—"

"Lady, look around. We got five hundred people in this line, more by the hour. Every hotel room and church basement for literally two hundred miles is already full. You want our help, this is your only choice. Bus leaves tomorrow at noon."

"But where are we supposed to stay tonight?"

He gestures with his hands to indicate the fairgrounds. Daphne spins in place, taking in the swarming throngs, the open-air buildings and pavilions, the paddocks and animal stalls. In a field to the north, families quilt the grass with their belongings, claiming space.

"You want the seats or not?"

She feels the weight of it, how her entire existence has narrowed, in a single day, to this. Shelter, food, safety. Right now she cares more about finding a secure place for her children to sleep than whether Brantley is safe, or even alive. The animal realization chills her.

"We'll go." Relief in the saying of it, the submission. The delivering of herself and her family into the care of others, however unknown. "Four of us. Two adults, two kids."

He types in their names and hands her four bracelets, blue for adults, green for minors, each imprinted with a barcode. "Keep these bracelets on until you're checked into the facility in Oklahoma. They're your ticket for entrance, shelter, meals, all of it. Next!"

Daphne walks away clutching the four bracelets like they're winning lottery tickets. She gathers the kids and makes them fasten the bands around their wrists as she fields their questions about what's next, questions she cannot begin to answer. They find an open spot in the field, stopping on their way for a stack of blankets and a plastic tarp to cover the ground.

The late afternoon brings a drenching heat and hours she will never forget, her family packed in with thousands on acres of sandy loam that breaks like piecrust in the hand and makes her long for the cool moisture of her clay. When evening comes there are bouts of weeping as the displaced mourn their dead and missing.

Yet through it all there is kindness, a luminous generosity born of common peril. People swap food, families intermingle. Parents of infant twins share a handful of diapers with a struggling mom. A boy two blankets over becomes obsessed with Cricket's panting and comes back with a water bowl rigged up from his Dolphins cap and a freezer bag.

True night comes on, and with it an interval of gradual quieting, an unspoken consensus to cease chatter, extinguish lights, comfort children. Coughs still. Laughter dies. A hush descends, and a low, rumbling voice lifts in song.

Amazing grace, how sweet the sound . . .

Scattered voices join him for the second line.

That saved a wretch like me . . .

Daphne's lips form the next words, and in an instant dozens are singing, and now hundreds, now thousands, and the earth seems to tremble with the swelling hymn, her body with unexpected prayer. The family spends the second night beneath the stars, and Brantley never calls.

16.

"We've got an all-hands-on-deck situation," says the douchebag on the screen. "This storm will affect homeowner, auto, personal property—every policy we sell. If the reinsurers collapse, we are well and truly fucked, guys."

The agents slump glumly around Norm's laptop and listen to Southerly's regional coordinator issue dire warnings about the imminent collapse of the reinsurance market. The event involves hundreds of agents gathered in branch offices across Texas and the American South to attend a morning Zoom as Luna begins its churn across the Gulf. They could all be sitting comfortably at their own computers but Norm corralled them into this stale-aired break room as a show of "branch solidarity," a sentiment Tate's finding it hard to conjure at the moment.

Reinsurance: a concept foreign to Tate when he started but now it's all anyone in the industry can talk about. Who knew that the huge national insurance agencies like Prudential and Southerly carry insurance themselves, that events like upper-category hurricanes sometimes require primary insurers to dip into massive transnational reinsurance pools, that even these reinsurers now face the prospect of a meltdown given the recent chain of domestic catastrophes here in the US of A. The deep freeze in Texas back in '21, the Front Range inferno last year, the California fires every year, the rain bombs flooding random towns and cities twice a month, the ongoing western gigadrought—and now a massive hurricane chewing up South Florida, all in the midst of a global recession.

"And if you think the feds are going to swoop in and save us, you haven't been paying attention. There's just not enough capital out there to shore things up. Triage is on us. We have to choose winners and losers. Otherwise, we're done. So how are we going to make these difficult choices within the boundaries of insurance law?"

Tate's phone hitches in his lap. He looks down.

Home early. Dinner on stove.

He smiles at the screen. Jessamyn doesn't like holding her packages longer than she has to. They arrange a meet at the parking lot of the recording studio in Montrose where her band is cutting an album.

Tate taps Norm on the shoulder. "Got an errand. Be right back." His boss half turns and sags deeper in his chair.

Yury says they're changing things up," Jessamyn says in his car.

"What's that mean?"

"No more pills, no more cookie boxes. They're moving to something more efficient. Sublingual tabs."

"You mean—"

"Wildfire," she says, like an incantation. Tate has heard the whispers in recent months, rumors of something novel on the rise. *Wildfire*. A new synthetic analgesic with ten times the potency of OxyContin, spreading like its namesake among smoke-breathing users on the West Coast; and now, it seems, making its way east.

"They want us to up our game," she says.

"I'm listening."

"Instead of a bag I'll bring back a whole carload. Half the time, twenty times the payoff."

"That's . . . a shitload of drugs."

"Your chance to go big-time."

"How's it work?" He ignores her mocking tone.

"Instead of driving to Saint Louis, I fly. They have their own car loaded up. I'll be back that night."

He considers it. "You don't know anything about the car, the stickers. If you get pulled over . . ."

"A put-together white chick, alone on the interstate? I smile, bat the eyes, show some shoulder." She bares her upper arm.

"That'll work," Tate says neutrally.

"Oh yeah?" She slow blinks. Her lips seem to self-moisten as they part. He almost leans in, but again a certain reluctance pulls him back. Jessamyn feels it, he can tell, the turmoil in him, the mystery of whatever this is. She's probably just messing with his head anyway, with no intention of letting things progress beyond a mild flirtation.

Showing the skin but keeping the forbidden fruit out of reach. And thus it's been since the Garden of Eden. It's a match we're losing, lads, and losing big. My advice? Don't play it at all, this pussy game. Sure, take the fruit when it's offered, but don't let them suck your brain dry along with your sack. The lassies' ll be after you soon enough. Never forget: we're animals, all of us. Let nature takes its course, me lads.

Jessamyn reaches into her bag for a lipstick, the spell snapped. "So, are we in," she says as she applies the gloss, "on this wildfire jag?"

He swallows, a tight ripple down his neck. "We're in."

"Text me the details." She puckers at the visor and pinkies the bubble of her lip.

Back at the office the agents shout on their phones as hurricane coverage blares from the TV. A meteorologist's dire comparisons, astonishment at what Luna did to Miami. A group photograph of a now-dead family. The dad a teacher, the mom an attorney, three bright-eyed kids mugging for the camera.

The sight inspires Tate to text Nora.

I'll take Connor Saturday.

Twenty seconds later: Like hell.

I get weekends.

Since when? You've missed 47 of the last 50.

Bitch, he types, but his thumb hesitates over Send. Instead he types NVM and pockets his phone. Probably not the greatest weekend for father-son bonding anyway, given the Luna sitch.

Norm comes out with his proprietary branch manager remote control and ups the volume. The footage just insane, the chyron a scrolling apocalypse. MASSIVE DESTRUCTION IN SOUTH FLORIDA . . . THOUSANDS FEARED DEAD . . . UNFATHOMABLE DAMAGE TO INFRASTRUCTURE . . . LUNA BARRELS OVER GULF OF MEXICO . . .

The gargantuan blade saws across the screen.

17.

The driver stands at the bus door with a clipboard. Her hair is green, her skin emblazoned with tattoos that Daphne, usually fascinated by body art, doesn't have the energy to scrutinize closely. She shows her wristband.

"We have four, plus her." She tugs at Cricket's leash.

"Sorry, no animals."

"That can't be right." Daphne searches her memory of the last evacuation. "Don't household pets have to be accommodated?"

"That law's been suspended by our sainted governor, bless her heart. They're doing shelter intake over there." She points toward the north end of the parking lot. Daphne stares down at Cricket, panting contentedly at her feet. The driver squats to pet her. "Sweet thing."

"She is." Daphne bends her knees to join them, grateful to share this private moment, to make it about Cricket rather than herself.

"From what I hear," the driver says, looking up, "they got no-kills lined up for most of them."

Most of them?

Daphne turns to Gavin and her children—and sees they've heard the exchange. "Kids, we need to—"

"No." Mia stamps her foot. "They're *not* taking her away."

Oliver's eyes go wide. "We can't take Cricket? We cuh-cuh-can't—" A crescendo, his voice one long keen.

"We can't," Daphne says, bawling herself now. "And we have to go."

"It's *evil*." Mia shakes with rage. "This is an *evil* thing you're *doing*, Mommy. It's *evil* and it's *mean*."

"Mia, we don't have a choice. I wish we did, but—oh God . . ."

It's Gavin who saves them. "You guys, you guys." He goes down on one knee to gather his siblings in. "Remember we put Cricket in that kennel when we went to Paris last summer?" They nod. "And went to pick her up and she refused to leave that dog run?"

"She made doggy friends," Oliver sniffles.

"And she'll make a lot more this week until we pick her up. She'll be okay."

Gavin glances at Daphne. She mouths a thank-you, but he turns his head aside. "We don't deserve her anyway," she hears her stepson mutter, and her heart breaks a little. He's not even fighting this, just giving in to the inevitable for reasons of his own.

Oliver insists on walking over with her. In the animal line, a man berates his wife. Daphne gathers that the woman came over to surrender the dog. Her husband has other ideas.

"Dammit, Rosie," he growls, "I been telling you about this FEMA plan for years. *Years*. Hell if we're going to that camp. Hell if I'm getting on that bus. Not handing over Roscoe P neither."

His wife puts a hand on his arm. "Deke, listen—"

"You think they'll keep the gotdamn dogs alive when they're throwing people in camps? No-kill shelters my sweet white ass." He stalks off into the crowd with the dog tagging at his heels.

Daphne looks down at Oliver, nosing Cricket's face. At the table she adds her name to a long list of owners and gets a written receipt. No barcodes for dogs.

"And these are no-kill shelters?" she softly asks.

The volunteer hesitates. "We'll do our best."

"Seriously?"

He puffs his cheeks, blows out. "We've got a lot of dogs, ma'am. Awful lot of dogs."

It is one of the worst moments of Daphne's life, handing over this beloved member of her family like Shelley at the gas station handed over two bills, if less willingly. She runs her fingers through Cricket's soft pelt, the smooth length of her sides, but she won't look at the dog's face, she can't, only kisses it with her eyes closed, afraid to see the animal's infinite trust even in these last moments, or the dawning sense of betrayal as she tugs at Oliver's hand to pull him away from this sweet perfect being who would do anything for any one of them, but would never do this.

The phone battery is dying. Daphne types one last text to Brantley— On bus to Oklahoma w kids. Will charge phone when I can. I love you—then calls her bank and can't get through. She tries the Willows again but Mia's phone dies on the second ring. (Thoughts of her mother-in-law are hardly pure: whatever has happened to Brantley, Flo will have working credit cards, ready cash, resources to help right the family ship.)

The bus leaves the fairgrounds along the same gravel road they walked hours before. Air freshener mingles with the chemical smell of the toilet. Daphne feels nothing at first when she sees the Odyssey, parked where they left it yesterday morning, with its windows shattered and its contents strewn along the side of the road.

But then she sees Brantley, peering up from the ground. She twists her neck and smashes her cheek to the glass for a last look at the photo, taken on their wedding day; but the car and the butterflied album are gone. When she turns from the window Gavin is standing in the aisle by Oliver's seat, his face ashen, phone clutched against his ribs.

"No." She thrusts out her palms to ward him off. "Don't say it, Gavin. Don't say it."

He shakes his head. "It's not Dad. Sorry. It's—this."

His hand is shaking when he gives her the phone. Daphne tries to figure out what she's seeing on the screen: looped helicopter footage shot from high above Miami, the skyline from a distance. The angle changes to show the coastline, a shot of the water over—but where is Key Biscayne?

Now a wider angle. A peaked roof juts up above the lingering surge, only a few feet visible below a cross and steeple. She recognizes the structure. Coral Gables, that Catholic church on Main Road, a few hundred yards up from the shoreline.

The camera pans down the coast, following the watery trail of Luna's devastation. Great rafts of debris. The grill of an upturned truck. Other structures peek above the lingering surge. Here, perhaps the top of the gatehouse at Pineapple Isles. Another looks like the gable of the guest suite above her own garage. A new lagoon has formed where their portion of the city once sat, their house and neighborhood swallowed by a rough and lapping sea.

Daphne hands the phone back, leans her cheek against the window, and lets her head bob on the glass as the coach trundles on past the stream of evacuees. Some walk alone, some in pairs, others in large groups. Thousands of displaced trudging through a rough and unfamiliar world, caught up in a thickening flow.

THE GREAT DISPLACEMENT
A DIGITAL CHRONICLE OF THE LUNA MIGRATION

The Megashelters

This interactive map visualizes the eighteen megashelters jointly operated by the Federal Emergency Management Agency (FEMA) and the American Red Cross in the months following Hurricane Luna's landfall. The map tracks the fluctuating populations by date. Users can sort internally displaced persons (IDPs) by demographic variables such as age, race, sex, income level, and other categories.

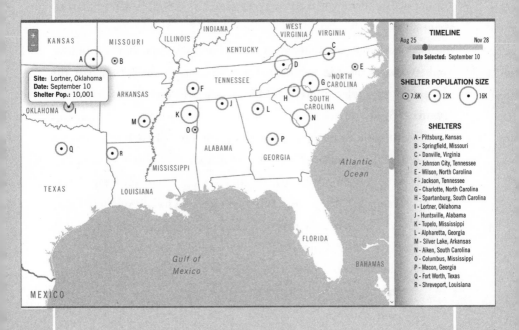

Site: Lortner, Oklahoma
Date: September 10
Shelter Pop.: 10,001

TIMELINE
Aug 25   Nov 28
Date Selected: September 10

SHELTER POPULATION SIZE
⊙ 7.6K   ● 12K   ● 16K

SHELTERS
A - Pittsburg, Kansas
B - Springfield, Missouri
C - Danville, Virginia
D - Johnson City, Tennessee
E - Wilson, North Carolina
F - Jackson, Tennessee
G - Charlotte, North Carolina
H - Spartanburg, South Carolina
I - Lortner, Oklahoma
J - Huntsville, Alabama
K - Tupelo, Mississippi
L - Alpharetta, Georgia
M - Silver Lake, Arkansas
N - Aiken, South Carolina
O - Columbus, Mississippi
P - Macon, Georgia
Q - Fort Worth, Texas
R - Shreveport, Louisiana

18.

The bus driver has ropy arms with tattoos that crawl up her neck and cover practically all the skin you can see. Even her flip-flopped feet swarm with vines, and snakes twine up her legs. Her hair reminds Oliver of a skunk's, he whispers to Mia, except the stripe is green.

Back at the fairgrounds, their family was near the front of the line and Mia and Oliver got seats in the second row. Which means they're close to the AC vents. Which also means they're the first to get the mini bottles of Gatorade when the driver opens a cooler and starts handing them out.

Which also means that when the driver, whose name is Roberta Grimes, starts talking and then keeps talking as the bus speeds up along another highway, Mia and Oliver are her closest, most attentive listeners.

"You folks're my fifth load of evacuees so far. Day before yesterday I drive over from Leisure City on the Reagan but nobody's collecting tolls. Pick up a load at some church and drive up here and head down for more and that's when they send me to get you folks. And here I am, bound for the Sooner State easy as cobbler, your magic carpet ride. You kids comfy? Another Gatorade?"

"Yes, please," says Oliver.

"Oliver, you can't have that," Mia whispers.

"Yes I can."

"You *know* that's too much sugar."

"You're not the boss of me."

"Mom!" Mia calls over the seats, but her mother is curled up in the next row back and across the aisle, staring out the window and turned away from Gavin, who's sprawled out with one leg in the aisle that will probably trip Oliver on his way to the bathroom, which he'll have to visit ten times today because of all the Gatorade. Gavin slits his eyelids at her and makes his gross lip face. Mia flips him off.

"Craziest part's how I ended up with this beast." Roberta Grimes pats the steering wheel. "Got the call from a buddy in Lauderdale, used to be a state boy in the highway patrol. Tells me pull out all the stops, Robbie, and asks if there's more buses. I tell him hell to the no, FEMA's called up every frikkin coach in Florida. Then I remembered one of ours was in for a body job so I motor over to the shop. Nobody's around but I got the extra key on my ring, so just left those folks a note and zam damn thank you ma'am and here I am."

She keeps giving Oliver winks with her spidered eyelids. At first he hides his face against Mia's sleeve but soon starts ogling Roberta Grimes as if she's a movie star. "I hope it's a long bus ride," he says, peeling the sticker from his third bottle of Gatorade.

Mia walks back to pee, touching the seats for balance. Behind Gavin and Mom sits a white couple, asleep. Almost everyone else on the bus is black or brown—except one other white family in the middle that includes a boy in the aisle seat who looks about thirteen, with a camo ball cap and a phone held six inches from his face. The last five rows are filled with Latino kids, maybe fifteen in all, with only two moms to watch them. The younger mom nurses a baby while the older one fans herself with a magazine.

The bathroom is occupied. While Mia waits in the aisle, a girl in the last row glances up and runs fingers through her hair, which is glossy and thick and falls halfway down her back. The oval of her face reminds Mia of Charlize. Mia smiles but the girl frowns, obviously too pretty to smile back.

Before sunset the bus pulls in at a shopping mall. A huge crowd mills around in the parking lot, lined on two sides with buses, Red Cross trucks, a few military vehicles. Soldiers stand around with their feet up on fenders. Smoke clouds up from a line of grills.

"They're cooking," Oliver says. Gavin points out two ice cream trucks.

Roberta Grimes tells them they can leave their belongings on the coach, and for the next hour everyone enjoys an amazing cookout by volunteers in a parking lot for all these evacuated people, probably a couple thousand. Oliver follows Mia around as they go get a burger, a hot dog, two ice cream bars each, then join a big disordered game of tag over by one of the National Guard trucks. Mia sees the cool girl from the bus again, speaking fast Spanish with her friends.

After a while Gavin walks up and finds them in the crowd. "Mia! Ollie! Come on, freaks, it's time to go."

They follow him back to the bus, where Roberta Grimes does a head count as a crew of volunteers loads some coolers. The passengers start filing on.

Oliver stops at the bottom of the steps. "Where are we going, Roberta?"

Mia rolls her eyes. Her brother always gets himself on a first-name basis with grown-ups as soon as he can.

"I'll be driving you folks on to Oklahoma, Ollie." She pats his head. "FEMA's got it handled, no doubt. I got a cousin in Stillwater. His name's Mike and ho-boy are there some stories about him. This one time in middle school . . ."

The story continues as the passengers settle in for the ride. In every seat someone has placed a blanket and a tiny pillow like the one Mia got on the family plane trip to Paris last summer. People quiet down as the bus gets back on the highway. Even Roberta eventually stops talking when she realizes the passengers behind her are asleep, or pretending to be.

"I want Dad," Oliver murmurs, for about the thousandth time today. Mia lets him snuggle up against her side, something he never does anymore. At home Oliver ignores basically everything she says, blowing into the house on a smelly breeze of annoying boys. So far during the evacuation, though, he wants to be with Mia more than anybody else in the family, probably because Mom's acting psycho and Gavin's being a dick. But she doesn't mind this new version of her little brother, for now.

"What will it be like?" he asks with a moist yawn against her arm.

"It's just Oklahoma," Mia says. "The main exports are meat and wheat and it's the twentieth-largest state. The state bird is the scissor-tailed flycatcher and the state flower is the Oklahoma rose."

"How do you know all that?"

"Oklahoma was my state project in fourth grade."

Nothing for a while; then, "Mia?"

"What?"

"Will you play my skull?"

An old game from Michigan, when they shared a room and Oliver used to pad across to her bed and ask for pictures to be drawn on his back, words to be spelled on his arms, music to be played in his hair. Mia taps out a rhythm on her brother's narrow shoulder blades, makes snare brushes through his hair and soft taps on the smooth cymbal of his forehead, thumps on the timpani skin of his lower back, all in time to the strange tuneless songs hummed by Roberta Grimes.

Snoring starts behind them, big mannish saws through the nose. Her little brother sleeps like Cricket slept when she was a puppy, curled head to toe over the seat with a skinny arm dangling to the floor. For hours Mia stays awake above him, a watcher in the dark.

19.

Five in the morning, the bus hellishly cold. Twice Gavin's asked the driver to raise the temperature. But people in the back have been complaining about the heat and he didn't pack sweats so now he's huddled up against the armrest, trying to cover himself with a miniature blanket that smells like ass. He's sitting with his sister because Oliver woke everyone up an hour ago and insisted on switching around so he could be with Daphne. The problem with Mia is she wriggles in her seat every two minutes and startles him out of already shallow spurts of sleep with sharp elbows and smacking lips and tiny moans sparked by her dreams.

Oklahoma swishes by in the night. They passed the sign last time Mia jabbed him awake.

WELCOME TO OKLAHOMA: DISCOVER THE EXCELLENCE.

Roger that. Literally the only thing Gavin knows about the place aside from its obvious excellence comes from his high school musical senior year, when he played bass in the band for *Oklahoma*. Now, as he writhes in this suspended state of half sleep, the show tunes earworm through his skull, the wind sweepin' down the plains and the scurryin' chicks and ducks and geese and the corn as high as an elephant's eye eating his brain tissue and causing him to thrash in the seat, which he hasn't reclined because he's not the kind of alpha prick who puts his seat down without asking, but the huge guy behind him is snoring like a sated bear so maybe it's not *quite* an accident when Gavin's elbow jabs the release lever and the seat shoots back into a pair of kneecaps.

A loud grunt, then—

"What the *hayul*?"

A hard shove from behind and the seat bucks him forward, almost smacking his face against the plastic surface in front of him. Gavin looks back at his offended fellow passenger. "Sorry, bro."

"Sorry, bro." Mocking him. The guy shoves the seat again.

"Get a life, asshole," Gavin murmurs.

"Gavin!" Daphne snaps from across the aisle. Too late.

The guy pulls himself into the aisle, blocking Daphne and Oliver from view. All Gavin sees is loose jeans sagging from a bulging waistline. The guy bends over so his unshaved face almost touches Gavin's.

"What you say to me?" Stale breath a wind on his cheeks. "What you say, you punk *bitch*?"

"Nothing, man. I'm sorry, it's cool."

Gavin shrinks away but now the guy has his hands anchored on both sides of his seat, pinning him in place.

"You listen, you piece a shit." Voice like peach fuzz. "You listen real fuckin' good."

"Okay," Gavin squeaks.

"You keep your goddamn seat up and your goddamn legs and whatnot in your own motherfuckin' row and you don't stick so much's a shitass pinkie finger in the aisle or I will rip your soft little hand the fuck off with a goddamn anvil pruner and shove some nice rusty rebar up your weak ass, you get me?"

A semitruck starts to pass in the left lane. The clatter drowns out the subsequent threats, but Gavin can smell the oily end of the huge finger, see the fury in the guy's droopy eyes and in the scissoring of his bared teeth. ". . . every bone in your scrawny-assed body," he finishes, then whips the constraining arm away from the inner edge of the seat and just like that the terror is gone and Gavin can almost breathe again.

Mia, flattened against the window, is the only other person who actually heard the guy's sodomy-and-death threats, which Daphne clearly didn't because she's now issuing mewling apologies to the guy as her stepson sits here with sensations of dismemberment churning his bowels.

After his stepmother finishes placating Mr. Deliverance, she squats in the aisle. Gavin stares straight ahead.

"Listen, Gavin."

"Don't."

"Gavin—"

"Just *don't*."

Mia knuckles her eyes. "What did Gavin do?"

"Gavin, you need to apologize."

"I already did."

"Why was that man being so *mean* to you?"

"And you need to watch your mouth," Daphne says, ignoring Mia. "We're not in Coral Gables."

"Neither is our house."

His stepmom bows her head and clasps her hands on his armrest, praying for something. "This is hard, I know," she says. "But we have to be smart, careful, and—we just do."

Because we're not in Kansas anymore, Gavin wants to say, then thinks: *But we kind of are.*

20.

She can't stop thinking of her art. Even more than her home or her husband, she obsesses over her ruined work, every swirl and every gouge, every hue of fired porcelain. The process, the industry, the beautiful mess. Those glorious blisters that sizzled up in a glaze five years ago and cratered two pieces that she kept anyway and showed last week, the unintended flaws exposing the ugly interiors, like torn muscle and cartilage over fresh-cracked bone. Those long collaborations with the clay.

Miles of interstate pass before the atmosphere on the bus goes back to a sleepy normal, though not for Daphne, who sits bolt upright in her seat with Oliver's warm body a comma against her side and an angry hardness lodged in her jaw. Her TMJ is back, the same stressy clenching that came on during the disorienting move from Ann Arbor, when they all spent three nights in that empty house before the furniture came, crashing on the five luxurious air mattresses picked up at REI. Mia and Oliver wanted to build a fire at the foot of the enormous stone chimney, even went outside to hunt down kindling. When they came back in with scratched arms full of dried palm fronds, Brantley already had the gas flames hissing over fake logs, clicked on with the touch of a wall switch. *A fireplace in Florida?* she had wondered; but Brantley wanted a fire next to his Christmas tree, even in Miami. So they had one.

What Daphne wouldn't give, now, for those fake logs. For one of those sleeping pads, for the four full baths and three half baths in their obscene house, for the Thai takeout and the Paulie's pizzas, a soak in the pool at the Pineapple Isles clubhouse with the swim-up bar and the tiki umbrellas skewering the flesh of a halved strawberry afloat on the surface of a daiquiri—

But no, that's wrong. All she wants is a sleeping bag. The rest of the bullshit can go. Sleeping pill, sleeping bag, sleep. Right now, if she knew her husband was alive, these would be enough. She swallows against a cold dryness in her throat.

Sometime later the driver's voice crackles over the PA. "Folks, we got one last haul in front of us. I need gas, you need breakfast, so we're pulling off at this shopping center. They got a Waffle House, IHOP, a 7-Eleven. You can eat, charge phones, do some sunrise yoga."

Scattered laughs. Passengers stir and a pang of hunger stabs Daphne's midsection like a long needle.

"Can we go to IHOP, Mommy?" Oliver breathes into her neck.

Daphne's jaw flares again. "I wish we could, sweetie. But we're going to have to make do with what they have here on the bus."

"PB and J?"

"Yes."

"Again?"

"I'm sorry, Oliver, but we don't have any money. We have to wait for your dad to finish with the patients he's helping and then you can eat all the IHOP you want." As the words leave her mouth, Daphne feels their fakery; but hunger distracts. The thought of a strip of crispy bacon or a mouthful of cream-covered pancake right now is almost more than she can bear.

"Hey, Mom." Mia's tweeny voice pierces the tired silence. "Let's go to Waffle House. Daddy says they're sketchy but I went to one with Sariah Foster-Sorenson after swim practice and it was really good."

An older woman in the front row turns and gives their family an are-you-fucking-kidding-me scan. Daphne cranes the upper half of her body out across the aisle.

"Mia, please keep your voice down. That goes for both of you. *All* of you."

Gavin ignores her, eyes closed, back in his shell. Mia starts to cry, and now Oliver amps up about peanut butter and jelly for breakfast, about his scratchy blanket, about the throw-uppy smell of the bus, until finally the driver pulls into the shopping center.

"Stay in your seats," Daphne orders. Gavin huffs out an adolescent sigh, Mia and Oliver continue to whimper. As fellow passengers rise and filter by, the hulking guy in the seat behind Gavin caresses his stomach.

"What you think, Rosie?" he says loudly—for Daphne's benefit, she feels sure. "Waffle House or IHOP?"

"Up to you, Deke."

"IHOP it is." Deke drums his gut. "I could use me a skillet breakfast, tell you the God's honest. Some hash browns maybe. They make a hella cuppa, too. Welp." With a performative grunt he pushes himself into the aisle. "Let's go, babycakes."

He leads his wife past their row with a loud sniff and hock. The other evacuees file by until Daphne and the kids are the sole passengers remaining. The driver lingers in her seat, texting, while Daphne seethes at this assumption that everyone, even if they have lost everything, at least has enough for a short stack of pancakes.

Finally the driver notices them. She startles. "You folks getting some chow?"

"Hopefully." Daphne keeps her voice bright. She steps forward, close to Roberta. "Just wondering if you have more of those sandwiches."

"Wait, you mean—" She lowers her voice. "You don't have money, ma'am?"

"No."

"They didn't put you on FNS?"

"I'm sorry?"

"FNS transitional meal vouchers. They gave them to persons without means."

Persons without means. Daphne would never have thought of herself this way, but at least for now, of course, she is.

"No one said anything about vouchers."

Roberta looks her up and down and Daphne sees what she sees. The designer jeans, the expensive blouse in a subtle cream, a ruby-encrusted diamond gleaming from her ring finger. A wealthy white woman somewhat the worse for wear but not exactly hard up.

Roberta reaches into a waist pouch. "You got three kids, Ollie and Mia plus this fella?" A nod at Gavin.

"That's right."

"Here's four vouchers. They're only redeemable for ten bucks apiece, though, so I'd go for Waffle House."

Daphne thanks her profusely and takes the vouchers. "Let's go, guys," she calls back to the kids.

"Where?" Gavin asks.

"Waffle House." She waves the vouchers. "It's on the government."

Most of the passengers have also chosen Waffle House, forty-odd Floridians overwhelming the waitstaff, tired but kind, asking about their evacuations, the state of the homes and neighborhoods they've left behind. From table to table over the next hour the displaced swap news and make tearful phone calls, voice their fears and the little they know about their present destination, the planless state of their lives.

At the next booth a middle-aged couple talks on speakerphone, hovering over the mobile like eager birds.

"Honey, no," says the mother. "There's no need for you to be here right now."

"We're just fine," the father adds.

"But I can take a furlough, Dad. Lots of soldiers in my unit are coming home to help."

The couple share a look. *Home*, he mouths. The mother shakes her head.

"You stay put, Elena." He traces around the rectangular shape of the phone, a delicate gesture for such large hands. "We'll let you know if we get in a pickle."

"Are you sure?"

"Absolutely."

When they disconnect, Daphne remains staring at their phone, replaying the family's conversation. She feels the couple's gazes on her and looks up, embarrassed.

"Sorry. Just a little out of it."

The father leans over the aisle. "Our little girl's stationed in South Korea," he says proudly. "Camp Humphreys, the big airfield there."

"Is she a pilot?"

"Flight engineer," says the mother. "I told her, if she took a leave, what could she do for us? No place to go, our work's gone for now—"

"We own a hardware store in Little Havana and Overtown."

"Three locations."

"Insured though. Machines, buildings, property. We'll get our check, but it's going to take awhile with all this." He twirls a hand tornadically over their table.

All this: a phrase Daphne has heard more than once since yesterday from fellow evacuees. *All this*: a murky stir of storm, loss, and indeterminacy. She turns back to her family as her sugar buzz starts to fade.

Mia's phone has charged to 51 percent. Nothing from Brantley. Daphne steps outside to make some calls. She phones the Willows to see if she can reach Flo. Busy signal, again. She tries the switchboard for the hospital in Miami but that, too, appears to be down, which seems impossible, that the complex wouldn't be answering its phones. She searches the browser for *medevac jet* but finds only general news about FEMA's vast search-and-rescue efforts. Commentators are framing the catastrophe as epochal and world changing, as if a nuclear warhead has detonated in South Florida, flattening a city she has barely come to know.

Back on the bus, the mood has changed, from the fleeting comfort of breakfast to a cautious expectancy. Daphne feels a stir of curiosity at the prospect of spending a night or two in Oklahoma, and along with it comes a burst of empathy toward Deke, the riled man who will be her neighbor there. She looks back across the aisle. His eyes are closed but fluttering.

"Sir?" She lightly taps his wrist. "Sir?"

He looks at her, bobs his chin.

"I'm sorry about Roscoe P."

His nostrils flare. "Excuse me?"

"I saw you at the animal station before we left. We had to give up ours, too."

For a moment the skin around his eyes softens and smooths. Then he leans forward so the upper half of his body projects halfway across the aisle. "You don't know jack about my dog, you hear? You don't know *squat.*"

Daphne rears back, shaken, and sits rigid in her seat for a long while. Later she steals another glance. Deke's eyes have closed, and a meaty hand presses against his mouth. His cheeks are moist and his shoulders buck forward with each sob. Through slitted eyes she watches him, this angry mountain of a man, weeping for his hound.

21.

Rain stands on the rise above the main gate and gazes down on two thousand tents. Work crews expand the grid of streets southward by the hour, to the bank of a narrow creek. At the center of the shelter rise four giant pavilions, three for dining, the fourth intended as a mixed-use gathering place. Three flatbeds coast down, hauling eighteen more portable toilets.

Her orders: to construct an open-air shelter on this twenty-acre smear of land capable of housing up to ten thousand evacuees for a period of four weeks, possibly longer. The plot is the former site of Tooley Experimental Farm, a short-lived extension of the Oklahoma State Arboretum, closed down years ago after a lawsuit involving the Muscogee Nation and still technically under the tribe's jurisdiction. Tooley Farm has several things going for it, including water hookups and a site only ten miles off I-40. An old barn perches near the southwest corner of the property, which is surrounded by chain link bisected to the east by the narrow creek.

On the other hand, the crew is building the shelter practically from scratch. Other FEMA task forces are repurposing shuttered military bases with existing dormitories and dining halls. Two megashelters will occupy closed-down liberal arts colleges in Tennessee and Alabama, Rain has heard. Others are more isolated, out in distant suburbs or remote facilities: rural airfields, summer camps—and places like Tooley Farm.

Ten thousand IDPs. Not refugees, Washington has admonished, because refugees by definition cross national boundaries, forced from their homelands, fleeing across borders to seek new homes in foreign states, clustering in camps. There are massive compounds in Jordan and Sudan where cholera and dysentery are rampant, where food is scarce and potable water scarcer, where children die every day.

But the messaging from headquarters is clear: Tooley Farm will not be a "refugee camp." Its residents—its guests—will not be "refugees." These folks will be treated with dignity and compassion, despite the scale of the evacuation. No one here will starve.

Dubious about the semantics, Rain buries herself in the logistics, guzzling lukewarm coffee by the quart as she oversees the endless cycle of request and requisition stirred through the alphabet soup of government agencies, NGOs and national charities and local organizations, churches and ad hoc volunteer groups. It's a battle of bureaucracy against need with no time to waste on hand-wringing, no red tape that can't be cut.

As a teenager in Indiana, Rain attended Carmel High, one of the largest public schools in America, with four lunch shifts and a student body of five thousand. Tooley Farm will be twice that size—though when she thinks of it this way, Rain finds the prospect somewhat less daunting.

Two high schools. I can run two damn high schools.

At least with the right crew in place. She's put Butch in charge of shelter requisitions, because the competition for supplies and facilities is fierce. Tents and trailers, mobile homes and Winnebagos, beds, blankets, cots, camping pads, pillows: whatever can be slept in or on or beneath. Butch can get on a phone and holler up almost anything, knows everybody in the state emergency offices, has a velvet touch when he needs it, a sledgehammer when required. One time Rain watched him strong-arm the COO of an outdoor apparel chain into donating two thousand sleeping bags worth a quarter million retail. He can guilt caterers out of their portable event pavilions, get a red-faced U-Haul manager to pray with him as he requisitions ten moving vans from the guy's lot.

But FEMA's supply of trailers and mobile homes and collapsible dome shelters is already cashed out, Butch announces, on the road to Florida to house the hundreds of thousands of IDPs who remain in-state. Tooley Farm will be stuck with tents: one thousand six-person domes and four thousand two-person pups, with all their vulnerability to the vagaries of the Oklahoma weather.

Unsettling. One of the guiding mandates in the disaster relief community post-Katrina had been the need for adequate mass temporary housing for the displaced. No more Superdomes, no more formaldehyde-leaking trailers. But that storm was over fifteen years ago now. Since that time, the agency and its partners have made major investments in temporary shelter, warehousing countless modules in a massive readiness exercise for a future sure to come.

Now that future is here—yet that store of shelter is already depleted. Even if it weren't, twice that number of trailers wouldn't be capable of handling the millions displaced from Miami-Dade. So, tents it is.

What about the perimeter?" Rain asks at one of a dozen staff meetings prior to the arrival of the first IDPs.

Jed Stricker opens one of his binders. Stricker the Stickler, as he's known around Region IV, real management type with a nose for best practices, detailed in reports he hauls to disaster sites in bindered hard copy, because you never know when "National Disaster Housing Strategy" or "Disaster-Related Food Needs" or "Housing Sex Offenders in Emergency Shelters" or fifty other pertinent government docs will come in handy when the networks go down.

"On it," Jed says. "We're repairing the existing fence line, filling in the gaps."

Rain says, cautiously, "We do need to make clear that folks are free to come and go as they like, Jed. We don't want a bunch of conspiracy types spreading rumors about FEMA concentration camps again. Do we need to fence the entire farm?"

Something crosses Jed's face. "This is a federal operation with a large population over an indeterminate time frame. We'll need a clear perimeter that shows the bounds of FEMA's authority. Otherwise we're looking at chaos."

Butch says, "I understand your reservations, Rain. But how are parents supposed to keep an eye on their kids if we don't have some kind of boundary? And let's say a load of folks shows up and we're already tapped out. How do we keep from being overrun? Plus look at the forecast for the Gulf Coast. This bitch ain't done yet."

Rain plays the scenario out in her head, how much worse this could get if Luna makes a second landfall somewhere heavily populated. So much to manage, such a vast scale.

Now, hours after that last meeting, Rain feels an unfamiliar shiver in her ribs. She's spent half her career amid endless whorls of devastation and carnage, coming in on the vanguard of rescue, shipping out with the first whispers of recovery. Water, fire, wind; death, destruction, collapse.

This is different. For the first time in her adult life, Rain is building something, creating this new place out of nothing. Putting stakes in the ground, raising pavilions to the sky, all to welcome thousands of her fellow Americans in need of shelter and food and services. In need of dignity.

A light rain swept through overnight, drying the air. She wonders how the new arrivals will manage being thrust together. Rain has witnessed it countless times, this resilience, how people pull together after disaster, lift one another's burdens and build castles out of ash. In catastrophe there can be progress, if only those affected can find their hope, that spirit within themselves to—

Christ almighty, what kind of sentimental sap is she? Rain needs some of her daughter's Gen Z cynicism. But part of her can't help it. Standing at the crossing and looking down on Tooley Farm, she feels more than anything like a camp counselor, waiting for the kids to arrive.

THE GREAT DISPLACEMENT
A DIGITAL CHRONICLE OF THE LUNA MIGRATION

Webs of (Dis)Organization

One of the greatest challenges in the wake of Luna was the coordination among dozens of federal and state government agencies with NGOs, non-profits, churches, and many other bodies in responding to the needs of the displaced. This force-directed graph expresses the relationships between these organizations as they worked together (often at cross-purposes) to manage the flow, settlement, and resettlement of IDPs. Each node represents a separate organization, and users may orient the network to visualize these complex and changing relationships as they functioned over a period of months.

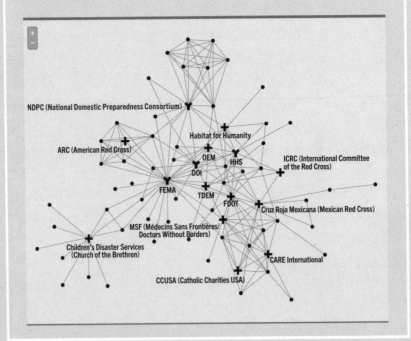

THE GREAT DISPLACEMENT
A DIGITAL CHRONICLE OF THE LUNA MIGRATION

KIANA ROBERTSON, RENTAL CAR CLERK

The Rockies are hazed with smoke from the Twin Sisters Fire to the north and the Shawnee Fire to the south. Kiana stands against the mountains gazing west from the rental car lots where she has worked since evacuating Miami in the days before Luna's arrival. She lives in Jefferson Park, a neighborhood of Denver, with her family. She is twenty-seven years old.

Play audio file:

Transcript:

We got out fast and we got out early. Thing you have to understand is we were all in the Superdome during Katrina. Isaiah was ten and Michael was eight. I was little and don't remember it, just some flashes I probably made up.

But Mama, she'll still go on about the Superdome, how the news called it a hellhole, called all the folks in there animals, like it was their choice to do what they had to. Fifteen thousand people in a closed stadium with no food, no water, no toilets, no light, and the main part of it my mom remembers wasn't what folks did to each other but what folks did *for* each other. Trying to get sick folks to hospitals, formula for babies. National Guard soldiers crying because they can't help the people dying. Mama says I was in the same diaper for three days. She had to scrape it off, wring it out. Three days, one diaper. She still talks about that

diaper, even mentioned it in her toast at my wedding, which,
I mean, no. Just no.

After Katrina, FEMA moved us to Mississippi. Ten mobile
homes in a Kmart parking lot outside Tupelo. There's seven
of us in one trailer, and that I do remember. Mama, my
brothers and me, my mother's sister and her daughters. A
neighbor shot himself right there between the trailers.
Isaiah was the first one came out and saw him. Mama lost
half her hair from the stress of that place.

Flash forward twenty-odd years and we're all living in Miami
and Luna builds up and they're saying it'll miss us. But
that's when Mama decides, five days before it hits. She just
knew in her bones. For some reason we all believed her.

At the time we were renting a place down in Goulds. She
makes all three of us and Isaiah's wife walk off our jobs,
go withdraw our money from the bank, settle any bills. She
rents a twenty-foot Ryder for the whole family and makes us
prioritize our things, pack efficiently, crate the dogs.
Methodical, you know? All in one day.

Next morning we caravan out of there, four cars and a Ryder
truck heading up I-95 when there's still only a hurricane
watch. We were probably the first people in all Florida to
full-on evacuate, which means there's plenty of gas on the
route, no problem getting a motel. Mom like Noah, got her
family in an ark. She decides we're going to Colorado.
Denver, she says. The promised land.

So by the time Luna turns and hits we're already in Kansas
City, away from all that. We watch CNN over beers in the
lobby of a Hyatt, all of us looking at Mama like she's some
kind of prophet while home's getting carpet-bombed. Took me
a long time to find work again but now I'm at the Avis at
DIA and it's a good job because folks always need cars. But
Florida, Louisiana? Mama says she'll never go back, not even

for funerals. Didn't fly down to Tupelo when her sister passed last year. You just don't want to feel that way again. The south's dead far as she's concerned.

▶ **ISAAC CARTER, DENTIST**

He likes to recline in his examination chair to put himself in his patients' place. Isaac and his wife, Sue, moved their dental practice from Miami to Decatur, Georgia, in the months after Luna. Both have reduced their schedules in recent months to ease into retirement. Isaac was sixty-one when Luna made landfall.

Play audio file:

Transcript:

It all came down to what you could fit in the car. We'd evacuated six, seven times by that point but you got the feeling this one was different. We get the photo albums, we get my insulin, luggage for a week. Then we lock up and drive over to get my father at the house. Mom had passed the year before so it was just Pops. He was getting by, still cooking for himself, had a garden to putter in, workshop in the basement.

There was this one section of wall in the house, a post embedded into the sheetrock by the kitchen. It's where our folks measured our heights over the years like parents do. You could see our names and ages, even stains from the backs of our heads. There was me at two, Mary at five, Jarrell at six, me at six, and so on, all the way up to when

Mary was fourteen, which was her last birthday so I reckon they decided to stop measuring us after that. But the post was still there, names and ages and head stains and all.

Anyways we're over at the house, out front loading the car and we've got the front door propped open, and that's when I hear this big cracking sound from inside. What the hell's that? Sue has no idea. We run back inside and we see Pops going at the wall with a crowbar, trying to tear out that post. Man's eighty-four years old and the biggest hurricane in the world's coming on and he's remodeling the damn kitchen. So I grab the crowbar from him and have a turn going at that post but I can't budge the thing. Then Sue takes a turn, and she's the one finally pulls it free. She let us know it all right, all the way up the peninsula, these two big men of hers can't work a crowbar but look what she went and did. We loosened it for her, that's what Pops says.

We've got Pops in assisted living here in Decatur but he's still got that post up behind the adjustable bed in his room. I imagine we'll bury it with him.

▶ TOM MATSUMOTO, STATISTICIAN

His office in the Department of Homeland Security headquarters looks down on C Street Southwest, two blocks from the US Capitol. His grandparents lived on Capitol Hill in the years following World War II, much of which they spent in an internment camp in California following Executive Order 9066 under FDR. Tom was sixty-four when Luna made landfall.

Play audio file:

Maybe it all started when my grandma told me about the war.
This was the late sixties, I was nine or so. They had two of
those Ansel Adams prints from Manzanar. The first was shot
from the guard tower over all the tents, with the Sierras in
the background. The other was a shot of the mess line.
There's this one kid in the picture standing off by himself
and staring up at the camera. I used to imagine myself as
that kid, had these crazy stories in my head about meeting
my grandparents when they were in there.

When my grandma told me about internment it was the numbers
that got to me. A hundred and twenty thousand people,
displaced from their homes and penned up for three years. I
guess I had some bad dreams about it, and I vowed that I
was going to count to a hundred and twenty thousand whether
they wanted me to or not. I only made it to two thousand
but it helped with the dreams.

So, numbers. There's fifty, say sixty thousand hotels in the
United States, which translates to five million rooms total.
On any given night, 60 to 70 percent of those rooms will be
in use. That occupancy rate spikes in the summer, especially
those last weeks of August. Let's say we had one million
hotel rooms available in the United States in the two weeks
after Luna hit. Now, if we'd sent evacuees to every vacant
hotel room in the continental United States—I mean
everything from the Four Seasons in Manhattan to the Ramada
Inn in Sheboygan, Wisconsin—we still wouldn't have had
enough space to house all those IDPs.

We did the math. It wasn't a back-of-the-envelope thing. We
pulled in the COOs of Motel 6 and Super 8 and you name it.
That's to say nothing about how we'd pay for it. FEMA always
provides transitional vouchers to help folks through those
first days and weeks after a major disaster. But you can't
put a million-plus people in hotels for an indefinite time

period. And you can't ask the hotel chains to donate the rooms because that puts them out of business.

Same thing with the potential indoor megashelters: basketball arenas, convention centers. Some of these facilities had emergency sheltering plans in place. Those might be feasible for a week, but then what? We'd already shut down spectator sports and big trade shows and so forth during COVID and now you're asking the entire NCAA to cancel its basketball schedule, or the NFL to cancel another football season, or twenty convention centers to tear up a hundred million dollars' worth of contracts just when big conferences are coming back? Remember, we were in a recession, the economy needed to churn, state budgets are already squeezed dry. But all those IDPs can't go home, not now, most of them not ever.

So we knew what we were facing. These situations are legend in the disaster relief community. The example we always use is Italy, back in 2016 after the earthquakes in Abruzzo, when they had to empty all those towns because of collapsing buildings. Nobody remembers this, but they put thirty-five thousand folks in tents for over a month. Berlusconi's telling everybody to treat is as a "camping weekend," laughs it off. Then it starts raining and nobody's laughing anymore. Imagine. Thirty-five thousand Italians living in camping tents for a month.

Here in the US we used to go on about our "First World problems." Nobody's pretending folks wouldn't be worse off if a storm like Luna had made landfall in Dhaka or Lagos. But the point is, it hit here, twice in ten days. And when the choice is between nothing and something, most folks will settle for a tent and three squares any day. Situation like that, your so-called First World gets real small, real fast.

22.

In the shade of a trailer Daphne chews her cuticles, fingers raw. The temperature hovers in the mid-nineties but a chill pimples her skin. Since the bus unloaded, she has kept her eyes averted from the wider enclosure, absorbing every word of instruction from the FEMA officials—the wiry black woman in charge, the two white men at her sides. Daphne took four copies of the handout. The front provides guidelines for meal service, shower facilities, mobile laundry units "with the capacity to complete thirty (30) loads per day." The reverse is bullet-pointed with "Rules & Regulations for Tooley Farm." At least forty of them, some pleas, some threats.

- Food is not to be moved from the mess tents.
- Residents are asked to eat meals ONLY during their assigned dining shift.
- Firearms are STRICTLY PROHIBITED within shelter boundaries and WILL BE CONFISCATED by administration.

The rules feel exigent, urgent. She wants to make the kids study the list like Gavin studied for his APs.

But when the staffers instruct everyone to line up at one of the two tables for "shelter assignment," she can't bring herself to move. Oliver and Mia have already found new friends, playing soccer tag with a group of kids dashing between the trailers. Gavin stands alone, staring off into the surrounding fields.

She scans back through her last twelve texts to Brantley. They read like a litany, a plea for grace from a neglectful saint. Her eyes blur and the actual texts on the screen fade into a sequence of imagined pleas, whispered in her voice.

Write back, Brantley.

Where are you, Brantley?

Text me, Brantley!

Call me, Brantley!!

Bring cash, Brantley!!!!!!

The shade darkens. She looks away from the screen and up at the wide and friendly face of a vested FEMA official.

"Ma'am?" he gently says.

"Yes?"

"I'm Butch. We're assigning shelter now. It's you and . . ."—he looks over his shoulder at the scattered pack of kids—". . . some of those?"

"Two," she says. "Plus that one." She nods at Gavin, now hunched down against a trailer and noodling on his bass.

Butch scans her bracelet and asks her to call the kids over. Once the four of them have been checked in, he tells them their tent number and gives them rough directions from the Square. "You'll be on first dinner shift. Four thirty."

"That early?" Gavin complains. "Nobody'll be hungry by then."

Butch gives him a bland smile. "You'll get used to it, son."

Gavin starts to object but Daphne shoots him a look. She doesn't need him tangling with yet another man three times his size, this one a federal official.

"Believe me, folks, y'all are the lucky ones," Butch informs them. "You arrived early so you've got your own dome tent, four cots. By tonight folks'll be assigned pup tents. Count yourselves fortunate, would be my advice."

A line of buses appears at the top of the rise, coming south off the crossing. Butch lets out a long, wearied sigh. "We'll have our first two thousand in by sundown. Maybe more. You folks take care." He jogs off toward a trailer, tablet and clipboard bouncing at his sides.

Daphne blinks up at the sun. A light breeze whisks down the hill bringing the smell of manure from the surrounding fields. She leads her children in among the tents.

23.

The streets have names, stenciled on signs at every crossing. AVENUE A1, AVENUE B2; COLORADO STREET, NEVADA STREET. Oliver is the first to figure out how the grid layout works, annoyingly predicting the name of every upcoming street and running ahead to confirm. Mia hangs back with her mother, cowed by the newness of it all.

They round a corner and pass a group of kids from their bus. Oliver is already talking to a boy holding a soccer ball, standing next to the beautiful girl who frowned at her. Mia stops when she reaches them.

Oliver points to the ball. "Dónde compraste la globo de fútbal?"

The boy laughs, some of the other kids with him. Mia, embarrassed, rolls her eyes at the girl. "Lo siento, mi hermano cree que puede hablar español." She says it slowly, enunciating so the girl will understand.

"He's actually pretty good," says the girl coolly—and in unaccented English. For a few seconds Mia worries she's already blown it, that now she'll have another SCB in her life. "I'm Luz," the girl says. She hip-bumps her brother. "He's Bembe." A skinny boy, nerdy-looking with thick glasses and socks pulled halfway up his calves.

"I'm Mia. And this is Oliver."

"You want to play later?" Bembe asks Oliver.

"I have to go to my tent."

"Come to the Square. Twenty minutes."

"What's the Square?" Oliver wants to know.

"Where the buses dump you off." Bembe points back the way they came and the boys agree to meet.

Mia exchanges a look with Luz. They don't say anything but Mia knows the sisters will both be there.

The family hasn't been camping since Michigan. Her father's favorite place was Bingham Lake, but Mia always preferred the common area in their neighborhood, the grassy expanse between the houses. Neighborhood dads would come out on those nights with a portable fire pit and guitars and sit around singing ancient songs and drinking beer until it was time for the kids to get into their sleeping bags. Home was a twenty-second skip away.

Those wild nights come to mind when Mia discovers where they'll be staying until they go home again. The tent is glorious, with four low cots, the floor thick and pillowy-soft so you can hear the grass beneath the crinkling plastic. The heat gives the interior a canvassy smell.

Mia tosses her backpack on a cot and plops down and cups her head in her hands. Gavin takes the bed across from hers, Oliver and her mother the cots in back.

Outside, along the grassy avenue, people trudge toward their assigned tents. Small families, large families, couples, other people all alone. Some of the kids turn and look inside Mia's tent as they pass. Mia waves, and most wave back. But the adults don't even turn their heads. They look so grim, like soldiers in a TV show.

"Should we unpack?" Oliver asks. "Mom, should we unpack?"

Their mother doesn't answer. She's sitting on her cot with her elbows on her knees, staring at the floor.

"Just keep your shit in your bag," Gavin says. "We won't be here that long, and it's not like there are dressers."

Mia tries knee-bouncing on the cot, hoping it's rubbery like a trampoline. Which it's not. She looks at the roof.

A stillness in the tent. A songbird calls from nearby, some faraway machine hums to life. Mia thinks of her father and thinks of Cricket and starts to tear up, but then she remembers Charlize and the Stone Cold Bitches and school. She really likes this tent.

In a soft and unfamiliar voice, Gavin asks, "So what are we supposed to do?"

No one answers.

After they arrange their cots and luggage, Oliver announces he's going to meet his new friend Bembe at the Square, and Mom says she'll walk him and Mia there. To ask some questions about food and computers, she tells them, though Mia suspects she just wants to get away from Gavin for a little while. They've all been crammed together for three days. Gavin stays behind while Mia and Oliver walk with Daphne back toward the trailers.

Another bus has just unloaded and people are milling around in the Square: new families, more kids. Oliver finds Bembe in the patch of grass between the Square and the perimeter fence. A swarm of kids plays tag—or not quite tag but a tag-like game with rules Mia can't yet understand. No sign of Luz.

"Oliver, no," Mom says. "I'm not comfortable just letting you guys go wild."

"There's a fence," Oliver whines. "We'll be fine."

Mom gets her worried look but lets them go play. The game is complicated, something involving "leapers" and "squads," and no one agrees on the rules. Mia soon grows bored and finds a spot to sit against a trailer in the shade. She's thinking about going to find her mom when Luz appears. Mia's heart speeds up as Luz sees her and strolls over. "Hey."

"Hey."

They sit in the grass and talk about their evacuations. Mia tells her about their sunken house, their ruined TVs, their smashed-up minivan. Her stories make Luz laugh, a reaction Mia likes, so she tells the part about the purse. Sparing no detail, she describes the long wait at the gas pump, the way her mother begged for money from a total stranger, how she screamed at Gavin.

"What did your dad do?" Luz asks.

Mia hesitates. "He wasn't there."

"Is he—like—"

"He's an important doctor and really busy because of the storm. He'll be here to pick us up tomorrow or the next day."

"Oh." Luz looks actually disappointed.

"But my mom is really mad at him," Mia says quickly, "so it could be longer."

"Your family's fucked up."

The observation gives Mia a thrill. "What do you mean?"

"Not in a bad way. My parents are always too tired to fight. They just pick shit all day."

"Pick?"

"Whatever's in season. Right now it's berries. We're in Florida until October, then we go up to Maryland, then California." The kids from the bus are all Guatemalan, Luz tells her, most of them cousins who go from state to state, following the crops.

"Do you ever go to Michigan? That's where I used to live."

"In May a couple times," Luz says. "Asparagus."

Luz's mom and dad, it turns out, had to wait out the hurricane on a farm back near Okeelanta.

"Why?"

"The buses didn't come and there was only room for the younger kids and two of the mothers. My tía Aldina and also Vicenta got to come, because she has a baby. She's a bitch though."

"Are your parents okay?"

"No one knows."

Mia has never met anyone who works on a farm before. Strange how easily it's happened, making this friend when she has basically no real friends back in Florida. And they have so much in common already, like parents who are missing, or maybe dead.

"Ew," Mia says, looking over Luz's shoulder. A boy is staring at them, taking a wide stance with his beefy arms folded.

Luz glances, ducks back with a shudder.

"His name's Kyler. Just some gross white boy from our bus. Sorry," she says, but Mia isn't bothered. Kyler inserts himself into the game and chases after Bembe, the obvious target in the group.

She looks at Luz. The way she watches Kyler reminds Mia of the way she always felt watching the SCBs. Wary and worried, as if they'll attack her at the slightest provocation.

"Hey."

"What?"

Mia leans over. "My dad says there are different kinds of white people."

"Oh yeah?"

"There are white people like, you know, like us." Mia makes a circling gesture with her hand, including both of them.

"What do you mean?"

"People who are smart and speak different languages and aren't really fat."

"Oh."

"But other white people are just stupid. They eat fast food every day and don't get vaxxed and buy groceries at Walmart."

"My family goes to Walmart."

"But, I mean, whatever." Mia rolls her eyes. "That's different, that's like a whole different—thing." She looks back at Kyler Biggs. "That kid . . . I know what my dad would say."

"What?"

Mia leans closer still, and in a low, secret-sharing voice: "He's white trash."

CARL LEE EDMUNDSON
@texasclimateguy

Weather guru, speaker, author, father, husband,
Texas State Climatologist
@UTAustin he/his

582 Following   **215.9K** Followers

Carl Lee Edmundson @texasclimateguy · Sep. 4

Houston, we have a problem. I've been tracking hurricanes
for the last 20 years: grad student in EnviSci at UC Boulder,
now a prof of atmospheric science at UT Austin. Not
bragging, just giving creds. (1/)

Carl Lee Edmundson @texasclimateguy · Sep. 4

We all saw what's happened to Miami over the last week.
Now Luna is bearing down on Galveston/Houston—an area
with a population of SEVEN MILLION. (2/)

Carl Lee Edmundson @texasclimateguy · Sep. 4

Could be we'll get lucky. Maybe she'll click south for Mexico.
But the most likely track puts her directly over the Bolivar
Peninsula by lunchtime Wednesday, strengthening again to a
Cat 6. (3/)

Carl Lee Edmundson @texasclimateguy • Sep. 4

In other words, a Direct. F*****g. Hit.
By the world's first Cat 6.
On the nation's fourth-largest city. (4/)

Carl Lee Edmundson @texasclimateguy • Sep. 4

This is the #HoustonApocalypse. A direct hit by a Category
6 on the Ship Channel and the Port will destroy the city, the
islands, peninsulas, waterways, rendering much of this
major sector of the Gulf Coast uninhabitable for decades.
No exaggeration. (5/)

Carl Lee Edmundson @texasclimateguy • Sep. 4

We saw this on a smaller scale with #HurricaneHarvey in
2017. 50 inches of precipitation, flooding, devastation. Much
more lasting were the environmental impacts—which, years
later, are only beginning to show their full effects. (6/)

Carl Lee Edmundson @texasclimateguy • Sep. 4

Here's how the Environmental Integrity Project described
Harvey's effects on Houston's air: "After the heavy rains
hit the Houston area, eight area plants shut down
within 24 hours, triggering a dangerous pulse of 1.3 million
pounds of un-permitted air pollution." (Link here: www
.tinyurl.349d0) (7/)

Carl Lee Edmundson @texasclimateguy • Sep. 4

Imagine this "pulse" multiplied by twenty. That's 20 million
pounds of air pollution floating around while the ruined city
tries to recover. (8/)

Carl Lee Edmundson @texasclimateguy • Sep. 4

Water pollution was even worse. During Harvey, Exxon shuttered two huge facilities, including the Olefins plant that released 12,000 lbs of noxious chemicals—xylene, benzene, etc. The Baytown plants also released—no joke—500,000,000 GALLONS of industrial wastewater into Galveston Bay. (9/)

Carl Lee Edmundson @texasclimateguy • Sep. 4

And then there were the Superfund sites, "only" 13 out of 41 of which were flooded during Harvey but nearly ALL of which will be flooded by Luna. (10/)

Carl Lee Edmundson @texasclimateguy • Sep. 4

Example: the San Jacinto River waste pits in Crosby, a narrow spit of land between Burnet Bay and the river. Right next door to major residential areas, including a huge mobile home park and large public housing complexes. And these environmental disasters inordinately impact poor communities and ppl of color. (11/)

Carl Lee Edmundson @texasclimateguy • Sep. 4

In addition to all the environmental damage (I've listed a fraction), Harvey caused catastrophic destruction from flooding due to 40 inches of rain. #Luna is expected to follow a similar stall pattern—but with as much as SIXTY INCHES of precip. (12/)

Carl Lee Edmundson @texasclimateguy • Sep. 4

And remember: when Harvey hit Houston, it was "only" a Cat4—and her eye came ashore at Rockport, 200 miles SE of Houston. At Harvey's closest pass to Houston, it had already been downgraded to a tropical storm. (13/)

Carl Lee Edmundson @texasclimateguy • Sep. 4

Luna, OTOH, looks like a direct hit. (14/)

Carl Lee Edmundson @texasclimateguy • Sep. 4

Since the Great Storm of 1900, Houston has never experienced major storm surge. The surge from Hurricane Ike (2008) crested at 18 feet. Bad, yes: did some serious damage in Bolivar. But Ike turned at the last minute and the Ship Channel and the industrial complex were largely spared. (15/)

Carl Lee Edmundson @texasclimateguy • Sep. 4

Now, there are huge projects in the works to protect against surge, e.g. the Coastal Spine, the Galveston Bay Park Plan, which calls for dredging from the Ship Channel, building a levy and "surge gate," etc. But none of these protective measures will be built for years. Meanwhile the city lies open and vulnerable. (16/)

Carl Lee Edmundson @texasclimateguy • Sep. 4

If #HurricaneLuna stays on track (a smaller "if" now than when I started this thread an hour ago), the Galveston surge will be 35-40 feet—far outside the bounds of worst-case scenarios studied by the Army Corps of Engineers. (17/)

Carl Lee Edmundson @texasclimateguy • Sep. 4

Watch those YouTubes of the 2004 Indian Ocean tsunami, those tidal waves destroying coastal communities in minutes. That's what Houston is facing. (18/)

Carl Lee Edmundson @texasclimateguy • Sep. 4

Haven't even talked about the wind but you've all seen how #HurricaneLuna shredded Miami—and we can expect the same in Houston. Refineries, petrochemical plants, fuel tanks: the Ship Channel may be a total loss. (19/)

Carl Lee Edmundson @texasclimateguy • Sep. 4

Economic impact will be staggering. The Port of Houston is the busiest port in the country for foreign tonnage. It's THE container port for everyone between Mississippi and the Rocky Mountains. Want to talk about supply chain issues? The port's destruction will make our current recession look like a blip. (20/)

Carl Lee Edmundson @texasclimateguy • Sep. 4

No one will want to live in Houston, work there, rebuild there for a generation. Why would they? What will be left? (21/)

Carl Lee Edmundson @texasclimateguy • Sep. 4

Apologies for dire tone, but this is not trauma porn here. I love the Lone Star State, I love the Gulf Shore and Houston.

But I am devastated.

I am terrified.

You should be too.

#HurricaneLuna #HoustonApocalypse (end/)

24.

Tate passes a dime over and under his knuckles as his eyes flit from the side windows to the rearview. Jessamyn's late, the parking lot breezy and barren. Any moment a squad car could round the corner and force him along. Evacuees pack the highways around Houston, the radio says, rivers of panic and haste. The city is emptying like a funnel half-clogged.

A sedan appears in the rearview, and Jessamyn pulls up. She curls a finger to get Tate in her car. In the passenger seat he waits out her chatter by staring at the dashboard clock.

"So where's the load?"

"What's your hurry?"

"I need to take care of some shit before I get out of here."

"They were joking about it in Saint Louis," she says, "how they'd never trade a hurricane for the floods up there. One of those guys, though, the bald one?"

"Vadim."

"He asked Yury how they're supposed to find you if Luna swallows Houston."

"Bigger question is how I sell the load."

"I could take it back, tell them you'll deal it later," Jessamyn says.

"That's not how they operate. It's strictly a no-returns policy."

"What if I told you there's two million worth of wildfire in this car?"

"Bullshit."

"Okay."

"In the trunk?" His hand on the door release.

"It's literally *in* the car, its guts. I saw them finishing up. Imagine fifty reams of half-size label paper, welded into the door panels, sewn into the seat cushions."

Now it makes sense, why she waved him over.

"How am I supposed to get it out?"

"This chop shop in Sugar Land." She hands him a folded paper. "They'll take it apart, remove the sheets, and give you yours. They take the rest."

"During a mass evacuation?"

"All I know is what they told me."

Tate glances at the address. Saint Louis never sends excess. He distributes what they give him, takes his cut, and leaves the remaining cash at his drop. Everything about the relationship is regular. Drugs in, drugs out. Cash in, cash out. Lather, rinse, repeat.

So why this sudden change in procedure? Now he has this extra car to deal with. Are they planning to get the shipment to the chop shop then put a bullet in his head?

Tate says, "Show me this new format."

Jessamyn reaches over him to open the glove compartment, her cool arm brushing his. She slides out a sheet of pink filmy plastic and hands it to him. Four columns and five rows of peel-off tabs, twenty in all. Not pills, not powder. Postage stamps, like old-style acid hits.

"Saint Louis has an entire garage full of these things. They think you can move this format three times faster. They want it done by Halloween."

He looks at her. "So take one."

"Yeah right."

"How do I know this shit is legit?"

"Don't be so paranoid."

"Every king needs a taster."

A beat. "You're serious."

"Dead."

"Tate, I'm not one of your milky little junkies. You eat one if you're so worried."

He could shove his gun up under her chin and make her do it if he wanted to. But there's an easier way. He almost laughs.

"Fine," he says. "We'll do it together. Same time, same dose."

A nervous frown.

"One bump never hurt anybody. I just need to see what I'm dealing with here."

"This is bullshit."

"If you want your cut we're doing this. Right now."

She reaches over and peels off a tab. He takes one, too, and together they hold their right hands up, tabs perched on their fingertips like tiny moths.

"You ready?"

An angry nod.

"Mark, get set, go."

They put their index fingers on their tongues—though not before Tate performs a sleight-of-hand knuckle roll and hides the tab against his pinkie. He watches her swallow.

"Satisfied?"

"Pretty much." He drops the tab between his seat and the door. "Now we wait."

They sit back. Outside, the world has gone still. This moment always has its own thrill, watching someone else's brain chemistry transform before your eyes.

After a minute Tate says, "Man, this shit works fast," and though he doesn't experience the rush himself, he's not lying. Regular users are already acclimated when they take a hit. But Jessamyn's system isn't used to the dopamine rush. Her skeleton seems to puddle in the seat. Easy to forget what opies do to fresh brains.

"So how many doses do I have to distribute?" he asks, just to see if she's still there.

"Quarter million, give or take?"

"No way I can sell that fast."

Her eyes narrow. "Then don't."

He laughs, then realizes she's serious. "What are you saying?"

"You know exactly what I'm saying."

"*Steal* it? Do you have any idea—"

"Listen." Her body makes a wriggle in the seat, everything fritzy with the drug. "They were worried about sending a big shipment toward Houston. But what are they supposed to do? If they can't move product, the guys above them can't either. Everybody shipping to the southern United States is flying blind. Imagine if last week you'd flown fifty kilos of brown into Miami. Who's going to sell that much heroin in a city that doesn't even exist anymore? Same situation here, except instead of reacting after the fact, you can anticipate it. Plan for it."

"Still, you don't mess with these guys."

She opens an app. "Look at this. Just look." Manic, she shoves her phone at his face.

A chain of hurricane icons tagged with category numbers— 5-5-6-6-3-2-3-4-4-5-5-5-6-6—ascending as Luna nears Miami, weakening over the peninsula, strengthening again over the Gulf. Pac-Man about to swallow Houston whole. "This entire place?" Her free hand makes a frantic circle. "In thirty-six hours this place is gone. Saint Louis will never track us down."

Tate feels himself flop and weaken on her hook. "What, we just take it?"

"How would they ever find us?"

"They know my name, they know your . . ."

"We have other names, thanks to you." She whips out a fake license that Tate purchased for her last year from an ID mill in Dallas. She holds it up next to her face. "Hi, I'm Kaitlyn and this is Steve. What's your name? Yeah, we're just so happy to be safe, you know?"

Tate runs a palm over his face and she moves her body close, so he feels her heat. "We're talking two million. Your dealers are all gone, you'll have no network, no buyers."

"Why didn't you take the load yourself, then? Head off into the sunset."

She angles away. "Because I'm a lowly mule, asshole, as you're so fond of pointing out. And where am I supposed to sell it, from my parents' guest room in Saint Paul? Because that's my evacuation plan."

Tate thinks of his son, the boy's future when everything in the world looks so damn bleak. He's seen the damage estimates in Florida, the catastrophe models from the actuaries, he's read the Twitter streams about what Houston is facing in the coming weeks, the multiplying effects of Luna on the recession.

Now, in this darkened parking lot, another decision point, another equation needed to balance market value and mortality assumption. Two million worth of wildfire sounds great. But a load that big is worthless if you don't have a way to distribute it. Regular buyers, runners leaning into car windows.

"Well?" Rubbing her thighs. "We doing this or not?"

"We need buyers."

"I've got a plan for that," she says. "I'm a regular Elizabeth Warren."

"Are you now."

A big smile. Maybe she's right. Obviously they can't stay in Houston.

"No motels," he says. "That's the first place they'll look."

"I'm all over the accommodations part."

"So where do we go?" he finally asks.

She jumps him, and after all these hints and come-ons they are finally entangled, her body like putty in his hands. And all it took was a single dose.

They pull up in front of Nora's house. His ex-wife paces the driveway with her healthy daughter perched on her hip. Behind her, David edges out the door with his arms full of bags. New baby, new husband, same house. Moving on but staying put.

As Tate strides up, Nora lifts her shades to look behind him and Tate imagines what she's seeing. Hottie in the front seat, beating the steering wheel to some thrashing track.

"What is she, fifteen?" Nora says.

"She's a colleague."

"Oh, I bet she is."

He looks at the FOR SALE sign in the yard, the UNDER CONTRACT insert along the top.

"Finally sold the place?"

She grimaces. "They backed out yesterday on account of all this." She twirls her free hand. "We'll keep the earnest money. Whoop-de-do."

They walk up the stubby driveway where David is now loading the station wagon. Their plan, Nora says, is to spend the next week waiting out the storm at her in-laws' place in Tucson, until they know the extent of the ruin.

Speaking of ruin. Tate leans against their car.

"How is it lately?" he softly asks.

The baby claws at Nora's cheek. "They've got him in a trial on this new med. The walking's better and he's sleeping through the night again, so."

"Well that's good."

"It's kind of washed him out though. You'll see. Connor?" she hollers toward the house.

Tate waits. A choking builds in his throat. The screen door whines open and his son struggles out with a suitcase. It's been weeks—okay, months—since Tate's seen the kid, just shy of his seventh birthday. He's wearing a lavender T-shirt and mismatched flip-flops and his hair's chopped in a buzz cut, which Tate hates because you can see everything. His skin is the shade of a receipt left too long on the dashboard.

Tate walks up to the porch and squats. "Hey there, little buddy."

Connor stares at him bug-eyed through the thick lenses of his glasses, struggling to recognize his own father. Tate puts a hand on the fragile jaw and grazes his ear and the edge of his hairline, avoiding the jagged scar parting the top of his skull like barbed wire. The touch of his son's warm skin shudders up his arm with the pull of that slender pharmaceutical thread that once joined them as Connor's pain ate him from the inside out, the grim-faced nurses and the breezy doctors and the tightfisted anesthesiologists and the impotent "pediatric pain management specialists" whose stingy bullshit he had to fight every day. Which he did, with everything he could lay his hands on legally; and after that, by any means necessary. Oxy, Vicodin, fentanyl, black market morphine to supplement what the nurses doled out. Pills, pulped tablets ladled on the tongue, furtive sips of codeine syrup from a Dixie cup.

Connor: his only child, his first customer.

Our sons. The fruit of our loins. Give him everything you've got, me lads. Your strength, your drive. Don't turn your son into one of these transmetro who-the-fook-knows, some feminized pile of shite that passes for a man these days. Give him a stern word when he needs it, a box to the ear. Raise them to be chips off the block of you, hale and genuine men. Because our sons, they're the image of ourselves. Remember what Machiavelli said: We raise our sons in a forge of steel.

Tate slides his hands down Connor's arms, soft as noodles, then pulls him into a gentle hug, careful not to squeeze.

"Ouch," he says anyway.

Tate drops his arms. "You excited for your trip?"

Connor stares blankly. "What trip."

"You and Mom and David and your little sister. You're all going to Arizona."

"What's Arizona."

Jesus. Connor nailed his multiplication tables in second grade and now this. The memory problems are getting worse, not better. It's like the kid has freaking Alzheimer's at seven years old.

"So listen," Tate says quietly. "It might be awhile before I see you again, buddy."

"Why."

"You'll be in Arizona, and I have no idea where I'll be."

"Arizona is not home."

"You know I love you, Connor, right?"

"What's love you."

You have my number," Nora says. Connor and his sister sit buckled in the back. David waits behind the wheel with the engine running.

Tate gives Nora an ex-husbandly squeeze and bends to wave into the back seat as the family drives off. The baby returns the wave from her backward car seat but not Connor.

Tate looks up at the house. He used to hold the mortgage on the place, the homeowner's insurance policy in his name. He takes in the windowsill where Connor rested his chin, the shade of a live oak where he took his first steps, the door frame where he smashed three fingers, his screams echoing down the street.

The house can go, as far as Tate's concerned. He sees Luna clawing for the place, flattening the rafters, ripping out the guts, sweeping it away like dust.

He thinks, *Let her come. Let her take it all.*

25.

Luna makes her approach, just as her forebear closed in more than a century ago. A hurricane unnamed, known afterward as the Great Storm of 1900. No one alive today was there when she came ashore that September morning, though the land preserves faint vestiges of her fury, still etched in the shoreline rock, remembered in the silt.

Over six summer days she swept in from the Atlantic, coursed through the Windward Passage, teased the Cuban coast, and arrived on the heels of a great building boom that had transformed Galveston from an island byway into a thriving city forty thousand strong.

No warnings reached Galveston from abroad. As the Gulf sky darkened, residents of the narrow island settled in for a September squall.

The truth came with the water. A storm surge twice a tall man's height swept the streets. Mules swam the churn still harnessed to carts. Winds turned tiles into missiles. Whole families were swallowed, neighborhoods drowned in the hellmouth of the surge. Twelve thousand dead, one of Texas's largest city reduced to rubble.

Survivors migrated across the bay, doubling the inland settlement's population, though Houston would not remain landlocked for long. The growing city's need for a deepwater shipping route only intensified with Galveston's devastation. The following decades saw the channel dredged from the mud beneath Buffalo Bayou, piled into bird islands and salt marshes that rendered the fifty-mile course a marvel of engineering and sustainability.

Galveston, meanwhile, fortified itself against the sea. In 1904 builders completed a three-mile section of the Seawall, a barrier seventeen feet high that would extend seven miles more by the 1960s—only to be overtopped by Hurricane Ike in 2008.

Now, as Luna bears down, the sister cities lie open and vulnerable. Refineries and petrochemical depots stand like inverted paper cups against her force. Luna peels free their lids with the ease of a kitchen can opener. Their contents—combustible, viscous, toxic—gush forth into the channel waters and over inundated land.

Her eye follows the Ship Channel into the heart of the city, where her wall gorges on the waters of Trinity Bay. She tears at skyscrapers, submerges highways, roots out the foundations of old bridges and crumbling infrastructure. A city unready for its demise, victim to the torrent of the winds.

Twelve days after landfall in Florida, Hurricane Luna dies over Texas, fragmented by the dryness of the land and by westerly winds that dissipate her bands. From here her remnant rains and winds will move east in the coming days to fill rivers and flood streams until finally dispersing over the Atlantic, the sea that breathed her into life.

26.

They love their guns, each turn-in a reluctant surrender. Example: this SIG Sauer P238 micro-compact, cradled like a Fabergé egg in the owner's hands.

"It's a beaut," Rain assures the Floridian. "I carried a .380 for a while. A Ruger."

The evacuee cracks her first smile. "Practical gal."

"That's me." Rain checks the chamber, lets the owner close the piece in its case, and walks the weapon over to the gun shed, a structure of galvanized steel erected behind the trailers. Already the shed is bristling with weaponry: rifles and shotguns stand upright in parallel racks, pistols crowd shelves and pegs. She finds a spot for the SIG Sauer, stores the cartridge boxes, and secures the outer lock.

Guns: an early test. Residents must surrender all firearms and ammunition at Main Gate, to be stored until the owner leaves the facility. Uncontroversial, Rain would have thought. Walk into any Field & Stream and you're asked to announce your firearms. The idea that residents shouldn't have to check and store them here—surrounded by children, living in tents—is bananas.

At the last staff meeting Jed had other ideas, tapping on a binder, quoting federal law: "'Neither the Governor nor any official of a municipal or state entity shall prohibit or suspend the sale, ownership, possession, transportation, carrying, transfer and storage of firearms, ammunition and ammunition accessories during a declared state of emergency, that are otherwise legal under state law,'" he read. "That's directly from federal statute."

"Doesn't apply here," Rain objected. "This is a Red Cross facility, not a government entity."

"That's just window dressing. This is a FEMA installation, under the jurisdiction of DHS. It's bullshit."

Maybe not bullshit, but they've had to split the hazelnut in these megashelters. Federal and state law on the one hand, Red Cross policy on the other, tribal sovereignty waving a third. Sure, a litigious gun owner could take them to court. But by the time the case is resolved this facility will be shuttered.

The next owner has brought his teenage son to the Square. The man is a real piece of Florida work. Loud Hawaiian shirt on a wiry frame, a sunburned face, a loud mouth, and two guns. One looks like an old Browning A-Bolt, a deer rifle slung over his shoulder. The other's a holstered pistol, maybe a Glock.

"What's the deal?" he's asking Nila, a liaison from Oklahoma Emergency Management. "I been here three days already and I haven't shot up a single mess tent." Nila says something Rain can't hear. The man responds: "No damn way I'm giving these up. You crazy?"

Rain checks his name on Nila's screen. *Chester Biggs.* "Mr. Biggs, if you don't relinquish your weapons we can't allow you to stay."

Biggs speaks loudly, so any other gun owners around will hear: "Only reason you even know about them is the lady in the next tent snitched. If I'd've kept these babies in their bag, I wouldn't be standing here now."

"Need your ammo, too," says Rain, speaking calmly but tensing everywhere.

The man looks about to explode when his son steps up to his side. "Come on, Daddy," the boy murmurs. "We'll get 'em again when we leave. Hell, come Thanksgiving we'll be back up at Big Cypress spotting white-tails."

The man's face changes in an instant. "Fine then," he huffs. "Let me just say goodbye." Biggs unstraps the Browning and looks back and forth between his guns. He plants a wet kiss on each barrel. "Take her. Just take her." He thrusts the rifle out toward Rain and turns away dramatically, drawing some nervous laughs from the crowd behind him, also a few rough claps from some other men nearby. Now the Glock. "Her, too."

With the handover complete, Biggs slaps his son's back. "Come on, Kyler. Let's enjoy all the comforts of this gun-free zone." He gives Rain a stare before walking off toward the pavs.

When they're out of earshot Nila says, "He's a carpenter. Maybe he'll be useful."

Rain grunts, watching his back. Charismatic guy, though she senses a harder element beneath Biggs's clownish charm, something gristly, reluctant to yield; also the sad slope of his shoulders as he puts on a good face for his boy. She's seen it before, how humiliating it can be for alphas like Biggs to lose control, to admit defeat in circumstances like this. And now he's got a black chick confiscating his guns.

"Keep an eye on that guy," she says, more to herself than anyone else. Nila nods.

Meanwhile Butch is checking in two volunteers from Houston. The man is about Rain's age with a round face, graying buzz cut, and a slight paunch, the woman perhaps ten years younger. Butch points a stylus at the guy. "This fella's in insurance," he tells Rain.

"Oh yeah?"

"And personal finance. Name's Steve," the new arrival says, reaching to shake her hand. "And this is Kaitlyn."

Rain asks, "If I gave you a dedicated phone line and a desperate-people line, could you give us some help over the next few days?"

"Anything you need."

"Excellent. We've got lawyers coming in but not until next week. Lot of desperate people getting off these buses."

"I can imagine."

She looks at Kaitlyn. "How about you?"

Kaitlyn twists at the waist, showing an orange mat strapped to her back. "Yoga. Vinyasa, hatha, basic stretching if people want."

For a moment Rain thinks the woman has a rifle case on her other shoulder, but what she's packing is an electric guitar. The instrument's head pokes out through the zipper.

"Is that a Gretsch?" Rain asks.

Kaitlyn lowers her shades. "D series. You play?"

Rain taps her left hand. "Used to. Nerve damage."

Kaitlyn looks at her more closely. "Have we met?"

Here it comes. "I don't believe so."

"I've seen you before. Wait." She snaps her fingers. "You're the flood lady, aren't you? From the magazine."

"That's me," Rain admits.

"Wow. These people are in good hands, babe."

Kaitlyn stares at her, almost girlish, until Steve nudges her arm. "Let her do her job."

She aims a shy smile at Rain, hoists her guitar, and takes Steve's arm. The couple leave the Square to find their patch of ground.

27.

The apex of the tent resembles a meringue, egg whites whipped into hard peaks. When Daphne muscles the pillow against her ears the sounds muffle to near silence, all but the liquid beat of her heart. Over these first days at Tooley Farm this has been her go-to pose, cocooned on her cot with her ears pressed into submission by her pillow. Move her elbows out half an inch and the racket comes flooding in. An infant's screams, tinny music, a couple screwing ostentatiously in a nearby tent. Beneath it all the low but constant buzz of the quadrant generator.

She pushes the pillow tight again. Quiet. Now loosens. Noise. Quiet. Noise—

"Just give in," Gavin says. Her stepson is slumped on his cot with his bass cradled in his lap. Mia has taken Oliver to the commissary, where the Larsen-Halls have qualified for a $250 credit for "indigent residents," another lovely category defining Daphne's new existence.

She slips Mia's phone from beneath her pillow. "I need to make some calls."

"See ya," Gavin says.

Daphne zigzags among the tents as she tries to make connections, beginning with the Willows. The line rings into an emptiness. A facility housing four hundred well-off retired Floridians, now severed from the world.

Like Daphne herself. She should have people to call, *someone* to extract her family from this place. Yet this cutting of threads happened long before Luna, she sees now, long before Gavin's return from California.

The isolation had been fraying at her marriage for months, for years. The move from Ann Arbor, the cutting of all those ties. Also Brantley's controlling temperament, the subtle ways he's nudged her away from teaching, from socializing on her terms, often without Daphne even noticing.

There was Flora Kalling, an attorney and the mother of a girl in Mia's class. They met during back-to-school night, hit it off, then Daphne invited Flora and her husband to dinner. Brantley came home late from the hospital, went up to shower following cursory handshakes with the couple, and didn't come back downstairs for half an hour. For the rest of the evening he was distant, incurious to the point of rudeness. When Bill and Flora left, he put on one of his pretentious jazz records while they cleared dishes.

"Those two are a walking argument for an obesity tax," he said over the sink.

Flora reached out the next week but Daphne didn't return her text, not wanting to expose the couple further to her husband's boorishness, nor to feel again her own shame.

Is she some kind of abused wife? Brantley has never hit her or grabbed her, rarely raises his voice. Yet somehow she has been living cut off from the world, suspended between her husband's will and the dopamine drips of her phone. And now all this.

She turns up Wyoming Street toward a dilapidated barn. Standing in its shade she tries the hospital, for the twentieth time.

"UMed switchboard. How may I direct your call?"

The connection is so unexpected that for a moment Daphne thinks she's hallucinating. "I'm looking for Brantley Hall. Dr. Hall, in General Surgery."

"Let me see—you know we're short-staffed, and departments aren't really functional. Can I connect you to someone else?"

"My husband was on a medevac plane from Miami."

A pause. "His name again?"

Daphne tells her.

"Ma'am, I'm going to let you speak to the doctor running our recovery. Can you hold for a moment?"

"Yes."

The phone system plays a recorded message Daphne has heard many times before. Now its banal commonplaces shade into a surreal description of a world that no longer exists. *Our renowned campus in downtown Miami features a medical plant equipped with state-of-the-art surgical facilities, cutting-edge research centers, and a patient-centered approach to care unrivaled on America's Eastern Seaboard. Our dedicated doctors and staff work across specialties to bring—*

"This is Bettina Duggan."

Daphne flattens a hand against the barn's rough siding, overwhelmed by the sound of a familiar voice. *So how is Gavin enjoying Stanford?*

"Bettina," she says.

"Yes?"

"Bettina—it's Daphne. Brantley's wife."

A gasp. "Oh God, Daphne! For a few days there we were all afraid you hadn't made it."

A ringing begins in her ears. "Brantley hasn't called us," Daphne says. Her own voice sounds small, remote. She rubs the rough board until a splinter wedges in her skin. She looks at it, dark against her fingertip.

"Daphne, give me a second so we can talk."

A dull clunk, a door closing. The hospital hubbub gives way to an awful silence.

Bettina comes back on. "I'm so sorry. We've been leaving messages on your cell. I'm so glad to finally connect. Brantley . . . Brantley didn't survive, Daphne. It happened at the airport, during evac."

"A crash?" She hears herself whimpering. She hears Bettina exhale. From a tent nearby she hears a zipper.

"No. Brantley delayed the ICU transport decision."

"He was incident commander," Daphne says dully.

"The plan for ICU was to take half the patients by ground transport, the other half by jet. Brantley—well, he was convinced they had enough time to get everyone moved before the winds came. But once they reached Miami International there was a ground stop. They thought it would lift. But the storm strengthened, and by the time they got everyone on the jets and hooked to life support, Luna was just—there. We lost three doctors, six nurses, and eleven ICU patients."

"And Brantley was one of them." Daphne needs to clarify this.

"Yes. There's going to be an investigation, though the important thing now is continuity. It's all so horrible, unthinkable really." Bettina pauses. "And I am so sorry for your loss, for your kids."

Daphne clutches the phone. "Where is my husband now?" She envisions Brantley's face, his picture from the wedding album abandoned along with the car, his image strewn with dirt.

"They've been bringing the remains here, to Jacksonville, where we've all relocated for now."

Daphne looks off toward the fence line, distantly aware of a stark detachment from this news, along with a righteous chill settling into the spaces between her organs. How *dare* he die and leave his children like this?

"You can claim his body here. If you can't get to Jacksonville we can have him driven or flown somewhere. For a service, or whatever you plan."

She wants to laugh, sob, scream, hurl the phone at the side of the barn, because the notion of planning a memorial service for her dead husband with no way to claim his body, no way to pay for a casket, no black dress, no money for cucumber sandwiches and whiskey at the reception, above all no Ativan—

"Daphne?"

"Yes?"

"Do you want to think about this overnight, talk to your children about arrangements?"

Arrangements. It is somehow easier to believe and accept the truth of Brantley's death after all that has happened this last week. Daphne's expectations of normalcy have entirely dissolved.

"We were evacuated and I don't have a car. It might be difficult to get there for a while. And the house is gone."

"Of course. I understand. Ours, too." Daphne remembers a cocktail reception last year at Bettina's home in Coral Gables, a few neighborhoods north of Pineapple Isles. An impression of cool marble and glass. "We have a condo in Snowshoe," Bettina adds, "plus the lake house in New Hampshire but those aren't exactly—" She catches herself. "I'm sorry, Daphne. Take all the time you need. There's no rush."

Repulsive somehow, to learn that one of this woman's biggest problem in the wake of Luna is owning two intact homes instead of three.

Bettina starts going over details, the morbid logistics of severing her deceased co-worker from his workplace. ". . . to talk about the life insurance, his other benefits. We have someone from HR doing all the cases early next week, so we'll have more information for you then as beneficiary, though there are obvious complications."

But the only word Daphne hears clearly is *beneficiary.*

Beneficiary.

Life insurance.

Benefits.

In the maelstrom of the evacuation she simply hasn't let herself think of such things. But Brantley had life insurance. And there is a retirement account, a 403-something, administered through UHealth. She heard him talking about it any number of times, the importance of maxing out preretirement contributions for the best advantage at tax time. Even if her home can't be salvaged, her family is protected. Of course it is.

The awful call to Bettina has conjured a lifeline back to her former existence, or at least some semblance of it. Eventually there will be a check. Multiple checks. Enough to buy a car, rent an apartment, get them back on their feet in a new place. Or an old place. Maybe Ann Arbor, where—

"Daphne? Are you there?"

"What about his salary, Bettina?" She hates having to ask, hates how money has become her sole obsession. "Could we possibly get an advance on his next paycheck? I haven't been able to reach our bank, and my purse was lost."

"Well . . ."

When Bettina doesn't continue, Daphne finally tells her. "We're really desperate here. We're in one of these huge FEMA shelters, out in Oklahoma. I honestly don't know what we'll do."

Bettina hesitates. "As I said, Daphne, the HR end of things is complicated. In fact, Brantley tried to take a salary advance earlier this summer, and—"

"What?"

"I really can't say more. But you might want to have your attorney on the line."

"My attorney."

"Yes."

Daphne clutches at her stomach, eyes squeezed shut. She remains in the shadow of the barn when the call ends. A wave of grief knocks her against the building's side and she kneels with the phone pressed against her cheek. She stays like this, letting it come, then walks back to the tent, her feet mechanical, leaden. She opens the flaps and when she sees Gavin cross-legged on his cot with his fingers moving along the neck of his bass an almost formal feeling comes over her.

"Gavin," she says, her voice different now, older and ceremonial, the voice of a widow, because that's what she is now, a widow, and when Brantley's son looks up he already knows.

PART
THREE

28.

For hours he wanders alone among the tents, a left on Arkansas Street then a left on Avenue D10 and a right on who knows, staring at the dusty packed gravel and trying not to lose it as other equally pathetic refugees trudge around him. Part of him doesn't care if they see him crying but part of him does, because this place is like a prison and if you cry in the joint you're just a bitch, as he learned this summer while binging all five seasons of *Prison Break*. That guy on the bus practically skull-fucked him just for leaning his seat back and now he lives next door, all because Gavin left his mom's purse in the driveway while his dad was dying at the airport like a goddamn war hero.

That's what Daphne called him. *Your father is a hero*, she said. *He died trying to save the lives of his patients, did everything he could to rescue them, but they couldn't get out in time.* Mia and Oliver took it hard, and Daphne's face was a slathered mess while she was telling them. But Gavin held it together, even when she took him aside to talk to him about what happens next, all the belt-tightening they'll need to do.

He almost laughed in her face. She really has no idea, not a clue how much worse it's going to get.

Vermont Street dead-ends at a large tent identified on a posterboard sign with the Sharpied word LIBRARY. A library, in the middle of a goddamn refugee camp.

Inside he's greeted by the most normal-looking person he's seen since getting here, an oldish lady with polyester pants and a peach blouse. Reading glasses dangle from a chain around her neck. She's a staff librarian in Lortner, she tells him, a town up the road fifteen miles, volunteering for the Red Cross by starting a library with a bunch of donated books stacked spine side up on five cafeteria tables in the shape of a capital E.

Gavin asks if you need a library card. She tells him to help himself.

He looks around until he finds a book he recognizes. Emerson, *Selected Essays*. He flips through until he locates those sentences from "The Young American" he recited to his father over the phone one night from Palo Alto. *I call upon you, young men, to obey your heart, and be the nobility of this land. In every age of the world . . .*

The surge of those American words in his throat. He first discovered them in February, during his last quarter at Stanford when he took a class called "Literature and American Experience(s)" taught by this kooky prof with frizzy hair and huge pink glasses who was always trying to get them to talk about what was "problematic" in the books they read, how the class should be understood as a series of "critical interventions" into the "imperialist idioms of American exceptionalism."

She said all the right woke stuff in lecture, but you could tell she was really into all the dead white guys on the syllabus. The Puritans with their howling wilderness, Natty Bumppo and the American Adam, even that bit from *The Great Gatsby* where the guy imagines himself checking out the "fresh green breast of the New World," a passage the prof made Gavin read out loud.

But he loved that class, how it made him see things. There were these two guys in his dorm from Shanghai. When he stood with them for the national anthem at the Stanford football games he'd think about Sui Sin Far and what she wrote about the democracy of the Chinese in America, how, even when surrounded by thousands of racist white people like Gavin, they could build their own urban Edens in their adopted land.

He leaves the library bookless and walks up along the fence line.

From here, Gavin can look down on the whole of Tooley Farm, the ranks of tents crisscrossed by clotheslines hung in the dead air.

Down to his right a hole gapes where some of the chain link has bent from the post. Easily big enough for him to squeeze through—though where would you go, dumbass, and what would you do? Maybe hitch a ride to the nearest town. Rob a convenience store, steal a car. He'd probably end up rotting in a field somewhere like a diseased steer, wandering off to die alone.

He sits for a while on the grass trying not to remember his father, which only makes him remember his mom. A night out with some friends, ice on the road, a truck. Her death in his face, he even went with a neighbor to identify her body. This is different. Just news, disembodied information, nothing to see or smell. Abstract and unreal, like the changes in the world that caused it.

He thinks about Zia, this girl he was just getting to know before he left Palo Alto. Even before Luna, it was hard to separate how he felt about leaving Stanford from how he felt about warming, which was all his classmates wanted to talk about, especially after the evacuations first quarter. The fires lasted a week, a week Gavin spent up in Marin County at his roommate's folks' house. When everyone came back to campus the faculty held all these flash seminars on the climate emergency, aka How Truly Fucking Fucked We Are. One seminar, "Geoengineering for Idiots," was led by three profs from environmental sciences talking about last-ditch plots to slow the rate of warming with emerging carbon-capture technologies and geoengineering schemes. The profs tried to put an optimistic spin on things but ended up making stupid jokes about the futility of solar radiation management. Half the students were crying by the end.

Zia had raised her hand and brought up that statistic about how guys supposedly think about sex once every seven seconds. "Well, that's how our generation thinks about climate change now," she scolded the profs as all the students nodded. "Every seven seconds. It's our future. It's everything. Fuck sex."

A very Stanford way of putting it, Gavin wanted to say, though right now Stanford feels not like a different world but like a different planet, one without nanoplastics tumoring the fish and gigadroughts torching the forests, without melting glaciers and father-killing hurricanes and methane sizzling up from the permafrost to expose extremophile bacteria and prehistoric viruses, this coughing earth and this sick joke of a country that's burning it all down just so Gavin's generation can come along and suck up the swill with a compostable straw.

"Fire! Fire!"

A distant scream. He turns his head, a sick part of him hoping to see some asshole burning alive. Down in the camp, thick clouds of black smoke swirl up from one of the tents. The canvas gusts into flames and two people run out waving their arms. A crowd gathers with blankets and water bottles and goes to work until the fire dies.

Probably an idiot lighting a joint, a kid messing around with Sterno. There's more yelling, some harsh laughs, before everything goes back to normal and people walk away, leaving a charred mess to smolder in the sun. The stink reaches his nose.

America. From a shining city on a hill to a tent city in an Oklahoma cow field.

Welcome to your new Eden, motherfuckers.

29.

No one will remember how it began, whether it was born in Tooley Farm or brought in from outside, or who started those early arguments over squad boundaries and the principle of aging out, or who first named the Demigod and came up with the rule of second capture.

All that matters is the game, the heat and rush and thrill of Range.

One thing Mia will always remember about her first round is that it happens the night she learns her father died. In the tent her mother makes them hold hands and say a prayer even though they never go to church, and Oliver is the only one who believes in God.

They all share a memory. Mom talks about the time they first met, at a party in Michigan. Gavin's story is about how cool their father was about letting him drop out of Stanford. Mia can tell it's a lie, but Mom just smiles. Oliver talks about Daddy's hot fudge sundaes. Mia tells a story about camping. A moment of silence, they all hug, and it's over.

Early in the night, after sundown. Gavin is off somewhere, Oliver running around with Bembe. Mia's mother sprawls on her cot staring up at the dark.

"Mom." Mia pokes her in the foot. "*Mom*."

"Oh, Mia." Her voice is weary, distant. "Let's go to sleep. I love you."

"It's not even nine o'clock."

"Please. I can't—think I—" And she mumbles something.

Mia starts sobbing, loudly, and Mom reaches for Mia's head and strokes her hair and they cry each other to sleep with their hands joined over the gap between cots.

Something grabs Mia by the ankle. She shifts her feet. A clawing.

Mia sits up, heart pounding. But it's only Oliver, standing with Bembe just inside the tent. Even in the dimness she can see their lips are coated with something dark and when her brother gets closer she smells the sweetness on his breath.

"What, brat?"

"You have to come," Oliver whispers.

"Where?"

"Range. It's *huge*. Plus there's popsicles."

"I'm not in the mood."

Because she remembers and already hates being awake.

"Everybody's up past the barn." He grabs at her arm.

"Go away," she hisses, pushing him into Bembe, hating her brother for not being sad. Oliver sticks out his darkened tongue and the boys slip through the flaps.

She listens to the darkness and waits for her father's features to appear but she can't remember them, not even his eyes. It panics her, this forgetting, which is worse, in its way, than the earlier remembering. She almost wakes up her mother but then she remembers her father's smell, which helps her see his face.

Yes. That's him. Whiskers on a Sunday, a twirl at his waist, faint chemical whiff of hospital in his hair.

Distant shouts and laughs come gliding over the generator hum. She glances at her mother. No movement, only breath. Mia puts on her shoes and pushes out the flaps.

Y̲ou have to be in a squad." A boy named Hamid explains the rules, which are complicated, but if Oliver can understand them so can Mia. "There's a new squad forming right now."

Luz, already a member of Hamid's squad, stands nearby.

Hamid says, "It's Dragonflies, and the leaper is that guy." He points to a blond kid. "He might let you in."

"Okay." Mia swallows. She's never been good at introducing herself.

Then: "Can she be in Crow Squad?" Luz asks, and Mia almost starts crying again.

For the ritual of initiation she has to steal a piece of fruit. The mess pavilions are guarded at night so you have to break in. Hamid sends Luz along to make sure Mia goes through with it.

Mia has never stolen anything in her life. Trying to look casual, they stroll all the way around the mess pavs until they pass a tired-looking lady with a Red Cross cap and a flashlight.

"Goodnight, girls," she says as they walk by. They start giggling once they pass, then they reach a spot along Pav2 where the lights don't reach. Luz shows her where to slip beneath the walls. Mia gets on the ground and wriggles under and now she's inside the pavilion. She was expecting complete darkness but instead the space is lit by two buzzing bulbs.

The fruit bins are on the far side, behind a line of serving tables. She steals around the outer edge of the pav. Halfway there she freezes.

The glow of a laptop screen, the back of a woman's head. She sits at a table in the darkened part of the pavilion, typing away. NanoBuds glow from her ears.

Mia forces herself to move. As she nears the fruit she has to step in front of a line of crates stacked against the wall. If the lady turns around,

Mia will be in her direct line of sight. She takes a deep, steadying breath and runs for the first bin, reaches for an apple, and—

"Who's there?"

Mia falls to the floor and scoots between two bins. The smell of apples and ripe bananas tickles her nostrils. She reaches up and pinches her nose so she won't sneeze.

"Butch, that you?"

Mia makes herself small, smaller still, and shoves the apple down the front of her shorts. Her mind searches for a way out. She'll count to fifty then she'll dash for the spot where she came in, covering her face as she runs. She counts down from twenty. *Three . . . two . . . one . . .*

When she pushes out the FEMA boss is standing by the bins, waiting.

"What's your name?"

Mia swallows. "Mia Larsen-Hall."

"And my name is Rain Holton. Did you take a piece of fruit from my bins, Mia Larsen-Hall?"

"No, ma'am," Mia lies.

"Mm-hmm." Rain Holton tilts her buzz-cut head then squats so her face is just two feet away. "Let me tell you a story, Mia. Few years back I was at a place called Yida, in South Sudan. Sixty thousand refugees in that camp. They had a nice central market but most of the food there was lentils and sorghum. MREs on occasion, but mostly lentils and sorghum. One day, during a bad season, this boy no older than you was caught stealing two MREs from a World Food Program storage depot. Enough to feed himself and his little sister for maybe a week if they were careful. He was running off and somebody tripped him up. In half a minute two Sudanese police come up on him and kick this kid to a pulp and leave his body to bleed out in the dirt."

Mia stares at the woman's face, imagining Oliver kicked and bleeding on the ground.

"Reason I'm telling you this story, Mia, is not to threaten you with death for swiping a banana. This is America. But a lot of people have gone to a lot of trouble to bring this food here to Tooley Farm. The folks I work with, they have to account for every banana and every packet of Saltines, you understand? There are folks living in this place, Mia, your neighbors, who came here with nothing but the clothes on their backs. And if food starts to run scarce, which it very well might down the road because I know how bureaucracies work and I have no illusions about where our country is right now, if that happens I am going to need to account for every last apple and every last cup of powdered potatoes and every last MRE. And if we let one person in here steal food, other people will start to steal food, and then where will we be if things get desperate, if folks get truly hungry? I need you to think about these things, Mia Larsen-Hall, the next time you get it in your head that it's okay to steal food from the mouths of your neighbors. Now scat."

Mia, too terrified to cry, leaves her hiding place and walks stiffly back to the other side of the pav, trying to ignore the trickle running down her leg. Luckily it's not too much and you can't see it in the dark and she's able to wipe most of it away before rejoining Luz outside.

They come back breathless to headquarters. "She passed," Luz proclaims. Mia, ears still burning, hands Hamid the stolen apple. Hamid gives her three taps on her right shoulder and two on her left and a last one on her right and his thumb makes a dirt X on her forehead, and now she's officially a noob. By tomorrow or the next day she could already be a scout.

Instead of congratulating her Luz steps up close and says, "I heard about your dad."

Mia looks away.

"Oliver told Bembe. I didn't want to say anything until after your ritual. I'm really sorry."

"Thanks." Mia's eyes well up again. She wipes them with her arm, and it's a good thing Hamid calls everybody in for the next round because she doesn't want to cry in front of her new squad.

"Okay, round three. Everybody go to your stations," Hamid orders. The Crows circle up for the squad cheer and fan out, and the game spirals in the night.

Kyler Biggs is the leaper in Leopard Squad, a group that likes to capture rough and break rules. They call themselves the "Snow Leopards" because they're all white, Luz tells her, confirming Mia's first impression of the boy. Tonight they're holding two blocks of Arkansas Street but nobody wants to mess with them. Kyler stands at the crossing of Arkansas and Avenue D7 puffing on a cigarette he probably stole from his mom.

"Come and get us, bitches!" he calls out. "You know you want it!" Still no one attacks.

Then it happens. Bembe jumps out from between two tents and runs at a girl about his age. She turns and sees him coming.

"No!" Luz yells. Too late. Bembe dodges to the side but one of Kyler's sidekicks sprints after him and he sprawls to the ground. Four Snow Leopards drag him roughly off to their base.

Mia watches the whole thing from behind a tent two avenues down. She hates the unfairness of it, that a buttsuck like Kyler Biggs can bully everybody, that he can still have a father when hers is dead and his probably murders deer for fun.

Later Mia walks with Luz back toward their tents, elbows bumping as they move along the avenues. "Kyler is such a dick," Mia says.

"Yeah," Luz agrees.

"You don't have to be afraid of him, you know."

"I'm not afraid."

"Yes you are."

"I'm just—" Luz goes quiet.

Mia moves closer; whispers, "You don't have to let him mess with you." They stop in the middle of a crossing. "There are things we can do."

Luz's eyes go wide. "Like what?"

Mia thinks about what the Stone Cold Bitches would do about it, this very interesting problem of Kyler Biggs.

"Just . . . things."

30.

Strings of mini-lights crisscross the avenues in sagging lattice patterns that change from block to block. By night Tooley Farm could be a massive street fair but for the bugs and the wafts of manure gassing off the surrounding fields. Music swarms from the tents in a thousand variations, tinny songs streamed from phones.

"God, these people," Jessamyn says at the north end of Avenue C2. Double ranks of tents march south. She's been pushing to get sales going but Tate has been sussing out the place, running light recon on the security arrangements while enduring several long shifts helping residents sort out their insurance claims, not that there's much to recover.

Never has he seen so many so fucked. What they want is reassurance, some glimmer of confidence that normalcy will return. What they need, he suspects, is a fix.

Jessamyn is wearing Daisy Dukes and one of Tate's dress shirts tied off above the navel, an outfit that gets her some looks, though most everyone in the megashelter is showing skin. Some have brought their cots outside, hoping to catch a breeze. Five shirtless men play a loud game of poker on an orange traffic barrier pulled in from the access road. Naked toddlers skitter among the tents. The evening quiet is punctuated by muffled sobs and urgent conversations gleaned in fragments as they walk along. English, some Spanish; here a torrent of angry French.

On Avenue D2 a fortysomething chick drags out a cot. Her back is bent like an old woman's, her skin spotted; a body that works hard. She has to take a half step to avoid falling. Tate braces her arm.

"Bad knee." A grimace of pain.

"Here, let me," Jessamyn says. They lower her to the cot and help her arrange a pillow. "You want something for that, the pain down there?"

"Hey—" Tate starts.

"I might know a guy holding some stuff."

The woman's eyes make a hopeful flash. "When?"

Jessamyn says, "I mean." She side-nods at Tate.

He looks up and down the avenue, feeling exposed. "Maybe tomorrow."

"Please."

"Someone'll drop by."

"Make it early." She paws at Jessamyn's knee. "Morning if you can."

Jessamyn waits until they're out of earshot. "What the fuck, man?" she says under her breath, walking sideways. "We had a sale back there."

"Never sell direct, not in here. This shit takes time, some patience. We need layers, okay? Deniability."

"Layers," she harumphs, unconvinced.

They're moving along Avenue D3 when they hear it. *WHAP-do-WHAP-WHAPPITY-do-WHAP.* Someone's shredding a bass guitar. No amplifier so the notes are indistinct but the rhythm is catchy, complex.

"Hold up," Jessamyn says. She tilts her head and talks to the tent. "Hello?" The music goes on. Closer, with her mouth against the flaps. "Yo, Jaco Pastorius, you in there?"

The slapping stops. The flaps part to reveal a gangly kid in sweat shorts and a Florida State tank top. Scraggly hair, a sparse semi-beard. The body of a long-neck electric bass rests against his crotch.

"You need something?" he asks.

"Just listening to you whack," she says. "You sound amazing."

"Thanks." He looks away but not for long, because it's hard to look away from Jessamyn, plus everything she says seems to have a double meaning.

"Fretless, too." She stands on her toes to inspect the instrument's neck, shirt inching up her belly. "I'm impressed."

The expert observation gets his attention. "You play?"

"Guitar."

"Cool."

"How long you been playing?"

"Maybe four, five years."

"You got a band, Jaco?"

"I did for a while."

"Who the fuck is Jaco?" Tate asks. Together they look at him, then at each other and start laughing.

She shifts her hips and sets a hand down there, notched against the bone. The kid pretends not to notice her bare stomach. "I'm Kaitlyn. This is Steve. We're volunteers from Houston."

"Gavin," he says. "From Miami. Actually Coral Gables, which is now basically Atlantis."

Tate nods at the tank top. "You go to FSU?"

Gavin glances down. "Got it from a donation bin." His spine straightens a few degrees. "I'm at Stanford actually."

"No shit?" Jessamyn rears back. "Jesus, dude. What's a Stanford student doing in this du—" She lowers her voice. "In a refugee camp? Shouldn't you be starting the semester?"

"We're on the quarter system. Classes don't start till the end of the month. I doubt I'll be going back anyway."

"How come?"

His shoulders slump and he swivels his head to look at their surroundings. "We had to abandon our dog," he goes on, an octave higher. "Plus my dad died in the storm."

"Jesus," Jessamyn says. Tate watches the kid's face, the quiver in the lower lip.

"You know," he says, sharklike, "I could maybe set you up with an amp."

"Seriously?"

"Maybe a distortion pedal."

"In here?"

"Why not."

"That would be amazing."

"I'll run into town. There's a Walmart."

"Good idea." Jessamyn slips an arm around his waist. "Should we keep walking?"

The kid looks panicked.

"Come visit us," Jessamyn tells Gavin, reaching to squeeze his skinny arm. "We'll play some tunes. We're in Staff Camp down from Hawaii Street. We aren't going anywhere, that's for sure."

They share a laugh that ends abruptly when a woman's voice asks, "Can I help you?"

"They don't need anything, Daphne," Gavin says, suddenly uptight.

Tate turns to see the narrowed eyes of a forty something MILF. First impression: this chick's as out of place in a relief camp as a rose pearl in a sardine can. That desperate face enjoys regular Botox and chemical peels. Smooth hands and a massive stone on her left ring finger. She reaches up to brush hair away from her eyes. Her fingernails are a mess.

"We were just listening to your son play," Jessamyn says. "He's really talented."

Daphne licks her chapped lips.

"I'm Kaitlyn. This is Steve. We're volunteers."

"Daphne."

"I'm so sorry for your loss, Daphne. Gavin told us."

"Thank you."

"This place." Jessamyn gazes around wide-eyed. "Please let us know if there's anything you need."

"That's so nice," Daphne says. Wistful, less like an automaton. They talk for a few minutes. Daphne doesn't bring up her husband, and Jessamyn and Tate don't ask. Gavin stands slumped, unspeaking.

A girl runs up, trailed by two others roughly the same age. "Mom, this is Luz and this is Carly and we're playing Range but Oliver ran away with Bembe and we don't know where he is."

Daphne smooths the girl's hair. "This is Mia. Gavin's sister."

"Ah," Jessamyn says.

The girls lose interest in the adults and rush off.

"Welp," says Tate. "We should head back."

He takes one last look at Daphne as they say their goodbyes. The shape of her nose, also the row of tiny wrinkles on her upper lip, the hollows of her eyes.

The massive stone on her ring finger.

The next morning Tate is outside the tent swiping on news reports and delaying his volunteer shift when Gavin wanders into Staff Camp. Jessamyn rests prone on a blanket, nose in a fashion magazine she swiped from a donated stack in Pav4.

Tate grins at the kid. "It's only been one night, bro. I don't have that amp quite yet."

Gavin gestures at the bass strapped across his back. "I just thought we could maybe play some stuff." He looks down at Jessamyn. "If you're not busy."

She muscles up. "Suppose I can squeeze you in." She ducks into the tent and comes out with her guitar. They sit together on her blanket cross-legged, admiring each other's instruments before messing around on some tunes. The long neck of Gavin's bass points like a shotgun up the avenue. The body, a capri orange polished smooth, warbles in the sun. Jessamyn's guitar is a jet black, dull and unreflective.

"*Damn*, you're good," she says after Gavin fingers through a complicated riff. He slaps out another, eyes closed over the sad scruff on his face.

She winks at Tate. Now back to the kid, playing him like she plays her guitar as they work through songbooks in their heads. Their music sounds good. Not acoustic but not amplified either. Somewhere in the soft between, hovering just below the camp din.

Gavin responds to Jessamyn's kindness like a whipped dog. Tate can tell he craves the attention, some note of feminine approval that doesn't come from his uptight mom.

What the kid really needs is a job.

31.

Hours slip by, days. Shock and guilt ebb and surge. Daphne's parents died in quick succession years ago. The experience was shredding and taught her what it means to feel alone and that the stages of loss are something like the stages of a rocket, each burning through and leaving a new part of you blackened and adrift.

She sits up on the cot. Her thighs spasm with inactivity. She stands, squats to fire her muscles. Her body craves a run, earned sweat streaming down her back. Instead she splashes bottled water on her shiny face, runs her fingers through her disgusting hair, and walks up to the Square, where the Red Cross has arranged for help with insurance claims, banking, and so on. Volunteers at two trailers offer appointments on a first-come, first-served basis, with lines twenty deep. She considers coming back later, but the new buses slotting through Main Gate convince her to stay. Tomorrow the wait will be longer.

In line she speaks to a Cuban couple from Lemon City whose entire apartment complex was leveled. The woman behind her is a waitress named Dorianne, a fiftyish divorcee whose parents are feared dead inside a state-run nursing home in Wynwood. Dorianne evacuated with her son, John Junior. "They're saying they'll find five thousand more bodies in Miami-Dade." She chews on a length of braided grass as she talks. "Haven't had a smoke in four days. I'd take John Junior's damn vapes if he had any left. Just something."

"There was a guy selling cigarettes this morning," Daphne says. "He came by our tent."

"I chased his skinny ass off. Twenty a pack that prick wanted. You think I got twenty dollars?"

"I know I don't."

Dorianne gives her a skeptical up-and-down, double-taking her engagement ring.

When Daphne's turn comes she steps into the trailer and the first cold hug of air-conditioning on her skin in days. The volunteer inside is the guy who was speaking with Gavin the other night.

He looks up from the booth. "We meet again. It's Daphne, right?" She nods. He gestures at the bench. "I'm Steve."

"Steve. Right."

"You're here about insurance?"

"I suppose." She rubs her arms, skin clammy from the AC. The booth is narrow and cramped. Her knees bump Steve's as she sits. "I just need to figure out a few things. Can you help me?"

"That's why I'm here."

They discuss her situation, which Daphne doesn't entirely understand, though even talking through it with someone knowledgeable helps.

"Let's start with insurance on your home," Steve says, "because that's where you can get the most immediate relief, housing vouchers and so on, once FEMA takes you off the tit. I'll put you through the databases. Homeowners, personal property, flood." He writes down her address and his fingers go to work on the keyboard. "Your kids are how old?"

"Eight, eleven, and nineteen."

"How they holding up?"

"The younger ones surprisingly well. It'd probably be harder if they were home, where their dad was." She sighs. "The older one, though, Gavin."

"The musician."

"He's struggling. He's been through a lot, and now this."

The computer pings. Steve squints at the screen. "Strange. Your address isn't coming up on NFIP."

"What's that?"

"National Flood Insurance Program. Government-mandated insurance you have to buy if you live in a flood zone. It's administered by FEMA, our generous hosts."

"Our house is—was—definitely in a flood zone," Daphne says. "We're a hundred yards from Biscayne Bay."

"Was there a recent lapse in coverage?"

"You mean—"

"Maybe you purchased private flood insurance? Or missed a payment?"

"I wouldn't know." Inside, a familiar shame leaps up and waves. "My husband took care of all that."

Steve leans back in his chair. "Let's approach this another way. I know a guy in the NFIP. He might be able to tell us something."

Steve makes a call turned slightly away from her as she tries to comprehend his side of the conversation. "And that's all the cross-checks? You sure? Okay, buddy. Thanks, Marcus." He disconnects. "Some bad news."

"Go on."

"Your house wasn't covered by flood insurance. Apparently it lapsed during a refi."

"My house was refinanced?"

"Twice." A pause. "Wait. Your husband didn't tell you about that, either?"

"Without my knowledge?"

He shrugs. "You would have to talk to the lenders your husband worked with."

Your husband your husband your husband. Repeating the phrase like a taunt, hammering her with Brantley's idiocy and lack of care.

Last winter, a conversation in the kitchen. Brantley going on about great interest rates, getting more capital out of their home. *I need power of attorney so you won't have to bother with all that crap, Daph, because do you really want to slog it down to the banks and title companies?* She had signed the power of attorney without hesitation, because what reason had Brantley ever given her to doubt him? Now the document she signed is one of a trillion pieces of paper swirling around in the Miami sludge.

"Next I'm going to check your homeowner's insurance and claims history," Steve says. "It won't cover the water damage from Luna. But at least it covers the structure, the roof, the land. You might also be able to claim wind damage, which in a storm like Luna would be hard to distinguish from what the water did."

Gavin's phone, those awful images of their submerged home.

"So the last listed insurer in the database is Progressive. Though . . ." She waits for it. "Shows here that your homeowner's policy lapsed in October." He side-eyes her. "Your husband again?"

"Jesus *Christ.*"

"Yeah, sorry."

"I thought lenders paid those policies automatically, as part of your mortgage."

"They have to be set up that way so the money comes out of escrow. Sometimes, if a house is refinanced a number of times, the policy can slip through the cracks."

"So you're telling me—" She claps a hand over her mouth. No flood insurance. No homeowner's insurance. Two refinancings of their mortgage in which she played no part. The massive house a total loss. How could Brantley have been so irresponsible?

She stands abruptly. "I should go," she says, feeling ill. "I need to sort some things out."

"Suit yourself." Steve butterflies his arms over his head. "And say hi to Gavin." She doesn't answer. Her hand is on the door latch when Steve says, "He's been playing around with my gal, you know."

"Playing . . . ?"

"Music," he says, with an easy grin. "Guitar, bass and whatnot. They're even talking about a band. He didn't tell you?"

"No, I haven't—we haven't talked about that."

"Gavin's got some real talent, Kaitlyn says."

"That's good to hear."

"And hey, good luck with all this."

"Thanks for your help."

"Here to serve, ma'am."

Steve raises a finger in a phantom hat-tip to match his cornpone accent. Daphne steps out into the heat.

32.

Every day Gavin looks for her. At meals, along the avenues, at open mic. He takes to getting up early so he can stroll by her morning yoga class in Pav4, watch from the shadows as she poses and instructs. Bodies of every shape and size contort on donated mats but he has eyes only for her. She moves among the others correcting and encouraging, stepping on the soles of feet.

What gets him is her kindness. Most of these people have never so much as thought of attending a yoga class before. They don't know what their joints can do. They laugh at themselves, ashamed of their body fat and poor form.

But this practice is for everyone, Kaitlyn wants them to know. This practice is for you.

Gavin tries the class, just once. During a balance pose Kaitlyn comes to adjust his stance. One hand on his scapula, another on his knee. He shudders. She feels it, and her touch lingers for a second longer than necessary—though perhaps he imagines this.

They play music most days now. Gavin lopes into Staff Camp at lunchtime and they sit on milk crates outside her tent, or walk to one of the pavs. Kaitlyn writes her own songs, biting, self-referential lyrics on the plight of their generation, not overtly political but sharp-edged and unsentimental. They play covers, too, old classics, new hits.

And doesn't he deserve this, after everything he's lost these last four, five years? Gavin tries never to feel sorry for himself but come on. His mom, his Oregon home, his Oregon friends, an in-person school year, his first sort-of girlfriend ever, Stanford, his Florida home, his Florida band, his dog, and now, the cherry on top: his dad.

Though he has no illusions about what this is. Kaitlyn lives with her boyfriend, probably fucks him every night for hours with all that chaturanga energy. Hard to know what she sees in the guy, this dull-witted insurance agent with his smirking self-regard and that pillowed rim of waistline fat he tries to hide with loose T-shirts. At night Gavin fantasizes himself into the form of a young bull moose, bucking horns and chasing his aging rival from the herd.

Gavin is shuffling along the dinner line when Steve bumps his shoulder.

"What's up?" Gavin says.

"Want to get out of here?"

"You mean—?" For a moment Gavin lets himself imagine Palo Alto, his gone life.

"Kaitlyn's doing a stretch class. I'm grabbing some chow in town."

"Um . . ."

"My treat."

They drive into Lortner for burgers and beers at a TGIF. Gavin tries to order a Heineken and gets carded but Steve shares his glass. Gavin takes furtive sips, peering over the top of the booth. Together they finish five pints.

On the way home Gavin is sprawling in the passenger seat, pleasantly buzzed, when the car sways.

"Fuck me," Steve says.

"What?"

"A flat. Feels like the front tire on your side."

They pull over on the shoulder. Gavin stands with his hands in his jeans pockets watching Steve remove the spare and some tools from the trunk.

Steve says, "Pop that hubcap for me, will you?"

Gavin points his phone light at the flattened wheel, pondering his assigned task. The hubcap is the metal disc in the middle, he's pretty sure. He sticks a finger in a crescent-shaped gap and gently tugs.

Steve rolls the spare up. "Is it stuck?"

"No, I just, I don't really know how to, like . . ."

"To change a tire?"

Gavin shrugs.

"Bro, you don't know how to change a freakin' tire?"

"My dad always had Triple-A."

"Well, tonight you're changing a tire, my friend. Now grab that lug wrench."

Gavin looks down at the array of tools and chooses the thing that looks most like his image of a wrench. Steve shows him how to pop the hubcap, how to jump the bolts, how to find the little reinforced rib in the undercarriage where you place the jack. The whole procedure takes about ten minutes start to finish. Once the car is lowered Gavin sits back on his haunches, breathing heavily.

"Outstanding." Steve slaps him between the shoulder blades. "Now do it again."

Gavin looks up at him. "Seriously?"

"Practice makes perfect, me lad. Now do the hubcap. Pop that fucking bitch, bro."

Gavin does, going through the whole routine a second time, with no instructions. When he's done his hands are smeared with rubber and grease and his skin is slathered in sweat. Blood pulses through his temples and the country air tastes deep and clean.

Steve offers him a cigarette. Gavin smokes the whole thing on the shoulder of the road without coughing once.

"Better than sex, am I right?"

"Wouldn't know."

"Oh man." Another hearty slap to the back. "The things they don't teach you at the fancy colleges. Gotta get you laid. I've met some skanks from Miami in the insurance line. I'll set you up."

"Gee thanks," Gavin says, giddy.

Back at Tooley Farm he follows Steve into Staff Camp, hoping for a glimpse of Kaitlyn. Steve goes in to check on her. His head pops out half a minute later.

"She's not feeling great." Steve's voice low, tense. "Probably on the rag. Let's call it a night."

"Okay."

"Next time the beers are on you, buddy," Steve says with a wink.

Gavin thanks him for dinner, though as he walks off he suspects that Steve isn't joking. Next time, he will be expected to pay.

33.

The National Bank of South Florida holds their checking account, their savings account, three Visa cards, Daphne's debit card. NBSF is their family bank. She has visited at least three of its many locations in Miami-Dade. There is even a favorite teller at the Merrick Park branch where she took Oliver just weeks ago to turn in a jar of loose coins.

She spends two hours on hold with customer service before deciding on a different approach. The task will require her to use one of the twenty-odd desktop PCs set up on flimsy folding tables along one side of Pav3. Even the sign-up sheet requires waiting in line. She writes her name down, then heads to Pav1 for lunch. On the way she bumps into Mia and Luz leading their little brothers along.

"You guys want to eat?"

"Me and Oliver are having lunch with the Calels," Mia says.

"Oh."

Luz says, "You can eat with us, too."

"Are you sure?"

Mia looks miffed but Daphne doesn't want to eat alone. Everyone grabs shiny zip-sealed meal packets and water bottles and takes seats at conjoined tables in the center of the pav, where two women oversee a passel of fifteen kids ranging in age from Vicenta's nursing baby to Hector, the teenage son of Aldina Calel, Luz's aunt. Mia and Oliver have already told Daphne something of the group's situation, the evacuation of a berry farm, a levee burst on Lake Okeechobee. It's unknown whether the other parents have survived.

Daphne looks around the pavs, struck by how few adults are here by themselves. Families, partners young and old, wives murmuring to their husbands. Gavin sits at a nearby table with Steve and Kaitlyn, already getting chummy with the odd couple. She imagines how Brantley would have reacted to Tooley Farm, the looks of smirking disdain he would have cast over the residents.

"I am sorry about your husband," says a voice through the hubbub. Daphne turns to meet Aldina's steady gaze.

"Thank you."

"Will you pray?" Aldina wants to know.

Mia stares, mortified.

Daphne surprises herself by nodding. "I will, actually."

Aldina raises her right hand and silences the children with a hiss. Daphne expects a Catholic prayer, maybe an Our Father in Spanish. Instead Aldina spools out a string of indistinguishable syllables, her eyes aflutter. Spellbound, Daphne stares at first before tucking her chin and whispering her own anodyne prayer. At one point Aldina's trembling hands leap across the table and grab Daphne's praying fist. The incantation crescendoes until finally the woman's grip loosens and her eyes open. She pats Daphne's wrist.

"Was that an indigenous prayer?" Daphne asks when the eating resumes.

Aldina frowns. "Como?"

Luz translates for her. Aldina's eyes crinkle. "We are Evangélicos. Eh—"

"Pentecostals," Luz explains.

Aldina gives an arch smile. "Sí, Pentecostal."

"It's a big thing back home," says Luz.

Daphne rearranges hunks of unidentifiable meat in her stew packet. "We visited Guatemala once, when I was pregnant with her." She nods at Mia. "Guatemala City and Antigua. My husband was on a junket but I just stayed in the hotel room."

"Por qué?"

"Morning sickness. It was awful." Daphne mimes a pregnant stomach and the act of throwing up. Aldina whispers another prayer.

Daphne asks, "Are you a minister of some kind, Aldina?"

"Just a Pentecostal," Luz answers for her, not bothering to translate.

"And your family, Luz?"

"We're Catholic," she says glumly.

Aldina peers down at her niece and sniffs.

In Pav3 Daphne waits a polite distance from her designated desktop, occupied by a distraught guy muttering at the keyboard. A banner on the screen reads FILING FOR UNEMPLOYMENT BENEFITS IN TEXAS; below, a spinning clock. Similar symbols appear up and down the computer line, the iconography of flooded systems and overwhelmed bureaucracies.

Five minutes go by before Daphne gently requests the terminal. The man looks almost relieved. "All yours, lady." He quits the browser and logs out.

Daphne uses her IDP code to log back on. The internet is rumored to be sluggish at Tooley Farm—though she couldn't have imagined quite how slowly the computer would respond. Several minutes tick by before the browser loads the bank's chat box.

Hello, this is Eliza and I'll be assisting you today. May I have your account number?

Daphne types: I don't know it.

That's okay. How about your name and the last four digits of your social security number?

Daphne enters the information.

What can I help you with today, Daphne?

I need to access my accounts.

Have you tried logging in with your username and password?

I don't remember them.

Not a problem! You can request a reset by selecting the My Account menu above. I'll wait while you try it.

Daphne obediently clicks through. A notification pops up: A username reset has been sent to the designated email address for this account.

Daphne's jaw flares. Back in the chat box, she types, I don't have access to my email. I'm in a FEMA shelter.

Would you like me to send a six-digit passcode to your linked devices?

My cell phone was lost in the hurricane.

In that case I can send the reset code to the email address on file.

But as I just explained, I can't access my email.

Let's try this another way. Would you like me to send a six-digit passcode to your linked devices?

A bot. She's chatting with a bot. An artificial intelligence incapable of comprehending how an actual human might have lost her smartphone in the midst of a national catastrophe and thus might not be capable of accessing her email account because her computer always used to log her on automatically, and how in order to reset her email password she would need to request that a security code be sent to one of her "linked devices," the only linked device to which she might have had access being her phone, which is now corroding at the bottom of what used to be Biscayne Bay along with the credit card and the debit card issued by the National Bank of South Florida, which holds the balances that she can neither access nor withdraw because she can't log onto their system because she can't check her email because she doesn't remember and can't reset her password.

Daphne types, Are you a perky little bot, Eliza?

I'm sorry, I don't understand your question.

Fuck you, Eliza.

This chat has now concluded. Please contact Customer Service for further assistance.

Daphne opens up Gmail and starts a new account. She makes up a new username and a password she'll remember, sends an email to herself to make sure it works, and is promptly asked for a backup email account and a phone number for authentication. She types in Mia's number and hits enter. Mia's phone vibrates. The screen flashes with a new alert.

Your Verizon balance in the amount of $625.51 is now past due and your credit card for autobilling has expired. Please log in to your Verizon account and enter new payment information to avoid a disruption in service.

She cackles, an ugly barking sound that turns heads in the pav. She swipes away the Verizon notification and enters the six-digit authentication code and goes to her new in-box to email the bank. She explains her dilemma, acknowledges how busy they all must be in the wake of the storm, and asks how she can go about accessing her accounts given her situation.

As she types this naked plea, the cold reality of her family's precarity walks up her spine. Brantley's death aside, the subject of money has become all-consuming since the moment she discovered her missing purse. The jarring lack of it, the burning need for it, the inability to access it, the impossibility of getting her family resettled without it. Money: the focus and purpose of her waking life.

She can think of two potential sources.

First, her art. She recalls the night of her opening, Brantley's vulgar complaints in the car about Pilar's failure to pay her commission percentages. She searches for Gallery 25. Pilar's website remains up and unaltered, even if the hotel and the exhibit space themselves are surely long gone. Daphne emails ostensibly to check in, hoping a quick account of her situation will inspire Pilar to send along any owed funds remaining after the gallery's ruin. The place must have been insured, though given Daphne's recent experience on that front, who knows whether anything is covered.

Second, Flo, a wealthy retiree with enough savings to finance a comfortable lifestyle at the Willows along with regular travel. The retirement community's website remains down, the switchboard isn't answering, and a search reveals no further information about the fate of its residents. Daphne wonders if Flo even knows about Brantley's death. An old woman displaced from her home to molder in oblivion, waiting for a phone to ring.

34.

A celebrity chef leads a cooking demo in Pav2, instructing Rain's over-worked mess staff in the fine art of quartering onions. Tomorrow he will go on *The Today Show* or *Morning Joe*, no doubt. As the footage rolls he will wag heads with the hosts over the state of those poor victims down in Oklahoma. *Those folks have been eating MREs by the thousands, Mika, so I thought I'd offer them a fresh-cooked meal.*

The guy cooks for an hour before his entourage leaves in a cloud of dust. His locally sourced dishes feed maybe a hundred, though every-one seems wowed by the glam. No harm done, Rain supposes, though who knows what fresh onions will do to their digestive tracts.

PRVs. That's what Butch calls them: pressure relief valves that keep the residents as content as possible despite their dire situations. By the end of week two, Rain has established a variety of these functions, all more practical than a lightning visit by a famous foodie. A walking track around the perimeter, basketball hoops on the sides of the barn, yoga classes. A bar of sorts, a roped-off area in Pav2 where alcohol is permitted. An AV outfit up in Norman has donated an inflatable screen for outdoor film viewings. Religious services are nondenominational affairs led by volunteer clergy from nearby towns. Evening popsicle deliveries for the kids have been especially popular, though now the youngsters expect them every night. She's also arranged for a regular shuttle bus to Lortner, the nearest town, where residents can look for jobs, splurge on McDonald's, or catch a bus out of state if they've been lucky enough to find a home elsewhere.

And turnover. By now hundreds of evacuees have already left

Tooley Farm, bound for the houses of friends, siblings, distant cousins willing to take displaced kin. Just this morning they put a family of seven on a bus to Seattle, where the father's brother has a construction business.

But others have already taken their places, new arrivals every day. Staff worry about increased demand on food, shelter, medical care, everything.

There is also a kind of unspoken separatism taking place through tent-swapping, a self-selection of portions of the population into ethnic enclaves. By now they've got a Little Haiti just east of Pav1, a Little Antigua full of Guatemalans and some Hondurans. Little Havana because apparently the Cubans don't want to hang with the Guatemalans. A Chinatown has sprung up down below Medical. There is even a "Crackertown," as the whites congregating in the area southwest of the barn have styled their neighborhood, tongue in cheek but also with a dark edge of pride in their self-designation, though Butch doesn't seem overly concerned. Rain has her doubts but so far she's kept them to herself.

She pushes her way up to the table to swipe a sample cup of the chef's lamb stew. "Dang," someone says. "Haven't eaten like this in a long time."

"And won't for a while," says another.

Rain lifts the tiny plastic fork to her lips and chews on a scrumptious hunk of lamb, potato, carrot, a mingling of herbs. Dozens of IDPs share observations on the concoction, filling their mouths with these flavors from another world.

A celebrity chef. Maybe worth the fuss after all.

In the evening she uses some rare alone time to page through a recent issue of *Southern Living* plucked from the donation bins. Not to her usual taste but she finds a few odds and ends, like a ceramic coaster in a terrazzo pattern. She takes a photo and is adding it to her neglected feed when a text dings in.

Vanessa, asking to FaceTime. Rain hesitates. She craves this rare silence, especially now, and chats with Vani are guaranteed to agitate. But once they connect she's glad they did, for tonight her daughter's curiosity gets the better of her millennial self-involvement. The mega-shelters are all over the news, Vani says. She asks how the population is doing, how the shelter works. As Rain talks through the early weeks and shares a few stories Vanessa moves closer to the camera, chin on the sweet cup of her hand.

"You okay, hon?"

Vani's cheek twitches. "It's terrifying, all this."

"Most of these folks'll be okay. The ones I worry about are—"

"No, Mama. I mean *all* this. It's speeding up. Did you read about that air quality thing in China last week, that die-off? Feels like we're coming to the end."

"Please don't say things like that."

"I'm never having kids."

The blithe pronouncement knifes Rain between the ribs.

"News to me," Leila says offscreen. Vanessa wheels on her partner.

"You refuse to see the big picture, both of you." Head wagging back and forth. "I mean, don't get me wrong, Mama, it's great that you found little tents for those people and all. But that day-to-day shit is meaningless when you think about it."

Little tents. Rain bristles. "Oh yeah? My career is meaningless?"

"That's not what I meant."

"You're the one studying urban socialism or whatever it is."

"Sociology."

"What are you going to do with that kind of degree, sugar?" she asks, veering them onto more tempestuous ground. "Just a year ago you were thinking about environmental law, that program at Northwestern—"

"And now I'm in *this* program. What's it to you?"

Rain gropes for a response but now Leila is there, hands on Vani's shoulders as Vani glares off to the side. Leila looks right at the camera and rolls her eyes and Rain understands the depth of their connection, that maybe Vanessa has found someone who knows her as well as her mother does. *A keeper.* As for kids? They'll come when they come, or not.

Once, when Vanessa was four, she got into a pitched battle with Rain about a playdate that had to be canceled because Vani was feverish with strep throat. When it was clear she wasn't going to get her way the little girl screamed until the veins in her neck stood out like braided ropes and she puked her grape juice all over the floor then went right back to arguing her case.

Twenty-odd years later and you still don't win fights with Vani. You retreat and you regroup, and you consider yourself lucky if the fire is 15 percent contained.

"Maybe I could come visit you there," Vanessa says, placating. "What's the place called again?"

Rain, surprised, arches her eyebrows at the screen. "Tooley Farm, outside Lortner. Maybe you should."

"We'll talk and I'll figure out my schedule. Probably be a few weeks."

"You can help me set up more of my little tents."

Vanessa concedes one of her tilted smiles. "I'd love that," she says, and Leila kisses the top of her head.

That night a line of slow-moving thunderstorms blows through. Cracks of lightning on the plains, hours of sheeting rain on trailers and pavilions and the thousands of tents. The morning dawns with a humid fog and saturated ground.

35.

This place, this game, this squad, this friend.

Sometimes Mia will huddle with Luz in the shadows, shivering with the thrill of the chase, the warm sheaths of their skin nearly indistinguishable in the night air, and while they're hiding Luz will teach Mia amazing cusswords in Spanish and in Mam, the language her grandmother back in Guatemala speaks that has ten words for penis, like *baak* and *t'lok* and *I'ish*, which also means corn cob, and *lb'aj*, which is also a word for snake, but these are the only Mam words Luz knows because in the United States her parents make her speak Spanish and English so she won't get teased.

Mia wonders how she could have been happy for even five minutes of her former life, attending a school she despised with the SCBs and their mean DMs. With a swallow of guilt she'll think of her father. But then an enemy will spy them and Luz will grab her by the arm skin and pull her out across an avenue into the space between two tents and away they'll go, free as fish.

And Luz is *so* good at Range, faster than anyone else in Crow Squad, even Hamid, and she's figured out ways to get around the rules, like using Spanish. Crow Squad has five Guatemalans not including Luz. Their English is perfect but they can also talk among themselves in Spanish whenever they want. Mia understands some of it but almost all the other white and black kids are clueless.

Usually that's okay. Tonight, though, there's a huge shouting fight about it and Mia can tell the whole thing's about to get really bad. It started in the first round when Crow Squad surrounded this stray

Leopard named Dorsey. Luz shouted Spanish directions to the others so they'd know how to complete second capture. They took her to the Joint for the rest of the round. But once Kyler Biggs heard how she got captured, all the other Snow Leopards started demanding a ruling from the guides.

At assembly, Kyler and Hamid stand in the middle of a huge circle, speaking for their squads.

"Spanish is cheating, and it's bullshit," Kyler sneers.

"Then propose a new declaration, bro," Hamid says. "If you got the votes you got the English-only."

And no way does he have the votes. A new declaration takes a two-thirds majority. Kyler wants to keep arguing but some Cuban kids start taunting him in loud Spanish, and by now it's obvious that nobody's voting for a new declaration because it's an idiotic idea and they all want to keep playing.

The crowd disperses to get ready for round two. The Snow Leopards are scowling and shooting nasty looks at Luz and her friends. At one point Kyler mumbles something and the squad follows him down Wyoming Street.

A trick. Not half a minute later, as the Crows make their way up Avenue D4 toward headquarters, Kyler appears out of nowhere, angled forward like a bull as he heads straight for Luz. His weight sends her sprawling to the ground so hard that Mia hears her friend's back scrape on the gravel.

She runs over to help as Hamid steps up to Kyler, ready to fight. Two of the other Snow Leopards come out with their fists bunched. Big kids, probably thirteen, with ripped-off sleeves. A few of the grown-ups come out of their tents to watch the confrontation. "Not my damn kids," one of them mumbles.

The Snow Leopards move forward and the Crows move back. The

two squads bunch up in two tight groups in the middle of the avenue, Kyler and Hamid nose to nose.

"We use English here," says Kyler, chin up. "You don't like it, leave it."

That's so racist, Mia wants to shout, but she's too afraid.

"I was born in Florida just like your white ass, bro," says one of the Crows. Rammy is his name and he's even bigger than Kyler. The two of them shout over the heads of shorter kids, the Snow Leopards throw more insults, and the Crows shout back until eventually the squads move away from each other and hustle into position for the second round.

Mia feels bad about not saying anything, but it's maybe better in these situations to let Rammy and Luz and the other Crows of color speak for themselves. Last year her mother read a book about white fragility for her book club and made the family talk at dinner about how important it is not to center our whiteness all the time, even how we all need to try to "be less white." Daddy just laughed and Gavin pointed out how perfect the book was for an all-white book club like yours, Daphne. No one got dessert.

Mia didn't understand everything but it was an interesting fight. What she took from it is that white people aren't that smart in the way they talk about their own racism all the time without actually *doing* anything about it. Same thing at her school, where the teachers led workshops on racism that were basically just an excuse not to plan lessons for half a day, or at least that's what Charlize said. If Mia learned one useful thing from all the sessions about structural racism and white supremacy, it's that people maybe need to stop talking so much and *do the work*.

As the squads head off to their headquarters Mia thinks about all the grown-ups who didn't do the work tonight. Luz got pushed to the ground and Kyler shoved Hamid and the Snow Leopards said all this racist stuff and none of the adults did a single thing about it. They just stood there, like they were watching a school play or something.

Do the work.

In here, Mia understands, the kids are on their own.

36.

Here, I'll let you enter your password. How many times has he uttered that phrase? The smart ones know enough to log off and close the browser. But most don't take the simple step of securing their accounts. Some old guy enters his password, checks his savings account to see if his home-owner's payment has cleared—then slumps back in his chair, letting Tate turn the laptop around and do whatever the hell he wants. Other times he pulls a coin trick: open a new tab, distract them long enough to wire some funds, and voila! A hundred bucks richer.

Tate chooses his marks carefully, targeting only those clueless enough not to notice that he's poached from their accounts. It will take them days to get another appointment and by then they'll likely be too addled to question or even notice the missing sums.

By now appointments have been relocated to the pavs, packed today with residents flooding in to claim computer time or slots with the volunteers. At the next table sits a perky lawyer down from Memphis along with a handful of colleagues detailed from the American Bar Association. Tight ponytail over a round face, cute twang that glosses her weary charges with optimism. She calls them *sir* and *ma'am* and flatters them with a respect they probably haven't felt in years. *That's right, ma'am, I'm your attorney now and nothing you say to me goes past this table. It's all privileged.* (How long has it been since any of these sad sacks felt *privileged?*)

Tate chats her up during an instant-coffee break. Compliments her on her warm manner with the IDPs.

"So what firm are you with?" she asks him over the lipsticked rim of her foam cup.

"Say again?"

"Are you at McCann Lively?"

"I'm in insurance."

"Ah." A condescending smile. "Been fighting you bastards all week."

After that the bitch frosts him, so his mood isn't particularly bouncy when Daphne Larsen-Hall shows up at his table, if anything more bedraggled than last time. Gray roots showing, sweat stains in her armpits despite the big fans everywhere.

"You're back," he says.

Her mouth bunches up, exposing that row of little wrinkles. "You were so helpful last time. And I couldn't get a slot with a lawyer today."

"So appointments with me are, what, dime a dozen?"

"That's not what I meant. I just—"

"Hey, we're all just trying to help." He gestures expansively around the pav. "So, what can I do for you?"

"I saw they put you down for personal finance in addition to insurance?"

He leans his chair back. "I have some experience in that domain."

"I thought you might have ideas. I still can't get into my bank accounts—"

"Let me guess. Your husband handled all of that?"

Her Botoxed forehead tries to frown. "I just need to know how bad my situation is."

Again he notices the chunky stone on her finger. The chick must be loaded. Piles of cash somewhere, but hubby's croaked and she can't access it. He clicks open her file and scans down the notes he took last time on her insurance shitshow.

"What was—is—your occupation?"

"I'm an artist. A sculptor."

"Impressive. And remind me, your husband was . . . ?"

"A surgeon."

"Right, right."

My, how the mighty have fallen. Tate knows all about the Daphnes of the world. He's sold insurance to the Daphnes and he's sold pills to the Daphnes, and in his experience the Daphnes are all the same, sucking at the husbandly teat while prattling on about the virtues of strong women and their autonomy. *And there you have it, me lads. The degrading effect of feminism on today's wives, outclassed at every turn by the very men they've spent the last three decades hammering.* Same with Daphne Larsen-Hall, whose surgeon husband was obviously running circles around her for years while she was noodling with clay.

Tate probes a bit, getting a vague picture of the family finances. Daphne isn't as stupid as she looks, asking pointed questions about the legalities of her situation. What recourse does she have to insurance compensation given her husband's death? If both their names are on the house title, can she sue the insurance company for allowing her husband to let the policy lapse?

"Those are really more of a legal thing." He looks sidelong at Memphis girl. "Her tribe can probably help you out."

"I know we had an attorney in Miami at one point but I don't even remember his name."

Surprise, surprise. "I could run a credit check on your husband."

"Please."

Tate's credentials are still valid, allowing him to run the check through one of the credit companies. He angles his laptop so she can see the brutal details for herself. A string of missed loan payments, eight referrals to collections agencies since June, a host of other fiscal infractions. A steaming mess.

"Now I'll run you, if that's okay?"

She meekly nods. The report comes up. In some ways the state of Daphne's credit is even worse than her dead husband's. Multiple credit cards she's never seen but issued in her name, unpaid balances in the tens of thousands.

By the end of the appointment the chick's been reduced to a quivering mess. Tate can see it in her shiny face, this new awareness of her own impoverishment. Sure, maybe she's got a few grand lying around in an old checking account. But she has no way of accessing it at this point, and even if she did, who knows what kind of tax liens and investigations might be swirling around her affairs.

Daphne Larsen-Hall, artist, MILF, surgeon's widow: not even worth a rip-off.

When he returns from the pavs he finds Gavin and Jessamyn sitting on twin milk crates, singing through some ZZ Top. He stops to watch. Tate feels for the kid, already in the anticlimax of his life, shrunken in on himself like a dead leaf. The slumped shoulders, the sullenness, the affected disdain.

One thing's for sure: the kid has a mighty crush on Jessamyn. Whenever he looks up at her, his eyes get doggish. She'll smile at him, sway for him, put a little extra into her strumming. If the kid had a tail it'd be thumping up a cloud of dust, or else he'd be humping her leg. Makes sense, though. Gavin's much closer to her age than Tate is, by a lot of years.

"You two should start your band," he suggests, strolling up.

"Get us those amps then," Jessamyn says.

"Soon." He goes inside the tent. From the plastic box beneath his mattress he takes his sim card and his phone and powers up. He's been doing this once every few days, just to check on old contacts. Saint

Louis doesn't have this number but Yury has friends in Houston, or what used to be Houston.

When the phone powers on a single lonely text appears on the screen.

You still here?

The message is from Liberty, his first and only direct buyer. How about that. Waifish, strung-out Liberty, still in Houston. He tries to picture her walking the ruined streets of Midtown or picking her way across the shattered glass of the Galleria, looting perfume stores.

He reclines on his cot.

How are ya? he texts, as if an old flame has just gotten in touch.

Bad. I need something.

He thinks about his reply.

I've relocated out of state. Hope you find what you need.

Her next message a bleak four words: There's nothing here. NOTHING.

Christ. Liberty, one of thousands wandering around that toxic wasteland with the other zombies, looking for a fix. He slips out the sim card and stashes his phone. Outside the tent, a crate complains as somebody shifts position. Gavin and Kaitlyn launch into an old Clapton tune whose lyrics he once knew. After the closing cadence there is a stillness out there. He can feel Jessamyn's calculations like a cold wind. Today, they agreed earlier. The kid's as ready as he'll ever be.

"So Gavin," she says.

"Mm."

"I been thinking."

A strum. Her voice soft but focused. Eve in the garden, tempting the unsuspecting man. *A story as old as time itself, me lads.*

"You've had a rough go of it, Gavin. Losing your mom, your dad."

"I guess."

"You're the man of the house now."

"Man of the dome tent."

She giggles. "Seriously, though. It's like you've gone from a college kid to this scrappy caveman in a few weeks. You've got such a burden on your shoulders now."

She's touching him somewhere, Tate can almost feel the strokes himself. His upper arm, the space between his skinny shoulder blades. Kid's probably hard as a rock.

"So, what are you all going to do, once you get out?"

Gavin takes a moment to reply. "If we get out. I mean, we're totally broke. Busted. My dad fucked us in such a major way. My stepmom still has no clue."

Tate's ears perk up.

"That sucks," Jessamyn says.

"Yeah."

Her fingers jazz the strings. A plucked chord, a delicate strum.

"So listen."

"Okay."

Her fingertips tap the guitar like the scratching feet of birds. "You want to make some money in here?"

37.

They wake to chirpy burbles from their phones.

"What the fuck," Gavin groans.

Daphne touches Mia's screen. Your Verizon service has been suspended due to an unpaid balance on your account. Please contact customer service to arrange for payment. The bars are gone, an alarm icon now in their place. The clock still works, at least. Daphne dresses quietly and hustles up to the pavs for her legal appointment.

The attorney in Pav4 gets an NBSF official on the phone, then wheedles, lectures, threatens until Daphne has new login IDs and passwords for all her accounts. She signs up for a computer slot and braces herself for whatever she might find.

Which is, basically, zilch. Following the insurance revelations and the credit reports, what she discovers now comes as little surprise: negative balance in the checking account, zeroed-out savings, cashed-out CDs. Daphne's last withdrawal took the account down to thirty dollars and change. That was two weeks before Luna. A last check—a hundred and ten dollars, written to the house cleaners—came in three days after that. The result: a negative balance, with the additional goad of a fifty-dollar overdraft fee.

A low logistical hum enfolds the crowd as Daphne logs off and wanders the pavs. Couples and families are already planning for an afterlife . . . *so we'll stay with Lynette for a while, they got that converted garage with the . . . day after tomorrow is the soonest I could get a midsize . . . got her procedure rescheduled for Thursday. We should be there the night before . . .* These people face unemployment, housing challenges, food insecurity, debt. Yet many are already on to their next steps, however tenuous; and like Shelley at the gas station, they have working credit cards. Connections. Women with paid-up phone plans call sisters in Dubuque. Men with credit cards email cousins in Savannah.

Others are silent and glum, battered like Daphne by their miserable epiphanies. Coral Gables has devolved into some mythical utopia she no longer remembers, full of white wine and extra virgin olive oil, air-conditioning and predictable routines.

Routines. She collapses on a metal chair away from the crowd and imagines herself back in her lost life. Today is Monday, the fifteenth of September. If she were in Florida, what would the family schedule look like on Tuesday the sixteenth?

Her eyes snap open. In a corner of Pav3 blue-shirted volunteers from Best Buy dole out free prepaids. *Quantity limited.* Daphne waits ten minutes until she has a new flip phone. Five minutes later she reaches a friendly administrator at the Lortner County Public Schools.

"Hi. My name is Daphne Larsen-Hall and my family . . . we've just moved to the area. Can you tell me about the public school system here?"

"Welp, Lortner Elementary runs K through five and shares admin and the campus with Ponca Middle. Lortner High's across the way. How old are your kids?"

"I have a third-grader and a sixth-grader."

"Nice."

"If I come enroll them tomorrow morning can they start right away?"

"Absolutely. Just need you to fill out some forms and we'll slot them in. Fact, if you spell me out their full names I can speak to the teachers, get them set up with desks and cubbies and so forth."

The image of Mia and Oliver sitting at desks tomorrow makes

Daphne giddy. She waits at a help table and ends up speaking to a grand-fatherly volunteer named Bill. She tells him what she needs.

"Glad someone in this place gives a damn about their kids," he huffs. "I mean, most of these folks?" He raises his bushy eyebrows.

Daphne chooses to ignore the ugly insinuation. "I assume they'll take the school bus eventually. But for tomorrow I have to get them there myself somehow. Any ideas?"

"They've set up a bus to Lortner. It takes folks to the Walmart, the mall in town. But that's a couple miles from the schools."

"I see." Daphne, crestfallen, drums her fingers on her wrist.

He shoots her a conspiratorial look. "Tell you what, though. Let me give you and your kids a ride."

"Seriously?"

"Meet you at Main Gate tomorrow at seven thirty sharp."

The next morning she hustles the kids into clean clothes and down to Pav1, where they slurp cornflakes with a sullen affect. Oliver interrogates her about the school's lunch menu, the playground, the length of recess.

Mia picks at a yogurt. "Can Luz come?"

"Not today," Daphne says quickly.

"But what about all the other kids? Why are we going to school and nobody else has to?"

"Again, that's up to their parents. Just like this is up to me."

"Cole already has school," Oliver says.

Daphne looks at him sharply. "Who?"

"He's a leaper in Tiger Squad. His parents make him do math and science every morning in their tent and his mom calls him a big reader."

"Oh," Daphne says, rattled by this glimpse of another family's residual normalcy. "Well, good for him. But this is what we're doing. Now finish your breakfast and let's get going."

Bill, true to his word, waits outside Main Gate, leaning proudly on the hood of a glistening pickup with a double cab. He opens the rear door for the kids and the passenger door for Daphne. As they drive off Bill brags about his new truck—Ford F-150 with the SuperCab, platinum trim package, an eight-foot box—and previews his travel plans with his wife of forty-six years. An Alaska cruise next month if the fires calm down, a week up in Minnesota over Christmas to visit the grandkids, and hell, we've always wanted to see Paris so maybe Europe in the spring.

Daphne feels stung by the man's blundering indifference to her own family's plight but too indebted to show him anything. Clearly Bill doesn't intend to be cruel, and they'll be needing all kinds of charity in the months ahead. A half hour of insensitivity is a small price to pay for a round trip to a new school.

Bill drives them through downtown Lortner, a four-stoplight town with a dilapidated main street, then another mile to the school complex, wedged off from a wheat field that stretches toward the horizon. The drive splits between Ponca Middle School and Lortner Elementary, a single-story brick structure humped above the plain. Bill takes the left branch and eases up to the curb.

"Welp, here you are," he says.

Daphne's hand hesitates on the door latch. She hasn't asked Bill for a return trip, nor has he offered.

"I'll be right here," he says, and slaps the dashboard.

Daphne leads the kids over a glaring plane of concrete and through the front entrance. Voices of children echo from rooms along the main corridor, a soothing pedagogical babble. In the main office a friendly

admin leads them down a short hallway to an interior office belonging
to Wanda Harris, assistant principal of both schools, a stout white-haired
woman with pouchy cheeks and a permanent frown line. Daphne sits
and starts filling out registration forms while Harris goes over the day's
schedule with the kids.

"Mia, I think you'll get along real well with Miss Norbertson for
social studies. She hails from Florida, just like you, and she's new this
year but everybody says—hold on. Florida, you say?"

Daphne looks up. Harris is staring at Oliver's arm.

"What's that, young man? Have you been in the hospital?"

Oliver shows his wrist. "It's my IDP bracelet."

"Say again?"

"Oliver—" Daphne says.

"It's for Tooley Farm," he goes on, "so we can get in and out at Main
Gate and use the store."

Daphne watches Harris's face. The administrative freezing of the
features, the hardening of the eyes as she picks out the tell tale bracelet
on Mia's wrist, on Daphne's. The office goes suddenly hot.

Harris's lips tighten. "Hadn't realized you folks are Lunas."

Lunas?

"You seem more . . ." She spritzes her fingers in front of her face.

White? Daphne guesses. "Together?" she says instead.

"Something like that."

"Their father—my husband . . . he was a surgeon. He was killed in
the storm. That's why we're here."

"I'm very sorry to hear that." Wanda looks at the kids. "Sounds like
you've had a tough time of it."

Oliver nods and Mia's eyes well up.

Harris sighs. "I'm going to have to get Principal Stoltz."

"Why is that?"

"This is above my pay grade. You folks sit tight. Back in a jiffy."

She leaves them in a waft of flowery scent. Mia wheels in her chair. "Why did you tell that lady we're here because of Daddy?"

"Sweetie, I was just trying to—"

"We're here because of Gavin."

"Mia, that's not fair."

"If he hadn't left your purse in the driveway we never would have come to Tooley Farm at all but you just blamed Daddy even though he's *dead.*"

"I hate this school," Oliver says, in his lethal little voice.

Two men appear at the door. The taller one walks in with a hand extended. "I'm Sam Stoltz, the principal. And this is Superintendent Winkler."

She shakes hands with Stoltz but not with Winkler, who stays by the entrance with his arms folded over a shiny navy blazer. Wanda Harris edges in and returns to her desk.

Daphne crosses her legs. "I'm confused. The superintendent of the entire system has to approve new student enrollments?"

"Not much of a system, frankly," Stoltz says. "As you've probably noticed, we're quite small, a hair shy of eleven hundred total students across the district, K through twelve. We run on a shoestring. And I'm sorry to say, we just don't have room for your children."

"But we're county residents now," Daphne protests. "Aren't you legally obligated to enroll them?"

"Actually we're not." Now the superintendent, speaking from the doorway. "Lunas aren't legal residents of this county."

"Of course they are. What kind of nonsen—"

"They're displaced persons," Winkler goes on, "and as such they do not possess the legal right to demand nor does this school system have the responsibility to deliver the educational resources provided to our school-age population of bona fide residents."

"And who gets to decide that?"

"The school board and the county board of supervisors deliberated all of this last week and got Governor Robideaux's sign-off. Would you like me to get his office on the phone? Or we could call the secretary of education in Norman. I'm sure she'd be happy to talk you through our decisioning."

The rote legalese, the bureaucratic preening. They were prepared for this. Through the glass partition Daphne notices several staff members huddled in the main office, listening to the increasingly heated exchange. Probably the biggest happening in the school's office in years.

"Look," she pleads. "These two are smart kids. Great students, and they get fantastic test scores. They'll be no trouble for your teachers."

Summoning the worst of herself. *Look at us. We aren't like the other Lunas.* She'll throw the whole megashelter under the bus if it means getting the kids back in school.

Winkler looks at Stoltz, who leans over with his hands clasped. "Ma'am, if it were just these two? Hey, no problem. But if we let your kids in we have to admit the whole horde out there."

"Precisely," says Winkler. "Free-and-reduced meals for a thousand refugee kids from Miami and Houston? Gang activity in our peaceful schools?" A snort. "Hard pass, thanks."

They drive back to Tooley Farm in near silence, broken only by Bill's murmurings about the crops blanketing the endless fields. Here's hay, this one's sorghum, bit of cotton over there, kids, major soybean farm starts about here; to Daphne they all look the same. Just shy of nine o'clock and the acreage churns with the industry of harvest though no humans are in sight, closed off in tractor cabs or perched high in giant combines throwing long shadows on the earth.

THE GREAT DISPLACEMENT
A DIGITAL CHRONICLE OF THE LUNA MIGRATION

▶ **AMBER JONES, ADDICTION NURSE**

She supervises a staff of eight at Dallas Mercy, where she has worked since Houston Methodist was shuttered after Luna. She was thirty-two and evacuating along I-69 when the hurricane came ashore.

Play audio file:

Transcript:

First time I put two and two together was after the Front Range fires a few years back. Lord that was something. Half a million acres, then the blowup around Sugarloaf, all those people trapped. So many more just hopeless. That's the real spur to users, the gloom of it all.

I was with a detail that went up there with the Red Cross. I assumed we'd be dealing with burn victims, smoke inhalation, toxins. Turned out what we were triaging was mostly overdoses. People came in with the gurgling mouths and clammy skin, blue in the lips.

Shouldn't have surprised me, though. One of our research docs down there was studying the social causes of addiction. She had this big study that started up way back before Hurricane Harvey. Six emergency rooms in six hospitals in metro Houston. One of the nurses' jobs was to administer questionnaires to OD victims. What drug they were using, what got them started, why they relapsed. We'd ask recreational users about the factors that spiraled them into full-on addiction. You get the picture.

Turns out Harvey was the number one answer we got. The floods, the mold, the relocation, the PTSD. Makes sense. You're clean for four years then your roof blows off or you lose your home in a flood or you're living in a mold museum. Even people who didn't lose a house or get sick turned to using as a way to cope with just living in the aftermath.

Luna was ten times worse, a hundred. There's a patient I had, a four-peat. Caletta was her name, displaced from Houston. Her thing was street drugs, mostly the powder-blue fentanyl pills that were big around here for a while. Gal was quite the artist. Her fourth time in the unit she made drawings for me, super realistic and detailed. Cats, dogs, doctors. Anyway we talked her into rehab. Her counselor in the facility asked her group to draw their addiction, what using felt like. The counselor knew I'd seen this gal and after Caletta died he brought me her last drawing.

It's a picture of Hurricane Luna, a big blue spiral over the Gulf of Mexico. Gorgeous. But look close and you see that the spiral is made up of a zillion dots, maybe two thousand powder-blue circles.

I knew what those circles were. Last thing that girl drew was a fentanyl hurricane.

▶ SADIE BLACKBURN, HOMELESS ADVOCATE

A Nebraska native, she lived on the streets of Miami for eleven years, sleeping in church shelters and public encampments before evacuating to a megashelter in Arkansas at the former site of Silver Lake College. She turned twenty-six the morning Luna made landfall.

Play audio file:

Transcript:

Shelter life? You just get used to the rhythms, the food, the bedding. Young volunteers who show up the week before their college applications are due then you never see them again. But the population, you never get used to that. They let anyone in. You can be strung out on wildfire or meth, sick with flu, long criminal record and they'll let you in no questions asked.

The morning of the evacuation I'm over in a women-only shelter in the basement of a Methodist church in Brownsville. The lights go on early, five, five thirty. They tell us to go out to the street and get on these buses. We were lucky we had buses at all. The church, they'd arranged for transport a few days before, just in case. Lot of places didn't do that and a lot of homeless got left behind. So we all climb in, hundred gals with all their bags and rags. My gal Wendy remembered it was my birthday so the whole bus sang me the song and gave me a Hostess.

We got sent to this shopping mall outside Tallahassee, and from there all the way to Silver Lake, this little college a half hour outside Little Rock shuttered after the pandemic. It reminded me of Pardon, Nebraska. Whole town died when the farms collapsed. Now it's just abandoned buildings. Silver Lake, though, it had a nice campus, cute town, couple thousand dorm rooms. Most had mattresses and the plumbing still worked, for a while.

Everybody liked it at first. One day you're sleeping in a
Miami church basement with a hundred homeless sharing one
toilet and next day you've got one roommate, a real bed, a
shower you share with your neighbor. They opened the dining
hall and brought staff in from the public schools to cook.
The ladies started talking about going for their degree. Our
joke was, all we need is professors.

Then it changed. People started being their old selves.
Because it wasn't just us shelter gals in the dorms. They
bused in any old body. Ex-cons just out of prison, there
was some gang stuff going on. And local police started
treating the college like a no-go zone. You could call
911 to report a bleeder or a rape and nobody would show up
at Silver Lake for an hour, or at all.

Finally it got too much. I came back to Nebraska. I'm in
Lincoln now and working for the municipal shelters here. I
have my own room with kitchenette. I do a lot of stuff for
the organization, some fundraising, I've even testified to
the state legislature.

Here in the shelter we make it nice for the guests. That's
what we call them, our guests. I never felt like a guest at
Silver Lake.

38.

Daphne sits with her legs splayed into the avenue and a patch of earth between her thighs. She uses the edge of a plastic spoon to scrape away the base of the prairie grass then tugs until the soil crumbles free. Blade by blade she works her way out in a Luna-shaped spiral, raising a small pile of weeds torn up by the roots. The spoon breaks. She unwraps another.

"Impressive," says a woman's voice.

Daphne looks up and wipes her lips with a dirty hand, tasting soil, feeling insane. Her visitor is Dorianne, the resident from the insurance line complaining about twenty-dollar cigarettes.

"Thought I'd drop by for cocktails." Dorianne holds a short stack of cups in one hand, an unlabeled soda bottle in the other. "May I?"

"Sure." Daphne crosses her legs, making room.

"Hold this." Dorianne hands her a cup. Daphne watches as she pours two drinks.

They tap cups and sip. Cloying, with a burn going down, but Daphne's first nip of alcohol in weeks. Right away it blunts the spikes in her brain. "What is this?"

Dorianne grins. "Some guy in Quadrant III was selling moonshine. I added bug juice."

"There's a still in here?"

"Who knows, I mean this place?" she says in her husky voice. "Wouldn't be surprised if some prick's cookin' meth."

The booze eases Daphne into a wandering conversation with her evening visitor. Dorianne has a boy, John Junior, thirteen. She tells stories about the broken bathroom on her bus, her flirtation with a Red

Cross staffer in Florida. Soon she gets around to the circumstances that brought her to Tooley Farm.

"I was kind of in between already," Dorianne says. "Divorced, and the asshole wouldn't pay up. After we evacuated I was going to get a motel, wait it out, but there was nothing by the time we got north, even the churches were full, so they put me and John Junior on this bus to Oklahoma. And here we are. God, I'm not usually this gabby," she says through her fingers. "Sorry."

Daphne waves off a cloud of gnats. "I know exactly how you feel."

"Oh yeah?"

She raises her cup. "To shitty husbands, dead or alive."

"Shitty husbands," Dorianne says, and she takes a gulp. "Wait. What do you mean, dead?"

Daphne spills it all: the forgotten purse, Brantley's death, the lapsed insurance, the canceled credit cards, the school debacle last week. She doesn't censor herself, and as the fragments of her story converge and the moonshine goes to work, she is able, for the first time, to examine each of them in the context of the others, as if piecing the broken spoons back together after her excavation project, or assembling a vase out of mismatched porcelain shards.

Cleansing, this simple act of narrating all the horrible things. Almost delicious, to shit-talk Brantley for once.

"What gets me most, though, is the pretense. Like if he'd just told me a year or two ago, 'Look, Daphne, I messed up and we're broke and I need your help,' I would have been right there with him. We would have moved into a condo, or relocated back to Michigan. Whatever. But instead we have to maintain the facade, and the facade is—the facade is"—her voice rising—"a two-million-dollar house, three cars, a kid at Stanford on no financial aid because his family income's supposedly too high, and Brantley strutting around at all his 'benefits' and 'functions' but in reality he's a fraud who doesn't have the *balls* to declare bankruptcy or tell his wife what a lying sack of check-kiting piece of Pinocchio shit he is."

She looks at Dorianne over her syrupy cocktail. The avenue stills in the wake of her rant. The moonshine in her head tilts the world.

"Ma'am," Dorianne says quietly, "this is a Wendy's?"

The laugh erupts like a gunshot, a hysterical buckle from her gut that splashes the sticky drink out of the cup and over her knuckles. Soon Daphne is on her side, gazing up at streaks of sunset, orange contrails crossing a deep blue, streamed from jets full of people going about their normal lives, ladies on business trips heading for plush hotels or home to endless changes of clothes and bathtubs. Tonight they will snuggle with their dogs in front of Netflix and they will ignore or fuck their husbands and smooth their faces with creams and night masks and tomorrow they will have the pleasure of dropping their children off at school.

"Hey." Dorianne, smiling down.

Daphne struggles upright and reaches out her cup for another pour. "Going all insie," she slurs.

"Preach," says Dorianne. "Here, have a splash."

Her neighbors Larry and Colette, the nice couple from Waffle House, find her later, sprawled between tents with her face in her own puke. Her eyes crusted shut. The stench of spattered liquor smokes her nose.

"Come on now." An avuncular voice. "Come on."

Larry peels her up from the ground, making a grunt of effort as he helps her stagger to her feet.

"You're so nice." She tilts her head so she can see his face in the strung lights. Behind him on the avenue Colette stands watching, arms crossed. "So so *so* so nice."

"And you're nasty drunk," he says, averting his nose as he helps her into the tent. No one else is home. *Home.*

"Ha!" she barks.

"Watch yourself out there," Larry warns. "This place . . ."

"Where are my children? What have they done to my children?" Her cot. She climbs toward her pillow, collapses before she makes it.

"Drink this."

A plastic bottle appears in her hand. She takes four large swallows of water and retches it to the floor. Larry takes the bottle and sets it by her cot. "It'll be right here. Now sleep."

The peak of the tent spins like a flicked coin, a swift blurring fuzz. When her eyes close her stomach heaves, but this time a soft belch is all that comes up. Her hands cross on her belly and her right index finger traces the points and facets of a gem that isn't there.

She bolts upright.

Her rings.

A four-carat diamond, set with five emeralds. Worth thousands. A last insurance policy, against the loss of so much else. And her wedding band, a ring of white gold identical to the one still circling the cold finger of her husband.

Who? Who could do a such a thing?

Larry. No, not him.

Dorianne. That's it. Brings her spiked Kool-Aid, lulls her with trash talking about their husbands until she passes out, then slips her engagement ring off her finger. Thieving *bitch*.

Daphne swings her feet off the cot, set on revenge. When she tries to stand a spike of pain drills through her skull and she collapses with a moan, then nothing.

Later, in the tent, a scuffle of feet, whispers.

Oliver: "What's that smell?"

Mia: "Yuck."

Gavin: "Shut the fuck up, you guys."

Oblivion again.

Later still, Daphne staggers out onto the avenue for some air, along silent graveled streets past the outer tent lines to the banks of the creek. She slumps to the ground. The stars spin among the limbs and branches until she turns away from the sky and finds sleep again muzzled into the ground, and it is the damp and particular scent of this patch of earth that startles her awake.

Dawn. The sky is rust shot through with a galvanized gray. She has slept for hours, her face inches from the trickling water, her nose gathering microscopic particles into a familiar yet unexpected redolence. She licks her lips and tastes the brine of the bank.

Is it—?

Her hand strokes the moist apron of soil. She claws loose a handful, squeezes to be sure.

She sits up, the lingering pain of her drunk forgotten. She shakes the sleep needles out of her arms and pulls another wodge of soil from the bank. Presses the two hunks together. Rolls them into a ball. A snake. A round-edged cube that holds its firm but giving shape between her palms.

Daphne looks up and down the creek banks, stunned into gratitude. As the first sun breaks through morning clouds and touches the water the substance in her hands seems to redden and pulse with undiscovered life. So intimate, humble, everyday; yet, in this moment, a thing of unspeakable grace.

This earth, this muck, this scent, this rich and malleable clay.

39.

She's taking her time, this one, browsing in the far corner of the library tent, neatly reorganized by Gavin over the last several days. It was a kick going through those boxes of donations, coming across all the books he read during that Grisham binge, thinking he'd be a lawyer someday. Or all the Lee Childs he mainlined the summer before Stanford, which inspired fantasies about riding across the country on a Greyhound just messing around, though when Reacher gets on a bus he chooses where to get off, and somehow there's always a decent diner and an amazing chick. Gavin would probably be more like Don Quixote, except he'd know what the windmills were for.

She starts thumbing through a book.

"Would you like to take that one with you, ma'am?"

Her shoulders tense and the book goes back on the table. She leaves the tent. Gavin starts a whispered countdown. "Ten . . . nine . . . eight . . ."

And she's back, licking her lips. "You got any—sort of fantasy novels? Something short."

He plucks a thin book off his special table. *The Other Wind*, by Ursula K. Le Guin. Not the best Earthsea volume, but not the worst. When the lady takes the book she slips a ten between the cover and his thumb.

"Return it when you can." He pockets the bill.

The next two are a couple, also black, maybe Grandma Flo's age. They're obviously not here for anything but books. She chooses a romance. He goes for nonfiction about World War II.

On their way out they pass a skinny white guy in a Houston Rock-ets tank top with a small, ratlike face. His fingers walk a dozen spines. "You got some fantasy books?"

"Yep."

"What, like anal? Threesomes kinda thing?"

Gavin stifles a laugh. "Not that type of fantasy. Sorry, man."

"Whatever it is, I'll take it. Got this bum knee."

"You want something short or long?"

"Make it a long. It's hurting like a bitch today."

Gavin pulls out *The Silmarillion*, the only mediocre book Tolkien ever wrote. He hands it to the skinny guy and gets a grubby twenty in return. The guy clutches the Tolkien like it's a family Bible. The cover shows the peak of a mountain slicing through a blue moon.

His customer wants to chat. "Must've walked thirty miles to get out of Dade County, you know? Couldn't find a bus anywhere, tried to hitch but folks were just driving by."

"Yeah, that whole thing," Gavin says. "We had to leave our car and it got all smashed up."

The guy thumbs through the pages until he finds the wildfire and starts to tug it out.

"Not in here, dude. What the hell." Gavin cups his hands over the book and peers out between the flaps.

"Sorry, man."

The guy tucks the wildfire back between the pages. Gavin watches him slink off, looking around over his twitchy nose as he peels a tab off the sheet and slips it under his tongue.

Back inside Gavin grabs his bass and perches on his stool. The library was his idea. Freaking brilliant, Kaitlyn said when he suggested it. Steve thought the same, so now Gavin is officially peddling wildfire to the beleaguered population of Tooley Farm. Ten bucks for a half sheet, twenty for a full. The first day he cleared over two hundred dollars, the second day just north of five. Word is spreading, too. Today he's almost at eight, and it's not even three.

So this is actually a thing. Seems he's actually a drug dealer now. Why not? No chance he's going back to college. Plus he's pretty good at selling, doesn't get ruffled by the weird behavior of all these IDPs trying to escape the misery of their displacement for a while. If a sublingual tab of wildfire is what gets them off, well, so be it. The money even gives him hope for getting out of this dump.

Expect all cash at first, Steve says. They'll give you their bills and their coins, whatever they've got, down to their final dime. Then they'll start handing over their bling. Wedding rings, lockets that enclose the last surviving picture of their mom. Soon they'll try to barter with other things. Booze, food, cigarettes. Blow jobs. (*Yuck*, was Gavin's reaction. Mostly.)

The trick lies in how you dangle the bait, keep them coming back for more. You need patience, persistence, a certain kind of ruthlessness, Steve says.

Gavin starts to bang out "Give It Away" by the Peppers, with that quick slide up the neck. The rhythms fill the library and Gavin looks out over his field of books, twanging at the strings.

40.

"We need buckets." Daphne rubs her hands. "Big ones."

Mia and Oliver exchange a look. Daphne knows she's been absent, addled. Their father is dead. Two nights ago their mother slept in her own vomit. But now, for the first time since their arrival, her head is clear.

"Buckets," she repeats.

"I know where some are," Oliver says. He leads them down to the refuse zone at the lower gate, screened off from the avenues behind plastic sheeting. He squeezes through a gap and emerges moments later with two five-gallon buckets dangling at his sides. Daphne recognizes the labels from last week's MREs.

"Perfect," she says. "Now a shovel."

Their next stop is the equipment shed near the Square. Here residents can request new light bulbs, borrow tools. Daphne signs out a shovel and Mia carries it back to the creek. Daphne demonstrates the minor excavation project she has in mind. On the shallower banks the clay lies slabbed up against the creek bed. They peel it by the shovelful and drop it into the buckets. When they have enough, Daphne leads them back over to the water tank in Quadrant II. They fill up the big buckets almost to the brims. Daphne rolls her sleeves up to her shoulders and shows them how to loosen the clods of dirt.

"Oliver, you take this bucket. And Mia, that one's yours. Take out any rocks or sticks you feel. I shouldn't find any clumps in there when I get back."

"Where are you going?" Mia asks.

Daphne holds up the shovel. "I have to return this, and find a few other things." They ignore her, already competing to see whose slip will be smoother. Daphne returns the shovel, then heads to the Square. She knocks on the aluminum door of Trailer 1.

"Come," calls a woman's voice.

Inside, Rain Holton sits bent over a laptop. "What's up?"

Daphne leans against a cabinet. "I need to report a theft."

"Oh yeah?"

She describes the engagement ring, the wedding band, the experience of waking up to a bare finger.

"So someone slipped these rings off while you were sleeping?" Rain asks.

"Yes."

"And that didn't wake you up?" Skeptical, an eyebrow raised.

Daphne bites a lip. "I was maybe a little drunk."

Rain says nothing.

"Maybe a little passed out."

"Okay. And what was this woman's name?" Rain brings something up on her computer.

"Dorianne something. Her son is John."

"John Junior?"

"Yes."

"They left for Philly this morning."

Daphne looks out the nearest window, mad at herself for not stopping by yesterday. "Of course they did."

"Do you want to file a police report? The fact that you didn't witness her taking the rings . . ."

"I get the picture." Daphne sighs, and just like that one of her last hopes for ready cash floats away. Knowing Brantley, the stone was probably cubic zirconia anyway. She scratches at a window screen. "Could you spare one of these?"

"A window?"

"Just a screen."

"You want one of my window screens."

"It's for the kids. We're making clay."

Rain looks around the trailer, likely thinking about bugs and breeze. She nods at a window near the back. "Why don't you take that one."

Daphne goes to the window and tries to pop out the screen. The assembly is bracketed to the rail, held in place by eight screws along the sealant line. Rain slides a toolbox out of a seat cabinet and produces two Phillips-head screwdrivers. They work together until the screen comes free.

Back at the pump Mia and Oliver revel in the mud, churning slip as a dozen kids look on. Daphne makes them take turns so everyone has a chance to break up dirt clumps. She sends them for additional supplies. They fan out and return with food vats, ripped sheets, more buckets, clothes swiped from the donation tent. With the window screen on an empty bucket, Daphne slowly starts to sieve the slip. The mesh catches pebbles and other debris. The kids, getting the idea, gather around and pluck the flotsam off the screen. The bigger ones take turns pouring, three times per bucket. After pouring out the excess water, they fill the sheets and scrap cloths with the filtered mixture and tie off the ends, with baseball-size hunks of clay left inside to cure.

"Now we wait," Daphne announces.

"How long?" a little girl asks.

"Two days, maybe three."

Groans rise up from the young crowd. Daphne shares their impatience, which expands with her anticipation as she checks the bundles over the next two days. Meanwhile children stop her on the streets to ask about the clay. "Soon," she tells them.

On the third morning, Daphne commandeers a corner of Pav4, where she peels the cloth from the balls and dumps some ten pounds of clay onto a table. She divides it into manageable hunks and spends a joyful hour with thirty children kneading the clay, forming it into bricks and globes. Each kid gets a fist-size hunk to mold and shape. They make animals, cars, family members, likenesses of their lost homes and left-behind pets. Daphne shows them how to make pinch pots out of snakes. An older boy, maybe a fourth-grader, sculpts a clay penis and testicles and asks her what she thinks. "Very realistic," Daphne observes, acting unfazed. Next time she looks he's made a decent hippo.

There is something about this clay. Boxes of Play-Doh have emerged from the donation tent over these weeks, but most of it is now useless, the offensive brightness of its colors amalgamated into husked graying lumps. The homemade clay is superior in every way, pliable and smooth, peaty with the smell of the creek bank.

Around lunchtime, as the kids start wandering off, Daphne finds herself edging from lighthearted noodling into more serious work. A shrink-wrapped set of flatware furnishes a plastic knife and spoon, poor substitutes for the loop tools and scrapers and wire brushes abandoned in her studio, but they're fine for her immediate purposes. She gouges and scoops, coils and smears, integrating the molecules, eroding the high points. No rustiness to her technique, not now. Her adeptness comes right back, habitual, intimate, grounding.

A few older residents pause to watch. Only rarely has Daphne had an audience, most recently at an open studio session held in Pilar's gallery the week before her show, to attract advance interest. This feels different. She could be back in Coral Gables. Michigan even, making art from earth.

The finished piece is recognizable as a kind of cuboid bus, the windshield enlarged and smashed up against the rank of windows along one side, mirrors appended like the misshapen ears of an elephant. Crude to her eye, the equivalent of a rough study sketch. But the impromptu audience applauds when she sets it down, cooing over her work.

"It's gorgeous, honey."

"Paint it yellow and you could sell that."

"How'd you get the wheels to look so realistic?"

Daphne answers their kind questions, then starts to clean up, setting the bus on a far corner of the table and clearing the workspace of tools and cloths, wiping down the surface, stowing mounds of clay wrapped side by side in the bins. Finally she sits alone at the table. The familiar newness of her making settles in her bones.

Rain Holton walks up. "This you?" She hands over an iPad. On the screen is Pilar's Instagram page, florid with Daphne's pieces. She scrolls slowly down the feed.

"How did you find this?"

Rain shrugs. "I googled you. Wasn't hard. It's beautiful stuff."

"Thank you," she manages to say. To see everything arrayed like this, photographed in its glory—most of it half-forgotten and all of it gone, reduced to shards on the floor of an acidifying ocean. Her hands remember every curve in the clay and every notch, her eyes every shade of glaze. Two million turns of the wrist, ten million tiny decisions. Half a life of art. She hunches over Rain's tablet, drowning in the loss.

She is aware of the lunch line forming outside the pav, twenty steps away. A hand settles on her shoulder.

"Maybe we can find you a wheel," says Rain, and pats her back.

41.

The band springs up like an oasis in the desert, a fresh but constant delight. Every evening a group gathers in a corner of Pav3, bringing instruments deemed precious enough to rescue from the storm, dragged here to help their owners through it all. The aspiring players come to the pav with guitars, saxophone and flute, harmonica and mandolin, their voices.

Five make up the core of the ensemble. A white college kid on bass, the lanky young man who volunteers in the library. On electric guitar and vocals is Kaitlyn, the yogi with the Gretsch. Someone supplies a pair of amplifiers.

There's also a saxophonist from Houston, a fellow named Leonard with bushy eyebrows who reminds Rain of her dad in the severe looks he throws around when others mess up. The second guitarist is a fifty-ish guy laying down a solid rhythm with a Martin acoustic that looks like it's been living on a porch. Biggest surprise is the drummer, a stout maybe-Filipina named Loida. She was homeless back in Florida, Rain learns, earned a living busking on plastic buckets along the beachfront. In here she's rigged up a grungy kit out of camp junk. Loida can get busy, too, sticks blurring as she slams the surfaces of plastic, metal, and wood.

You'd think the group would welcome all comers. But by the third night the ensemble starts to winnow the less talented hopefuls. They shout down a poor girl who shows up with a clarinet that sounds like a hyena, nudge out an old Italian man naively thinking his accordion might be welcome.

Rain itches to step in. Why shouldn't the ensemble include a competent accordionist, an earnest clarinetist?

Yet she understands what lies behind the group's high standards, even admires it. Rain once served a six-week training stint with Doctors Without Borders in Nepal. Half her time in country was spent at a Bhutanese refugee camp five times the size of Tooley Farm. That camp, too, had a ragtag pickup band, but only a dozen folks survived the weeding process. She remembers the earned arrogance on the faces of the ensemble members, how proprietary they got.

As for the ensemble here, this isn't a middle school jazz band, some kumbaya-we-are-the-world bullshit where everybody's just as good as everybody else, all the miserable evacuees pulling together and harmonizing their differences through the timeless language of music. No, these players are total snobs, with impeccable musicianship and sharing a silent agreement that standards still matter in this changing world, despite everything.

Anyone is free to listen, though. With thousands of aimless IDPs in the megashelter, Pav3 becomes the place to be at night. Live music, board games and cards, some beers. Listeners will call out cover requests, and while the band tends to steer clear of the cheesier stuff, the string of familiar tunes spreads smiles. Listening to these musicians beneath the Oklahoma stars, maybe it becomes possible for her displaced residents to see a good future, to imagine that ruined cities can be rebuilt, that a dying earth might heal.

Aside from all that, the music provides a nice distraction from the national maelstrom. Rain is on daily calls now with FEMA senior staff about the need for a "controlled population" in the shelters. Things around the country are tilting off plumb. She can hear the tension in her colleagues' voices as they report in from Georgia and Alabama and Mississippi on the roiling discontent among their displaced. Spoiled food, horrible sanitary conditions, mini-riots here and there. The eighteen megashelters are so many powder kegs, ready to blow.

One evening, as the musicians pack up, Rain happens to swing by Pav3 as the band is plotting a concert. She pauses in the dark to listen as they discuss the proposal, jokingly at first, but the discussion turns serious as they consider how to get permission, refreshments, even ticket sales. (To keep out the riffraff, as Leonard puts it.)

"We need a name, though," Kaitlyn says.

"What about the Outer Band?" the bassist suggests.

Some like it but Leonard shakes his head. "Too space age. Folks'll think we're some goddamn Devo cover band."

Rain passes out of earshot and stumbles on a loose shoelace. As she squats to retie her boot, the drummer whips past her up the avenue, tapping rhythm on her jeans.

"You figure it out?" Rain asks her back.

Loida stops and turns around. "Huh?"

"Your band got a name yet?"

A girlish grin. Loida brings her drumsticks together and thwacks them against a palm. "It was Gavin's idea. We're the Displacements."

42.

Jessamyn emerges from the tent in a snit. She's overslept and missed her morning stretch class, which Tate doesn't think is a big deal, frankly. What's the Red Cross going to do, fire them? She claws her fingers through her hair and launches a battery of complaints. This place is hell, what are we doing here, this was a bad idea—also your idea, Tate helpfully observes, which gets him ignored through two bowls of cornflakes.

He doesn't see her again until happy hour, part of their daily ritual, when Gavin strolls over to the Staff Only Pavilion for a beer.

Tate rounds the corner as Jessamyn strides past, making for the johns.

"You having a drink, babe?"

"Bathroom run," she snaps over her shoulder. From behind she looks ill, shoulders slumped over folded arms.

In the SOP, loose gaggles of FEMA workers and Red Cross medical staff sit bullshitting at the tables. The big guy, Butch, known as a legendary storyteller, regales a table full of volunteers. From another group Tate hears murmured complaints about medical supply chains. In the back corner Gavin hunches over a book.

"Hey," Tate says. The kid spread-eagles the paperback on the table. Tate glances at the cover. Samuel Butler, *Erewhon*.

"Good book?"

Gavin shrugs. "Not as good as *The Way of All Flesh* but that's a high bar."

"Never been a big reader myself."

"Reading's overrated. I miss my Xbox."

Tate clinks his bottle against Gavin's. "I hear that," he says cheerily, then starts shooting the breeze. Gavin's an excellent student, eager and quick, and Tate likes teaching him the craft. Here's how you tell a new user from a die-hard junkie. Here's how you know if somebody's about to dine and dash. Most important: here's how you make sure nobody turns you in. Carrot and stick. Dangle more product in front of their noses, hint at what happens if they narc. Warn them about the men above you. Guys who make you look like a teddy bear by comparison.

The apprenticeship has turned into a twisted father-son thing, and Tate has to admit, he enjoys the chance to flex the paternal muscle. Gavin just lost his dad, his stepmom's broke and whacked, and he's clearly in need of some strong male role models. *Because that's what true men are at heart, me lads. Mentors. Templates. Archetypes for our sons. Warrior exemplars, through and through.*

Lately Gavin has started talking about what comes next. Enroll in community college? Barista somewhere? Start a band? And Tate nods along, happy to lend advice.

"You've got to have a five-year plan is what I always say, with contingencies built in. That's one of the things they won't teach you at a university. I mean, college is great and all, don't get me wrong. I went to junior college for my associates and I don't regret it for a minute. But you get a whole different set of skills on the street."

"Like how to sell drugs?"

Tate hesitates, detecting a possible note of condescension in the kid's response. He's coming up with a suitable rejoinder when Jessamyn slides down the bench, not on his side. The kid brushes the greasy dangle off his face, sits up straight. Posture is power, and Gavin's bent like a lobster unless Jessamyn's around.

"How are my boys?" she asks, her mood markedly improved.

"Just talking over Gavin's career options," Tate says.

"What've you got so far?"

Gavin shrugs. "I'm pretty good at sales."

"Nothing wrong with sales," Tate says. "Hell, I've been selling insurance for a dozen years and look at me."

"Yeah, look at you," Jessamyn snorts.

Tate decides to ignore her. "There's a podcast you need to listen to," he says to Gavin. "It's real helpful about this kind of stuff, life choices and all. I'll text you the link."

"I don't have a phone anymore," Gavin says. "The family data plan ran out and we can't pay the bill."

"Jesus."

"Fun times. I'm trying to console myself with analog immersion in various pretelephonic utopias." He taps the cover of his book.

"Going nowhere fast?" Jessamyn asks.

"And backward," Gavin says.

They laugh at some literary in-joke Tate doesn't get, the insult made worse when Jessamyn leans into Gavin so their shoulders rub. She's playing it up, giggling at the kid's jokes, dealing her flirty hand. Probably trying to get back at Tate for their fight earlier, but her manner is totally transformed from what it was ten minutes ago, almost like she's—

He looks at her more closely, the flush along her neck, the jerky movements of her hands. The eyes are different, too. Hard to see in this light but her pupils have shrunk into black dots the circumference of pinheads.

He thinks back to that last night in Houston. A tab of wildfire on her tongue, her exuberance after the dose. How she babbled during the stop-and-start traffic along the evacuation route, still surfing her high. Eventually she crashed, and when she woke up the next morning she was her regular self. She hasn't mentioned wildfire since, at least not as something she'd be stupid enough to try again.

But the signs are all there, radiating from the fevered gorgeous mess of her. How many times has an irritable Jessamyn gone on one of her "bathroom runs" and come back placid, her jagged edges smoothed? How many times has Tate watched her fingering through a lackluster tune then taking a quick break and returning with a vengeance, inspired to pluck out a new song for her ragtag band?

What an idiot he's been, not to see it coming. One little taste and the chick gets hooked on her own product.

Tate counts cash and does the math on his phone calculator. Gavin sells ten, twelve sheets a day. At twenty doses a sheet, this translates to fifteen hundred doses a week, and they've got just less than a million doses of wildfire stuffed in the car. Meaning they'll need, oh, six hundred and sixty-six weeks to get rid of it all. Thirteen years in an Oklahoma FEMA camp selling doses to climate refugees. Spectacular.

He stuffs the cash into his gym bag and feels that familiar itch of impatience. Back in Houston things had been ramping up in a big way. Tate was clearing four grand a week, easy. He'd started imagining what life might be like on an extra quarter mil a year. Take Connor on a luxury vacay in Hawaii, pay for any therapy he needs.

Then, Luna. A wrench shoved into his well-oiled gears.

It's not as if they expected to sell much. The whole point of coming here was to lay low for a few weeks, long enough to get Saint Louis off his back for good, then settle somewhere else. But he's starting to see the weak points in the plan. What good is a carload of product if you can't sell enough to make it worth the risk?

He complained about it last night after they fucked—or tried to. Hard to focus when your tent's surrounded by do-gooders and your back skin's Brillo-padding on cheap sheets, plus Jessamyn hasn't been as into sex as she was when they first hooked up—and now he knows why.

238 · BRUCE HOLSINGER

Just give it time, baby, she cooed in his ear afterward. We're not in a rush here. Be patient, okay?

What is it Jace Parkinson says about patience? Tate shuts his eyes, remembering.

Ah, Job, the poor sod. Loses ten children, loses his wealth and health, then bends over and says, "Arse me again, Lord." None of that for me, lads. You want a model from history on how to get what's yours? Take Genghis Khan. Now there's a proper man. D'you know, lads, genetic studies show that something like ten percent of men living in the former Mongol Empire share identical Y chromosomes, all down to Genghis? Bloke's got sixteen million direct descendants living today. Think on that. The great fookin Khan. Burning the crops, spreading the genes. Now that's a man.

So fook patience. Fook Job.

43.

She kicks the flywheel and guides the child's hands against the clay. Together they straddle the potter's wheel: a gift from Rain Holton's staff that now lives near Pav3 in its own canopy tent, where kids crowd in every morning for throwing sessions. Other parents have started teaching math, reading, science, an informal school day coalescing in the pavs.

Daphne has embraced her de facto role as art teacher—though the operation is already slipping out of her hands. Clay vessels are beginning to appear willy-nilly around Tooley Farm, flower vases on tables in the pavs, pots to hold hand sanitizer in the toilets. Last week a pair of enterprising teens from Little Havana convinced the staff to let them dig a pit to fire selected pieces. They've even set up their own Instagram account, @IDPCeramics, plotting to monetize the megashelter's budding operation if they can only figure out the shipping.

The girl in her lap, Jada, is five, a delicate little being determined to make the wheel work for her. Daphne once said to Brantley, soon after the move to Miami, that their house would feel like home only once her wheel was installed in the new studio. Two days later, surprise! A new wheel appeared, a premium electric model with adaptable speed control and "EZ-Feel Toggle Switches" to reverse direction. Also a high-end programmable kiln, its sides encased in stainless steel. Brantley preened over the fancy equipment, assuming his wife would respond with the appropriate gratitude. But Daphne had instantly hated the setup, and let him know it.

The conflict was part of a pattern that shaped their marriage over its final years. The overweening husband, assuming jurisdiction over every square foot of their enormous new house, even the studio, the one space Daphne had claimed as her own; the ethereal, acquiescent wife, always happy to yield to his greater command of logistics, who rarely even knew the right questions to ask—and still doesn't. Earlier this morning Daphne spoke to the lead counsel at UMed, who walked her through some HR legalities and hinted at her husband's various transgressions over his final months. In light of his death, the attorney assured her, the hospital would not be filing suit against Brantley's estate, though Daphne should be aware of the lien against his employer-sponsored life insurance.

The lawyer ended the call, almost as an afterthought, by informing her where the remains of the airport victims would be taken after the forensics team completed its arduous work. Did she prefer cremation? Yes, she did. A facility in Jacksonville, then, where she could pick up Brantley's ashes upon her return to Florida. Daphne imagines mixing them with her clay and casting her dead husband as a snake, slithering through the dirt. Maybe she will bring the ashes back to Tooley Farm, and scatter them over the site of the family tent.

No acrimony in throwing pots, though. She peers over Jada's shoulder as they lean together into the rotation, joined by the calming symmetry of the work. The wheel spins, Daphne kicks, together they thin the clay, and a long moment passes until she senses someone hovering nearby.

"Daphne."

She lifts her head and looks into the eyes of a ghost. Her feet freeze, the spinning stops. Brantley's mother stands back from the wheel, hands clutched over her sternum.

"Flo!"

She lets Jada scramble from her lap, then jumps up and embraces her mother-in-law, muddy hands and all. Flo's body is thinner than she remembers, more brittle to the touch.

"My God, Flo. How did you find us?"

"Long story." Her mother-in-law grasps Daphne's wrist. Through the muck of the clay Flo's sinewy hand trembles like an injured bird. Daphne can tell in one glance that she already knows about Brantley.

"Is there somewhere we can go?"

"Of course." Daphne grabs a clean rag from her supply and tenderly wipes her mother-in-law's hands, then her own. Putting an older kid in charge of the wheel, she leads Flo toward one of the empty pavs. They walk in silence at first, both overwhelmed. Eventually Flo clears her throat, as if expecting Daphne to begin.

"I'm so sorry," Daphne obliges. "About Brantley, about—everything. But I couldn't find you. I called and called at the Willows but there was never an operator."

"I know, dear." Flo pats her arm.

They have reached Pav2. Flo cups Daphne's jaw and plants a kiss on her cheek. "I can't imagine what you've been going through in this place." She looks around, her nose wrinkling in distaste.

Daphne bristles, oddly defensive of Tooley Farm, though this reaction soon gives way to a mollifying calm. Flo represents security, wealth, a way out; horrible but true. "We're doing okay, actually," she says slowly, aware of the need to please. "The kids are struggling with their father's death. What it all means."

Flo brings a hand to her mouth, and for the first time Daphne looks somewhere other than her face. What she notices first is the outfit, a mismatched pantsuit in which the stylish Flo wouldn't be caught dead on a normal day. Her Puma sneakers look right out of the box. Her hair is a bristly mess.

"You remember how unpredictable Luna was in those last hours," Flo says as they find chairs and sit. "There weren't enough buses for everyone, so they took us in two shifts up to this retirement community in Sarasota to wait it all out. That's almost four hours, an eight-hour round trip. You do the math."

"But Brantley said the transport could accommodate everybody. We could have taken you so easily, Flo, we had plenty of room."

And you had your purse. She wonders what these weeks would have been like had her mother-in-law been along for the ride. Even now, as Flo bends in a camp chair like an unwatered plant, Daphne finds herself obsessed with the state of her mother-in-law's finances. How much does she have? What is she bringing to the table?

"They accommodated all the bona fide residents. That wasn't the issue."

"I don't understand."

"They almost didn't take me, Daphne."

"What?"

Flo reddens. "My account at the Willows has been in arrears for months."

"But—didn't you make a huge up-front payment when Brantley moved you in there?"

"Half a million dollars."

"I thought that guaranteed you a spot for life."

"There's still the monthly fee. Five thousand and change. The fee covered my apartment and all my meals, the health club, the hairdresser. My accounts were set up to pay it automatically, and I never gave it any thought, until . . ."

Daphne sees it now.

"He had power of attorney over everything." Flo is whispering, as if any potential listeners would care. "All my affairs, since just after his father died. My retirement accounts, insurance—everything. A few days after I got to Sarasota, I was summoned to speak with the director. She gave me a week to find alternative housing."

"Is that even legal?"

"Perfectly, for folks still in independent apartments. If I'd been in assisted living I suppose they would have had to deal with me. I tried to call Brantley, then you. But I couldn't get through." Daphne's purse, Brantley dying at the airport with his phone in hand. "The end of my week comes, I beg them for a few more days, until my birthday has passed, at least—"

"The sixth, wasn't it?"

She nods. "I ended up in a shelter in the community hall of a Sarasota synagogue. That first stretch was very hard, especially after learning about Brantley from the hospital. But after a while I had the presence of mind to ask the right questions, and someone connected me with the Red Cross to look into your location. They put me on a bus and . . . well, here I am."

Daphne presses her hand. "God, Flo, what he did to you."

"I'm sure there's a perfectly sensible explanation." She smooths her hands down her thighs. "Brantley was a wonderful son, a wonderful husband and father."

Daphne doesn't know whether to laugh or cry. "Flo, he was a megalomaniac. In our marriage, at the hospital. I'm broke because of my husband's God complex. My children are in this camp because of it. Medical workers under his supervision died because of it. Don't you see?"

"What I see is a man who was a loving son, a good provider. Maybe he made some bad choices near the end. But that's how I'll remember him. You'll learn to as well."

Daphne sits shaken, awed by her mother-in-law's fantastical powers. Oddly she thinks of Steve, the schlubby insurance agent, wishing he were here to pop Flo's bubble just as he popped Daphne's.

"What about Gavin?" her mother-in-law asks. "Is he going back to Stanford?"

"Oh sure. With the spare hundred thousand I've got under my camp pillow."

Flo looks at her sidelong. "What about the 529?"

"You mean—"

"The college savings account. Brantley talked about it all the time, to me, at least." She sounds smug, in the know. "Were you not aware of it?"

"I guess I was, in a general sense," Daphne says, feeling familiar shame but a flash of hope. "Do you think he kept anything in there?"

"I suppose there's one way to find out." Flo rubs her thighs again and stands, unsteady on her new shoes. "Now when can I see my grandchildren?"

44.

Story hour was not in the plan. It starts on a drizzly morning in October when a teenage girl bursts in, holding two little boys by the hand.

"Our mom told us to get books," she grumbles, like she's been asked to clean toilets.

Gavin smiles. "What do they like?"

"Trucks, rockets. Boy shit."

"Right, right." He fingers through a row and tugs out a Thomas the Tank Engine title. "You guys like trains?"

The older boy glares at him. "I'm in third grade."

"Manny!" the sister snaps. "Be nice."

"And I'm five," says the littler one, spreading his fingers. He's obviously more like three but Gavin nods sagely.

"So you guys need something more sophisticated. Let's see let's see let's see . . ." He pulls out a paperback. "How about superheroes and underwear?"

"I guess," says Manny, dubious.

"I wearing underwears now," the little brother whispers. "*Spiiiiiider-man underwears*." He snaps his waistband.

"Then you might like this." Gavin shows them the cover. "*The Adventures of Captain Underpants*. A modern classic." He hands it to the sister.

"Read me now," says the little one—to Gavin, not to her.

"That's rude, Tyrique." His sister gently bops his head. "We'll read it back at the tent."

"No, Dasia." Tyrique points up at Gavin. "Him."

Dasia rolls her eyes. "Sorry."

"No problem. Guys, fall in." The boys follow him back to his stool and sprawl with their legs akimbo. Dasia leans against a stack of boxes, sketching with a pencil in the back of a battered copy of *The Lorax*.

Gavin opens to the first page. "Chapter One," he mumbles. "George and Harold."

Reading aloud is harder than it looks. He fumbles the book a few times trying to satisfy Tyrique's demand to keep the pictures displayed, and fields Manny's astute observation that maybe the characters shouldn't all have the same voice. By the third chapter, though, he gets into the swing of it. He invents distinctive dialects for George and Harold, reciting the narration in a sardonic TV announcer's tone that has the boys in giggles.

Mr. Krupp is formulating his plan to get even when one of Gavin's regulars pops in. Sherry is her name, a strung-out Texan with pipe-cleaner arms. She gestures at the fantasy table. Gavin mouths *Fifteen minutes* and goes back to the story. Dasia, taking a pause from her sketching, watches as Sherry leaves the tent. When she looks back at Gavin he ignores her, hoping she's too young to have a clue what's really going on in the library. Once he's finished with the book he hands it over to her.

"Okay, guys." He stands and brushes his hands together.

Tyrique doesn't budge. "Again," he says, low and threatening.

"Can't right now," Gavin says. "I've got patrons coming in. Maybe some other time?"

"Tomorrow," Tyrique says, clearly pissed.

Gavin looks at Dasia, busy examining her nails. Up to him, then.

"Fine," he tells the brothers. "Eleven o'clock, okay?"

The next day they bring friends, and by the end of the week story hour has become a thing, an hour of preadolescent literary edification in the space before lunch, moms and a few dads whisking by to drop off their brats while other children wander in on their own. Dasia hangs around to help, occasionally staring down a kid for getting too loud.

Tastes quickly gravitate toward the darker end of the children's book spectrum, like a Grimm's Fairy Tale collection with the original warped endings, or Roald Dahl's *The BFG*, all about kidnapping and cannibalism. A big favorite with the Tooley kids is a truly fucked-up volume called *Slovenly Peter*, which comes in a donation box with a stack of other old-fashioned titles, including *Raggedy Ann* and a banged-up *Mother Goose*.

The stories in *Slovenly Peter* are all about disobedience and its consequences. Cruel Frederick kills birds and throws kittens down stairs. Augustus refuses to have soup or anything else to eat. He gets thinner and thinner until finally—and here Gavin learns to look up and say, "All together, now!"—the kids chime in with the last line: "He's like a little bit of thread; and on the fifth day he was dead." In much the same spirit are the rhyming couplets in "The Story of Little Suck-a-Thumb."

> The door flew open, in he ran,
> The great, long, red-legg'd scissor man.
> Oh! children, see! the tailor's come
> And caught out little Suck-a-Thumb.
> Snip! Snap! Snip! the scissors go:
> And Conrad cries out—Oh! Oh! Oh!
> Snip! Snap! Snip! They go so fast
> That both his thumbs are off at last.

The accompanying pictures show a freaky guy in red pants streaking in and going to town with scissors as long as garden shears. Blood gushes from the fresh wounds, and in the lower panel you see stubs where Conrad's thumbs should be.

The story's unlikeliest fan is a Crackertown girl named Eliza, barely two years old, sitting on her sister's lap and sucking her left thumb. The first time Eliza sees the picture of the red-legged scissor man butchering little Conrad she pops her own thumb out of her mouth, screams at the top of her lungs, and runs out of the tent.

"Yo that book *works!*" Manny observes.

The next day, though, Eliza returns and "scissor man" is the first story she requests. Big crowd pleaser, this *Slovenly Peter*. Gavin reads it through every day, with no complaints so far from anyone's censorious mom.

Over the following weeks the library becomes a haven within a haven, a site of commerce and strange fellowship. Gavin anchors the place, aware of the new standing afforded by his proprietorship. When he walks into the dining pavs, grateful moms make him butt in line while his buyers give him quick, in-the-know nods. Even Oliver deigns to attend story hour once or twice. At breakfast one morning Gavin hears him boasting to some other kids about my big brother, the guy who reads.

One day Daphne stops by. At first Gavin thinks she might be a buyer, here to score. Which would be hilarious in its own brutal way, but it's clear she's here to observe. She stands in the back beaming down on the multiculti assemblage at her stepson's feet. Even in this place, the white benevolence positively glows from her skin.

"I've heard you're a natural," she says as the kids wander off.

"They're pretty cool mostly. Plus they have good taste." He replaces the day's books as Daphne strolls around to the fantasy/sci-fi table. "So what's up?"

She walks her fingers over a few titles, landing on *God Emperor of Dune*. Fan the pages, lady, and you'll be in for quite the surprise. Instead she looks at him. "Gavin . . . we need to talk."

"Okay," he says slowly. "Give me a minute or two to straighten up?"

"Sure." She waits for him out on the avenue. He plucks full sheets and half sheets out of eight books and hides them between some boxes.

Daphne leads him to the track for a purposeful hike around the inner perimeter. She takes him through it all, the lapsed insurance, the unpaid mortgages, the whole sinking ship, so much worse than losing our house, Gavin, you have to understand what this means, what happens when we ultimately leave here, because we have some difficult choices ahead of us, and that's where you come in.

He knows where she's going with this, can feel it coming on like a hurricane (*bwa–ha–ha*), and it's easy to stop listening because he's listening instead to his dad, that night he called last February for a "father-son chat." Gavin was home late from Green Library after a meeting with his Roman Decadence project group. Middle of the winter quarter, two hours head-buzzing about Juvenal's satires and their assignment on sex work in ancient Rome. Should they make a short film? A multimedia collage?

Gavin's idea was a hookup app for the Roman Empire, call it Tindrissimus or Grindorum, complete with online profiles of well-hung gladiators and vestal virgins ready to take the plunge. A weekday, so no beer, no California edibles, fine with him, he secretly preferred an unclouded mind, but the lack of substances didn't provide the clarity to register that it was almost two in the morning back in Miami, that someone must be dead because why else would his dad be calling him in the middle of the night?

The only dead thing, turned out, was the 529. For Dad the family 529 was like a vintage car in the garage. Something you occasionally gawked at and constantly bragged about but never used. Dad had explained it all to him once when Gavin was in eighth grade and his mom was still alive, because you're old enough now, son, to understand why it's important to take care of your money, and let me tell you, there's no

wiser investment than a 529 with the tax-free earnings, low maintenance, simplified reporting, that five-year gift tax averaging. Best of
all, it means you and your siblings can go anywhere you want. The
Ivies, stay in state, hell, go abroad. Soon after his mom died, Gavin happened to sneak a peek at a 529 statement open on his father's desk and
got goggle-eyed at the balance: $345,689.80, a sum still etched on his
optic nerve.

All gone, his father told him.

I've made some mistakes, Gavin. Nothing that's not ultimately fix-
able, but with the recession, and, well, the long and short of it is, I had
to drain the 529 and we're going to need you to take a break from Stanford. We're paid up through the current quarter but after that . . . Other
thing is, and I need your help here, we need to keep this from Daphne
for a while. She's had a hard adjustment to Florida, had to leave all her
friends behind. Let's call it burnout, okay? You were traumatized by
the fires, the campus evacuations, and—no, I'm not asking you to *lie* to
your stepmother. Just delay the truth. Meanwhile who knows? Could
be I'll straighten some things up in the finance department and we can
send you back to Stanford in the fall.

"I'm really, truly sorry, Gavin, about everything," his stepmother
says now. "Especially my own idiocy, how blind I've been to what was
going on." She takes his arm. "We're going to have to pool our resources to get back on our feet. And the biggest asset we have left, I
hope"—here she looks at him—"is the 529. It's a lot of money, Gavin.
And since your father was the sole owner and you're the beneficiary, I
can't withdraw any of it without your consent."

He lets her go on for a while. She's been reading about the procedure
for tapping the college account, the penalty for early withdrawal, the
possibility that they'll need to use only part of the balance, and that's
the best part, Gavin, because maybe there's enough money in there to
get us settled somewhere, tide us over until I can find a job.

The mantra rattles in his skull: just rip the fucking Band-Aid off. Tell her about the 529, about why you dropped out, about how you helped Dad bullshit his wife for half a year. Just tell her. And finally, after all these months of lying to his stepmom, sneering at his stepmom, condescending to his stepmom, hating on his doormat of a stepmom, he does.

45.

School goes from nine thirty until eleven thirty then again from one thirty to four, which means basically five hours a day in the pavs sitting on wobbly chairs or hard benches that hurt your butt. The teachers are mostly stressed-out parents who've never taught before, and even the few "real" teachers aren't getting paid and *got they own shit going on*, as Mia hears one of them complain. Back at her school in Florida, sixth graders were supposed to start dissecting frogs this fall. Mia would have been allowed to use a scalpel to cut through skin and organs just like her father did with people.

Worst of all, her mother's now the art teacher, with a line of eager beavers who want to make crappy bowls out of the clay they dug from the creek. It's *so* embarrassing having your mom work with all the kids you know, her hands on their hands, issuing instructions in her fake-patient voice.

One morning, Mia gets in line as soon as school begins, surprising her mother.

"Can I try?"

Her mom's smile is a little too wide. "Of course you can."

Mom guides her at first, adding water, helping her pull. Mia feels a cup rising up in her hands. She imagines drinking out of it instead of plastic. Others gather around to watch. Femi, Hamid's little sister, peeks over the wheel, tiny fingers grasping the edge of the splash pan.

"Hi, Femi." Mia smiles at the toddler. Femi's eyes widen at the sound of her own name.

Mia presses slightly on the sides. The walls thin as they rise. She decides to make a vase, one of those bay-blue vessels like the ones her mother left at home. Taller, thinner, reaching up toward Mia's nose . . .

"Not too much pressure, sweetie," her mother says. "Watch the edges there . . . Mia, it's tilting a little can you—wait, don't—"

The clay wobbles. Mia touches the lower part of the wall to correct the tilt. She can fix this. But no. A thwack against her right hand and the clay flies off the wheel, causing dirty water from the pan to splash in the toddler's eyes. Femi starts wailing and shoves her tiny fists into her eye sockets.

"It's just water," Mia says, furious at the brat for messing her up.

"Mia!" Mom scolds. "She's a baby."

Femi's mom comes rushing up and Mia's mom helps her wipe the little girl's eyes. By the time they calm her down, Mia has already gathered the collapsed clay for a second go.

"Know what," says her mother, "why don't we let someone else take a turn."

"I need to finish my vase."

"I know, Mia, and maybe later you—"

"You give everybody else three tries and you're not even giving me two."

Her mother says, in a sharp, mean voice, "Mia, put the clay down."

"It's not fair."

"*Now.*"

Mia smashes her clay ball onto the middle of the wheel, making the whole apparatus shudder and rock.

"Mia—Mia, wait."

She ignores her mother's pleas as she stalks out of the tent and bumps into Oliver.

"Come on," he says, grabbing her arm, "we're skipping school today."

"You're eight years old. What do you know about skipping school?"

"Come *on*."

"Why?"

"Grandma said it's a surprise. Hurry up or we'll be late."

Back at the tent, Grandma Flo sits up on her bed with a creepy smile on her face. Powdery makeup cakes her cheeks.

"We're going to the mall in Lortner," she announces, almost vibrating.

Buses go back and forth every day from Main Gate to Lortner. People can get a long-distance bus from there to anywhere they want. You can also sign up just to go look around.

"How did you get tickets?" Mia asks, thrilling to the prospect of a day in a town, walking in and out of stores.

"All in the timing." Grandma Flo sounds almost like her old Florida self. "I asked at just the right moment, when some others had canceled."

"Go, Grandma," Oliver says.

"Can Luz come?" Mia asks.

"I have four spots but Gavin's busy in the library. I don't see why you couldn't ask your friend."

Mia dashes out to go find Luz. At the first corner, she bumps into Gavin.

"What time's the bus?"

"Grandma said you weren't coming."

"I'm taking a day off. A working man needs his sabbath."

"Oh," says Mia, deflated, and it doesn't help when they get to the Square and she discovers they'll be riding in a school bus, painted white with a big red cross on the sides. The road is narrow and bumpy, and by the time they reach the outskirts of Lortner, Mia is ready to puke.

Big boxy stores and chain restaurants line the sides of a boulevard. Taco Bell, a Western Sizzlin, a Dollar Tree. Then a Staples, a Denny's, a shoe store, a Bath & Body Works, the long shared front of a Walmart and a Lowe's spread out behind them. The bus slows and turns.

"This is a mall?" Mia says, crestfallen.

Gavin puts his head over her shoulder. "What were you expecting, Aventura?" Aventura Mall, an outdoor complex on the far side of Miami with an amazing food court, art galleries, even a hundred-foot tube slide. They used to go sometimes for a special treat.

Mia stares bleakly at the passing storefronts. The bus makes a lazy circle through the parking lot and pulls up in front of Lowe's.

Today half the town must be here. When the bus door opens, dozens of people turn to gawk at all the IDPs gushing out onto the pavement. Mia blushes in the glare of the cars and the judging eyes of the real Oklahomans.

"Keep your head up, dear," Grandma Flo says. They make their way down the rows of cars. The looks aren't mean exactly, but full of pity, and something else. Lots of raised eyebrows and wrinkled foreheads.

A man closing his tailgate nudges his wife, whose lips make a cooing circle at them.

"How are you all doing out there, folks?" the man says. "FEMA taking care of the Lunas?"

"Surf-n-turf every night," says Gavin, not even glancing aside.

"Well, God bless." The wife steps forward and clasps Grandma Flo's hands. "God bless all of you."

Grandma Flo stares down at the tangle of fingers and smiles weakly at the couple.

In the Walmart, it's Mia's turn to gawk. For the first time in what feels like forever her body is *inside* somewhere, under an actual roof, though the walls are so far apart and the roof so high that the store feels like an immense pav, stuffed not with IDPs and tables but with toys and fluffy towels and home storage bins and megapacks of soft drinks and especially new clothes, maybe an acre of them. She browses the racks for a while, remembering the smell of undonated shirts and dresses and pants, then wanders through the store until she finds Oliver in

Electronics standing in front of a television, his eyeballs shining with the glow of a cartoon.

After an hour Grandma's ready to leave. Long distances separate the stores and their grandmother is slow, so it takes a while to get to the Dollar Store. Mia surveys the shelves with a sinking in her chest, because there is literally nothing, even in the bargainiest bins in the Dollar Store, she will be permitted to have. A girl in the candy aisle looks at her IDP bracelet and Mia can tell she knows what it means.

She turns down an aisle of hair products and pauses in front of a display of clips and bangles and tugs a package of three ponytail barrettes from the rack. Her fingers trace the delicate hinges. The clips would look perfect on Luz.

The curved mirror at the end of the aisle shows distorted reflections of Mia with the package of barrettes, the clerk at the front helping another customer, Grandma with Oliver in the next aisle. Gavin must be waiting outside. It's almost an accident when the package slips down the front of her jeans.

An endless field of asphalt stretches between Dollar Tree and the Staples. Halfway there Grandma Flo drifts right, toward the Denny's. "Let's get some lunch."

Mia looks at Gavin. Gavin looks at Mia. They both look at Oliver, then at Grandma.

"Seriously, Grandma?" Mia says. "But how—"

"I want to take my grandchildren to lunch and damned if I won't."

Gavin says, "Gram's still got that swagger, yo." Everybody laughs, even Grandma, though there is something crazy and frantic in the cackles she makes while crossing the lot.

"Table for four," Gavin says in the Denny's, fingers in the air. When the hostess sees his bracelet, Mia can swear the lady's nose wrinkles, but the food tastes amazing and Grandma doesn't even make them order off the value menu. Mia gets chicken tenders with mashed potatoes, Oliver gets a grilled cheese with French fries, Gavin gets apple bourbon pancakes, and Grandma orders a steak. She insists on sharing bites with everyone else. They even get dessert.

"I'm gonna hurl," Oliver says, rolling in the booth. Grandma makes him sip her fizzy water. When the bill comes she takes out a credit card and hands the plastic tray to the waitress.

A TV over the bar starts showing Miami Beach, the piles of lumber and steel and endless mounds of ruined buildings shot from a helicopter.

"That's fucked up," Gavin murmurs.

"What?" Mia asks.

"They're not even bothering to clean it up. You see any bulldozers or dump trucks down there?"

He's right. The beaches, too, look deserted. The waves lap the shore as always, the water back to its silky blue. But on shore it's all a long pile of wreckage and junk.

The waitress reappears. "I'm sorry, ma'am, but this credit card was declined."

"Oh dear." Grandma starts fishing in her wallet. "Try this one."

The waitress takes it up to the station. Mia tries not to watch her over there, fiddling with the machine. In less than a minute she comes back. "Same problem, ma'am."

"Oh. I'm afraid—well I'm afraid I don't have any cash. Are you sure it was declined?"

The waitress taps her foot. "Should I get my manager?"

Families at the surrounding tables look over. *Lunas*, Mia hears someone murmur. Sweat breaks out in her armpits and she thinks of the SCBs.

"I—I don't know," Grandma stammers. "Let me just—"

Three twenties appear like magic on the table. "Will this cover it?" Gavin says.

The waitress glances at the check, swipes up the cash. "Sure will, hon. I'll get your change."

"Keep it," says Gavin, sounding almost *exactly* like Mia's father.

"Okay then." The waitress slips the cash into a pocket of her apron, and the bad moment is over.

Grandma Flo stares at her water glass. Mia turns to Gavin and whispers, "Where did you get all that money?"

"Nowhere," he says, which makes literally *no* sense. His eyes look like they always do when he lies.

"Did you steal it?"

"Seriously?"

"Well *did* you?"

"Fuck off, shoplifter," he softly snarls. "And don't be a narc and tell Daphne or I'll beat the shit out of you."

How many times has Gavin said this to her? Probably a thousand.

For once Mia believes him.

During Range she gives the package to Luz while huddled behind a tent off Avenue E9. Luz examines the barrettes beneath the dangling lights. Mia helps her fashion a smooth ponytail above the nape of her neck. She makes the job take longer than it has to, luxuriates in the silky texture and sweaty scent of her best friend's hair.

"You look older," Mia says when it's done.

Luz shakes her head, testing. The gift stays put, holds as fast to her hair as the two girls to each other, Mia believes, in a friendship that never has to end.

46.

Flo wakes up complaining of abdominal pain. Not severe, she assures Daphne; probably gas, from the awful food. As they walk to the pavs for breakfast Daphne matches her mother-in-law's gimpy pace. Flo is suddenly fragile, an old woman rather than a fit and spry retiree. Her infirmities mean more responsibility for Daphne, a fourth dependent; another soul in the flock, with no help from her depleted accounts or Gavin's 529 or any other source.

They fill their trays and join the kids. Powdered eggs again, clumped and oily in their reconstitution, sopped up with bread the texture of an old sponge.

"Prison chow," Gavin mutters, and Daphne thinks longingly of the Norwegian MREs served last week, dried plums and the tang of salted fish.

Flo sets down her fork. She puts her hands on the table with her fingers interlaced. "I can't eat this."

"Yeah, the eggs suck," Oliver says cheerily. "Mom should have warned you."

Daphne studies her mother-in-law, moved by the wholesale change in her, a depressed shell of the old Flo—though isn't the more surprising transformation, the truly startling metamorphosis, the one happening inside Daphne? The prospect of a morning at the kickwheel gives her a rush of vitality, an energy missing from her life in Miami, where she struggled some days just to get out of bed and walk through a house someone else cleaned, where the simple tasks of grocery shopping and transporting her overscheduled kids around exhausted her.

Daphne would resume her old life in a heartbeat if given the choice—but here, in Tooley Farm, she knows she will come back to her family's platform tent at the end of the day bone tired, terrified for the future, yet somehow she will also be—*better* isn't the right word. But more centered, more focused; more, perhaps, herself. The world sharp and clear as it hasn't felt in years. Her skin, the air, the rough texture of the tent, the weight of her body on the cot. A density missing from her former life.

Surely it's immoral on some level to find strength or even romance in this new impoverishment, to sentimentalize the leaking, sinking ship her life has become, as if they wouldn't all still be addicted to their screens if they could afford smartphones again. But there is an odd contentment in the bare essentials, the absence of all the trappings and glitz. As in graduate school, financed with student loans and two part-time jobs. No furniture, a candle stub drizzling over a Chianti bottle on a bare floor, nothing in the fridge but a four-pack of yogurts and a case of Leinenkugel. Over those years with Brantley, it was scenes like these that would come to her along with a stinging awareness that she was living his vision of their accumulative life. That it has taken a world-changing catastrophe to uproot her from these circumstances seems both fitting and sick, yet another measure of her false consciousness, this pleasure she takes in her own capacity to get by with so little, convinced no doubt by the sheen of her former wealth that all will turn out well in the end, because it always has.

Yet the Larsen-Halls are hardly the only family coping in here. There is general composure among the diners, these many others who have lost everything and now sit at thousands of folding chairs babbling over institutional oat circles and freeze-dried eggs. Rain Holton moves among the tables, stopping to speak to families and individuals as she goes, answer questions, hear complaints, each grievance received with a calm demeanor and quiet authority. Yes, the food is wretched, the showers are never hot enough, the sheets and blankets are scratchy, there is a constant low stink, and no one knows what comes next. But somehow this woman and her staff are holding things together, keeping the threads from fraying away.

She turns to Flo. "Can I ask a favor?"

Flo pats her mouth. "Of course, dear."

"Would you mind taking the kids to Pav3 after breakfast, to make sure they're doing their school work? I'm afraid they're turning feral."

"I suppose I could do that." Flo's face brightens. We are a team, Daphne wants her to know. A family. This woman won't be let down again, Brantley be damned.

Flo sets a slug of powdered eggs gingerly on her tongue and chews with exaggerated chomps to make her grandchildren laugh. But when she stands to throw away her garbage, she bends at the waist, wincing.

The med tent is an olive domed structure fully enclosed on all sides. Beneath the awning a nurse triages a line of residents ten deep. Rows of folding chairs sit beneath a canopy, most of them taken. An hour passes before a nurse comes out and guides Flo into the tent.

By now Daphne has the seat closest to the check-in nurse, identified as Sandy on her name tag. Medical staff come and go, some pausing to complain to Sandy in murmurs of subdued alarm that Daphne begins to interpret. The local hospital, it seems, overwhelmed with the influx of displaced, has been rejecting Tooley Farm's recent requests for ICU beds, sending patients miles away to the adjacent county; what happens next time a resident needs immediate treatment?

She scans the waiting area, crowded with ailing Lunas. Continuity of care: a phrase she heard Brantley use countless times. The longer a patient sticks with the same family doctor and sees the same specialists, the better the prospects for long-term health. Yet for the middle aged and elderly here, the disruption will soon have dire consequences, severed as they are from their cardiologists and their gastroenterologists, their neurologists and their ENTs. And there must be hundreds of evacuees here in the middle of chemo or radiation.

A thirtyish woman stumbles toward the Red Cross tent, helped along by an older man Daphne takes for her father. A smear of vomit slathers her shirt. Her head lolls to the side and her eyes are half-closed, unfocused. Her nails scratch furiously at a reddened patch on her arm.

"Another one," Sandy says with a heavy sigh. She stands and signals to an orderly. "Take her right in, guys." Two staff members come and lead the young woman into the treatment tent. The father takes a chair and slumps over his knees.

"What happened to her?" Daphne asks softly.

Sandy, typing on her laptop, doesn't look up. "Just an OD."

"You mean—"

"Fentanyl maybe." She shrugs. "They'll give her Naloxone, an IV. But there'll be more coming in."

"How do you know?"

"Logic of supply. When there's two there's ten." Nothing she doesn't see every day in her regular job, Sandy says, getting chatty. Before this Red Cross gig she worked in an ER in San Francisco, where the opioid epidemic remains at a peak sustained by the recession and the in-flood of urban dwellers displaced by fires up and down the state. No reason to think a few hundred folks in the megashelter won't have brought their full supplies of oxy along; be a shock if they hadn't. Some selling pills, or bartering them for needful things. Others pushing the envelope in their dosages.

"I mean, me?" Sandy toys with her foam cup. "If I were stuck in this place involuntarily I'd be shooting up every day, too." She looks sidelong at Daphne. "Sorry, sweetie." Daphne waves off the apology.

Behind Sandy the tent flaps part and Flo emerges, clutching a bottle of MiraLAX.

"All set, dear," Flo says.

"You okay?"

She pats her stomach. "Nothing too drastic."

Daphne, relieved, walks with her mother-in-law back toward their tent through the strange music of this place. Conversations sieve through tent walls into a wordless humming. The burr of the generators mingles with the coughs of a bus, the crunch of gravel underfoot.

47.

A shower pump has gone down in Quadrant III, rendering an eight-stall unit unusable until Maintenance can get a new part. The lines are twelve deep, eighty-odd IDPs shuffling over to the next unit, compliant and beaten. Some stalk away, saving a shower for tomorrow.

"Tell you what." Rain raises her voice over their mumbling. "All you folks waiting for this unit, fall in behind me. Come on, now."

She walks backward until she has the residents herded up, then leads them toward the staff showers near Medical, enjoying their relieved babbling. Rain will hear about it later from Butch. But keeping order in this place entails small compromises and minor flexibilities. No one is telling Rain or her staff how long this whole thing is expected to last, how many more weeks or months they'll be sheltering these folks.

She notices Chester Biggs in one of the lines, picking at a cuticle. Rain hasn't said more than a hello to the man since their initial exchange when he handed over his guns, though she's marked the charmer in him, his garrulous way with the friends he's accumulated in here. As she passes by the line she catches his eye.

"You got a minute?"

He straightens up and appraises her. "Crazy day at the office but I can squeeze you in, I suppose." His eyes narrow. "Why?"

"I could use your input on something, that's all. Walk with me?"

He looks longingly at the shower line, shrugs, and falls in beside her. Biggs walks at an amble, intentionally sluggish, hands loosely clutching the ends of the towel yoked over his shoulders. A little show of resistance to Rain's authority maybe. But that's okay if this is what the man needs.

She leads him down past the barn and over the creek to the junk-yard, as her staff have taken to calling the debris-strewn area just inside the secondary gate, home to Tooley Farm's four dumpsters, filled with mess trash and other waste produced by the thousands of IDPs. Emptied every Thursday and overflowing by Tuesday, with the inevitable scatter of plastic, paper, and other refuse teased from the bulging containers by breezes or curious kids. The port-a-john company keeps one of its vacuum trucks parked here. A faint sewage smell seeps from the tank and hose apparatus.

Rain points to a pile of odds and ends stacked up near the fence. Colorful lengths of plastic, steel poles and wooden beams, metal pieces of various hues and shapes.

"What's all this?" Biggs says, taking it in.

Rain lifts a boot and sets it on the rail of a ladder that was once sky blue, now flecked with chipped paint. "This, apparently, is two deconstructed play structures, from some park renovation outside Tulsa. A parks-and-rec crew brought it all by in a flatbed couple days ago. Now it's ours."

"Quite a gift," he quips.

"Yeah."

"Feels like regular Christmas morning."

Chester circles the heap, bending down here and there to assess the soundness of an orphaned sliding board, the health of a four-by-four. At the end of a second circuit he straightens, hands parked on his waist.

"You'll need some new posts, hardware for sure. Lotta rust in some of them bolt threads."

"Right, right," Rain says. "You think it's salvageable, though?"

He waggles a hand. "Most of it, I'd say."

"Great. Thanks, Chester. Appreciate your time."

"No big."

She starts to walk away.

"Hold on, now," he says. She stops and turns back. Biggs hasn't moved from the edge of the pile. "When you planning to set the thing up?"

"We've got a work crew that can probably handle it," Rain says. "They might get to it next week."

He lifts a hand to his jaw, rubs at his whiskers. "Be a shame not to get it up and runnin' sooner, all these kids in here and whatnot." Chester gives her a side-eye, a gleam of humor in it, letting her know he's onto her clumsy manipulation.

"We've got a full arsenal in the tool shed," she says. "Hammers, wrenches, post hole diggers."

"Let me round up some of my guys." Biggs turns to walk away from the junkyard with a new bounce in his step.

My guys. Rain marks the phrase, this subtle confirmation of Biggs's leadership role among the white folks sheltered along North Dakota Street. He's not wrong. He manages to corral a dozen men and boys and sets them to work creating a new playground in the lot on the far side of the barn. By dinnertime they have eight posts sunk in the dirt waiting for concrete, which they mix and pour the next morning from two wheelbarrows. A staffer drives Biggs to the Home Depot in Lortner for new bolts and Butch arranges for a few yards of mulch to be delivered to cushion any falls.

By the third day twin play structures have risen at the edge of Quadrant III, colorful beacons for the younger kids—and some of the older. Biggs's son, Kyler, is the first to climb to the platform, where he beams in triumph with a sledgehammer raised to the sky.

"I am Ragnarok, god of destruction!" he yells with a growl, playing for cheers. The kid doesn't have his dad's natural charisma, though when he descends back into the crowd Chester throws a protective arm over Kyler's shoulders and gives his head a rough noogie with his knuckles, letting his own intentional goofiness erase any memory of his son's performance.

"Good worker, this boy," a sweaty Chester loudly proclaims, as delighted youngsters assay the monkey bars and slides and the earthy smell rises from the fresh cedar mulch. Grateful parents come by to slap Chester on the shoulder, shake his hand, and he makes every one of them give the same credit to his son.

Rain watches the man work the crowd, his beaten-down sorrow displaced, for the moment, by an earned pride.

She's walking back to the Square when a familiar rumble sounds from far up the road. Buses? Tooley Farm is already at capacity, swollen with displaced. She checks her messages. Nothing about another load of IDPs.

A line of military vehicles snakes west. She wills the convoy not to slow at the crossing but they take the turn one by one, kicking up barrows of dust as they descend toward Main Gate. At the fence line a commander in the lead vehicle, a lightweight Humvee with its top down, makes a circling motion above his head. Other units trundle off into the grass outside the fence. Four of the Humvees boast .50-caliber mounted machine guns. Also in the mix: two M3 Bradley fighting vehicles, hulking blocks of steel with turrets. By the time the lead Humvee pulls to a stop in the Square the whole facility is essentially surrounded, a vehicle stationed every hundred yards around the outer fence line, NCOs and specialists spilling out.

Rain scans the commander's badge as she strides up. "Good day, Staff Sergeant."

"It's a beaut," he says. His eyes heavy-lidded, neutral.

"What brings you to Tooley Farm?"

"Orders."

"The governor's?"

"We're augmenting security for the megashelter. We'll take over entry searches, detentions, that kind of thing."

"Where's your unit based?"

"We're out of Sand Springs, the 279th."

"So you're a combat team," she says, stating the obvious.

"Most definitely, ma'am."

"This is a resettlement facility, Staff Sergeant, and we already have a paid security detail. Why not send us a CST from Oklahoma City?"

"They're all still down around Houston with FEMA's best and brightest. You're stuck with us."

A chuckle from his driver, a pencil-necked specialist.

"Stewy Brothers, is that you?" a voice calls out from behind her. The staff sergeant leans left to look behind Rain as Jed Stricker approaches. The guardsman's sunburned face cracks a smile.

"I'll be damned." The two men clasp hands and thump chest to chest. They know each other from their high school days, Jed explains, when they were standouts on rival football teams in Tulsa.

Rain thinks: *Small fucking state.*

She asks Jed to give Sergeant Brothers a tour and the two men stroll off. Pencil Neck stays behind, picking at a boot tread.

Rain walks slowly back to the Square, keeping a wary eye on the Humvee. For normal FEMA operations, the National Guard will send its civil support brigades to assist local first responders. Engineers, health technicians, chopper pilots with experience extracting flood victims from rivers and roofs. The unit dispatched to Tooley Farm, on the other hand, is part of an infantry brigade. No reason those .50s have to be mounted as they are, no justification for those Bradleys to be bristling with guns. Doesn't help that the unit's men look a little ragged. Under-slept and scruffy-faced, without the tight discipline you'd expect from a Guard brigade called up.

Her phone kicks. She takes it out and reads a text from Vanessa.

How's next week? Fly in Tuesday to OKC and rent a car?

Rain types a return message. What about classes?

It's fall break

Ok then

Love u

You too V

Rain lifts her head and looks around at the deploying Guard unit. Pencil Neck gets a scratchy order on his radio and starts the Humvee. He touches the brim of his cap to Rain. The vehicle's wheels kick up a cloud of orange dust that settles over the Square.

48.

Mia stares at the fake warrior up there and wills the play structure to collapse. The posts to crumble, the platform to melt under his feet, the plastic to dissolve, the whole thing to come crashing down onto the mulch and bury Kyler Biggs in a coffin of twisted metal and wood. Instead he raises his hammer and does a ridiculous war cry and when he climbs back down his father gives him a big hug and starts acting like Kyler built the two structures all by himself, like the whole thing was his idea.

His father. This is the part that hurts. This is the part she hates, a loathing that snicks through Mia like a swallowed piece of glass. That a father like Kyler's got to live and a father like hers had to die. If she hefted that sledgehammer right now she could kill them both.

After the adults drift off, Kyler and his Snow Leopard assholes basically take over the new playground. They stand guard at the bottoms of the ladders and the bases of the shimmy poles and won't let anyone climb up unless they know the password, which of course no one does except the kids on their squad.

But eventually someone gets through. It's Bembe on the second play structure, the bigger one, clambering backward up the tunnel slide. Mia can hear him struggling inside the plastic cover before he emerges on the platform pushing up his glasses, delighted with himself. Her heart soars.

"Kickass, Bembe!" Luz yells, cheering her brother's show of resistance.

Now Kyler spies him from the other platform. He makes a growling noise and hurls his hammer to the ground, almost hitting a little Toad Squad girl. He slides down a pole, sprints toward the second structure, and gets up the ladder in two seconds—but not before Bembe slides back down, giggling madly.

Kyler jumps off the platform and chases Bembe around both structures, getting some help from the other Leopards. They almost have him when Luz, appearing from nowhere, sticks out a leg and sends Kyler sprawling into the mulch. She grabs Bembe by the arm and runs around the barn with Mia and Oliver in close pursuit.

"I'll get you, bitches!" Kyler yells as they flee.

The next day, he does.

The attack takes place behind the bathrooms just inside the perimeter fence in Quadrant IV. Nobody is around except Mia and Luz; no toilet lines for a change. After this they're going to the pavs to watch You-Tubes.

A stall door slams. While Mia sanitizes, a gruff laugh comes through the vent.

"There's our little mamacita. Hanging out by the shitters, right where she belongs."

"Get your hands off me, you dick."

Mia bangs out of the stall to see Luz rubbing at her wrist. Kyler's in her face and two other Snow Leopards flank her as she backs toward the perimeter fence.

"Leave her *alone!*" Mia shouts.

"These are Crackertown toilets." Kyler ignores her. "You and your avocado pickers can use the toilets in Quadrant III."

"Or just dig a hole like back home," says one of the others.

"Stop!" Mia shouts.

Now they have Luz pinned against the chain link. One of them starts shaking the fence behind her and another grabs at her hair and suddenly they don't look like thirteen-year-olds anymore.

Kyler says, "Come on, now."

"Fuck you, asshole," Luz says.

"Fuck *me*? You wanna fuck me, mamacita?"

He lunges. Luz kicks him in the knee.

"You little *cunt*."

Kyler swings and misses and the other two close in and Mia stands frozen against the stall door, watching as the boys grope at her best friend like a pack of wolves. Her ears roar. Luz lands a punch to a face, another kick, but then one of them gets ahold of her right arm, and another has her left, and Kyler's just about to throw a punch to her stomach when a man's voice booms out.

"The hell's going on here?"

The struggling stops and Mia turns to see one of the directors, the big friendly one named Butch, making for the fight. The boys sprint away along the fence as Luz crouches on the ground.

Butch bends down with one hand on his knee and the other on Luz's shoulder. "You okay, sweetie?"

Luz wipes at her nose, looking furious and ashamed while Butch squints down the fence line. "I know those boys. I'll speak to their folks."

"That's not enough," Mia says, finding her voice at last. "They should be arrested."

"You think?" He looks amused.

"It's not funny. They *assaulted* her, it was *sexual assault*."

"Okay, but—"

"No, it wasn't," Luz interrupts him. "It was just a stupid fight."

"Luz—"

"Stop, Mia. Just *stop*."

"What did *I* do?"

"You need to shut up, pendeja."

And her beautiful friend darts off, half-bent at the waist.

Mia huddles between two sheds with her fingers curled around half a broken brick. She imagines hurling it at Kyler's thick skull. What would it sound like? How amazing would it feel to see his dirty tank top slathered in blood?

And his dad is even worse with those looks he gives Luz and the other Guatemalan kids, the sneers on his tobacco-stained lips when he's sitting around with his Crackertown buddies. Those people are all racist, *really* racist, and nobody's doing *anything* about it.

She presses the rough surface of the brick as if she can squeeze the unfairness into it, this rage rushing down her arm, rage at the SCBs, rage at her father for staying behind and dying when he should have evacuated with them, rage at herself for not defending Luz, even rage at her mother for not letting her have a second chance at the kick wheel. She remembers that warm ball of clay, how she wanted to smash it in her mom's face. Now she wants to smash it into Kyler's, smear the brown mud down his neck and make him—

The plan fills her like a Christmas morning thrill.

She sees it all at once. The sickening surprise, the disgusting beauty of it. Like one of her mother's sculpture installations: a world all its own, but of Mia's creation.

The next night, during Range, Mia waits until the squads disperse before second round. Luz has basically quit playing because she's too afraid of Kyler, but that's convenient for Mia's plan because it means her friend won't suspect anything, and never has to know.

She steals off to the storage tent behind Pav2, where they keep the cooking equipment. Finds a gap under the ground flaps and slips inside. Swipes a ladle and a saucepan and slides out beneath the flap. Next she heads over to the rank of broken toilets by the fence. The strip of yellow OUT OF ORDER tape comes off in one pull. Deep breath. *Now.*

The stench blankets her but she lifts the toilet lid and reaches down until the ladle hits the top of the squishy mound and with no hesitation she takes a scoop, lifts it out over the lip of the seat, and dumps it in the bucket. A second scoop, then outside to retch and spit. Gushes of oxygen fill her lungs.

Mia repeats the grim process until the saucepan is nearly full. She drops the ladle into the tank and takes the pan outside. She puts the lid on and carries it over to a spot by the fence where she can hide it for a few minutes. Now up the fence line to the working toilets, where she pumps out sanitizer and bastes her arms and face and neck, reveling in the sting and reassuring scent of the antibacterial gel.

Once she feels less disgusting Mia retrieves the saucepan from its hiding place and moves through the camp. If anyone stops her to ask what she's doing, she can say she needed manure for the garden, the little plot of vegetables some residents planted on the far bank of the creek.

She crosses between rows of tents, stepping carefully over ropes and ducking behind laundry and making quick dashes from street to street with the pan of waste hugged to her middle, going through half of Tooley Farm until she reaches Crackertown and the stretch of North Dakota Street between Avenues F4 and F5.

Kyler's tent, and she can tell that people are here. A flashlight or electric lantern casts a glow on the sides. Low murmurs float around from the front. She hunches over her pan and waits.

". . . got the whole thing set up in the first place."

"You mean the trailers, the sheds?"

Two men are talking, one of them Kyler's dad.

"Because who's watching the watchers, know what I'm saying? The other day Bed Larimer has this guy on about these camps on the Greece–Turkey border where they got no clean water, no toilets, they got kids young as ten offin' themselves, and Bed, he says how's that any different from where this is going here in the USA? Way FEMA's got us penned up like cows and you think we're any different than Syrians, Moroccans, all them? You seen what happened in Birmingham. How long till this place goes down the same way? We got National Guard on the perimeter, for fuck's sake. Use us for target practice if FEMA orders it."

A cough.

"Some of those guys, though, they seem all right."

"You think?"

"I could see an arrangement."

One of them slaps a knee. "That's what I'm telling you, man." Almost whispering now. "It ain't all black and white, if you take my meaning."

Gruff laughs.

"So what are we talking about here?"

"Home rule, brother," Biggs says. "Our own flag, our own rules. We seen it done before, Bundy up in Oregon, the militias on the border. All we need is Betsy Ross and a—hell, we both know what we need."

No talking for a few seconds. A sniff.

"You smell that?"

"What? Oh that. Jesus."

"Broke latrines again."

"Want to head down to the pavs for a cold one?"

"I'm in."

The dangerous mutterings continue as the men wander off. Mia hefts the saucepan and steals along the side of the tent until she faces the avenue. Six tents up, a woman sits on a broken chair, her head nodded over her chest. In the other direction the two men are just rounding the corner. Otherwise, no one.

She shifts slightly and peers inside, hoping Kyler's mom won't be passed out on a cot. But the tent is empty. Mia pushes aside the flap, enters the family's dwelling, and goes to work.

THE GREAT DISPLACEMENT
A DIGITAL CHRONICLE OF THE LUNA MIGRATION

TESTIMONY OF CARLTON BAINE

Deputy Associate Administrator

Office of Response and Recovery

Federal Emergency Management Agency

before

The Ad Hoc Subcommittee on Hurricane Luna Recovery

of

The Senate Homeland Security and Governmental Affairs

Committee

. . .

Senator MARCUM (R-OK). Mr. Baine, I'm a bit confused. Why isn't the administrator here today?

Mr. BAINE. Senator, Administrator Kellstrom has been called away on an urgent matter.

Senator MARCUM. And the nature of this urgent matter?

Mr. BAINE. Senator, I'm not at liberty to say.

Senator MARCUM. Would you consider this hearing an urgent matter, Mr. Baine?

Mr. BAINE. Yes, Senator.

Senator MARCUM. But clearly not as urgent as the matter that called Administrator Kellstrom away from Washington.

Mr. BAINE. I couldn't say, Senator.

Senator MARCUM. I'd like to hear about these compounds you've been running. Because I'll be honest with you, sir, I've received more calls from my constituents about this subject than anything else since Luna hit. Have you visited these camps?

Mr. BAINE. Senator, we call them megashelters, as the word "camps" has some unpleasant connotations that we would rather—

Senator MARCUM. Has Administrator Kellstrom visited any of these megashelters?

Mr. BAINE. I believe she has.

Senator MARCUM. What was her impression?

Mr. BAINE. You would have to ask her that directly, Senator.

Senator MARCUM. I'd love to, Mr. Baine, if she'd bothered to appear before this committee. But let me broaden the question. What kinds of discussions have you had with your colleagues at FEMA about these camps? What have you learned about how they're operating?

Mr. BAINE. I believe they're doing an excellent job given the circumstances, Senator.

Senator MARCUM. An excellent job.

Mr. BAINE. Yes, Senator.

Senator MARCUM. Would you go so far as to say they're doing a heckuva job?

Mr. BAINE. Senator?

Senator MARCUM. Have you read this story in yesterday's *Washington Post*, Mr. Baine? "Mississippi FEMA shelter suffers from sanitation woes, spoiled food." Mr. Chairman, I believe this story is entered into the record?

Chairman DIAZ. That's correct.

Senator MARCUM. Mr. Baine, have you read this story?

Mr. BAINE. Yes, Senator.

Senator MARCUM. What is your reaction?

Mr. BAINE. Well, I can tell you that—

Senator MARCUM. Because you want to know my reaction, Mr. Baine? Outrage. Disgust. Just listen to this. "At one point, the lines for the portable toilets were so long that camp residents set up a latrine of their own, digging holes for waste and using draped sheets for privacy. When a rain storm flooded the makeshift latrine overnight, the streets nearby filled with raw sewage." Raw sewage, where hundreds of kids, American kids, run around and play. What do you have to say about that?

Mr. BAINE. Senator—Senator, the men and women of FEMA are responding to the worst natural disaster in American history. The health-care situation alone has been staggering. Emergency rooms in four states overwhelmed, stores of antibiotics depleted, first responders tapped out.

Senator MARCUM. But my question, Mr. Baine, is about conditions once the displaced are in your shelters. How is it possible in this day and age that there aren't enough toilets to accommodate the basic sanitary needs of the residents of a facility run by the federal government of the United States?

Mr. BAINE. That's really a procurement question, Senator, and—

Senator MARCUM. A procurement question? Are you serious?

Mr. BAINE. Senator—

Senator MARCUM. This is a moral question, Mr. Baine. What is FEMA doing to ensure the safety and health of the hundreds of thousands of American citizens in its care?

Mr. BAINE. Again, Senator, we're doing everything we can to—

Senator MARCUM. If these reports are true, FEMA is creating impossible conditions in its megashelters. You're going to have mass revolt on your hands, or else people abandoning the place to face God knows what.

Mr. BAINE. Which is their right. These are not internment camps, Senator Marcum. They're relief facilities. The IDPs are free to come and go as they please.

Senator MARCUM. How are they supposed to leave? Most of these folks came in on buses, and some of these camps are miles from the nearest town. Many have lost everything, homes, family members, jobs. All wiped out.

Mr. BAINE. Our responsibility is to the residents of the shelters, Senator. That's FEMA's jurisdiction. Once they move beyond the perimeter—

Senator MARCUM. Yes?

Mr. BAINE. Once they leave our perimeter they're on their own.

Senator MARCUM. In other words, if they leave, they die.

. . .

49.

Outflow.

By late October, two full months after Luna hit, people have started leaving Tooley Farm in droves. For weeks these departures have been spaced out, isolated goads to those who remain. But now the true exodus begins, with regular departures from the Square. A couple boards a shuttle to Tulsa. Two families crowd into a rented panel van bound for Chicago. News of a HUD apartment in Cincinnati for that quiet couple over on Arizona Street, rumors of a job in Fayetteville for a guy down the block.

Daphne attends a housing meeting in Pav3. The leader, Butch, outlines the government's working plans to secure more permanent shelter for the displaced. Her family may soon be relocated to a mobile unit outside Charleston, South Carolina, she learns. Once settled they can apply for welfare, though Butch warns them about growing resistance from state governments to funding the influx from Luna. A familiar refrain, this fraying safety net, made worse by the perpetual gridlock in Washington and the nation's failure to manage the rising populations of displaced.

For Daphne, it's all starting to feel a little too personal. What qualifications do these other residents possess that have allowed them to find gainful employment in far-flung towns she's never heard of? Warrensburg, Missouri. Fairplay, Colorado. Leesburg, Virginia. Daphne has applied online for at least thirty jobs but so have hundreds of others, thousands. Stocking shelves, busing tables, cleaning houses—she would take any paid work. But the jobs are elsewhere and she is here, and who wants to hire a receptionist who has to relocate from out of state before her first shift?

She reaches out over email to everyone she knows: classmates remembered from her MFA program, old neighbors in Ann Arbor, even childhood friends to ask about employment prospects in their areas. The replies so far have been friendly but distancing, generic well wishes of the sort she might have typed herself just a few months ago. No offer of a spare room. No mention of a job.

The email from Pilar is different. The last time Daphne spoke to the gallerist was on the morning of the evacuation. Pilar's family has resettled in Asheville, North Carolina, where her daughter is in school and her husband is working construction. Pilar hopes to open a small gallery soon, she writes, because people still need art, now more than ever.

> I wish I could have saved your brilliant work, D. I did bring along "Unflight," which I shipped to Stoneham in Manhattan last week. He gave us three thousand—that plus your portion of my insurance payout will come to just over 12K, which I'll wire to you next week when I have the final figure. Same account as last time? Meanwhile love to you and the kids, and I'm so sorry again about Brantley. You are in our thoughts.
>
> xxP

Daphne rereads the sentences, pinching herself. All her work was destroyed by Luna, she had believed, and there would be no proceeds from the show despite selling out. What she hadn't factored in, of all things: insurance.

But twelve thousand dollars! Enough to buy a beater car, rent an apartment somewhere, reestablish something of a life. She checks rental listings in Ann Arbor and finds a two-bedroom apartment for eleven hundred a month, including utilities; another for eight hundred if they're willing to live on the edge of town. And that isn't counting housing assistance, welfare, other forms of public aid. A job in a town she loves, Mia and Oliver back in a great school system . . .

She is starting a reply to Pilar and already imagining a substantial balance in her checking account next time she logs in when Mia appears at her side. "Mom."

Her daughter taps her arm. Daphne's fingers don't stop. "Not now, sweetie."

"Mom, I need you."

Daphne glances at the screen clock. Three minutes left, and already the next user is behind her, bouncing on his toes. "Just give me a sec, okay?"

"I have to *tell* you something."

"Just a minute," she snaps, and Mia recoils, spins, and darts away. Daphne calls after her, half rising from her flimsy chair before returning to the terminal. Mia's crisis can wait, whatever it is. This can't. She finishes the message and sends it off, her mind filled with the future for once.

Outside, she looks for her daughter. *There.* A flash of brown hair, a face red with anger. She calls her name but Mia won't stop. By the time Daphne reaches the bottom of Florida Street her daughter is nowhere to be seen.

Crack.

A loud report rips through the low hum of the shelter.

Two more:

Crack.

Crack.

Firecrackers?

Distant screams, from the direction of the barn.

She sprints up the lane. Already the byways churn with other residents, pushing, crowding, calling. She rushes along avenues and streets, darts between tents and through the pavs and around the Square, plunges back into the depths of the camp, shouting for her children.

The loudspeaker whines and the voice of Rain Holton booms over Tooley Farm.

"Shots have been fired in Quadrant III. We ask everyone to remain calm and return to your tents. We are investigating the situation and we need the streets to be clear. Again, please return to your tents."

Almost by accident, she reaches the library. She lifts the flaps and steps inside.

"Gavin!" Voice ragged with panic, outside sounds muffled by the books. Her stepson bobs up from the other side of a table. "Have you seen Mia or Oliver?"

"No."

"Go to the tent, see if they're there. I'll keep looking."

Gavin glances back at the tables. "I'll stay here in case they show up."

"But—Fine. If they do, bring them to the tent right away."

She pushes out and smacks into the helmet of a guardsman. He continues up the avenue with three other troops, barreling toward the source of the gunfire.

The PA again: "The situation on Wyoming Street has been contained. Residents of Quadrant III, please remain in your tents until the scene is cleared. Repeat, please stay clear for the time being. We'll make another announcement when the quadrant is open."

Daphne circles back to the tent. She pushes aside the flap and there they are, Mia curled on her cot, Oliver perched in Flo's lap, his cheeks wet with fright. Her mother-in-law looks up and her nostrils tighten, as if Daphne has carried in a bad smell. Mia springs off her cot.

"Mia—"

"You're so *mean*," her daughter says, with one of her signature heel-kicks. Daphne reaches for her but she slips through her hands and out the flaps. Daphne steps out into the avenue but Mia has already disappeared, again.

Back inside she glances at her mother-in-law, expecting a string of passive-aggressive snits. But Flo's expressions can change on a dime. The curling distaste has been replaced by a clear-eyed sympathy that surprises her.

"I'm going to Bembe's," Oliver announces, and drops off Flo's lap and out the flaps before she can stop him.

Daphne collapses on her cot. A bird settles on the top of the tent and a rhythm clicks from its beak and its shadow slides across the canvas. She puts her hands behind her head and closes her eyes. One crisis slamming into the next, into the next, and the next . . .

"What about a funeral, Flo?" she says. "It's been weeks. Is that something we should do for them, some kind of service?"

"And for us."

"I suppose."

"What about his body?"

"He's being cremated in Jacksonville, I know that much. But I should get copies of the death certificate so I can officially inherit all his debt. Ugh, what a pain."

Silence, then a choking sound. She turns to see Flo's head bowed into her hands and her shoulders shaking. In one movement Daphne goes to her.

"Flo, I'm sorry." An arm over her frail shoulders. "That sounded cold. Forgive me."

Flo nods, accepting the embrace. They cry together. Easy to forget, in all the residual anger, that Brantley was Flo's only child. Easy to forget how much her mother-in-law has devolved over these long months from that prissy matron in Daphne's kitchen sweeping potato chip crumbs off the counter.

Once she's calmed down, Daphne tells Flo about the email from Pilar, the small sum she is set to accumulate in the coming weeks. The money will provide a small nest egg for the five of them to build on. They will reclaim the Odyssey in Florida or buy a used car, rent a modest apartment somewhere, and try to find work. They will muddle through, five souls caught up in these strange new drifts.

Later in the afternoon Daphne wanders over to Pav3 and finds a donated copy of *USA Today*. She had been so used to reading the news on her phone that its absence has meant weeks of near oblivion to world events. She scans the headlines. The economy has passed its fifth consecutive quarter of negative growth. The House is debating a carbon tax, again. The football coach at a Big 12 university has been suspended in a recruiting scandal.

But not a single story about Miami or Houston or Hurricane Luna on the front page, no mention of the megashelters. She recalls those weeks and months after 9/11, living in Ann Arbor that year before meeting Brantley. She and her roommate, Jen, got their news from NPR and the papers. Daphne subscribed to *The Detroit News*, Jen to the *Chicago Tribune*, and they had no TV in the apartment. When not in class they were both glued to the coverage in the papers until one morning in mid-November, while Daphne was sipping her tea, Jen looked up from the *Tribune* and said, "Wait."

"What?"

Jen spun around the front section of that day's *Tribune*. "No 9/11."

Daphne scanned her paper. "Same," she said, showing Jen the *News*, and they sat together in a wondering silence and pondered how a cataclysm so all-consuming could take second or fifth or eighth place to the repair schedule for the Ambassador Bridge, or another loss by the Lions.

She feels something of that bafflement now, scanning over the front page of *USA Today*, the catastrophe already hazing into the past. She can see it, how all this plays out. The displaced less pioneers than parasites, too many new mouths to feed and needs to accommodate as a fracturing nation absorbs their numbers. Look at COVID. A million Americans die and things just move on. Same with the Lunas. Soon enough their shared displacement will be swallowed by indifference, as her home has been swallowed by the sea.

At dinner, word spreads about the shooting. A murder-suicide, says a man at the next table. Guy just couldn't take it anymore. A resident put a pillow on his wife's face and shot her, then offed his own father, then swallowed a massive dose of opioids and shot himself. A desperate man with a loaded gun, weeks of hopeless nothing, then a decision.

The shooter's name, Daphne learns, was Bobby Snowe, his wife was Leonora Snowe, his father was Thomas Snowe, and they were from somewhere in Miami-Dade, the only facts about them she will ever know, aside from the manner of their deaths.

Outflow.

The Snowes, too, have left Tooley Farm for good.

50.

On Wyoming Street, yellow crime-scene tape has gone up around a tent where a grim-faced soldier stands guard. At lunch the mood is somber as the morbid tidings spread. No official announcement, but residents know which tent has been cordoned off, who died where. Someone saw body bags. Someone else mentions drugs.

Withdrawal rage, speculates a sun-damaged chick hugging a two-liter Diet Pepsi that Tate suspects is spiked. "Fella ran out of vikes or whatnot. Seen it a thousand times."

"Don't think it was pills," says her neighbor. "There's other stuff folks can get in here."

"Yeah?"

"I mean, you hear things."

What Tate hears is risk. He tosses half his sandwich and heads out to the car.

His family once lived outside Odessa, in the flattest part of Texas where you could see across the scrub for impossible miles. They owned a dog named Clyde. One afternoon he had Clyde out on the county road when three dogs appeared a quarter mile downwind. The hounds got the scent and started sprinting, kicking up eddies of dust. Tate had no chance of outpacing the strays so he stood there with Clyde, waiting for whatever was about to happen. Closer now. Lolling tongues, snouts flecked with froth. Tate picked up some rocks.

The dogs were fifty feet away when Clyde rolled over, showing his belly. The display of submissiveness slowed the dogs' approach. The beasts padded in small circles as they neared, whining. Bare patches in their mangy fur, a missing ear, an empty eye socket. No collars. The strays feral, capable of anything.

Tate followed Clyde's example by getting down on the ground and lying still. Soon they were on him, nosing around Tate's neck and crotch. The dangerous carrion stench of them. What they must have gotten in to smell that way, like demons passing over as he cowered in the dirt, waiting for that first bite, the bloody break of his skin.

Instead they nuzzled at his hands until he scratched their ruffs. The smallest dog tried to get Clyde to play by sticking its butt up, jumping in the air like a kid on a pogo stick until a shotgun blast lifted its body clean off the road. Another blast followed and a second dog crumpled. By the time the third blast came the biggest dog was already away and running fast. The slug splashed up its spine and the animal toppled forward into the side ditch.

"You all right?" came a woman's voice. Mrs. Kellum, owner of a neighboring farm, emerged from the scrub with a shotgun veed over the crook of her elbow.

Tate nodded.

"Been tracking those mangy shits for weeks. Help me get them in the truck."

She walked back into the scrub and a minute later drove out her pickup. With a lot of mess and curious sniffing from Clyde they loaded the dead dogs in the bed. Tate got in front with Clyde and Mrs. Kellum. The woman dropped them at home and went to take the bodies off somewhere. While he washed himself and Clyde with the garden hose Tate thought of that dog shot while running away.

You never want to be that last dog, me lads.

At the CVS in Lortner he buys a prepaid phone and dials the number for Sam Hawley in Dallas. An unassuming middleman, Hawley moves guns, surveillance equipment, and the like—and makes the best fake IDs in Texas. There are guys like him in every state. Facilitators with clean hands and cold hearts who will sell anything for a cut. Tate always pictures Hawley in a darkened basement hulked in front of three computer monitors, using one hand to game, the other to deal refurbished AR-15s.

Some clicks, then Hawley comes on.

"Yeah."

"Your friendly neighborhood insurance agent here," Tate says.

A beat. "You got some balls."

"How's that?"

"They're looking for you, bud. Those Saint Louis guys."

Tate's cheek tics. "I'm not surprised."

"What's the occasion?"

"Who do you know in Oklahoma City?"

"Street corners not doing it for you?" Hawley asks.

"I'm sick of the piddly shit. And you know what happened to Houston."

A snort. "Tell me about it. We got my sister-in-law's whole family living in our cellar. Goddamn drain down there clogs twice a day."

So much for the basement theory. "Anyway," Tate says, looking out across the boulevard. "I need to dump this load."

"Always nosin' for shortcuts." Hawley clicks his tongue. "Tell you what. I'll give you a name and a number in OKC but don't call here again."

"Usual commission?"

"Double it. You're a steaming potato, my friend."

After they disconnect Tate waits for the text then makes the call. He reaches a nameless voice and explains what he's selling and how much of it. The voice is noncommittal. If the buyer's interested Tate will get a call. Might be an hour, might be a few days. Might be never.

He drives back to Tooley Farm with the new phone burning through his pocket. When he reaches the final turn for the parking lot he's tempted to keep going. Why not try his luck in some stretch of California, or along the East Coast somewhere? He thinks of Liberty, her texts from the ruined bowels of Houston. Yury, Vadim, the crew in Saint Louis: the Russians have long arms. They'll be looking for him, their stringers asking questions in the church basements, in the megashelters. How long before one of them starts to hear rumors about a ready supply of sublingual wildfire in an Oklahoma FEMA camp?

He parks and loads a packet of sheets into his gym bag and trudges back into Staff Camp, pausing at the top of the street. Jessamyn paces the gravel in front of their tent, white-faced with need as Gavin looks on. It's bad today, he can tell at a glance. Should have left a little something behind.

Jessamyn spies him coming. She motors into him, savage.

"Where the hell were you?"

She pats him down like a rookie cop, jerking her head to look at his bag.

"Scouting. Always smart to plan ahead."

"The car was gone," she says, "and there was no—everything was gone. *You* were gone."

"And now I'm ungone." He glances at Gavin. "You're out?"

"Totally cashed."

Tate pats his bag and nods at the tent. "Inside."

They go through the flaps, Jessamyn scoping the bag the whole time. She's starting to remind him of his Houston regulars. Dropping weight she doesn't have, losing hair. No longer bothering to hide her habit.

He slips out a sheet. "Just one."

She takes two, practically ripping them off the sheet. He grips her wrist but she's already eaten the tabs and protects them with a childish pride, a hand against her lips and a triumphant squint. Her forearm fragile in his grasp, like the bone of an overcooked chicken.

"Jess—just ease up, Kaitlyn." Forgetting himself in the rush of her dosing. "Get some control."

"You her fucking doctor now?" Gavin says. The kid's got his fists balled up at his sides but beneath the tough-guy shtick Tate recognizes a fearful longing he knows too well, and knows how to satisfy in a small way. A guy will do almost anything to free a loved one from pain.

"Easy, buddy," he says, clapping a hand between Gavin's shoulders and steering him back into his lane.

The wildfire goes to work. Once the initial rush hits her bloodstream, Jessamyn takes out her guitar and starts strumming aimlessly. Tate lowers himself onto his cot and a few seconds later Gavin joins him there, his rage dissolved with her sated need. They sit together watching her noodle around in a world beyond their reach.

51.

Her daughter spins a pirouette when she sees her, thrilling Rain somewhere deep. She glues an arm to Vanessa's shoulders as they walk through the terminal toward parking. They chat amiably during the drive, though as they near Tooley Farm, Rain's enthusiasm dims. The three bodies are still warm. Vani searches her profile from the passenger seat.

"What's going on, Mama?"

Rain flicks her a glance. "Something happened the other day, in the shelter. You should know about it before we get there."

"I'm listening."

Rain tells her about the shootings, the dark mood. Some folks can't take traumas like this, she explains, and they seek other remedies to counteract the effects. Drugs, suicide, even murder. Vanessa probes a bit, asks if there have been other incidents at the megashelter.

"Not even close," Rain says. "We've had some vandalism, some robbery. Drugs going around. But no violence to speak of. I was ready to show off the place, brag to my daughter on how we've kept ten thousand evacuees safe and housed."

"And then this."

"Then this."

Butch is waiting when they arrive. He gives his FEMA niece a bear hug but immediately hustles Rain into Trailer 1 for a conference call, leaving Vani to discover the strange world of Tooley Farm on her own. Not the welcome she deserves, though she's a resilient girl.

Late at night Rain researches the victims while Vani sleeps on the

294 • BRUCE HOLSINGER

spare bunk. She finds only the barest bones of their lives: dates of birth, a Miami address for a home long gone. The three bodies have been stored in a mobile morgue for now, joining a man who succumbed to a heart attack two days ago. Rain tracks back through the last few weeks, agonizing over what she and her staff could have done differently to forestall this. Random tent searches for weapons or contraband, as in a prison? But how do you balance the safety of your residents against their civil liberties and freedoms? A conundrum, for now unresolved.

The next morning, after a hurried breakfast with Vani, she calls a meeting of senior staff and ticks through items: a memorial service led by the chief chaplain, counselors for those working through issues around suicide and self-harm, maybe an active shooter drill.

Butch brings up an ugly vandalism incident in Crackertown. A family's tent was smeared with feces, he says to wrinkled noses.

"I've heard some ugly accusations about that," Nila says quietly.

"Oh yeah?" Rain prompts her.

"From the boy, Kyler. There's this Guatemalan girl he roughed up. Luz Calel."

"I saw the tail end of that," Butch says.

"He's convinced she did it. The father's all revved up."

"Chester Biggs," Rain says.

"That's the one."

"We put them in a new tent," Butch says. "It's being investigated."

The discussion turns to drugs. Someone's clearly sitting on a large supply of opioids, Medical reports, with an active trade going on in the camp. Rain asks everyone to listen for rumors of a supplier, ask some discreet questions, though the Guard detail isn't trained for vice work.

"On a cheerier note," says Nila, "the Displacements want to put on a concert. Open up the pavs, have a dance floor. Maybe get some kegs."

"Dear God," says Butch to general laughter. Rain feels tickled by the plan. Another relief valve, and Tooley Farm needs one about now.

"Let's make it a benefit," she suggests. "Invite locals here for the evening, raise a little money for school books."

Staff Sergeant Brothers saunters in at twelve minutes past the hour, chewing gum and twiddling his thumbs, literally. Rain ignores him for the moment while moving through a few more items. The subject now is guns. She orders more rigorous ammunition and firearms checks at point of entry, more thorough searches of bags. Brothers mutters something.

Rain looks at him. "What was that, Staff Sergeant?"

He clears his throat. "I said, maybe you should loosen up your firearms policy. Second Amendment and all."

"I'm familiar with the Constitution."

"These people have lost their homes, family members, everything," Brothers says. "Now you take away their only means of protection, in *this* place?" A grand gesture with his arms. "As my grandpop used to say, don't bring a pea-shooter to a jungle."

He eye-fucks her on the word *jungle*. She imagines herself taking up Butch's Sharpie and drawing a little Hitler mustache below the asshole's nose. But that's the danger of complacency, isn't it, treating the man as a cartoon character, just as Rain has been regarding residents like Chester Biggs as more clownish than dangerous, her nonchalance both a coping mechanism and a keep-the-peace management strategy bolstered by the glib reassurances from her senior staff and the pressure of more immediate priorities. Hey, if we're letting the Cubans have their Little Havana why can't the white folks have their Crackertown?

But now, she realizes with a quiver of alarm, this tactical indifference risks becoming a form of complicity. Just look at the facts on the ground: a murder-suicide, an enclave of white separatism, a budding interracial conflict over an act of disgusting vandalism—and a National Guard unit led by a couple of good ol' boys getting a little too lax on security measures.

She returns the sergeant's stare. "We need to talk about how that gun got into Tooley Farm."

He cocks his head.

"I checked the records. That man, Robert Snowe, arrived two days after your unit took over entry searches. Wasn't a little .38 he had. That was a .480 Ruger. Big piece, way too big to go undetected. So what gives?"

"You got your methods, we got ours."

"Look," says Rain. "I'm a veteran. I understand things aren't always clear-cut when it comes to regulating civilians. But we need to be on the same page here."

"Last time I checked, the Constitution gives every American the right to life, liberty, and the pursuit of hap—"

"That's the Declaration."

"Pardon?"

"That's the Declaration of Independence, Staff Sergeant, not the Constitution. But hey, what's the difference?"

He bristles with the insult. Butch steps in to keep the peace but fuck this guy. For the rest of the meeting Brothers keeps his trap shut.

Afterward she finds Vani in Medical talking to an elderly man. Rather than eavesdropping Rain goes inside the med tent to check in on the staff. Now that the population has thinned the supply chain is less in crisis, though insulin remains in short supply, and the staff have handled three more overdoses in the last forty-eight hours.

Vanessa waits for her by the nurses' station.

"So you're interrogating my IDPs now?" Rain teases as they walk.

"Just asking a few questions. This place is amazing."

"That's one word for it."

"I had no idea what things were like in these shelters. It's this whole little world but nobody knows what's going on. Like, is anybody taking notes?"

Rain hooks her daughter's arm. "In my experience, folks want to forget this kind of thing. Refugees will jabber all day about their hometowns, the streets they grew up on. But ask about getting by in the camp and they'll change the subject." A lesson she learned on a UN training mission in Maicao, a Venezuelan refugee settlement along the Colombian border. Children with their bellies swollen and burns across their backs, the wind-scraped desert making lonesome howls through the tents. But all their parents wanted to talk about was getting back to Caracas once the conflict blew over.

"What gets me is the scale of all this," Vanessa says. "The tiny stories embedded inside the huge sweep."

"The micro and the macro."

"That's it."

They crisscross through Tooley Farm hitting as many streets as they can, Vanessa coaxing nuggets from the residents, Rain stewing over the staff meeting. Her daughter leans against her. "I brought you a little present."

"Oh yeah?"

Vani just smiles. Back in the trailer she pulls out a stack of magazines and sets them on the table. *Abitare*, the glossy is called.

"It's Italian," says Vani. "Guy in my program had them at a party. Says his dad's the managing editor or whatnot."

Rain sits and starts looking through an issue as Vani plays an album on Spotify, some new young thing with a dovelike voice and a softer style than her daughter's usual taste. They linger for a time over the magazines, sharing a welcome calm as the pages whisper past.

52.

Could be the murders, but lately he's had more buyers than ever. They step in looking all messed up and jonesing; but even before their first lick a blissful look comes over their features. The shakes slow, facial muscles relax into dopey half smiles. Gavin feels like a god, doing this.

Yet there is a new bite to the hustle. Buyers have seemed edgier lately, more hostile. Steve warned him about this, these transformations you'll see in users over those first months. Gavin hadn't wanted to believe him. It's all about pleasuring these folks, lifting them away from their troubles. And there's so much hurt in this place, dense and durable pain, Gavin an anesthetizing force for the good.

All a delusion. Obviously he's making things worse for these people, not better.

Kaitlyn stops by the library most mornings now, hinting for a dose. She'll sidle up with her hands in her back pockets, elbows splayed, pushing out her chest. So far he hasn't given in to her clandestine needlings, which he both desires and fears. The curvature of her neck, the peculiar vibrations when she's in the tent. It's a sick codependence, and so far he's the one staying well.

Pages rustle off to his left. Peering around a stack of books he sees a gorgeous skinny chick thumbing through a paperback. Pink glasses, starburst of coily hair, a slightly cleft chin. How has she escaped his notice all these weeks?

He straightens up. "Hey."

Her eyes stay fixed on the book. "Hey."

"Help you find something?"

"Yeah, no, I'm good."

Obviously not a paying patron of this fine establishment. He lets her read for a few more minutes before ambling over until he's close enough to see the title. Cormac McCarthy, *The Road*.

"We're not there quite yet," Gavin says.

She looks at him. "Soon, though. Another handful of cat sixes—"

"Add a cup of million-acre forest fires—"

"A dash of mass extinction—"

"Pour in one megadrought and stir."

"Bake for twenty more years."

"And voila! Dystopian apocalypse."

She smiles. "I'm Vani."

"Gavin. You new? Just off the bus?"

"Visiting, actually."

He scoffs. "Nobody 'visits' Tooley Farm."

"I do."

"Why?"

"My mother." An eye roll. "She runs this place."

"No way. The *Time* magazine FEMA lady?"

"You got it."

"Where are you here from?"

"Santa Cruz. I'm in a grad program out there."

"I was at Stanford until March."

"Graduated?"

"Dropped out. Father issues."

"Sounds tough."

"So how are you killing your time in Tooley Farm?"

"Listening, mostly. Lot of interesting stories in this place."

"Enough to fill a library tent."

"The kinds of things people will open up on, the stuff they'll tell you." She leans back on a table and knuckles her glasses up her nose. "The other day I was sitting with this guy about eighty, here all by himself. His whole theme was, I'm a survivor. Survived a grenade in Vietnam that blew off my leg. Survived a car crash that killed my first wife. Survived COVID-19 that killed my second wife, my son, my sister. And damned if I won't survive this motherfucker. That's how he put it."

She reminds Gavin of the enthusiastic girls at Stanford, full of verve and zip, ready to talk about anything.

"So what's your story?" Vani wants to know.

"Nobody wants to hear my story."

"Don't be so sure."

"You're humoring me, I can tell. Parachuting into a refugee camp, mingling with the distraught locals."

"Just like my mom."

"Ouch. You two on the outs?"

Vani does a pretty shrug. "She's okay. Just a little too charmed by the rules and regs."

"Probably has to be, to run a place like this."

She looks at him carefully. "You, though. Stanford dropout in a FEMA camp? That's a whole novel right there."

"I could do it as autofiction. Though honestly I'm not one of those guys who thinks his own life is significant enough to sustain a whole book."

"Hey, I'd read it."

Gavin hasn't bantered with anyone like this since those late nights in the dorm lounge, though the more she tries to draw him out, the more he resists her friendly urge to probe, the further he surfs from the interesting stuff. His dead father, his bankrupt stepmom, his shoplifting sister, his strung-out crush, his opioid-dealing gig, the little kids who gather at his feet every day to hear tales of death and dismemberment.

He says, "Maybe we could hang sometime." *Where did that come from?*
"Yeah, no, I'm good." Same as her first four words.

She's leaving day after tomorrow anyway, she tells him. Vani holds
up the McCarthy and taps the cover with a finger. "Thanks for the
book."

As she leaves the tent with her nose in the novel she passes one of his
regulars: Gail from Galveston, a fortyish white woman with a grubby
sundress and a bandanna tied around her head, cancer style. Two weeks
ago the dress was clean and Gail in pretty good shape. Now she looks
undead, with parchment cheeks and eyes sunk in dark hollows.

"What'll it be?" Meaner than he intends, but she's freaking him.

"Whatever you got."

"You know the price."

"Don't got no more cash."

"Not my problem."

"But I got these," she croons, grabbing her breasts. He backs away
but she's coming on strong. Her breath reeks from the gap between her
lips, grayish and chapped.

He grabs two volumes, Terry Pratchett's *Wintersmith* and something
else. He thrusts the volumes at her and she attacks him like a grateful
child. Her emaciated arms wrap him in a weak hug and the full smell of
her rotting body washes over him. He goes to push her off but she's
already wheeling away, all her attention on the hidden treasure in the
books.

Gavin's stomach gurgles something up and he retches the sour bolus
onto the floor of the tent. He stays like that until the blood flows back
into his head.

His last visitor of the day is a wiry Latino guy with inked skin. Twin
studs in one ear, a toothpick wedged between flaky lips. At first he

picks up random titles, flipping through the pages before slotting them back in place. Gavin has seen the guy around the camp once or twice but never in the library, and he's not giving off junkie vibes.

"Help you find something?"

The guy shows his teeth. "Yeah homes, you can help me find something." A raspy voice, high but with a hard edge. "You got books of fantasy, homes?"

Homes? "Yeah. But first, 1995 called, homes. It wants its slang back."

The smile fades. Before Gavin can apologize the guy's in his face.

"You don't like the way I *articulate*, bro?"

"Sorry, man." Gavin shows his palms. "Didn't mean any offense. My bad."

"It's cool, it's cool. No problem." The guy uncoils as quickly as he sprang. He looks over his shoulder. "How much for your sheets?"

"Ten for a half, twenty for a whole."

"Give me a whole."

He pulls out a wad of cash, more bills than Gavin has seen on anyone in here except Steve. As his visitor tugs a twenty from the stack, Gavin notices the writing between his knuckles. Ten fingers, twenty letters, words he doesn't want to read.

They make the swap. Gavin pockets the bill.

"So where you get your shit, homes?"

"I've got a guy."

"We all got a guy, homes. We all got a guy." His chin lifts. "So who's your guy?"

Out on the avenue someone laughs and someone coughs. A fly lands on the inked man's neck and starts tasting a diamond of purpled skin. The guy doesn't feel it there, or doesn't care. Maybe he likes the thought of Gavin noticing his non-reaction.

Gavin kicks at a table leg. "It's just . . . a guy," he says. The buyer starts a slow nod that doesn't stop until the fly lifts off.

THE GREAT DISPLACEMENT

A DIGITAL CHRONICLE OF THE LUNA MIGRATION

▶ **BEDFORD F. ("BED") LARIMER III, TALK SHOW HOST**

A graduate of Liberty University School of Law, "Bed" Larimer hosts *Bed-Time*, the most popular show on American radio, with eight million daily listeners. Originally housed in Larimer's home studio in Palm Beach, Florida, the show and its host relocated to downtown Atlanta in the storm's aftermath. Larimer was forty-two years old when Luna made landfall.

Play audio file:

Transcript:

They have an app for your phone now, the FEMA App. Look it up. They say it directs you to the closest shelter in case of emergency. Who would put that thing on their phone? A FEMA megashelter's about as safe as Mogadishu during the Clinton adminstration.

What always amazes me is the left's hypocrisy about the various agencies of government, their moral pendulum. Take the CIA. For decades the left despised the CIA for supporting anticommunist regimes in Latin America. But as soon as the CIA engineers a plot against a Republican president, now they can do no wrong. Same with the FBI. For decades the left hates on the feds for what they did to MLK, to Nixon's enemies. Then the FBI plans a coup against a duly elected president the libs don't like and the FBI's suddenly untouchable. The peacock director goes on MSDNC spouting all this self-righteous illegal bullshit and now he's a Democrat hero.

Even the military isn't immune. Vietnam? Our soldiers are rapists. The War on Terror? Our Marines are torturers. But as soon as they turn against the president, the military brass are like new gods to these people. General worship. It's the idolatry of our age.

Then the whole cycle repeats itself around FEMA. For years after Katrina the libs did nothing but bitch about FEMA. You're too young to remember but there was this whole lib line about how George Bush was murdering black babies in the Superdome. Then Luna comes along and we're supposed to believe this huge government bureaucracy is capable of sheltering, what, five hundred thousand Americans, for how many months? And if you raised some red flags around what FEMA was up to with these camps, you're propagating "conspiracy theories," which is the Democrat phrase for facts they refuse to see.

Here's what I know about the FEMA camps, and I can see that little smirk on your face but hear me out, because this is crucial. It's all there, out in the open, the what, why, and how. Go back and read the amendments to the Insurrection Act and Posse Comitatus, which allow the military to be deployed domestically in the event of a public health emergency. Before that there was the Garden Plot. You still hear them using that as a model for rounding folks up. Everything they need is already right there in written law. During Luna they were just testing it out for next time.

It's no surprise to me what went down in Oklahoma, how things got out of hand the way they did with the Tooley Five. You don't forget a thing like that. The government couldn't just brush that under the rug, much as they tried. Americans don't want to be told what to do, whether with free speech or vaccines or the Second Amendment. Don't tread on me, don't tread on my Constitution.

You ask me, FEMA had it coming.

53.

A cat has stolen into Tooley Farm. A stowaway with a resident, or a visitor from a nearby farm. Definitely not a stray: she wears a flea collar and her fur is glossy and full. Her appearance inspires the kids to talk about their pets back at home. Dogs, cats, goldfish; rats, mice, hamsters. One girl claims to have a cousin who once owned a de-stinked skunk.

The day is windy, big cool gusts rolling in beneath high clouds as Mia and Luz wait for the cat to slither their way. "I was the one who took Cricket on her dinner walks," Mia says. "I brought a slice of organic turkey and always shared it. Always."

Luz says, "I read somewhere that dogs transfer cells into their humans."

"Seriously?"

"How long did you have Cricket?"

"Six years."

"You probably have a lot of her cells in your blood."

Mia gazes at her beautiful friend. Luz always knows the right thing to say, a secret kindness that comes out of nowhere like an unexpected gift. Mia's own secret is almost unbearable now, like a breath held too long. For days everyone has laughed about "the toilet tent" and Kyler Biggs is the butt of new jokes, even among the Snow Leopards. Mia tried to confess to her mother the other day and now she's bursting to tell Luz what she did but hasn't worked up the nerve.

Finally the girls get their turn to share the cat. Mia runs a finger beneath the animal's chin while Luz scratches at the bony space between her ears. They've just sunk their fingers into the luxurious belly fur when a shoe comes down on the kitty's tail. The cat claws at Mia's arm.

"Ow!"

The kitty darts off. Three bloody lines rise on Mia's skin. The shadow of Kyler Biggs blocks the sun.

Luz springs up and gets in his face. "You hurting cats now, cerote?" she snarls. Luz is a foot shorter than Kyler but right now she looks taller, meaner, stronger, the wind kicking her hair up into a wild swirl. Mia swells with pride and fear. More Crows step up, ready to fight.

Kyler flicks his hands. "Adios, muchacha."

"What's that supposed to mean?" Mia demands.

"Adios and bone diaz to all you motherfuckin' muchachitas."

"Luz! *Luz!*"

Bembe and Oliver come tearing around the corner of the barn.

"Luz, tienes que venir!" Bembe wails. "Nos están llevando! A todos!" He tugs at Luz's hand. Tears cut the grunge on his cheeks.

"What do you mean they're taking you?" Mia says, almost laughing at the sight of Bembe's dusty face and his glasses, crooked and steamed. "Taking you where?"

Kyler snorts. "Like I said, adios, bitchachas."

Oliver hops on one foot and points to the Square. "It's *ice.*" Her little brother wipes an arm across his snotty nose. "It's because ice is here."

But there's never ice in Tooley Farm, not even an ice machine—

"Mierda," Luz says softly, followed by a stream of Spanish too fast for Mia to understand. The farm kids all start running from the barn, first down Nevada Street then left on Avenue B5 past the pavs and into the Square. Between the trailers and Main Gate, a long van and a white bus idle. The medallions painted on the vehicles show twin eagles with wings sheared in white. A shield covers their breasts and blue letters scream from the sides:

HOMELAND SECURITY

US IMMIGRATION AND CUSTOMS ENFORCEMENT

At least a dozen agents cluster nearby, the words POLICE ICE embla-zoned on their vests. Their utility belts sag with clubs, spray cans, guns. They've set up a table and chairs sheltered from wind by the trailers and already four people stand in line, a Mexican family that includes a boy, Oscar, from Elephant Squad.

Rain Holton is arguing loudly with the head agent. Two guardsmen stand by and Mia can tell they're on ICE's side. The agents wear camou-flage jackets under their vests even though there's nothing at Tooley Farm to camouflage themselves *from*, it's obviously just a stupid style statement by losers who want to pretend they're in the army.

In the chaos of the milling crowd none of the ICE agents have seen Luz and Bembe yet. A surge of protectiveness gurgles up into Mia's throat and suddenly she knows what they have to do.

She grabs her friend's arm. "Let's go."

"What?" Luz shakes her head and blinks, confused.

"You need to hide. Come on!"

She pulls a stumbling Luz along behind her as Bembe and Oliver start to run from the Square and the other kids scatter in different di-rections, and for a moment the familiar thrill of the chase returns. They will turn onto the avenue up ahead, then dodge left down the next street and keep running until they reach those abandoned ragged tents in Quadrant IV where it will be impossible for ICE to find them. Crow Squad will bring them food and any other supplies they need until it's safe to come out.

But before they reach the first corner she senses the absence. Luz has released her hand.

Mia stops, turns back. "What?" she says, already panting through the wind. "Aren't you coming?"

"Bembe, no," Luz orders, loud but calm. Ignoring Mia. Their brothers skid to a stop at the corner. "Don't be stupid. We have to go."

"What?" Mia gasps. "I don't understand."

Luz glares at her. "This isn't a game, *Mia*," she says, biting off her name. "This isn't Range. ICE isn't an 'enemy squad.' Our tía isn't a 'Leaper.'" Luz makes mocking quotation marks with her fingers while thrusting her hands at Mia's face. "No more 'scouts,' no more 'declarations,' no more 'captures,' okay? Grow up. This shit is real." She glances at her brother. "Bembe, start packing your stuff. I'll go talk to them."

Luz starts walking back toward Main Gate. Mia follows, too afraid to say anything, so she stops at the edge of the Square and just watches. Vicenta and Aldina are walking toward the trailers, the baby wailing on Aldina's hip. Luz joins them near the table and soon the other Guatemalan kids come back along with maybe another twenty IDPs who line up at the tables.

It takes a few minutes before Mia understands what's going on, how this works. At her school's monthly Equity Assembly last year a visiting speaker showed a movie about the plight of undocumented workers in Florida. The film included footage of ICE raids when agents swarmed into factories and farms like an invading army, slamming people up against brick walls and making them lie facedown on the pavement or the dirt, leading them away by the dozens with plastic ties around their wrists.

This raid doesn't go that way. For one thing, no one tries to flee. All the people questioned seem resigned to whatever's going to happen. And where would they go anyway?

For another, the agents aren't storming around arresting brown-skinned IDPs at random. They don't bother any of the Little Havana people, they don't hassle any black residents except for a few Haitian families but they all seem to have the right documents. The agents act like they know who they're here for as they check papers and ask questions. They're organized, methodical, cold, and they seem to have a list.

The crowd grows. A few residents start yelling at ICE, and some are filming with their phones, but nobody throws anything and there's no real protest. Soon the processing is done. Altogether about two dozen people will have to leave, including Oscar's family, a few other Mexicans—and all the Guatemalans. The agents issue instructions and the residents who have to go start trudging back to their tents.

Mia follows Luz to Little Antigua, where Aldina, Vicenta, and the kids have been ordered to get their belongings. The officers hand out trash bags and tell the residents they can each take only what fits in one, and leave everything else behind.

Mia slips into Luz's tent and finds her squatting over the floor shoving clothes into her bag.

"Where are they taking you?"

Luz won't look at her.

"How can they *do* this?"

"They do whatever they want." She shoves handfuls of Bembe's clothes into the second bag. Toothbrush, toothpaste, comb. She picks up the barrettes that Mia gave her, stares at them for a second, tosses them into a corner of the tent.

Mia's stomach churns and a little cry escapes her. With it comes a dark thought. *Adios, muchacha.* "But how did Kyler know?"

Luz makes an impatient sound. "His dad probably called ICE or something."

Something twists in the pit of Mia's stomach. She has to ask. "Is it because of their tent, when I—when it got messed up?"

Luz's hands freeze. In a slow, awful movement she turns her head. "That was you?"

Mia's mouth moves but no words come out.

"They thought it was *us*. Those whites blamed *us*." Jamming a thumb right at her heart.

"I'm sorry, I—okay? I'm sorry."

"'I'm sorry,'" Luz mimics. She knots the bags shut.

"But what can I do now?" Luz goes for the door. Mia blocks her. "Luz, what can I do?"

"You did it already." And her friend shoves her aside.

Back at the Square, the crowd has grown and an actual shouting match has broken out, Rain Holton and a few of the Tooley Farm staff on one side, ICE and some National Guard soldiers on the other. The big guy, Butch, looks defeated as he tries to calm everybody down. His face is beet red and he's huffing like he might have a heart attack.

Mia peers through the milling bodies at Luz. The best friend she's ever had, who welcomed her into Crow Squad and fought at her side every night and taught her the world's dirtiest words in three languages, is about to leave her here, in this place that now seems ugly and stained. The guilt swarms like wasps needling down her legs and crawling into the pit of her stomach, making it hard to breathe in the suffocating mass of IDPs.

Luz and Bembe climb into the bus. Their silhouettes move against the windows as they find seats. Aldina and Vicenta follow them down the aisle with the rest of the Guatemalan kids. The door of the van opens and more detainees file on, and all Mia can do is wait for the inevitable.

Which comes in less than a minute. The ICE agents divide between the bus and the van, and with a grinding of gears the vehicles move, taking a wide turn past the trailers and through Main Gate and everything has happened so fast, so crushingly fast. Less than an hour ago Mia was with Luz at the barn tickling a cat and now her best friend is

THE DISPLACEMENTS · 311

on a bus to who knows where and she doesn't have a phone number for

on a bus to who knows where and she doesn't have a phone number for her and neither of them has a home address because neither has a home.

As the rumble of the ICE vehicles fades the crowd thins, the voices soften, and Mia, gutted and alone, stares up at the road. The wind lulls and a gruff chuckle breaks the new calm. Chester Biggs stands with some men in front of Trailer 3.

"Justice, boys," he says, playing it up. "Like my mama always said, you start throwing shit around, shit will most definitely get thrown back on you." And the whites around him laugh and laugh. Mia gazes over their heads at the distant fields, her eardrums throbbing with the last words Luz spoke to her, and probably ever will.

You did it already.

Oliver appears at her side, his face apple red. She reaches to hug him but he slaps her arms away.

"Bembe just told me what you did. Now everybody knows," her brother snarls.

"But—

"They should have taken *you*."

54.

Rain stands alone in the lee of Trailer 3, sheltered from the gusts. The DHS vehicles are gone, and with them any semblance of her control over this place. Vanessa wouldn't even look at her just now, stalking off after the raid. The lingering residents act shell-shocked, as if a bomb just vaporized two dozen of their neighbors. *Phht*, and gone. Moms, dads, kids, whole families, and not a thing Rain can do about it. The National Guard colluding in the roundup, ugly gang of Crackertown folks cheering them on, the whole machinery of enforcement making a mockery of her supposed command. She has never felt so weak.

She reaches Joe Garrison on the phone and demands an explanation, which comes in bureaucratic dribs and ass-covering drabs. He speaks of belt tightening throughout the agency, the inspector general's concern about jurisdiction over foreign nationals, a general desire to expend American emergency funds on *actual Americans*, a phrase that makes Rain seethe, for the response to Hurricane Luna has been an international effort, from the teams sent to Houston by Cruz Roja Mexicana to those shipments of MREs from Norway that fed the residents of Tooley Farm for a full week.

"It's nothing personal, Holton," he goes on. "It's not about Tooley Farm. ICE is doing these pickups in all the megashelters this week."

"So you knew they were coming today," Rain says to her boss, who sputters for a moment before heaving a theatrical sigh.

"They'll be fine. They're being taken to the base up in Stillwater for processing. They'll have dorms, mattresses, indoor mess. They're no longer your concern."

"But who authorized the raid in the first place, Joe, and when? Who signed off on this in the middle of the biggest relief operation in—"

"The fuck knows. But listen up. Congress is not going to renew the displacement funds in this new appropriation. If the states want to pick up the slack that's on them. But the federal government's out of the megashelter business as of next month. As for the illegals, honestly it's cheaper to house and feed these folks as detainees rather than honored guests."

"Honored guests? My residents are living in tents and shitting in portapotties."

"At taxpayer expense."

"Taxes they paid, just like the rest of us."

He mumbles something officious and disconnects.

After dinner Rain drives her daughter to Tulsa International for her flight back to Oakland. On the interstate, Vani lets it rip.

"I don't see how you can justify working for this administration. I really don't."

"Vani, stop."

"Those people were sitting ducks. They arrested those mothers in front of their children. They put little kids on a prison bus. That baby's probably sleeping in a cage tonight thanks to your friends."

"They're not my friends."

"They sure as hell pay your salary."

"Just stop it."

"That's always your solution. Just stop it, Vanessa. Just moderate your views, Vanessa. Know what? Not anymore. I'm sick of pretending around you just to keep the peace. Maybe what wingnuts like Bed Larimer are saying about these FEMA camps is true."

"So now I'm the Nazi?"

"If those migrants hadn't been penned up in here in the first place maybe they wouldn't have been detained."

"You think this is easy? You think others haven't thought through these same sets of problems?"

"Don't see much evidence of that, if I'm being honest."

Rain grips the wheel with both hands. Ten and two, flexing her fingers to keep her voice steady. "Let me be honest, then." Ten and two. "Because what I do, disaster relief? It involves compromise, Vanessa. Practical compromise, political compromise, and yes, moral compromise. The job is impossible without it, whether you're working for a government or a private corporation or an NGO. That's why the Red Cross maintains neutrality in the middle of wars. Neutrality means giving shelter one month to people whose village is being burned, even if those same people helped massacre a neighboring village the month—"

"Neutrality is a smokescreen. It's called complicity, Mama. Com. Pli. Ci. Tee. It's just an excuse not to be self-critical. This whole humanitarian paradigm you like to preach—"

"Oh God, is that what they're teaching in graduate school these days? The 'humanitarian paradigm'? Must be nice to sit back deconstructing the world instead of getting your hands dirty."

"Only dirty thing I see around here is your paycheck."

"God*damn*it." Rain's hands jerk on the wheel and the car pulls to the shoulder. She lets it idle as she turns in her seat to face her daughter.

"You think this shit doesn't break me, Vani? You think I don't lie awake nights staring at the ceiling thinking about all the mistakes I made that day and what they might cost?" Her voice is cracking but she pushes on. "And yes, for your information, compromise is how it works. You spend a whole day giving food and medicine to folks starving in a refugee camp but then you're going into town with your team two hours after watching six children die from malnutrition and you're drinking until you can't see, because you have to go in there again the next day and try to preserve as many lives as you can. And Tooley Farm? That place is my responsibility now. Those lives are my responsibility. And in there, I have to hold it together. In there, I have to act the strong, silent, capable type, can't show the belly because that's what they want, my boss with his little post-racial quips, even Butch and my staff are watching for mistakes, and I have to just eat it up because the people we're helping are more important than whatever I'm going through, whatever I might be feeling because who's gonna give a goddamn about that? Not my daughter, I guess."

"Mama—"

"But meanwhile I can't control a goddamn thing, like a man offing his wife and his father and himself, or a goon squad coming in and taking away kids under my care. And now my own daughter thinks I'm taking blood money from this government? *Seriously?*"

Rain starts slamming her palm on the steering wheel, so hard she feels the impacts in the bones of her hand. Her eyes well, everything blurs, all these weeks rush in and she lets them come as she takes it all out on the unyielding circle of vinyl and steel. Eventually the strikes slow and weaken until finally her arm rests shaking on the wheel, wrist angled loosely at twelve o'clock.

Vanessa stares at her slack-jawed.

"What?" Rain says between breaths.

"I shouldn't have said all that."

"It's fine." Rain looks down at the hamburger she's made of her hand.

"I'm sorry, Mama, I had no right to—"

"Like I said, it's fine."

"It's not." And Vani reaches over and takes her bruised hand and cradles it on the padded armrest between their seats. Rain's palm is numbed with the violence, but her daughter's caress soon livens the

316 · BRUCE HOLSINGER

blood. When she feels recovered she flexes, squeezes Vani's hand, and puts the car in drive.

"Thank you, hon," she softly says.

"You okay?" Vani asks.

Rain nods, sniffs. "I think so."

"Good. But damn, Mama." Vani shakes her head. "You need to yell more. Process that shit."

"You think?"

"It's okay to lose it once in a while. I do with Leila all the time. Doesn't it help?"

Rain moves her head side to side, makes circles with her neck. "You know what? It kind of does." She turns, gives Vani a smile, and puts on her signal. By the time the car merges back into the right lane Vani is humming a wordless tune, batting her knees with the flats of her hands, the brutal exchange already forgotten.

As Rain accelerates her heart throbs. She steals a glance over at her daughter, this proud mercurial girl singing it all away.

PART
FOUR

55.

The raid has shattered things.

Mia, inconsolable, resists Daphne's every attempt to comfort her, or even talk about what happened. Her skin goes pale, she stops eating more than a nibble, her eyes sink into hollows. If Daphne so much as mentions Luz's name she gets a snarl and a *Stop!* Daphne, intent on normalizing things, lets her daughter be, attending to the basics without forcing a discussion. In the short term, weak parenting keeps the peace.

Oliver's affliction, meanwhile, is an unwholesome, almost prurient need to know the gory details. Is Bembe in a cage? Where did they take him? Are there real toilets? Are there TVs? Where will he sleep? The questions go on for days and Daphne has no answers.

The kids seem more destroyed by the detention of their friends than by the death of their father. They've made a whole little world here all their own, a world now threatened from all sides.

Rumors spread following the raid, speculating that a fellow resident called in ICE. The most likely suspect is a father in Crackertown. Someone scattered a bucket of human waste around the family's tent, Daphne hears, ruining cots, clothing, everything. His son was in a long-running dispute with Luz Calel and the other Guatemalan kids involved in Range. Once the vandalism escalated things, the father took matters into his own hands.

Such rumors are certainly untrue: Daphne has seen more than one news report about the removal of undocumented residents from the other megashelters. Yet some version of this account has overrun Tooley Farm like a virus, with resentments flowing in all directions. Interactions feel poisoned or otherwise off, IDPs fragile and liable to snap. Now, when the Crackertown whites come to meals, they enter the pavs with wagons circled against what they perceive as a hostile throng. At breakfast one morning Daphne watches as Deke, the man who confronted Gavin on the bus from Florida, accuses a diminutive Haitian man of butting in line. Pushing and threats ensue until two of Deke's neighbors make him back off. But the damage has been done.

The behavior from this crowd makes Daphne ever more conscious of her whiteness, the burn of shame on her pale cheeks. She's tempted to tape a sign on her forehead, or Sharpie one of her T-shirts: *Not from Crackertown*.

A chill and rainy afternoon. She huddles with Oliver in Pav3 drilling him and a boy from Galveston on their multiplication tables. Mia sits with a group of middle schoolers down at the far end of the pav, overseen by Flo and one of the Houston dads. Two tables over, Gavin works with Kaitlyn on a poster for their concert.

Quite a pair, her stepson and this wild older girl. For weeks Daphne has marked Gavin's growing and unmissable infatuation, how he looks up when Kaitlyn walks by, how he skitters off to band rehearsal with a puppy-dog eagerness. Daphne feels for him. Anyone can see the crush is not mutual—yet Kaitlyn is keeping him on the line, toying with him. They stand over the table with their faces close, soft words mingling as they plot and plan. When the poster is done they hold it up together for the nearby tables to see.

THIS FRIDAY AT 8 P.M.

COME OUT AND HEAR

THE DISPLACEMENTS

IN CONCERT!!

AN OLD-TIME ROCK-AND-ROLL SHOW TO BENEFIT
THE DISPLACED RESIDENTS OF TOOLEY FARM

$10 AT THE GATE & FREE PARKING
DONATIONS ACCEPTED

The poster will be taken into Lortner for copying, then stapled on telephone poles, thumbtacked on bulletin boards, handed out in flyer form at churches and Costco in hopes of bringing in a respectable audience. Kaitlyn sashays the poster around the table, a hand on her flat stomach.

"Looks great," says Steve, cockily strolling in from a corner of the pav. He slides an arm around Kaitlyn and inserts himself between her and Gavin, whose posture slackens at the other man's appearance, air going out of his chest.

Steve catches Daphne's eye and gives her a knowing smile. *I've seen your credit report, lady.* His scrutiny feels almost pornographic. She shudders.

Steve offers Kaitlyn an open bag of trail mix. Not the birdseed from the commissary, but a luxury blend picked up during one of the couple's jaunts into town, the plastic heavy with chunks of white chocolate and candied fruit. Nearby kids ogle the bag.

"Should we go?" Kaitlyn asks him, crunching on a mouthful of the stuff.

"Give me a sec, babe."

He strolls over to Daphne's table, popping a malt ball between his lips and offering her the bag. She reaches in for two handfuls that she scatters on the table behind her. The kids pigeon for the chocolate and nuts.

He gets the message. "Here you go, guys," he says expansively, setting the bag down in the middle of the next table. Kaitlyn and Gavin start packing up the art supplies, the sizzle between them gone.

Steve folds his arms. "How you holding up?"

"Doing okay." Daphne's response is curt, Gavin-like.

He props his left foot up on a chair, splaying the denim vee of his crotch. "So what's the family plan? You folks shipping out of here soon?"

"We'll see. How about you two?"

A loose hand dangles from his thigh. "I figure we'll hang for a couple more weeks. We're both really fortunate, Kaitlyn and me. That's one of the reasons we've stuck around. To give something back, you know? Not that Houston's in any better shape than Miami."

She blinks.

"Sorry. Hits a little close to home, I guess." A palm to his forehead. "God, there I go again."

"Hey, no worries on my account," she says. Though they have to be deliberate, his juvenile taunts.

"What's Gavin's plan? Will you ship him back to Stanford after all this?"

She bites the inside of her cheek. "Unlikely," she manages to say.

"Shame he had to drop out. Good kid, lot of smarts. Gotta be really hard for that generation right now. I mean, after COVID, you know?"

"I suppose. Well anyway." Stretch of the arms, crack of the knuckles, anything to ward him off. "Thank you again for everything. You were very helpful."

"That's muh job, ma'am. Bein' helpful and all."

Exactly what he said that first time he helped her. Is this schlub actually *flirting*? His bland face and smirk-smiles remind her, in a perverse way, of her dead husband: Brantley brashly self-assured in the face of his family's economic ruin, Steve here to help the destitute yet unable to mask his condescension.

His girlfriend sidles up, saving Daphne a reply. "Can we go back?" Kaitlyn twists girlishly on her feet. Gavin has already left the pav, slouching back toward the library.

Steve finally releases his leg. He stands there looking between them, the same cheesy grin on his lips while Kaitlyn jiggles at his side. She claws at his wrist. "Babe, I'm serious. Let's go."

It starts to rain, a light tippling on the pavilion roof. Kaitlyn bends her knees as if needing a pee, Steve pats her butt with a lewd ostentation, though by now Kaitlyn is practically clawing at his arm. Another dorky hat-tip from Steve, a nervous fluttering smile from Kaitlyn before they leave the pav.

At the computer bank, a woman has abandoned her terminal seven minutes early. A message from Pilar sits in Daphne's inbox, brief and to the point: *Wired you this morning. 13.2K.*

Daphne leans against the back of the chair. Thirteen grand. She feels filthy rich. Her chest swells with the change, and she almost laughs. Around her sounds a pre-dinner hum, air thick with the cold smell of the crowd, the roof of the pavilion ornate with shadows of the rain.

She logs into her bank account—and almost chokes.

Balance: one dollar and twenty-four cents.

The wire hasn't cleared yet. Surely that's the issue.

But the scrolling list of transactions says otherwise. The deposit from Pilar is there, all thirteen thousand and change. The sum came in this morning at 9:17 a.m. Then a withdrawal, at 3:42 p.m. A large one, for nearly the entire balance of her checking account.

Daphne stares at the screen, willing the figures to reverse themselves, to divulge something other than the screaming truth: that her new fortune is already gone.

56.

Oklahoma City hasn't called. A problem. Back in Houston Tate had all the connections he needed, a network that kept his operation running like a high-end German auto engine. Out here in the wild it's a different story.

Not that he's lacking resources. With a carload of wildfire and his brainpower, Tate can get by just about anywhere if he has to. Hell, he almost took off on his own days ago. He's got an ID, wheels, limitless product, cash reserves pilfered from random Lunas. The world is there to eat.

You've got to suck that tender flesh out of the oyster shell while you can. Don't let the deadweights of the world hold you down. Fly like the falcon. Carpe your per diem. Reach and seize, me lads. Reach and seize.

First, though, he's got to get the hell out of Dodge. By now he's sucked the withered breast of Tooley Farm as dry as it can be sucked, shifted every shiftable dollar out of these losers' accounts and hidden his tracks as best he can. Only a matter of time before some stray drooler sniffs him out. By then he needs to be on the road. He figures he'll swing through Arizona to pick up Connor and go from there.

He stops by the library just before five. "Walk with me," he says. Gavin packs up and falls in beside him like a loyal dog. It's been days since Tate's last chitchat with the kid. Gavin's been avoiding him, probably blaming Tate for Jessamyn's little problem.

"So how are things going?" he asks fifty yards along. "Still got 'em lined up out the flaps?"

"I guess, though . . ."

"What?"

"I don't know, man. I just—that guy who shot himself, the rumors going around? I've been thinking we should stop."

Tate looks sidelong at him. "We're in the final stretch."

"But—"

"No sudden moves, understand? The timing's not right. When you've been in the business long enough you get a spidey sense about these things. We've got a big payout coming. You'll get your cut."

"Seriously?"

"Damn straight. Just hang in there for another three, four days, maybe a week. Then we close up shop and let these lovely enthusiasts get their fix somewhere else."

"There *is* nowhere else. That's the thing. These people depend on me."

"They depend on the wildfire. Believe me, the freaks always find an alternative. Maybe they'll scam a few oxy from the folks at Medical, or hitch into Lortner and hook up with some brown behind the McDonald's. Capiche?"

"I guess," Gavin says. "What about you guys?"

Finally Mr. Stanford gets it. "We'll be shipping out once I get rid of this load. You should, too." Gavin's step falters. Tate slings an arm over the kid's shoulder. "Hey, man. You made a nice chunk of change, learned a few things. That'll stand you well when you're back out in the world."

"Yeah, okay."

Gavin's eyes are moist, his lips pooched out as if he's trying to hold back a blubber.

"Don't be a pussy now."

"Probably just as well," Gavin mutters. "That guy freaked me out the other day."

"What guy?"

"That Latino dude. Kaitlyn didn't say anything?"

They stop walking. Tate's pulse spikes in his neck. "Tell me."

"He came into the library, got up in my face," Gavin says. "He bought a full sheet and wanted to know where I got it."

"When was this? When exactly?"

"It was—I don't know." He palms his forehead. "The day before that ICE raid I think, when they came and took everybody. Not him, though."

Tate counts on his fingers. "Thursday, Wednesday, Tuesday . . . this was five days ago and you're only telling me now?"

"Like I said, I told Kaitlyn. And don't we get our shit from Russians or Ukrainians or whatever?"

"*We?* Are you fucking—" He feels his hands spasm into fists. The kid backs away. "What did you tell him?"

"Nothing."

"You sure?"

"Hundred percent."

"And if Rain Holton or that Butch guy come poking around, what will you tell them?"

"I'm not a rat."

"Not saying you are, it's just . . ."

Tate's voice trails off as he puts it all together. Rumors of an overdose tied up in that murder-suicide, and now a thug acting just a tad too curious about his sourcing. How long until the guy drops a dime, or uses what he knows to curry favor with the next level up?

So, a slight adjustment in the plan: more caution, an acceleration. Calculated risk, exponential reward. Gavin will give his regulars a little bonus to keep them off his back for a few days, because the last thing they need is a bunch of junkies dropping dimes. Meanwhile Tate will wait to hear from Sam Hawley's contact in Oklahoma City. Four days max. He sells or he doesn't. Either way, he cuts and runs—maybe by himself this time.

A commitment's less important than a good exit strategy, me lads. Always have an exit strategy.

Let Gavin and Jessamyn be the last dogs. Tate will be the lone wolf, howling at the moon.

57.

"We got trouble in Crackertown." Butch, leaning into Trailer 1. He comes inside and glances at Nila.

"You want me to scoot?" she asks.

"Nah, you should hear this." He sits heavily across from Rain. "Went over there with Jed just now. Crackertown's a fortress. Clotheslines strung around a perimeter, guys searching anybody who wants to get through. They've put up a Sharpied piece of wood that says 'Checkpoint Charlie. No Trespassing.' Thought it was a joke at first but then these old boys step out with saps, and we—"

"Saps?" Nila says.

"Like blackjacks, these leather weapons weighted with rocks, homemade jobs but you wouldn't want one of those sumbitches upside your head. Then some other boys start floating in, this one fella steps up on Jed—"

"Seriously?"

"Thumps the chest, asks our business, like we're Crips and Bloods. Finally I get to asking them how they're doing, what we can do for y'all. We're just doing a walk-through is what I say, and they let us by."

Rain listens in disbelief. "That's not acceptable."

"Maybe not," says Butch, "but it's what it is."

She shakes her head. "We can't have that kind of thing going on in here, Butch, as if they own the damn quadrant. We need to send in the guard, get the perimeter taken down. Put a stop to this separatist nonsense before it gets any worse." She thinks of Vanessa, her youthful certainties. Maybe her daughter was right. Letting ICE haul those folks away only exacerbated tensions already thick on the ground—though it wasn't as if Rain had a choice. (Vani, screaming in her ear: *You always have a choice.*)

Butch's eyes harden.

"What?"

"Wouldn't go that way, Rain."

"I'm listening."

He puts up a finger. "For one, the vandalism, that incident with the waste. It was a godawful thing for that family to come home to. The daughter had a little cold so didn't smell anything. Apparently she crawled right in bed on top of a pile."

Nila makes a gagging sound.

A second finger. "Two, they see what happened to their tent as an attack on them. Not just on the family but on the whole community. They say it's a racial thing."

"Say again?"

"An attack on an ethnic minority, is how Biggs put it."

"You are absolutely fucking with me, Butch Jansen. An 'ethnic minority'?"

"Well, Rain, in here they actually are."

"But we have no idea who even did it. How does he know it wasn't one of his own people?"

"They're convinced it was an outsider." Butch shows his hands to forestall her protests. "I know, I know. Important thing right now isn't who did it but who they *think* did it. They've got all the paranoia ginned up about FEMA, the deep state. If the government can't protect us we'll protect ourselves kind of a thing. My worry is, we send the Oklahoma goddamn National Guard in there to take down some rinky-dink clotheslines we're going to look heavy-handed. Thus proving their point."

"Their point being . . . ?"

Butch shrugs. "Their point being they want the right to defend themselves. 'Protect our own' is how Biggs put it."

The phrase gives Rain a chill, conjures Branch Davidians and wingnut militias and QAnon. She looks at Nila.

"What do you think? Remember, we've got this concert coming up in three or four days, there'll be people floating through. Is this the right time to play it loose? Or should we be clamping down?"

Nila slots her eyes toward Butch. "Give it a few days. Show them we're taking the investigation seriously. Go down there and interview the family yourself, Rain. Make them see how outraged you are that someone would do something like this. Let them keep their little ropes up, we'll show them it doesn't bother us."

"I mean, compared to an ICE raid, a bucket of shit is pretty small potatoes," says Rain.

"As it were," Nila adds.

"For God's sake, don't say that!" Butch shouts, his eyes going comically wide. The women start to laugh, but his baleful expression sobers them up. "Don't minimize this. Don't pretend it's less than what it is. There are hundreds of people in that little pocket over there. Women, children, old boys mad as hell."

"But what are they trying to accomplish, Butch?" Rain parries. "What's the goal? You don't see the Cubans putting up barriers around Little Havana. The black folks in here aren't warning people off."

Butch's face goes slack. He looks almost disappointed in her. "Do I really need to explain, with everything that's happened in this country the last six, seven years?" The question sits between them, ugly but unavoidable. "They've got nothing more to lose than what they've already lost. You got to remember, Rain, these are their homes now. And they'll defend them any way they can."

Their homes. And that gets to Rain, lodges a shiv of empathy somewhere in a hardened part of her. To have your home desecrated like that, to be forced out of your meager shelter when you've already lost so much.

When Butch leaves the trailer she watches him out the streaked window, that wise head of his, the ambling gait. Nila is right: Rain needs to see this for herself. Keeping her distance, she visits the four corners of Crackertown in turn. At each crossing there is a barrier, a warning sign, a menacing guard. It would still be possible to enter the improvised neighborhood by dodging between the tents, but that's not the point.

Butch's assessment was spot on. Must be two hundred white folks inside the perimeter, many armed with saps, sticks, baseball bats. Could be a handgun or two slipped through.

The whole place coiled, primed to strike.

58.

On the morning of the concert, the Displacements meet for a sound check. They run through their set lists, test the amps, the PA, a breakfast group meanders in to listen, and it's all such a rush that Gavin barely notices at first how bad Jessamyn sounds. When the band hits Zeppelin's "Ten Years Gone" she misses some of the syncopated chords near the beginning. They have to start over, twice. Loida's getting pissed.

On the third try Gavin smiles encouragingly across the low stage, but Kaitlyn's blank look withers him. Her movements jerky, her rhythm off. When rehearsal ends she packs up her guitar and stalks out of the pav.

"What's up with that crazy girl?" Loida stacks up her buckets.

Gavin doesn't answer. Low blood sugar maybe, or she slept poorly or got in a scrim with her fuckface boyfriend. But he knows the truth.

He heads into Staff Camp, on her scent like a hound. Outside their tent he stands listening until he's sure she's alone. He parts the flaps. The hunger is already scraped off her face. That telltale look, the pinprick pupils.

"What's up, cutie?"

Tears pool in his eyes. "I'm done." He stanches his snot with the side of a hand, sniffs. "I'm not doing it anymore."

"You're quitting our band?"

He shakes his head. "I'm not selling for him anymore. Steve can fuck off."

She grabs his arm and pulls him down onto the cot. Her drugged-up body presses hot against his side. She places his hand on her knee and pets it like a cat. "Tell me," she says, stroking the fuzz above his wrist.

"It's hard to explain," he begins, but once he stutters out a few words it's not so difficult. Everything comes out in a flood: the jonesing buyers, an old man handing over his watch, the Galveston chick with the rancid smell. He explains his terror that a user will die on his watch. He looks at Kaitlyn. "Especially you."

She gazes up at him through a messy curtain of hair. Her eyelids flutter over her tiny pupils. "Me?"

Their noses are inches apart. "You're using every day, Kaitlyn, like three or four times. This shit is killing you. *He's* killing you."

"You're worried about me? Little old me?"

"We could leave, just the two of us. I'm nineteen now, and—"

"My big man." She reaches up and runs her fingers through his hair.

"Seriously though, seriously," words stuttering out, "I've got four thousand dollars. We could take the money and leave the shit with him and just go, get out of here. To the Bay Area maybe, or New York, who knows. You could get clean, we could start another band—"

"A band."

"And we could get jobs doing whatever. Waiting tables, I don't know."

"Gavin, I'm afraid to go to sleep." She squeezes his hair and locks eyes with him. "Last night I had this dream. I was making my dad's head out of clay, like I was your mom. I molded his whole head, did his ears with my fingers. But then I put my thumbs in his eye sockets and just pushed until his eyeballs shot out the back of his skull."

How gone she is. Her gaze flicks away but the intensity of her touch picks up. His breath hitches; he gasps. More than her fingertips now. She's massaging her whole hand up and down his forearm, basically stroking off his wrist.

"Let's do it," he says. "Me and you."

"Gavin. Gavin that is *so* sweet. And *so* tempting."

"Will you think about it though?"

"Already am, baby."

He's desperate to see it in her half-shut eyes. To escape this place with her. He's never felt desire like this, the simplicity of what might be. She shudders, lips so close. If he cocks his head four degrees they will meet, finally their softness on his—

"Hey, Gavin." The stroking pauses. She glances down at the bulging crotch of his jeans. "Are you a virgin?"

"Why would you say that?"

"Are you?"

He swallows. "Yeah."

"That's sweet." The upward look again.

"Why?"

"Just because . . . I don't know."

She falls into him and he runs his hands up her arms, around her back. The soft bump of her bra strap, the tautness of her ribs back there . . .

"Not here," she says, wriggling away. "Meet me after dinner, when it's getting dark. Over near Medical."

"But the concert—"

"We don't play till eight. That's plenty of time." She breathes against his face. Sour, the air of her sick and sweet at once. It reminds him of his dog.

59.

Daphne paces behind the Square, on hold with soft rock streaming over the line. In the middle of "Piano Man," a live bank representative comes on and she explains her dilemma.

"I can see the deposit made yesterday." She stares at the transaction record, printed out at the pavs. "Thirteen thousand plus. And then a wire transfer to some place called BancoGTM. All but a hundred and change, just—gone."

"You didn't make the transfer yourself?"

"Absolutely not."

"Didn't authorize a third party?"

"This is the only money I have in the world right now. Or was."

Daphne hears the play of keys.

"Ma'am, our system shows that someone with the correct credentials authorized the transfer."

"Excuse me?"

"Someone answered the security questions correctly, logged in, made the wire request."

"But who?"

"Our fraud department might be able to tell you more. Would you like me to put you through to them?"

"Okay. But where was the money wired to?"

More clicking. "To a bank in Guatemala City. I have the account number but we don't have access to the funds. The money may not even be there anymore. Often people will wire funds out of the country to one bank and then immediately move them to another."

The agent transfers her to someone in fraud control who promises to get back to her within forty-eight hours. If it turns out the funds were illegally withdrawn, he tells her, chances are good the full balance will be restored. Her money is insured through the FDIC, after all.

Insured.

Steve? She sees the sleazy insurance agent accessing her credit report, and therefore her social security number, her past addresses, who knows what else. He could have reconstructed the answers to Daphne's security questions from everything he saw, then logged into her bank account and wired all her money out of the country, leaving her none the wiser. Maybe he was flaunting his theft in the pav the other day, shoving his criminality, along with his crotch, right in her face.

But according to the bank, her account was accessed from abroad. Hard to imagine such a parochial man engineering a feat like that.

Guatemala City, though. So odd. She thinks of Luz and Bembe, the residents living in Little Antigua before the raid. The only other tenuous connection Daphne has to Guatemala came through that awful trip with Brantley. Nausea cresting in heavy waves, abandoned in a hotel room to puke for hours at a time; though her husband loved it there. The food and drink, the architecture, the rhythm of life—

A suspicion edges in, groping for purchase.

The surgery conference was something of a boondoggle, Daphne recalls, an all-expenses-paid junket with colleagues at Michigan to meet with counterparts in Guatemala City. There were seminars on technique, meetings with administrators, hospital visits. Afterward the two of them spent three days in Antigua. Brantley had been charmed by the colonial city, especially the luxury hotel repurposed from an old monastery. The Clintons once stayed here, he trumpeted; and one evening, at the height of Daphne's misery, Brantley had drinks with a group of local doctors. The pisco sours pitched him into a fevered vision of relocating to Guatemala, a fantasy she scarcely registered at the time. We could retire here, Daph. The cost of living is unbelievable! Invest in some real estate, buy a refinished colonial with full-time servants and a swimming pool in the courtyard . . .

Daphne hasn't thought about his zeal for the place in years. As usual with Brantley's big plans, nothing came of the scheme—perhaps.

In her notebook she finds the number for the crematory in Tallahassee, scrawled during that conversation with the hospital counsel. A woman answers on the first ring and Daphne asks about Brantley's ashes. There are no remains held under that name, the woman informs her. Daphne asks her to check the name against the hospital list. Same answer.

Her ears start to ring. She lucks into an open computer slot and starts searching in and around Antigua. The Hospital Nacional Pedro de Bethancourt, the Casa de Salud Santa Lucia: a mix of large public hospitals and smaller private facilities. The links lead her nowhere. Any American hospital would list departments and divisions, attractive pages featuring smiling surgeons and chief residents and senior administrators, with clear instructions for making contact. Most of the hospitals in Antigua don't even have their own websites. She jots down a dozen phone numbers before she has to log off.

Her halting Spanish moves her down the list as she burns through her prepaid minutes. With each connection she asks the operator about a doctor from the United States working in their facility. One gives her a brusque dismissal. Another laughs in her ear. A third puts her on hold and never comes back.

The fourth call is to a private clinic with a religious affiliation. A voice menu comes up in Spanish she can't understand. She hits zero and waits.

"Allo?" says a female voice.

"Estoy buscando un cirujano estadounidense en su personal," Daphne says carefully.

"Como?"

"Estoy buscando un cirujano esta—estadoun—"

"English?"

"Yes, thank you."

"You're looking for a North American doctor here?"

"Yes. His name is—"

"Doctor Hall?"

Daphne stops breathing.

"Brantley Hall, sí?"

"Sí." Daphne sees gray, red, black, white, starbursts and pinwheels of color. "Tell him it's Daphne."

"I get him for you."

No, she wants to say but can't. It was just a guess, after all, an impulse. But it's true. The phone is heavy in her hand but already the woman has come back. "He is with a patient. He calls you later. Daphne, sí? This your right number?"

"Sí," she manages to croak out. *He calls you later.*

She disconnects already framing her husband's uncanny resurrection, making tortured rationalizations on his behalf. *Brain injury. Psychosis. Amnesia.* You read about these things, like in Oliver Sacks. A piece of debris strikes Brantley on the head at the airport. He survives the ravages of Luna and is one of thousands rescued by the National Guard. Evacuation, a shelter, medical care, no identification. Somehow he makes his way to Central America, and then—

Or no. He believes we're dead, all of us. For weeks he strives to locate his family amid the national sprawl of mass displacement. Pulls out all the stops, searches for us high and low. Finally he can't take it anymore, the loss. Ravaged with grief, the bereft doctor leaves everything behind. He will start over somewhere else, put his skills to work saving lives in a still developing nation.

Or—or—or—

The absurdity of these justifications pitches her into a pure and howling rage. Hand clamping her mouth, rocking on the chair and uttering little screams into her closed throat, coming unhinged with the atrocity of it.

The coward. To abandon his children, leave his family penniless, fake his death, or at least allow everyone who knew him to believe and accept that he perished in the hurricane. And all to spare himself . . . what? Bankruptcy, opprobrium, humiliation. The appearance of weakness in the eyes of the world.

True, had Brantley somehow joined them in the early days of the evacuation, the family would be in similarly dire straits now. But at least they would have been together, the kids untraumatized by their father's supposed death, along with everything else they've endured.

And now this? Not only did he empty their bank accounts and engineer the total loss of their home—but he stole directly and calculatedly from *her*, from Daphne, *just yesterday*, wiring away a stash of money that might have stood the family back on its feet again in the coming months. Now even that reserve is gone, the sole legacy of her art.

The arrogance, to think he can get away with this, hiding out in Central America while his family lives in a displacement shelter in Oklahoma. He hasn't even bothered to change his name, as if he's showing off his resourcefulness for Daphne to admire. Did he think she wouldn't ultimately learn of his survival?

An appalling thought comes to her, as chilling, in its way, as the abandonment itself. Maybe Brantley *wants* to be found.

60.

Dry grass crunches beneath the soles of his battered Nikes as Kaitlyn leads him up the short rise to the same gap in the fence he saw all those weeks ago, when he learned his father died. He watches her perfect form bend and wriggle through. His shirt catches on a broken wire that rips his sleeve but his skin is untouched. Together they leave Tooley Farm behind and plunge forward into the darkening field. The dusk sky casts Kaitlyn as a faint shadow on the ground. He could reach out and touch her, the narrow width of her lower back. Steve can have his wildfire and his sad bullshit insurance life because I've got the finest—

No, that's not who she is, a mere piece of ass. She's more like the courtly lady in those troubadour poems he read in comp lit first quarter, the kind who messes with your head until you'd do anything to have her, no matter how humiliating. Lick her feet, scrub her floor while she kicks you in the face . . .

"Over here," she whispers. They approach an outcropping of rock in the shape of an iron, jutting up to block a wedge of stars. Still ahead of him, she glides around it. The air cool silk. She'll be quick with him, he speculates as he rounds the great stone, and she'll definitely be on top, no way she'd ask him to—

"Hey, Gavin."

A fist drills him in the gut. Gavin doubles over. Before he can lean away another punch catches him in the neck. Steve grabs the collar of his shirt and shoves him up against the rough surface of the rock.

"So let's hear about this plan of yours," he says.

"Wh-what plan?"

A knee rockets into his crotch. The pain blooms up through Gavin's balls and into the pit of his torso but he can't double over or even move his hands down there because Steve has him pinned by the shoulders with a forearm crushing his larynx. He moans, a pathetic baby sound silenced with a palm over his mouth. Steve's hands smell like metal and piss, his breath like dirt.

"The great escape, huh? The Bay Area? Sounds like a dream, man." Another knee, pulping him down there. "Kid's at Stanford and he's stupid enough to think he can steal my shit, get the girl, start a band . . ."

"I don't want your drugs, I just want out."

A scoff. "You're in this, kiddo. This is your life now, so suck it up and deal. You hear me?"

Gavin nods against the stone.

"Here's what's going to happen. You're going to walk back into that shitty refugee camp, you're going to go play your little concert, and tomorrow morning you're going to go back to the library with a nice stack of tabs and do what I told you. String them out. Understand?"

Steve lets go and Gavin slumps to the ground.

"Next time you try to weasel out of this I'll drive you to a nice cow field a few miles from here and I will put a fucking bullet through your skull." Steve squats down over him and Gavin feels the cold barrel of a gun against his temple. "But there's not going to be a next time, is there?"

"No."

"Say it like you mean—Who's there?"

A movement in the tall grass, over to the left. Something whizzes by. A rock. Another. They clatter against the boulder and ping off.

"Shit!" Steve yells as something hits his arm.

Now a volley of rocks, thrown by unseen hands. Steve staggers to his feet, gun swinging wildly. Gavin looks up and sees another rock strike him in the neck. Kaitlyn squeals as one hits her in the side. Steve grabs her by the arm and together they run out of the clearing, his gun held uselessly at his side. Gavin huddles on the dirt with his arms shielding his head. The pain worms through his groin and stomach and up along his rib cage and into his throat, still sore from the pressure of Steve's arm. He slips a hand down the front of his pants, expecting to feel blood, shredded cartilage, who knows. But everything's still there at least, intact but throbbing.

He senses a presence above him. Shape of a kid against the sky. His eyes unblur.

Manny, from the library, holding a rock the size of an apple. Next to him Tyrique sucks at the nub of a popsicle.

"Yo. You dead?" Manny says.

"I wish," Gavin manages to answer. Other forms loom through the late dusk. Four, five kids crowd in as he sits up, elbows on his knees. Whispers begin—*sister's a Crow scout . . . his brother's Elephant*—speaking in a code Gavin doesn't understand.

Manny asks, "Why's that dude have a piece?"

"Huh?"

"There's no guns allowed in Tooley Farm. That's what my pops said. But that dude's got a piece."

Gavin says nothing.

"Anyways this is Bear Squad's new HQ. You gotta clear out."

"I can do that."

Gavin gets on all fours to push up. The pain slides from his groin down his legs, which are weak and trembly. Tyrique reaches into his pocket and pulls something out.

"You having this," he says.

Gavin takes it. An oblong packet, cold and squishy.

"His second popsicle," says Manny. "We're supposed to take one but they always give my brother two. He wants you to have it."

"Eat it *now*," Tyrique orders, staring.

With his teeth Gavin rips off the seam and spits it to the ground. The popsicle is too far gone to hold by the stick so he slurps from the cellophane, freeze-pop style. A tangy grape, still frozen enough to cool the sour heat in his throat. He downs the slush in seconds and shoves the wrapper into his pocket.

"Thanks, man," he says, but Tyrique is already mingling with the other kids, issuing orders left and right.

Gavin hobbles back toward the fence with the popsicle stick wedged between his teeth and a sugar buzz stanching some of the pain. How will he share a stage with Kaitlyn after she's shredded him like this? But he can feel the adrenaline surging in anticipation, a counterpart to her opioid high. If she wants to burn her life away, that's her choice. Let her die driving off into the sunset with Cowboy Steve.

As he nears the perimeter fence he senses movement on either side. The hairs sizzle up on the back of his neck. Steve again, another sucker punch. His arms go up to fend off the attack, which never comes.

He looks to his left and sees the upper half of Tyrique's head. Beyond him, three or four other kids push along through the field; to the right, same thing. And he understands. Bear Squad is guiding him home. The protective phalanx breaks up only when he reaches the fence line and the kids disperse, jackrabbits bounding through the grass.

61.

Rain had her doubts, but the concert committee has knocked this thing out of the park. Thunderstorms are in the forecast for later; for now, the air is dry, the sky clear. Scents of cinnamon and cider waft along the avenues and the pavs glow like luminescent mounds. Local farms have donated dozens of pumpkins and hay bales that line the path from the parking lot all the way to the improvised ticket booth set up by Pav3. Once inside the venue, visitors can purchase cups of beer or mulled cider and spice donuts, the bills collected in tin boxes by volunteers.

With a pang she thinks of Vanessa. She should be here to see this little world at its best. This one magical night, Tooley Farm dazzles.

The parking lot attendants wave their flashlights as the first visitors come in by car. Three buses disgorge the elderly residents of a retirement community in town (Butch's doing, a sweet-talking call to the director of the place). The visiting crowd combines forces with residents to swell the pavs. The booming music thrills the children vying at Range. Their laughter spills through the streets.

By eight thirty the Displacements are well into their first set, a blend of classic rock and rhythm and blues. Rain leans against a tent pole in the back of the pav watching the crowd, old folks placidly taking in Creedence Clearwater's "Born on the Bayou" like it's Beethoven.

The one unexpected sour note comes from inside the band itself. Not many here will notice or even much care, but Rain has heard the Displacements rehearse often enough to be alert to a clunky show. The drummer is doing her best to keep them all together but losing the beat in certain spots. Gone is the group's smooth coherence, the attunement she's come to admire. Even Leonard's off tonight.

She scans their faces, looking for the source of the discord. Gavin, the Stanford boy thumping away on his bass without once looking up; and across the stage from him, Kaitlyn, oodles of talent in those slender fingers though tonight there is a halting stiffness to her performance. All in all a lack of blend. If Rain didn't know better she'd assume the two had never met.

She strolls away from the pavs up through the maze of supply tents south of Medical, saying hello to residents, stopping to chat with an elderly couple. The husband complains about the volume of the amplifiers. Another forty-five minutes, Rain assures them, and suggests a visit to Medical for cotton balls so he can plug his ears.

The moon glows down, blanching the tops of tents. On Nevada Street she comes upon two men heading out of Crackertown. One is Chester Biggs, the other she's met once or twice. Last name Pearson, she recalls.

"Evenin'," says Biggs, saccharine sweet. Pearson sweeps off his ball cap and gives her a little bow, a gesture that pushes one of his backpack straps off his shoulder. He nudges it back on as he straightens. The backpack's weight settles at the bottom of his spine with a dull metallic clunk. Something heavy in there; Rain thinks of horseshoes and hammers.

She plays it light. "You guys enjoying the concert?"

The men trade looks.

"Not to my taste, if I'm being perfectly honest," says Biggs.

"Same," Pearson agrees.

"You know what?" Rain says. "Ditto."

The men laugh, too readily. Another gentle clink from Pearson's pack.

"Where you guys headed?"

"Wherever the hell we want," says Pearson.

"Hey now." Biggs, with an easy grin and a placating hand on Pearson's arm. "We're friends here, ain't we? Neighbors and all."

Rain says nothing.

"We're just a couple old boys out for an evening stroll," Biggs continues. "Might be we head to the concert, might be we hit that refreshment stand by Main Gate for a coupla beers. For now we'll keep on keepin' on. That be all right with you, Mizz FEMA?"

The men don't move, their postures casual and menacing at the same time. Behind them the length of Nevada Street stretches empty into the night. A song ends back at the pavs to a burst of applause.

A soldier rounds the corner, a specialist from the 45th out on security patrol. A white girl with her hair bunched tight beneath her cap. Rain almost asks her to stop and help her search the two men when the specialist's gaze flickers toward Biggs. Her soldier's eyes crinkle at the edges—in kinship, in recognition, whatever; Rain doesn't want to know.

"Evenin'," Biggs says, touching his brim.

"Good evening, sir, sir," she trills; a slight hesitation, then, more formally, and to Rain: "Ma'am."

Rain nods. Pearson turns to watch the soldier pass with an ostentatious leer. The specialist is gone as quickly as she appeared.

Biggs tilts his face to the sky. "Looking to storm later."

"Oh yeah?" Rain says.

"Your people might want to check weather-dot-com," he says contemplatively. "Looks to be a big one."

"We'll do that," she says, and the men stroll off. A laugh from the next corner; at her expense, no doubt. Biggs turns his head and gives her one last look, his eyes shadowed beneath the sagging bulbs.

62.

Range isn't the same. A spark is missing, and even captures have lost their dangerous thrill. Crow Squad had to accept some remnants from disintegrated squads, slow kids who don't speak Spanish. It's just hard for Mia to accept it all, the guilt, the loneliness, the endless drag of a Luz-less life. Which doesn't mean things can't get worse.

During the concert everyone's getting ready for round two. The squads gather around the barn waiting for the guides to announce the Order of the Night. A bunch of kids have left to get donuts but not enough to ruin the game. The music carries through Tooley Farm. The air is at its warmest in weeks, reminding Mia of the last days before Luna came.

While the guides argue, a big group gathers near the barn, listening to someone. Isaac, a leaper from Tiger Squad, stands in the middle of a circle, describing a fight he saw earlier outside the fence. Two white guys, one older, one younger. The older one, Isaac claims, had a gun.

"What kind?" someone asks.

Isaac shrugs. "Pistol's all I know."

"Wait, who'd you say has a gun?" Kyler Biggs demands as he barrels up to the edge of the circle.

"Don't know his name," Isaac says. "He's a volunteer, works at the pavs. But I know the other dude. He was . . ." Isaac spins around and points at Mia. "Her big brother."

Mia looks behind herself, then back at Isaac. "My brother what?"

"Got his ass whupped."

"What are you even *talking* about?"

"The guy was shoving his piece right in your brother's neck. Kneed his rack, said he'd off him if he stopped selling."

"Selling what?"

"The shit he deals in the library. Wildfire."

Mia looks at him blankly.

"Drugs, dumbass." A sly smile. "Your big bro's a dope slinger."

"He's my *half* brother and it's not true."

"Sure as shit is."

"No, it's not." She stomps her right foot.

"Yes, it is." Isaac stomps his left, mocking her. Some laughs.

"It's true, Mia." A different, quieter voice: Hamid, the guide of Crow Squad. "Everybody knows it," he goes on. "Gavin's been selling that shit since like week three. People just didn't want to tell you because you're so *sensitive*."

Snickers. She sees the difference in Hamid's eyes. Why is he being like this? Doesn't he know she's one of his most loyal scouts? As the insult sinks in Mia senses a change among the kids in her squad—her supposed friends. It's a lesson she learned from Charlize and the SCBs but forgot, until now: once they turn on you it happens fast, and all at once.

She wishes Luz were here to defend her. "What does that mean?"

"Everybody in your family tries to get away with shit. And when I say shit, I mean shit."

A few low *ooohs* from the Crows, because by now they probably all know what Hamid is talking about. Kyler gets up in Hamid's face.

"Say again?"

Hamid, arms folded, just shrugs.

"You say something about *shit*, Mohammed?"

"The name's Hamid," he snaps back.

"Tell me what you just said to her."

Mia stares at Hamid, willing him to stay silent. Because if he doesn't . . .

"Wasn't those Guatemalans who fucked up your tent," he tells Kyler, giving in, but Mia can tell it's not because he's scared. It's because he's angry. Cold, hard, furious. "It was her." He points at Mia, and *everyone* stares. "We lost Luz and Hector and everybody else, and now Crow Squad totally sucks because of *her*."

Just then the guides swing around the corner of the barn, their conclave adjourned. They announce the Order of the Night and the squads organize themselves, but Mia feels frozen to the gravel. Her throat squeezes shut, everything seethes and spins.

Crow Squad is done with her. Finished. No one will look at her or talk to her and when Mia tries talking to them they pretend she's not even there. The idea that the Crows can just *ignore* her after all these weeks—

"Why are you guys doing this to me?" she calls after them. No one stops. "*Guys!*" she screams, squeezing together every molecule in her body. Finally Hamid turns around. The others wait for him.

"They're making a new remnant squad tomorrow," he says, sounding bored. "You can join that one."

Mia's fists tighten. Nobody wants to be in a remnant because remnants are made up of the newest and stupidest kids and they're eliminated early every night.

"It's just a game, Mia," Hamid says. "Don't be so fragile."

"It's not just a game." *It's everything.*

Hamid turns away, and the Crows leave her there, squadless and alone.

A blow to her shoulder. "Ow!" The impact pitches her forward to the ground. She catches herself with her hands as Kyler Biggs walks by with his posse. She can't tell which one pushed her but it doesn't matter.

Looking back, Kyler spits off to the side, glaring down as the loogey hits the ground near Mia's nose. He gives her a hideous smile. "Now you're the one in a world of shit."

63.

From the dark of the pav, Daphne watches, listens, frets. The bass hangs from her stepson's shoulders like an anvil. Gavin hasn't looked up once during "Rock You Like a Hurricane," the first song in a hurricane-themed sequence that delights the audience. But his performance is sullen and self-conscious. Cautious, as if he's suffering from a bout of stomach flu—or a psychic shock of some kind. Maybe Brantley, rather than returning Daphne's call, has reached out to his son somehow, before she could decide how, when, or even whether to tell him his father is alive.

She has been dreading the coming conversation. How did Dad survive Luna? No idea. How did he get to Guatemala? Beats me. Is he coming to get us? Your guess is as good as mine.

"Daphne." Flo appears at her side. Mia, her face a slathered wreck, clings to her grandmother's arm. "We need a word with you, dear."

"Can it wait?"

"No," Flo warns, "it can't."

What now? She follows them out past the drinks stand to an equipment cage. The Displacements remain in view beneath the pavs, the musicians posed like models in a distant diorama.

"So, what is it?"

Flo looks at Mia. "Tell your mother what you just told me."

Mia wipes a line of snot off her lip. "I got kicked out of Crow Squad and it wasn't my fault, I didn't even *do* anything, but now no one will talk to me and it's like the SCBs all over again."

"Mia, slow down," Daphne says, trying to be patient this time. "You're having some trouble with this game, the other kids?"

Flo touches Mia's shoulder. "Honey, you need to tell her what they said about Gavin."

"What about him?" Daphne says.

Her daughter bites her lip.

"Mia, will you just—"

"He's a drug dealer," Mia says.

Daphne laughs easily, dismissing it. "That's ridiculous."

"Daphne, you need to listen," Flo says.

"Mom, it's actually true."

"That's a crazy accusation, Mia."

"He gets them from that Steve guy who helped you with money. Plus his girlfriend, the guitar player." Mia points to the stage.

Something tightens at the base of Daphne's spine. "That's not possible."

"It's why he works at the library. People come in and he gives them certain books and the books have drugs in them. They're in sheets, like stickers."

"Oh come on."

"Isaac saw them. He said Steve had a gun and was pointing it at Gavin before the concert. Hamid said everybody knows Gavin deals drugs."

"Then Hamid is lying."

"Hamid doesn't lie. He's a guide."

"Mia, stop it."

"Daphne," says Flo, and the sharpness in her mother-in-law's voice stills her. Mia wraps her middle and taps her foot, and in her daughter's familiar gestures Daphne discerns the awful truth of it.

"He had cash that day," her mother-in-law says. "At the Denny's, the day we went into Lortner. My credit card wouldn't go through. Gavin paid for our whole lunch and gave a generous tip. I was too upset to ask where the money came from. But now . . ."

But now?

A sting in her eyes as epiphany hits. How close the apple has fallen from the tree. She backs against the cage and her fingers claw through the diamonds in the chain link. She sees that girl at Medical who overdosed. Vacant stare, grayed skin, scratching at the nothing on her arm.

"We have to report this," she eventually says. "We have to tell the authorities. I want those two arrested, taken away."

Flo grips her arm. "Honey, think about what you're saying. Gavin is nineteen. An adult. If you tell these people he's been . . . well, who *knows* what will happen to him. He could spend the rest of his life in prison."

"That's his problem."

"We have to talk to him," Flo says calmly. "We'll wait until after the concert and do it then. We'll keep him away from those people, and we'll do everything we can to help him." She pauses, then with meaning says, "We're a family. That's our job."

A family with something rotten at its core, only now exposed to the light. She wants to tell them about Brantley and yet what good would this do right now? Would it bring Flo joy, to know her son abandoned her? The unshared weight of this knowledge, a horrific revelation about Gavin—

"I need some time," Daphne says. "I need to think."

Flo takes her granddaughter's hand and they drift off, leaving Daphne alone against the cage, waiting for the music to end.

After the concert she lurks outside the pavs. When Steve appears she follows him twenty feet back, focused like a predator on the top of his spine. Her hands itch to throttle him, or plant a knife blade in the soft muscle between his ribs. That backbone willfully straightened, that cocky strut, the lofty glances aside at his fellow residents that again remind her uncannily of Brantley.

She tracks him into Staff Camp and down the last length of path to his tent. He pauses to untie the flap and turns at her approach. His ready smile fades.

"Daphne," he says.

"He's done."

"Say again?"

"Gavin is done. He's out of whatever you've gotten him into."

He gives her one of his puerile smirks. "That's not how this works, babe."

"'Babe'? Are you serious?"

"It's between Gavin and I, we're business partners. It's none of your concern."

"Between Gavin and me, and it most certainly is my business. Back off or I'm turning you in."

"Like hell you will," he snarls. After a quick look around, he reaches back and pulls out a gun, a snub-nosed pistol in a glossy black. He tucks it back into his pants just below his navel, the barrel pointing down at his crotch. He folds his arms and spreads his legs, going full tough guy on her.

Daphne arches her brow, looks down at the gun with a sniff. "What, you're going to shoot me now? Kill my son, my whole family?"

"Hey, if that's what it takes." He pats the pistol grip.

"Try me, then." Daphne thrusts out a hand and points over the fence, resolved now to flush this man out of their lives for good. "I'll go out there and tell the National Guard if I have to. You need to pack up your drugs and your overcompensating little pistol and you need to leave this place. Now."

"And if I don't? Your stepson's the one who's been selling directly. Just ask the junkies." A harsh laugh.

"If my son gets hauled in for this then he'll face the consequences just like you." Though repulsed, she steps closer. "First, though, I'll let him explain how he was coerced into dealing by a washed-up insurance salesman who preys on displaced hurricane victims."

A glimmer of doubt in his eyes.

Careful, Daphne warns herself.

"There were witnesses, you know," she says, "out there at the rock. A dozen kids saw you hit him, choke him. They heard every word you said." She takes a breath to calm herself, and as the night air sweetens her lungs she feels a surge of protective love for Gavin. "And you know what? Those kids adore Gavin. They genuinely love him, something you'll never feel from another human being."

His head jerks away. For a moment she believes he will reach for his gun. She believes she has pushed him too far. A shooting spree: he's just the type.

But then his chin tilts up and he gives her the same arrogant look she'll see from Gavin sometimes, that she once endured from Brantley. Masked insecurity, injured pride.

She shows him an index finger. "You have one hour."

64.

For a good five seconds Tate comes close to pulling out his gun and putting a nice hole in that narrow back so he can watch the bitch bleed out on the grass. He doesn't move for a while after she disappears, poised on the edge of a gaping pit, a lonesome knowledge that the hierarchies have all flipped. Here's this broke-and-woke widow getting up in his face, all over the fate of some sad-ass college dropout who doesn't even share her genes.

He pictures his own spindly son. From the pavs he hears Jessamyn shredding the lead-in lick to "Should I Stay or Should I Go." Tate picks up on the tune's question in her voice and decides to take it personally.

He goes inside and starts whipping his belongings into a bag. Once he's packed, he does a last sweep of the tent then slips a wad of cash beneath Jessamyn's pillow. Two grand, enough to get her settled somewhere else. He hesitates by her cot, slapping ten full sheets of wildfire against his palm. If he leaves her nada he'll be forcing her involuntary withdrawal, the illness and delirium and shakes, the days of sweating pain. Better to gift her a little for the near term. A hundred doses, give or take. At the rate Jessamyn's going, the supply should last her two weeks, three at a stretch, then she'll have to taper. Her problem, not his. He slips the tabs beneath the pile of bills and puffs up her pillow. Two minutes later, as final applause thunders from the pavs, he leaves Tooley Farm for the last time.

Once on the two-lane he calls his ex-wife.

A long, tired sigh. "What do you want, Tate?"

"You guys still in Tucson?"

"Sad but true."

"Thought I'd head out your way and hang awhile. I can be there tomorrow."

"Tate—"

"I've got a good thing going, some real cash coming in. I figure I'll find a place nearby. Take Connor weekends and give you guys a break." He hears the baby squawking in the background.

Nora blows into the receiver. "Tate, don't. I can't take your bullshit. And Connor, he won't know the difference."

He starts to object but clamps his lips shut. Just like that his big plans deflate.

"How is he?"

"We found him a nice place for his OT."

"That's good."

"Look, I should go. She's being fussy tonight."

Tate says nothing.

"Don't come, Tate. You aren't needed here." She disconnects.

Fine then. *Steer clear of the needy ones, me lads. The needlers, the depressives, the time-sucks. Spread your wings while they're beakin' at their own.*

He sets a hand on his gym bag. A hundred sheets of wildfire in there, and thousands within feet of him as he drives. Tate can feel the drug's potency, powering the car like a second engine. Millions on these four wheels. Be a shame to waste it all on a city full of anonymous strangers.

He props his phone on the dashboard and speed-dials a Houston number. When she answers he hears no words on the line, only her thin breaths.

"Hey, Liberty."

"Holy smokes. Tate?" The syllables scraped like ulcers from her throat. "That really you?"

"Sure is."

"Well wowee. You here in Texas?"

He grins, wrist warming the steering wheel. "On my way. And I've got a feast for you, Liberty. Turkey, stuffing, all the trimmings. Thanksgiving's in two weeks."

Those string bean arms, that translucent skin around her jaw bones. Maybe he'll actually do it. Take his junkie pet out for a turkey dinner in one of the northern suburbs that's still intact, put some mashed potatoes on her fragile bones. Maybe she can hook him up with a new clientele.

He notices her silence. "What?"

"I'm clean now, Tate. Going on three weeks."

"Jesus." He swallows. "Good for you I guess."

"I got a good church I go to, Riverbend. A community, you know? People are building things back down here."

"Right."

He swerves to avoid a smear of opossum.

Liberty says, "It's kinda funny."

"What?"

"You and me."

"How so?"

"When we texted a while back I somehow thought you'd come home to Houston. Swoop in, hook me up. Instead you were all, 'Tough shit, Liberty. I'm hell and gone.' I mean, not in those words but that's what you meant. I knew you weren't coming."

"Hey, if I could've I would've."

A big raindrop slaps the windshield. The on-ramp to I-35 is coming up on the right. If he wants to head south and back into Texas this is it. He needs to turn pretty much now.

"No, brother, it's a good thing," Liberty says with a gravelly laugh. "It was you cutting me off that finally drove me into rehab. Guess I should thank you for not being there when it counted. No offense."

"None taken." Tate passes through the interchange, staying on course.

The rain begins in earnest. Big splotches hammer the windshield, with lightning strikes every quarter mile. Tate flips on the radio. Every station has dissolved into emergency alerts. Three long staticky blares, a flatline tone, a robotic voice that comes in short bursts into the dark of his car—*six miles south-southwest of . . . combination of unusually warm air and . . . addition to the tornado, destructive hail has been reported in the vicinity . . . away from doors and windows and take . . .*

The first hailstones fall in a loose scatter. Spits of ice no larger than cherry pits ping the hood and windshield. Now golf balls, riddling off metal and glass. Few more miles and he'll be past it. He accelerates.

Acts of God. They spent a whole day on them at Southerly orientation, sorting though the exclusions and the inclusions and the emergency riders for hail. The PowerPoint included a quote from an old law dictionary that Tate afterward taped to his monitor: *In the law of insurance, an insurer is not liable to indemnify the assured against loss occasioned by an act of God; and a common carrier, being an insurer, is similarly privileged.* More than once he's read the sentence aloud to desperate clients, enjoying the panicky protests once they learn that no, Wanda, your homeowner's policy won't cover the utility pole spiked through your garage roof, that actually, Frank, your auto rider excludes the landslide that buried your new pickup. If you buy a house a hundred yards from the ocean don't expect Nationwide to rebuild after a hurricane takes it down. If you park your gold-plated Model S Tesla in an Oregon forest during a megadrought don't come bitching and moaning to Allstate when a fire reduces it to ash.

Tate reaches for the console and switches to *Me Lads*. All the way back to the first episode that hooked him. As the sky falls around him the voice of Jace Parkinson carries him through the thick of the storm.

Look at you. Y' feel stomped down by it all. Replaced by the dolts. Rejected by the ladies. Usurped by the unqualified. Aye, that's what this is, me lads. A usurpation. You're canceled, you're kicked in the teeth. And now, just as you're wrigglin' there like a worm on the ground, manhood drained by the world, you hear a voice.

THE GREAT DISPLACEMENT
A DIGITAL CHRONICLE OF THE LUNA MIGRATION

▶ JOCK BALTUSROL, CHIEF EXECUTIVE OFFICER, GULFLAND GASCO

We are in the cockpit of a Cessna 152 that Jock takes up monthly to survey the company's oil fields around the Permian Basin. Following his defeat in the race for US Senate, Jock returned to Gulfland with an ambition to build the company into the world's top producer of oil and natural gas. He is almost there.

Play audio file:

Not much to look at but right now we're producing ten
million barrels a day out here, from Midland in the east to
El Paso in the west, Tucumcari up in New Mexico down south
to the Mexican border around Laughlin Air Force Base.
Seventy-five thousand square miles producing. And ten
million barrels? That's more than the Ghawar field in Saudi
by a long shot. Biggest goddamn oil field in the world, and
no sign of slowing down.

Wish I could show you the depth of the shale, too. The
Spraberry, the Delaware, these layers go down two thousand
feet. There's a reason they call it fossil fuel. When our boys
drop their bits in the Avalon shale we're going through rock
that's a quarter billion years old. So you can buy all the
Teslas you want, eat fake meat until your soybean cows come

home. Fact is, America's now the biggest producer of crude in the world and we're expanding operations all the time.

And mostly that's thanks to Hurricane Luna. There was a bottleneck for a while back in the teens, not enough pipeline to get out all the crude we could extract. But now we got pipe running down to four deepwater ports on the Gulf Coast. Pretty soon Brownsville will be shipping more than Houston ever did. It's the one thing Houston's still good for, getting US crude out to sea. Without Luna, though, I reckon we'd still be at seven, eight million barrels. Big irony that a storm like that ends up increasing domestic fossil fuel extraction by fifty percent. Joke's on the Sierra Club, I guess. But those Lunas? Let me tell you, those folks work like dogs.

Not like all those jobs will last. You see that line of trucks? Two hundred self-driving tankers in a line straight as an arrow, just a hundred feet between them. No drivers. Fully automated macrofleet, operating twenty-four seven. Each one of those things makes thirty runs a day from field to pipeline. We're automating our distribution hubs, too. Biggest innovation in commercial transport since Malcom McLean invented the modern shipping container.

What's that? Safety? Hey, we've had maybe ten accidents in the last six months. Back in 2021 we had two hundred deaths on Route 285 down there. They called it "Death Highway." Last year we had five times the traffic but only thirty-two fatalities. And that's all down to innovation, to the investments Gulfland has made in safety, in protecting our workers and the communities we serve here in the basin.

We don't compromise on that shit either. It's what I tell my kids, my grandkids. At Gulfland, we're in the business of saving lives. We want a future just as much as everybody else.

▶ DR. ZEBULON CRANE, PASTOR

Riverbend Church sits on Chimney Street in sight of the husk of Williams Tower. Pastor Zeb has lived in Houston for seventy-three of his seventy-five years, having returned to the city of his birth following an extended period in Baton Rouge after Luna. He died just weeks after making this recording.

Play audio file:

Transcript:

There are still people here, thousands of them. Sometimes the sanctuary is as full as it was any given Sunday before Luna. Our congregants are more scattered now, but they worship just as hard. When you invite Christ into your life it doesn't matter if the earth lies salted beneath your feet. What matters is the abundance of your charity toward your neighbor.

We learn in Genesis that Adam was called to exercise dominion over all the earth. "Be fruitful and multiply, and fill the earth and subdue it; and have dominion over the fish of the sea and over the birds of the air and over every living thing that moves upon the earth." Lot of evangelicals hold that God is telling us to take what we want regardless of the consequences. That climate change is a hoax propagated by Satan, that Satan is using catastrophes like Luna to prepare for the end times. Our task as God's chosen ones is to multiply, subdue, dominate. Tear up the earth, destroy the air and water.

But there's another path. I was one of the original
signatories to the declaration of the Evangelical Climate
Initiative way back in 2006. I've been thinking about these
issues for a long time. As Christians, I believe we're called
to care about the climate because we love all of creation.
To damage this universe made by God is an offense against
God Himself. I really believe that. Christians must be
stewards of this earth.

Before the hurricane, when we were six thousand strong,
Riverbend was already working on climate care around the
world. We'd send our young people on missions of
environmental stewardship, to participate in reforestation
in the Amazon, say, or to clean up the banks of rivers in
India or the shores of African lakes.

Now we're turning inward, tending our gardens here. We're
scraping off condemned houses, we're planting native grasses
and wildflowers and trees. Reclaiming this ruined city from
within.

There's a lady comes here alone every Sunday, recovered
addict named Liberty. Such a musical name, and she has the
voice of an angel to go with it. At Riverbend we got her to
join the choir and she started writing her own songs. There
was one song Liberty wrote early on, it was about trash
pickup. I wish I could remember the lyrics. "Bottle by bottle
and bag by bag," something like that, but better,
more poetic. I remember the melody, though. Let me hum it
for you.

65.

The closing chords of the third encore—the Rolling Stones, "Gimme Shelter"—fade into cheers and whistles, but when Gavin takes his final bow the pain flares again. The fact that he made it through the concert at all is a miracle. He watches Kaitlyn case her guitar and slip out through the flaps behind the stage before the crowd can swarm.

"You got groupies," Leonard observes wryly as he twists off his mouthpiece.

Kids from the library cluster at the edge of the stage. Gavin lets them thwack the strings of his bass so they can experience the power of the amp. For a while he gives pointers on how to slide up the neck, how to slap, while Loida shows off her roughed-together drum kit. The impromptu master class takes his mind off his lingering pain.

Though not for long. Back at the family tent, Daphne waits for him, wearing out a patch of dead grass. From inside he hears Mia wailing, Grandma Flo trying to soothe her off a tweeny cliff. Daphne stops her pacing and blocks his way in.

"What's wrong with Mia?"

"She got kicked out of her squad."

"Bummer."

"And she feels bad for tattling."

"What do you mean?"

"On you."

Everything goes still. "Great show," someone says strolling by, but Gavin can't look away from his stepmother.

"He's gone, Gavin."

"Who?"

"Your dealer or supplier, whatever the hell he was." Daphne is seething; he's never seen her like this. "I told him if he didn't leave tonight, I'd turn him in."

"You didn't—" His balls start to ache again. "He'll kill me. Maybe you. Maybe *them*." He gestures at the tent.

"No he won't."

"How do you know?"

"I just know, believe me. Men like that . . ." She waves a hand. "Anyway I watched him through the fence while he drove away, just to be sure."

He pictures Kaitlyn returning to her tent. She'll understand that Steve has left with their car, all the money, all the wildfire—

"Wait, just wait." He squeezes at the roots of his hair, takes random steps in front of the tent.

"You've been through so much, Gavin." Her voice softens. "You've lost your mother, your father, you lost your college and your home. I know it hurts, and I can't imagine going through all that." She comes closer. "But you have a choice here, Gavin. What you do right now, I mean *right now*, may determine the rest of your life. Let me help you."

He blinks. He wants to hit her, like actually physically beat the shit out of her, but the look Daphne is giving him right now is so fucking *motherly* that he can't bring himself even to clench a fist.

"I don't need your help." He pushes roughly past her, ignoring the pleading-mommy look on her face.

Kaitlyn. Who knows what shape he'll find her in. It will be up to Gavin to hold her down to earth, help her push through the coming days and weeks, get her sober and ready to face the real world again. With Steve gone, Gavin's the only one in here who knows her, the only one who cares. The thought brings a terror and a thrill. Gavin will be her person now, because other than him, Kaitlyn has nobody.

He reaches their tent in Staff Camp and sees her guitar. The body of the thing sticks out into the avenue uncased, leaving only the neck hidden beneath the flaps. He stares at the exposed portion. It's supposed to storm later tonight. She would never leave her Gretsch out like this. It must be forty-five minutes since the concert ended, maybe an hour.

He goes inside and his soul unzips. In the tent there is no source of light save the terrible glow of her, skin pale as a crescent moon, the shape her body was holding in her last moments. Eyes open and fixed, mouth gaped and lips speckled with foam. Her frozen hands clutch a sheaf of tabs, a dozen or more. At least half of them peeled off from the top sheet. He imagines how it happened. One dose, a second, her exuberance as she gobbled up more, no one to stop her this time . . .

He turns his back on her and goes outside. Staff Camp is empty of residents. Gavin is alone. He takes a few steps and looks around, helpless. He goes back inside and stands there staring down at her. Leaves the tent for a second time and walks almost halfway back to his own family's tent before turning around and going back to hers.

He sits within the arc of her folded body and slips a sheet of wildfire from the small stack in her grip. He peels off a tab and puts it on his tongue, tasting the first sweet sting. He removes another tab and a third, as Kaitlyn must have done, and lays them next to the first, and now a fourth, a fifth, a sixth, and really it's as easy as licking stamps, and he is all but ready to swallow and do himself—when in one movement his upper teeth bite down on the back of his tongue and snowplow the tabs off his taste buds and into the front of his mouth where his lips gather them together and spit them out in one bitter wad onto the floor of the tent.

He gets a kick anyway. Wildfire, a good dose now goosing his system. Even that quick bump and the world seems to open. He sees Tooley

Farm from above, the antlike movements of the IDPs, the shabby expanse of the pavs, and he absorbs the heat of the drug as he sits back against her. Kaitlyn's bony hip pushes into the middle of his spine. He shivers. She is colder now, the chill of her death burning out through her clothes.

66.

Hours before dawn, Rain scans the radar. An ugly splotch of red covers the western half of the state. Bulletins warn of cumulonimbus clouds, rotating walls. A cyclonic line extends from the Kansas border down the I-35 corridor to Dallas. A freak storm for this late in the year; though after Luna, weather systems will never surprise her again. Tooley Farm has endured some heavy rains, but nothing like this.

She looks up from the screen at the staff bunched around the interior of Trailer 1. "I'm calling it. We need to evacuate."

Grunts of acknowledgment, some of them less than pleased. But they all know what even a weak F1 would do to Tooley Farm. The twisters this storm is throwing off have been clocked as F2s and F3s, even a possible F4 in the most recent report, with no sign of relenting. They can't possibly stay.

Rain walks outside and calls Joe Garrison in Georgia. Their exchange is brief, barbed, unambiguous. Washington has been looking for a justification to close down the megashelters, to make the Lunas someone else's problem. Mother Nature has just handed them an excuse on a silver platter. Garrison gives her new orders: evacuate the remaining residents to a sports arena in Oklahoma City and await further instructions. Washington is defederalizing this whole thing, he tells her. If the Red Cross wants to keep it going for a while, if private charities and NGOs want to step in, that's their business. But the federal government is pulling out.

The remaining population stands at just under three thousand. Lot of people to move in two hours, but it's better than ten thousand; half a high school, Rain tells herself, remembering that first morning back in August, and at least they have a fortified place to take their IDPs. Butch starts shaking the phone tree. Soon twenty buses are on the way, with dozens more vehicles of various kinds commandeered for the evac.

With the gears cranking along on transport, Rain goes to the intercom. "May I please have your attention. We have a very important announcement." She waits for her residents to rub the sleep from their eyes before going on. "Folks, I know this isn't the kind of news you want to hear at three in the morning. But the National Weather Service reports a major storm system heading our way. There are numerous tornadoes roughly eighty miles to our west. They'll be on top of us in just a few hours. What this means, unfortunately, is we're going to have to evacuate Tooley Farm."

A swell of protest through the trailer's open door. Butch walks in. She holds up an index finger.

"Now I don't want anyone to panic," she continues. "We have plenty of time to get you all out, and we've secured alternative shelter in Oklahoma City. But everyone needs to start packing up. The first transports will leave the Square starting in about half an hour, and we'll be calling you up by quadrant. I promise we'll get you all out safely and securely. Thank you for your cooperation."

She clicks off and looks at Butch. "What's up?"

"We got a bigger problem."

"Bigger than a line of tornadoes?"

"You wouldn't believe."

The look on his face. He leads her outside and over to the gun shed. A guardsman is sprawled against the side, blood streaming down his face as two medics attend to his injuries. Three helmeted soldiers stand before the broken doors, fingers on trigger guards. The padlocks hang loose, the hinge plates ripped from the frame. Inside, the gun racks are in disarray, with some weapons abandoned on the plywood floor, others stacked in random piles against the metal walls. Several of Rain's staff have started to inventory the remaining guns and ammunition.

"They took enough for a small army," Butch says.

"We know who did this yet?" Rain asks.

"I got my suspicions."

So does she. Biggs and Pearson, those dull metallic clinks from the backpack. A crowbar and a hammer is all it would have taken to brain the guard and snap off the door hardware.

With four guardsmen flanking them, Rain and Butch trot up Avenue B3 to the edge of Crackertown. A traffic barrier has been dragged across the way. Nailed to the crossbar, a piece of poster paper.

YOU ARE ENTERING
THE SOVEREIGN TERRITORY OF
THE TOOLEY PATRIOT MILITIA

ALL VISITORS MUST BE ANNOUNCED AND SEARCHED
-TRESPASSERS WILL BE SHOT ON SIGHT-

DEUS VULT

A crude symbol in Magic Marker: an outlined fist raised in the air, the Roman numeral III below the knuckles. Behind the barrier are two men bearing rifles. Biggs and Pearson, together again. Rain squints through the dim light and picks out what looks like a Bushmaster Predator across Pearson's chest. Biggs is carrying something similar. Gone is his old hunting rifle. These are serious guns, with enough rounds to take care of any intruders.

The soldiers fan out, their comms crackling. Rain shows her palms and approaches the barricade. "Mr. Biggs," she calls.

"Ma'am, don't," says the nearest guardsman. She waves him off.

Biggs watches her approach. His nostrils flare. Another two steps.

"Chester. Look," she says. "We have to evacuate this facility. We're calling in the buses, and the whole population is relocating to Okla—"

"Like hell." He shifts his rifle to his left arm. "Like hell we are."

"You're the one who told me to look at the weather, you remember? You were right. It's a bad storm. Anyone who stays here will be in danger."

"Read the sign."

"Your kids, your wife."

"Read the sign, lady. This here's sovereign territory. You get it? We got jurisdiction over Crackertown. It's ours, not yours. We ain't going anywhere. Not again."

"Well, Crackertown is, I can tell you that. Few hours from now this whole place could be gone, just like your hometown."

The reminder of his displacement rattles him. It's a long moment, drawn out by his slow movement to a position within a yard of the barrier. The guardsmen start edging in around her. Rain wants to crush this guy like a bug.

When Biggs finally speaks his voice is low and soft. "We can only take so much shit, you hear me, lady? Only so much. Now y'all move your asses along."

"Leave us be, don't tread on me," says Pearson. Like a motto. He spits in the dirt.

"Let's go," says Butch. Rain follows him back to the Square past the loading buses, out Main Gate, and up the hill to the access road, where the 45th has set up a command post to overlook the encampment and coordinate with the soldiers below.

Down in Crackertown, now moonscaped by the Guard's sodium lights, a dozen strapped men pace the streets, and those are only the ones Rain can see. She thinks back to tactical training, how she would defend a ragged field of tents. Hidden gunmen will be positioned strategically throughout the encampment, caches of ammunition ready to hand. If the National Guard storms Crackertown the outcome won't be in doubt, but there will be unthinkable collateral damage. Tents pierced by stray bullets and a dozen children shot up by Tooley Farm's own security detail. Body bags lined along North Dakota Street. Can't happen.

Though the decision, she understands as she arrives at the command post, is already out of her hands. Staff Sergeant Brothers watches her approach. "How many folks in that neighborhood?" he demands.

Rain looks at Butch.

"I'd guess eighty, ninety at this point," Butch says.

"So we've got a hundred residents and two hundred guns and ten thousand rounds packed into an area the size of a high school football field," Brothers says. "Outstanding."

Hey, you're the big Second Amendment guy, Rain wants to reply, but stays silent. She looks out over Crackertown, trying to channel her rage into sympathy for these diminished men, see them through Butch's eyes, emasculated by circumstance, groping for some measure of control over their precarious existence—though honestly if she had her Sako and a decent scope she'd be tempted to take care of the damn problem herself. For a while she lingers around the command tent as the guard officers and local law enforcement plot their approach. But the evacuation has a dual purpose now, and more urgency. The best thing she can do is keep it running smoothly.

As she starts back toward Main Gate, a news van pulls up near the command post, a CBS affiliate logo plastered on the side.

"Oh hell," she mumbles. Her phone vibrates in her pocket. "Yeah?"

"This is Kyra Blaine with *The Oklahoman*. We're hoping to get your comment on a story we're running tomorrow. Is it true that FEMA is closing down the shelters?"

"I've got no comment."

"Because a source at the agency tells us that—"

Rain disconnects. On the western horizon, a shimmer of lightning cuts the darkness. A text dings in from one of her staffers on an early bus to Oklahoma City. This is heading your way now. An embedded link leads to storm footage from the western part of the state, filmed just before dusk.

Butch looks over her shoulder. "That's the only goddamn SWAT team we'll need," he says with a grunt.

Rain silently agrees. On the screen, a tornadic supercell spawns multiple funnels. The twisters divvy up the sky, three slender fingers braided on the earth.

67.

Mia shivers in her cot with her covers wrapped around her, yawning so hard her jaw hurts. Grandma Flo folds clothes into her roller bag while Oliver stays asleep, or pretends to. The whole shelter is going to a stadium forty-five minutes away.

"Mia, you need to start packing," says her mom.

Mia clutches her pillow, listening to all the neighbors grumble. Will they even *be* neighbors tomorrow, or the next day? It seems insane that they're all just going to *go*, even more impossible than when they left Coral Gables, because at least then Mia was happy to get away from school and the SCBs for a while. And now that Crow Squad has kicked her out—

Wait. She looks around the tent. "Mom, where's Gavin?"

"I have no idea."

"But shouldn't he be packing?" Mia waits. "Mom, shouldn't he pack?"

"Yes, he should."

"So why isn't he? What if he misses the bus?"

"Then he misses the bus. He's an adult."

"But . . ."

"Mia, pack."

She grabs a pair of socks by the side of her cot. A shirt. She folds the shirt and rolls up the socks and sets the balled socks on top of the shirt. She looks over at her brother, still a lump under his blankets.

"Oliver's not packing."

"Oliver, get up," Mom says sharply. He whimpers. Mia shifts on her cot and kicks her brother in the leg. He makes a snarling sound and rolls over. Grandma Flo, kneeling on her cot, stares at two lipsticks in her hands.

Mia asks, "Grandma, do you know where Gavin is?"

Grandma Flo blinks and looks over at Mia. "I'm afraid not, dear. But I'm sure he'll come back in time. As you know, he's having a rough night."

Mom shoots Grandma Flo a mean look. Mia starts to worry that Gavin really won't come back. That he'll miss the bus, maybe on purpose. And Mia will know why: because she tattled. Maybe her mother even kicked him out of the family. He's not her real son anyway. Both his real parents are dead.

Oliver finally gets up. He gathers all his clothes and tosses them in his bag and starts chattering like an annoying little bird about what the stadium will be like and whether there will be basketballs and who will be on their bus to Oklahoma City and Mia just wants to slam her pillow in his stupid face.

She sees herself in the mirrored buckle of her little brother's roller bag. You're worse than a tornado, she tells the ugly distorted girl. You ruin things, you tear things down, you blow things up. You ruin homes and families and you send your friends to jail.

Mia falls back on her cot, pillow over her face, ignoring her mother's whiny pleas. She'll just lie here for a while, thinking about all the happiness she's killed.

68.

The storm rolls in from the west. The worst of it will descend on them in thirty, forty minutes, Butch warns. Rain leans out the bus door. In the split second of a lightning strike she imagines the dark mass, an immense void against the horizon. Cascades of rain drum every exposed surface of Tooley Farm. The evac convoy has shrunk to two buses, a National Guard personnel carrier, the commander's Humvee, and a news van parked askew. Once they're gone this place will be empty for the first time since August.

She slogs back toward Crackertown. The area is still surrounded by the guardsmen, though their numbers have also dwindled. The sodium lights sculpt quavering curtains of the rain. Tents lie sprawled across the ground, collapsed beneath the gusts and pulling on their stakes, waiting for the height of the storm to fly free.

Biggs sees her coming. He hollers something that telegrams up the sodden street. Men come hustling up from the checkpoints, jackets aglisten beneath the waltzing lights. They cluster behind the barricade with their rifles slung across their chests and their hands at the ready on the stocks and trigger guards.

Rain steps forward in the slop. Biggs mirrors her, followed by those behind, all moving toward the barricade in a shifting mass. Muted clink of steel, *chunk-chunk* of a cartridge.

She lofts her arms. "Guys, you don't have to do this," she shouts over the rain.

"Already have," Biggs yells back.

She points over their heads, twirls a finger. "Maybe five miles that way is a tornado a mile wide. You'll die here if you stay."

Biggs dog-shakes rain from his head. "So be it."

"Will you at least let the children go? Think of your son, your daughter. Let us take them."

No one speaks. Biggs raises his arm and gives a hand signal. The group disperses once more, back to stations around Crackertown.

"Go on now," he calls to Rain over the barricade. "We're done here."

She gives him a long look before turning for the buses, half expecting a bullet in her back. What do these guys have to lose? If they stay here they're likely dead. If they shoot her they're certainly dead. Either way this can't end well.

Rain makes it halfway to the Square when she hears the shouts behind her. Through the hammering rain come most of the residents of Crackertown, a straggled huddling line of IDPs flanked by guardsmen, some carrying the smallest children. Mostly women and kids and a handful of the saner men—though not the armed ones. Not Biggs, not Pearson.

At the Square the residents divide between the two buses and soldiers help them on. When the front bus is full Brothers slaps the door to send the vehicle on its way.

"What about the rest of them?" Rain yells.

Brothers shakes his head. "They want to die here that's their problem. We're moving out."

His answer, despite the conditions, pulls her up short.

"We can't leave those men."

She sees a female figure alight from the remaining bus and run in the opposite direction. "Hey! *Hey!*" Rain shouts after her. "Who the hell's that?" But the woman has already disappeared into Staff Camp.

"No idea," Brothers says. "Some random idiot."

Now another resident, a boy, jumps off the same bus and starts running in the opposite direction, back toward Crackertown. This one she recognizes.

"Kyler!" she shouts after Biggs's son. "*Kyler!*" But the boy won't stop.

The situation is cracking apart. Butch leans out the door, signaling. She follows him onto the bus. "How long till it's on top of us?"

Nila, working a laptop in the front row, squints at the screen. "Fifteen minutes, twenty tops."

Butch says, "And who knows which way the bitch'll turn. We need to haul it, Rain."

"Like now," says the driver, scanning his weather app.

Rain pictures Kyler's moon face, that constellation of zits and freckles swirled around his nose. "Give me two minutes. One more try. And see if you can figure out who that woman was."

Butch shakes his jowls. "Rain—"

"Two minutes."

A last sprint to the edge of Crackertown, where the armed group has gathered again at the bottom of the avenue. Biggs shoulders his stock and sights on Rain's chest. She sees the red glow from the scope and looks down. A laser dot quivers on her rib cage. She stares over the barricade at these steaming shells of men.

No one moves—until Kyler steps through the slop to his father's side. Instantly Biggs's face changes. The boy has that way of gentling the man somehow, like a trainer whispering to a foamed-up horse. Rain has seen it before, that day Biggs turned over his guns. Maybe some father-son alchemy can end this thing. Kyler puts his hand on his daddy's sleeve. Biggs is resisting, she can feel the tension in the man's forearm in her own. The barrel tilts down ten degrees, twenty—

Crack!

Current rips the air. Rain reels back blinded, ears ringing with the impact.

Ragged screams, pleas for help. When she stands she sees that six Crackertown men are down, four of them unmoving. A fifth writhes in the mud. Pearson. The others, including a wide-eyed Chester Biggs, cast their weapons aside, throwing the hunks of conducting metal to the ground. Kyler pulls at his father's elbow, urging him away.

The lightning strike has drawn some of the Guard back to the scene but there is no time. The twister. Rain hears the great monster coming, feels it in the small bones of her feet against the ground. Soldiers and residents huddle around the victims. A guard medic starts to administer CPR but two soldiers pull him off as others heft the casualties and huff it for the Square.

They stagger together toward the last bus. Rain's mind reels with shock, her body still lurching with the might of nature, that cruel and arbitrary motherfucker. The great tempest that drove them all here months ago, the menace now driving them away, saving some, killing others. Indiscriminate and miraculous at the same time.

They cross the Square and she catches a glimpse of Chester Biggs. His face a white twist of shock and grief, heavy with the men he's lost, the wages of his idiocy.

Crack!

Another strike, somewhere past the barn. Above them the dangling bulbs pop off, and the lights finally go out on Tooley Farm.

69.

The light cords whip like reins. By the time Daphne enters Staff Camp she is already soaked through. She checks the tents one after another, screaming Gavin's name through the storm.

She finds him in the seventh tent. When the flaps part she sees the body on the cot, and knows. The face glows a ghostly white in the near darkness, open eyes fixed on the tent's roof. A froth between the parted lips, dried foam crusted on the skin. Her stepson sits over the body with his legs crossed, rocking side to side in a catatonic rhythm.

"Gavin." The fabric of the tent muffles the wind. "*Gavin.*"

He looks up, his eyes blank. She shakes his near shoulder. "We need to go, honey. Right now."

She tugs at his arm, at the solid immobile mass of him. She takes his chin and tries to get him to look at her but his eyes are glazed. He has his hands wedged beneath Kaitlyn's back, anchoring himself to the cot with the corpse. Watching her body is a sacred duty, some final stand he has decided to take against the world. He will not leave her.

Then neither will Daphne. She gathers up the lower corners of the sheet and blanket. Wraps the cooled feet, the ankles, the legs.

"Help me," she urges.

Gavin's face contorts and she fears he will strike out, boot her from the tent. That she will have to leave him here after all. But her movements do not pause. Smooth, her bearing respectful and solemn. Nothing frantic, nothing rushed.

Finally Gavin springs into action. He crosses Kaitlyn's arms over her chest and helps Daphne shroud the woman's waist, the torso, the head.

When their work is complete Daphne takes the ankles and Gavin takes the armpits and together they lift. Daphne staggers under the body's weight but rights herself before stepping through the flaps.

They struggle over the first crossing. Lightning flashes to the south, awful and close. A popping sound and the lights go out, the camp plunged into a thick darkness. She thinks of Mia and Oliver in the bus, how she's risking their lives for this. She wants to drop the body and sprint. But they are jogging now, with the heavy corpse bent over the gap between them, and somehow she is finding the needed strength. Up a flooding street, left past Pav3 and Pav1, both billowed and ripped. The gravel squelches beneath their feet. Daphne sees the bus, a ladder of windows dimly lit.

A horrific rumble from the west, like a train bearing down. Now hail, hard balls of it. Daphne, battered, stumbles and almost drops Kaitlyn's feet. Gavin takes more of the body's weight. Together they stagger into the churning mud lake of the Square. When they have splashed halfway across, a brilliant light flashes on, blinding her.

Daphne blinks away the globes in her vision and sees a news crew capturing their progress. A news crew, filming this.

She looks up and sees her children watching from the back of the bus, dark faces pressed to the glass. Rain Holton sprints out to meet them and braces her arms beneath the middle of Kaitlyn's body. Two soldiers help them close the final thirty yards to the bus, where staffers and residents pass the sopping bundle along.

"Go, go, go!" Rain shouts, and soon the driver is accelerating up the hill and through Main Gate and now to the paved surface, away from the yawning storm.

"Bring her here, now," says a man's voice from the back. "Bring her on down here."

Through the streaming blur in her eyes appears Deke, the man from that first awful ride so long ago, now straddling the aisle.

"Put her here for now," Deke says, reaching. "Just put her right here."

Deke takes the feet gently in his hands so his palms cup Kaitlyn's heels and together they lower her to the slickened floor. There are additional victims arrayed head to foot along the aisle, one of them getting CPR from a medic, the others shrouded like Kaitlyn, already gone.

As the bus rumbles forward Daphne huddles with Gavin in a middle seat. Mingled smells of cold and wet, piss and fear, an awful hint of burned flesh. Singed cloth. Whimpers from children but no chatter. Windows steamed. Daphne rubs at the glass with the side of a fist and looks back down at Tooley Farm. A flash of lightning irradiates the churning white of the great pavilions, shredded by the winds. Another burst reveals the ghostly swirl of tents.

In the dark of the bus Gavin sits with his head bowed and his eyes closed, shivering. Daphne puts a hand on his back, and around them the displaced weep and a sad fug rises from bodies slumped in the seats. Up front Rain Holton stands astride the aisle, hunched forward to peer ahead. A silhouette against the windshield, a captain in the prow.

THE GREAT DISPLACEMENT

A DIGITAL CHRONICLE OF THE LUNA MIGRATION

Megashelter and Migration: An Interactive Map

Drawing on data from numerous federal agencies, this resource traces the populations of the eighteen FEMA/Red Cross megashelters from their points of origin pre-Luna to their dispersal across North America in the months following the closing of the shelters. By hovering over one of the geographical sites on the map, users can display IDP itineraries to and from each shelter. Clicking through will display more refined data by dates of arrival and departure, zip code of origin and destination, and other variables.

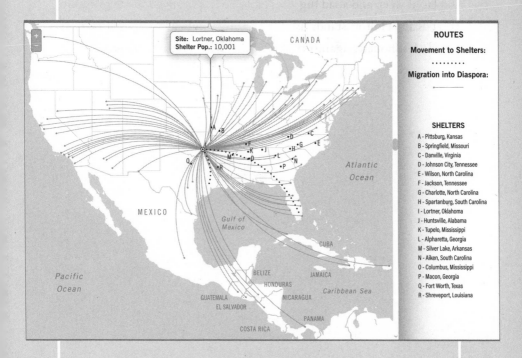

Site: Lortner, Oklahoma
Shelter Pop.: 10,001

ROUTES

Movement to Shelters:
....

Migration into Diaspora:

SHELTERS

A - Pittsburg, Kansas
B - Springfield, Missouri
C - Danville, Virginia
D - Johnson City, Tennessee
E - Wilson, North Carolina
F - Jackson, Tennessee
G - Charlotte, North Carolina
H - Spartanburg, South Carolina
I - Lortner, Oklahoma
J - Huntsville, Alabama
K - Tupelo, Mississippi
L - Alpharetta, Georgia
M - Silver Lake, Arkansas
N - Aiken, South Carolina
O - Columbus, Mississippi
P - Macon, Georgia
Q - Fort Worth, Texas
R - Shreveport, Louisiana

PART FIVE

70.

Section 321, row MM, seat 15 jams up against an apron of concrete with a full view of the basketball arena. The cavernous space rings with that familiar IDP hum, though the National Guard has given way to stadium rent-a-cops, locals in lime-green security vests patrolling the aisles. New volunteers sit at tables on the basketball court and dole out housing vouchers and debit cards. Only the second full day after the concert but already the lines are getting scant.

The finality of it. More and more families are leaving, the good-byes sudden and stark, everything about Tooley Farm fading away: the pavs, the Square, the shower lines, the sharp edges of the place. Even the faces are blurring now, except hers.

Gavin watches the footage for the twentieth time, the clips streamed on his cheap new phone. The chyron: UPROOTED AGAIN: FEMA CAMP EVACUEES NARROWLY ESCAPE TORNADO, SIX DEAD. First the National Guard phalanx and the men of Crackertown emerge from the torrent carrying the victims of the lightning strike, hauling bodies like logs over the splashing mud. And now Gavin and Daphne come stumbling across the Square, their pale faces stark in the rain, Kaitlyn's body suspended between them and the bedding plastered to her lifeless form.

What heroism, the anchor says, to risk their already fragile lives to honor the dead.

A uniformed cop wanders into the arena's main lobby around one, while lunch is being served along the middle concourse. Gavin, waiting for a hotdog, sees the officer talking to Rain Holton, who beckons him over. The cop introduces himself as Officer Nalley and leads him into a conference room off the concourse. When they sit the cop opens his little notebook.

"We're just trying to close the circle on the OD. You mind answering a few questions?"

"Nope," Gavin says. *The OD.* That's what she is now.

"You knew the victim?"

"We were in the band."

"You're the one who found her, after the concert."

Gavin nods.

"Knew her pretty well?"

He shrugs. "Well enough."

"Meaning?"

Gavin looks at a poster over Nalley's head. A gymnast in mid leap off a vault, upside down in that second before sticking the dismount. Her face frozen in concentration. A camera flash in the scoop of her neck. "Well enough to know she was using."

Nalley pulls out an evidence bag. Gavin stares through the plastic at the stack of wildfire, dog-eared and sodden. "You recognize these?"

Like the gymnast he blanks his face. "She took a bunch."

"We found the dealer in his car out off County Line Road this morning. Lot of cash and a boatload of this." Nodding at the tabs. "Shit out of Missouri's been spreading like crazy, no surprise it ended up killing some Lunas."

"You arrested him?"

"He's deceased."

"Oh."

"Wasn't pretty the way they found him. Fella's car got thrown a good hundred yards."

Gavin tries to feel something. "They were both volunteers, from Houston," he manages to say.

"Tragedy all around." Nalley asks a few more questions, then slaps his notebook shut.

"That's it?"

"Just closing the circle," he says again.

"What happens to her now?"

"We've already reached out to her parents up in Minnesota. They'll drive down for her, I guess. That's usually how it goes, if their folks give a damn. Lot of times they don't with the junkies."

"Kaitlyn wasn't a junkie." His voice falters on *junkie*, which comes out as a ragged squeak.

Nalley smirks. "Jessamyn, actually." He thumbs his phone and brings up a picture of her Texas driver's license. Gavin stares at the photo, at the full name, at the date of birth, these raw details of her mystery. He blinks rapidly, about to lose it.

The cop's face softens. "Luna, man, she did something to people. My sister and her husband lived down in Galveston and they lost everything. The house, their jobs. He had a heart attack few weeks back and she's drugged up on something or other, who the hell knows. She says it's prescription. Probably end up on a slab like this gal."

The officer stands, signaling the end of the interview. That's that, then. Gavin has officially gotten away with everything, and he didn't even know her name.

Back in his aerie he sees Daphne standing near the edge of the basketball court, astride the three-point line gazing up. From down there his face must be a smudge against the rafters. She walks off the court and picks her way stair by stair up to the second level and into the third, her upturned face less grim than he's used to lately. Something has changed inside his stepmother, something Gavin is seeing only now.

She slips into the row below his and takes seat 14, turned toward the front with her arms folded. They've talked to each other just once since that night, a quick and incredulous interrogation from Daphne. Did you store drugs in our tent? Have you been using yourself? What were you *thinking*? Her manner in the two days since the evacuation has been detached, almost cold, so unlike the simpering and solicitous Daphne of old, the stepmom who would knock softly at your door and never say a word about your filthy room, would gently remind you to brush your teeth even in a refugee camp.

"A few things," she says, in her new no-bullshit voice.

"Okay."

"I've rented a car for day after tomorrow. We're going back to Florida to get the Odyssey and take care of some things."

Dad's ashes, probably. Daphne can fucking have them.

"Butch found me a job in Sarasota," she says, "one of these set-asides for Lunas. I'll be the caretaker at an apartment complex. It comes with a two-bedroom in one of the units."

He tries to imagine Daphne noodling with a broken lighting fixture or plunging a toilet. She flashes him an upward glance. "Hey, it's a job."

A job. Good for her. This morning Gavin wandered down the boulevard and saw a HELP WANTED sign in the window of a grocery store. Once the fam's gone he'll do a search of his own. FEMA is giving them a full week before everybody gets kicked out.

"About your drug money," she says.

"It's gone."

She turns fully around.

"I put it all in the donation envelopes," he says, "before that big group left for Philadelphia, to be sure they'd find it." Hardly a pure gesture—he didn't want it on him when the police showed up. But still. The cash had been weighing on him. Now he feels unburdened, oddly less criminal. Also poor as fuck.

Daphne lowers her voice. "You gave away *all* that money?"

"Not all." He reaches into his pocket, pulls out a wad of cash, and holds it over the seat.

"What's this?"

"Two hundred. You guys can use it in Florida. Mia's birthday is the twenty-third so you could buy her something from me."

"Or . . . you could give it to her yourself?"

"But I won't be with you guys."

She tilts her head, squints. "Gavin, what on earth are you talking about?"

"Nobody wants a drug dealer around their precious kids. I get it."

The squint turns into a frown, and he sees the realization dawn on her. The bewilderment seems to glow from her face. "Gavin, did you actually think for one minute we would leave you here?"

"I maybe thought . . ."

"You think I'm some kind of monster, like your—" Her lips tighten over the unspoken word, and once again he sees the alteration in her, a new calmness around the edges of her eyes. She turns away and looks down at the court. "We have to split the driving, though. Your grandmother's useless and I'm exhausted."

Gavin makes a wince that turns into a hiccup and then a poorly suppressed sob. Daphne props her elbow on a seat back and rests a hand on his knee. Some time passes before she speaks again.

"I've been thinking about the kind of people I want in my life after this," she says, "and one thing I know for sure is the kind of people I don't. Like Steve with the gun and the hot young girlfriend and the drugs he's afraid to sell himself so he has to find someone more vulnerable to do it for him. Or that Biggs idiot, risking the lives of whole families to save—I don't even know what. It's the selfishness, the lack of caring about the world around them. It reminds me of the pandemic, that piggy look you'd see on the faces of guys walking into convenience stores without masks, breathing in the faces of clerks all day when people were dying by the thousands. Just the weakness in that, you know?"

Has Daphne rehearsed this? Would he be an asshole to ask? Or would a dose of his snark just prove her point?

"Do you remember . . . I'm sorry but do you remember how your father could be sometimes? There was this certain tone he would get with waitresses and flight attendants, or cab drivers. Even his nurses at the hospital. Don't be that person, Gavin. That kind of white man. Please don't. With the world as it is, all of this, we have to be kind, and even when we're too exhausted or broken to care we have to *act* like we do. And you're capable of that, Gavin. I've seen it so many times, the way you are with your siblings, the gentle way you were with those kids at the library. You have gifts you can't see. You're a good, good person. You just are. Anyway."

She stands abruptly, brushing nonexistent dust off her thighs. "We'll talk more later, okay?"

Gavin nods, speechless as Daphne tucks the bills into her waist pack, an ugly Naugahyde thing she fished from the donation bins and now wears buckled around her hips in lieu of a purse.

She catches him eyeing it. "High fashion." She pats the bag. "And less vulnerable to tires."

Later, a young voice wakes him from a snooze.

"Yo."

Gavin slits his eyes open and sees Manny hovering in the aisle. A dozen rows down, Tyrique rides piggyback on Dasia, spurring her hips.

"My sister said I gotta give you this." Manny hands him a book. Dr. Seuss, *The Lorax*.

Gavin hands it back. "Library's closed. She can keep it. Read it to Tyrique on the bus or whatever."

Manny looks down at his sister, who shows him a harsh nod. Back at Gavin. "Can you please just take it?"

"Oh-kay, big guy."

"See you." And the kid quick-steps down the aisle to the staircase. Tyrique looks up and blows him an actual kiss before the three siblings disappear.

Gavin pages listlessly through the book, remembering from some long-ago cuddle in his mother's lap the characters and the story line, the tragic but ultimately redemptive arc. The Grickle-grass, the Once-ler in his Lerkim, the tale of Truffula Trees and the ecological exile of the Lorax—and oh, my children, what we've all done to the trees, the earth, the sky! How unutterably tragic, this Dickensian factory rendering forests of majestic Truffula Trees into these useless truckloads of Thneeds.

But you know what?

He feels it coming, the sunny simplicity of the book's resolution. Look, kids! Don't we want the Lorax to return, the Swomee-Swans to sing again, the Bar-Ba-Loots to frisk again, the Humming Fish to swim again? Well, guess what? *We* have the power! Why, if everyone just plants one Truffula Tree and someone like you just fucking *cares* a little bit we can beat this thing, people! We can retrofit the dozen new coal-burning power plants coming online every year into twenty-acre meccas of solar-powered ingenuity. We can reclaim all that coastline in Bangladesh so sixty-five million climate refugees can finally return to their miraculously unsubmerged hometowns. Who knew that planting a mere Truffula seed would be enough to stem the seemingly inevitable global temperature spike of an apocalyptic three or four degrees?

He's about to toss *The Lorax* over the rows when something different catches his eye. A two-page spread inside the back cover.

A drawing. Dasia's work, he recognizes, intricate with detail and quirks. A tent full of books, its flaps open to the world. Inside, a wide-eyed guy sits on a stool with a book splayed, showing two illustrated pages with a screaming monster on one side, a spatter of blood on the other. Body parts scattered like pottery shards. A dozen kids surround the reader, their faces upturned to take in the gruesome tale.

But their profiles are indistinct, with mere hints of actual features. The person you see in detail is Gavin. His back is straight and his face animated with the story he tells. Dasia has rendered his mouth open and smiling, his free hand gesticulating wildly to match the vivid action on the page (she has even drawn swalloops around his hand indicating motion). Most of all, though, the reader looks happy: rejoicing in the pleasure he's giving these kids, all transfixed in this magical moment created by the teller and his tale.

Gavin stares at the drawing, bedazzled, thinking of what Daphne said about his worth. They're not nothing, these consolations. This knowledge that *someone* out there can still see you this way, as a useful creature, skilled enough to capture and hold attention, capable of giving joy and salving loss, if only for the span of a book. Who needs wildfire when you've got the Scissor Man?

Fuck the Lorax, though. The Once-ler is more Gavin's speed, that dour old guy stuck in his Lerkim and handing out seeds for the Panglossian suckers to plant while he hunkers down in the ruin of it all.

71.

To flush a real toilet again. The circling motion of the water reminds her of the kick wheel back at Tooley Farm, and also of the Luna videos where they speed everything up so you see the hurricane in time lapse as it charges over the ocean and the Gulf. A big wet whorl, but one that Mia can control.

She walks along the concourse past the fancy luxury boxes. Images of Tooley Farm still throb. Lunches in the pavs with the Calels, the sound of Aldina's prayers. That night she stole the apple, and became a Crow. The smell of the fields beyond the fence. So different from the concourse, carpeted and quiet, with hardly a smell at all.

"Fire!" someone yells.

A gush of water hits her face.

Batman leaps out and sprints ahead of her down the concourse. Mia starts to chase him but what's the point, it's just Oliver. Yesterday a store in the city donated a bunch of leftover costumes and water guns and all the little kids have been running around shooting each other even though Halloween was two weeks ago. *So* depressing, and why would anybody think it's a good idea to hand out guns?

At the next opportunity she walks down a level and finds two sisters from Lynx Squad, Tiana and Charlotte, sitting on a broken escalator and giggling over a new phone. They separate so she can pass but instead she sits two steps behind them.

"Is that yours?"

Charlotte nods without looking up. "Moms got us a new Trac."

"My mother says I can't have a phone again until I'm fifteen," Mia says.

"Damn."

Mia leans over and looks at the paused video on the screen. "What are you watching?"

Charlotte hits Play. A gymnast does a routine on the uneven bars. Mia looks more closely and realizes the girl is Tiana.

"You're amazing." Mia tries to square her previous impression of Tiana, a girl who's neither fast nor flexible, with the goddess on the bars. "Were you in the Olympics?"

"Uh-huh. Want to see my floor routine?"

"Sure."

Charlotte swipes to the next video and they watch Tiana tumble across the mat, do cartwheels and handsprings and aerial walkovers galore before taking her bow. In Range she wasn't even a leaper.

"Are you going back to it," Mia asks, "once you're out of here?"

The girls exchange looks and for a second Mia worries she might have offended them, like maybe Tiana had a bad injury. Charlotte snorts, Tiana covers her mouth, and they both start juddering with laughs.

"What?" Mia says, feeling left out. "You guys, *what*?"

Charlotte touches the screen. "It's this new app. You can deepfake any YouTube or TikTok you want."

"Seriously?"

"Here's me kicking this bitch's ass." Charlotte swipes and shows herself in a mixed martial arts fight, dropping a muscle-bound lady with a kick to the head.

"Can I try?"

Charlotte takes a shot of Mia's face and lets her mess around with the app. Mia first turns herself into Ariana Grande singing "Xylophone," then into Bela Zorne scoring in the Women's World Cup, then into

Greta Thunberg making her famous speech to Congress. The glittered pink case, the hot weight of the thing in her palm. She's about to become the president when Charlotte holds out her hand.

"We gotta go," she says.

"Where?"

"Chicago," Tiana says. "My dad's cousin's got a place for us."

"Oh." Reluctantly Mia hands over the phone and watches the sisters walk together down the escalator, their shoulders rubbing the whole time.

"Good luck in Chicago," Mia says. The girls wave and then they're gone.

Mia walks down a level and goes to a railing that overlooks the whole arena. No sign of Oliver. She'll find him though, and he'll pay.

Down below, Tiana and Charlotte stroll across the court bumping elbows. Other kids are scattered around the arena but not in any organized way, not in squads or teams.

On the stadium floor, looking for her mom, she spies Kyler Biggs lurking at the mouth of a tunnel. She steps back behind a banner before he can see her. With his arms folded on his belly he leans against the concrete wall looking bored. Here, at the stadium, Kyler is different. Not a bully or a harasser anymore but a sad sack, Mia's dad would have called him. Deflated like a cheap balloon. Same with his father, who for some reason never got arrested and now spends most of the day slumped in a middle row. Most of the other whites have left, and there's no Crackertown posses to prop them up anymore, just like Gavin doesn't have his drug customers and all the little adoring kids around to make him feel important.

There is a word Mia learned the last week at Tooley Farm, printed on one of the vocab flash cards some mom from Texas found in the school donation bins. CONTRITION. A big and formal word, one a priest or a school principal might use. For days Mia has been chewing on that word, mulling the synonyms printed on the back of the card. REGRET. REMORSE. COMPUNCTION. SELF-CONDEMNATION. Especially GUILT.

She feels all those words now, their sucking force, so strong it can seem as if that force is what pulled the tornado across the plains to Tooley Farm and brought them all here, to this cold, sterile, Rangeless place.

There's only one thing to do. She can't apologize to Luz so she has to apologize to Kyler. She still remembers the way his punches landed on Luz's body, how that rock felt in her hand and how she wanted to slam it through his skull until his brains spilled out. But it's the right thing to do, even if what Mia *wants* to do is climb into Tiana's deepfake app and become someone—*anyone*—else.

She blinks at a movement, the flash of a face. From behind Kyler, Grandma Flo comes shuffling out of the darkness. Her shoes are untied, and just as she passes Kyler one of her feet gets caught in the laces and she sprawls forward, arms out. But before she can hit the floor Kyler catches her, one hand on her shoulder, the other on her waist, and helps her stand again. Mia watches in amazement as he drops to his knees and starts tying Grandma Flo's shoes. When he stands she pats his shoulder and Mia sees her mouth form a *Thank you, young man* before she moves off across the court. Kyler just shrugs.

During all this Mia has come out from behind the banner. The surge of contrition is even stronger now, and she starts to walk toward Kyler, ready to apologize no matter how it makes her feel.

When he sees her the dull look in his eyes sharpens to a glare. His lips curl into a wet snarl, the cords tighten in his neck, and she thinks for a moment he will spring at her, that he will attack.

Instead he puts out his arms and mimes a fishing reel, his right hand spinning the imaginary line to raise the middle finger of his left. He keeps the bird there, rigid and hideous, until Mia turns away, hating him again. She squeezes her eyes shut and exhales. A relief, to have this particular plan thwarted. Luz would *never* apologize to that buttsuck, so neither will she.

She moves off the stadium floor and hears a musical sound. A girl's giggle, high and quick. Mia cocks her head, listening. Another girl, cackling back. They are out on the concourse somewhere, up to something. She turns that way and runs for the laughter.

72.

Again the phone hiccups against her thigh. Today he's finally decided to call back, five times so far.

They were all fleeing north the last time she spoke to her husband. For months that last wobble of his face on Mia's screen has come back in varied forms; a passing thought, a surging fury, a tremble of disgust. But the prospect of actually talking to him touches a chord she barely senses anymore, a tightened string only Brantley's voice could twang.

She looks down at the screen.

+1 502 76236518

Guatemala

She could still make it happen. An ice pick gouging out his eyes, a porcelain pike customized for his severed head and flaunted above the stadium marquee. The Surgeon Series, she'll call it, a celebration of spousal dismemberment. She'll grind his bones to mingle with the clay and make glaze from the lean gristle of his limbs. His flayed skin will make a leather binding for the exhibit catalog.

She picks up the phone. "Hey, Brantley."

A long, recalculating pause. What was he expecting, a sentimental mewl? A gush of wifely glee?

"Daphne," he says, and her name from his mouth has no effect.

"So you're in Guatemala."

"Antigua," he says. "You remember. It's beautiful."

"Mm."

"Daphne, how—how are the kids? How's Gavin?"

Daphne inspects a cuticle.

"I'm working at one of the hospitals," he goes on, "outside the city, but I have a place near *el centro*." She scratches at her knee. "Money goes a long way here. Plus they love American doctors, the training and specialization."

"Ah."

"I told them I'm a refugee from Luna."

"Hey, it's a big diaspora."

"Look." She hears him swallow, imagines the rippling of his skinny neck. "It's unforgivable, what I did."

"You think?"

"I made some mistakes."

"A few."

"I don't know how much you've figured out."

"Not everything." Now the dagger. "But Flo has helped me piece some things together."

A heavy pause. "You've talked to my mom?"

"She's been living in our tent for weeks, Brantley. Until we had to evacuate from our refugee camp."

"Jesus. I didn't think they'd throw her out on the street for a few missed payments."

"You thought wrong."

"It started after the furloughs, right before the move to Miami. I got a tip from a colleague that the Phase 2 trials on this new antiviral were airtight, so I got a home equity loan and—"

"Brantley, stop."

"—and put that and a bunch of our retirement money into the pharma. But the Phase 3s went south after we moved. Then in Miami we bought more house than we could afford, we got those new cars, we wanted a club membership—"

"Stop with the we."

402 · BRUCE HOLSINGER

"Fine. I refinanced our—the Coral Gables house—twice. But I was
barely covering the mortgage payments as it was, and the only thing I
was spending money on was servicing debt. So in the spring I took the
overage and transferred everything to a foreign bank."

"In April."

Again she hears him swallow.

"You planned this, Brantley," she says, surprised she can still be capable of shock. "You'd been planning this for months before Luna."

"You have to understand. I was so embarrassed, so humiliated. How
could I go from associate chief of surgery at a major hospital to a bankrupt schlub? What do I tell my kids? What do I tell my wife?"

"You had money. You had a phone. You had ways to move around.
You had fifty thousand dollars in a Guatemalan bank account, for
God's sake. Fine, you wanted to leave us."

"I didn't—"

"But at least you could have arranged to wire me enough to get your
family settled somewhere else. Yet you abandoned us in the middle of
the worst catastrophe in American history. And then you stole thirteen
thousand dollars of *my* money, couldn't even leave enough to get your
children out of a shelter."

"I took it for our new home, Daphne," he says. "I mean it."

"Our *what?*"

"You could come to Antigua, all of you. We can rebuild our lives
down here. The art culture is insane, Daph, there's a huge expat community, some incredible restaurants, a great bar scene."

To hear his voice again, the snaky confidence in it. The twisted
image of himself he somehow still believes in. An adoring, oblivious
second wife, a son who wanted nothing more than to please him, two
younger children who saw him as a god. He failed all of them. And yet
somehow Daphne is even angrier at herself for not seeing her husband
for whom he truly was. The kind of man who could wreak all this

destruction on his family and still think everyone would jump at the chance to join him in Guatemala.

She watches the second hand on a wall clock above the opposite bleachers, and for the next minute and a half tells him exactly what she thinks of his plan, points out the considerable weaknesses and blind spots of his plan, suggests where in the depths of his lower digestive tract he can shove his plan.

"Can I at least talk to the kids?" he asks when she is done. Petulant but resigned now, defensive. Daphne takes a breath. She has had time to think about this.

"Brantley, they still think their father is dead. They've organized their entire emotional lives around the fact that you're gone. If they learn you've been living in Guatemala all this time cruising bars in *el centro*? God knows how they'd react."

"You can't keep me from talking to Gavin, at least."

True, if Brantley can figure out a way to contact him. But Gavin deserves more. She wants to throw a cloak over his shoulders as a shield.

"You ruined his life, Brantley, far more than you ruined mine. You have no idea. Don't make this worse."

"I just want to talk to him, explain things a little bit. He deserves to know what happened, and why I did what I did. Besides, he's not your son."

"He *is* my son. I didn't abandon him. And I didn't force him to live a lie for half a year about why he dropped out of college."

"He needs his father."

"His father is dead. Besides, Gavin is stronger than you think. I'll tell him and your mother about all this once we're resettled but not before. If they want to talk to you then, it will be their choice."

"Fine."

He's being curt now, clearly hearing the anger in her voice. This conversation needs to end but she can't help herself. She has to know.

"Brantley—how did you get out?"

He has been waiting for the question; maybe they both have. In a flux of words he tells her about the chaos in the hospital, the rush to the airport, the fear of the staff as Luna approached. Then, the airport.

"We were in the medical hangar but the whole evacuation was running late. They were going to let us take off between the outer bands, we were all set to go. But she was too close, the pilots said the winds were impossible, then the control tower grounded us and bugged out with everybody else. By that point nobody wanted to risk going across to the underground shelters in the main terminal. So we stayed by the hangars, everybody found cover where they could. I climbed inside a dumpster with one of the nurses but she couldn't stand the smell. I don't know where she went after that but God, Daphne, once Luna hit I couldn't—half the buildings in the airport ripped up and flying through the air, the walls of the hangar basically Frisbees. The winds rolled the dumpster over the tarmac like it was a milk jug. The trash bags were cushioning me, and kept me from getting crushed against the walls. One of the lids cracked open and I looked out and the medevac plane had its wings sheared, they were just gone and the fuselage was lying on its side. I saw some bodies but I couldn't tell who they were. It was carnage, like a war. Then the winds strengthened even more. It got worse. I was in the air, like Dorothy in *The Wizard of Oz*, the dumpster was actually spinning."

Daphne realizes she has been holding her breath. She lets it out slowly as Brantley continues.

"Then the winds died. One minute I'm flying through the air, the next minute there's this incredible calmness. It was bizarre. So—quiet, so sudden. The sun came out, I even saw this sliver of blue sky. I was wet, exhausted, terrified, still buried in a mound of trash. But alive. So I pushed the bags off me and climbed out of the dumpster. The wind had died. There was no rain, not a drop. Luna was gone, just like that."

She hears his fingers snap and the harsh exit of his breath.

"But she wasn't done. Because I was in her eye. They say it was forty miles across with the strongest wall ever recorded and there I was, standing in the middle of Hurricane Luna with the whole world spinning around me. Everything was so still. It was like being inside one of your vessels, Daph, as if I'd shrunk down to the size of an ant and I'm standing on the base of one of your porcelains before you fire it, with these perfectly symmetrical pale gray walls towering miles and miles up to the bluest sky. Then, at the very top, the edges flare out at the lip of the vase. I saw it all at once, everything, and I was suspended there, alone at the very bottom of the most beautiful, terrifying thing I'll ever see."

His voice gone mystical as he describes the sublimity of the storm, comparing it to her art. Brantley was never close to articulate about her work, has never before captured something of its essence.

Then he ruins this brief illusion, as she knew he would. "I was at the center of the universe, or that's what it felt like," he says. "When the other side of the eye wall got close I climbed back into the dumpster. I somehow knew I was going to be okay, like I was meant to survive that thing. And then, when it was over . . . I just walked away."

A sadness flames up in her, quickly extinguished. Untold destruction and death, his family's sudden destitution—and in the end it's all about this man, his stature, his insignificant life.

"Brantley, you have twenty-four hours to return that money to our joint account."

"What?" he scoffs. "Daphne, let me try to fix this. Let me talk to Gavin, to my mom—"

"I'm sorry, but no. I've thought this out. I'll call the newspapers in Florida and Antigua. I'll call Bettina at your old job. I'll start a GoFundMe to raise money for an international lawyer to come for you. You think any hospital will hire you after that? You'll be an international pariah."

He backs off, tries to smooth things in his Brantley way but she stops listening, and soon his words are a drone in her ear.

73.

Talk about catastrophe. She scans headlines and op-eds and reads about the other megashelters closing down, but the debacle in Oklahoma embodies the worst of it now. With six deaths on its last night, five by lightning strike, one by overdose, Tooley Farm has already devolved into a metaphor, a symbol of everything wrong with disaster relief in this new era of rolling ecological crisis. The nation has to do better, has to find more humane ways to shelter these vast new flows of the displaced—

Rain looks up from her tablet and over the storm-ravaged remains. The barn is gone, the trailers scattered in great shards of aluminum. The pavs, bent and mangled, sprawl like massive parachutes abandoned where they collapsed.

News vans sit at odd angles in the wreckage of the Square. She hovers near a satellite truck and listens to Joe Garrison, just in from D.C., giving an anodyne statement. Plaudits to the FEMA staff for their hard work and the Red Cross for its partnership, the promise of an investigation into the circumstances of this senseless tragedy. As Rain skirts the rank of cameras he flashes her a look that says it all. The investigation will paint a target squarely on her back. She can already feel its itch there, like a fresh tattoo.

Rain walks with Butch out Main Gate and up the rise to the road, to the same spot where she stood while looking down on Tooley Farm that last week of August, at the beginning of it all. Butch throws a big arm over her shoulders. She leans in to gather his warmth.

"This wasn't about saving the coral reefs, Rain. This was about

keeping thousands of miserable Americans alive and fed for a coupla-
three months. You gave these folks ten weeks of shelter, and don't you
ever forget it."

"Not much danger of that."

"Pray with me, Rain."

"Butch—"

"Just fuckin' pray."

He bear-paws her shoulders and she puts her thin fingers on his, and
together they stand on the edge line of the road with their eyes closed
as Butch mumbles a half minute of prayer. When he squeezes her arms
at the end she feels lighter, steeled for what comes next.

Which, as it turns out, will be a lot of nothing. After the press conference Garrison orders her back to region headquarters for a full debrief next week. "Maybe hit the road today," he darkly advises. She
knows better than to push it. She books a red-eye through Dallas to
Atlanta, says goodbye to Butch and the rest of her team, and drives
to Oklahoma City to tie up a few last ends before handing things over
to Nila.

Rain is pushing out to the central lobby of the arena when Daphne
Larsen-Hall comes jogging from the main stairs, calling her name. As
she nears the turnstiles Daphne, breathless, reaches into her tote bag
and pulls out an object wrapped in a black T-shirt. The cloth parts to
reveal a ceramic sculpture covered in a swirled glaze of blue, green, and
aquamarine. The eight tendrils could be the legs of a spider and despite
their rigidity they seem to move, anemone-like, the effect of the single
droopy eye daubed subtly on every tip.

"It's stunning," Rain says, moved. She rubs her fingers along the
ribs.

"I made it years ago, during my MFA." Daphne shows her the ini-
tials and artist's mark carved into the base. *DL*, and between the two
letters the intricate figure of a woman half-transformed into a tree.

"Daphne?" Rain guesses. A story from Greek mythology, she remembers. A naiad or nymph pursued by one of the gods, then transformed into a tree when she calls on the river god to help her.

Daphne nods. "The piece has always been in my studio, so I can see it when I work." She presses it into Rain's hands. "I want you to have it."

Rain's throat is closing up. "I can't accept this, Daphne. It's too much."

"It would mean a lot to me if you did. Please."

She searches Daphne's face and sees the meaning of this exchange. The woman has next to nothing left yet here she is, offering up perhaps her only possession of real value as a simple gift. *Sell the damn thing,* Rain wants to urge. *You're an artist with a growing rep. Use the cash for a down payment on a place wherever you end up, or the first year of your electric bills. Be practical.*

But then she thinks of how Vani would react to the sight of the piece in Rain's condo, the conversations it might provoke. She sees the sculpture on her mantel with a stubby candle on either side, or cuddled in a nest of mini-lights. Herself coming home to this beauty after shrouding the bodies of the burned and the drowned.

"So does my new sculpture have a name?"

"It's called *Sentinel*. But you can call it whatever you want."

"I'll stick with *Sentinel*. I could use some good defense these days."

Daphne beams, tearing up.

"Thank you," Rain says.

"No," Daphne says with a sniffle, "thank you," and after an awkward hug they part.

At the airport a text pops up from Vani asking to FaceTime. Rain waits until she's settled in a quiet corner near her gate with a venti dark roast and the newest *House Beautiful*, purchased at a magazine stand up the concourse. No sense trying to sleep on the flight when she's already preoccupied with the debrief next week. A full-scale investigation of what happened at Tooley Farm, possibly an appearance before a congressional committee in Washington.

She pushes in her earbuds and makes the call with her phone between her knees, feet propped on her carry-on. Vani recounts a recent cycling trip with Leila through the Marin headlands and Sonoma County. It wasn't a pleasure tour, though, to scope seals and sample pinots. Instead they spent the week touring fire-damaged forests, camping in the charred ruins of wineries.

"We met this couple who evacuated from Houston," Vanessa says. "They'd been at this camp in Arkansas, at an old college campus—"

"Silver Lake?" Rain says, naming one of the other closed-down megashelters.

"That's the one. They were only there for a week but it got me thinking about Tooley Farm and what the two sites had in common, but also how different they were. Apparently there was a lot of crime at Silver Lake. Sexual assault, abduction, gang stuff. And that stadium in Tampa sounds like it was worse than Katrina."

"A lot of moving parts."

"Yeah. I've been reading this amazing book on shantytowns, the history of these undocumented landscapes around America. The shantytowns in Central Park, all the Hoovervilles during the Great Depression. The author even mentions FEMA trailer parks and that's when it hit me."

Rain's ears prick up.

"What you did in Tooley Farm, Mama. What all the little tents I was razzing you about must have meant to those people."

Rain glances at a monitor, trying not to cry. Been a lot of trying not to cry today. Her flight boards in a little while and she doesn't want this to end, but soon they say their soft goodbyes. Afterward Rain looks down at her phone, a favorite photo of her daughter laughing up through the app icons. She is stroking the scratched glass with the pad of her thumb when the gate agent announces a delay.

Only a fifteen-minute boarding pause at this point but her connection in Dallas is tight, and if she misses that second flight she won't get home by sunrise, which she planned to watch off her deck at Bougain-Villa with a mug of steaming coffee under her nose, and somehow this is the straw. Her shoulders start to hitch, a heat builds in her chest, and soon she is slathering her magazine and pawing around in her bag for a packet of tissues. She's used up half of them before she calms down and gets a grip, stops making a spectacle of herself. A girl in the opposite row stares at her slack-jawed. Rain stares back until the kid looks away.

Rain opens the magazine and snaps some shots, posts a few odds and ends, but her heart isn't in it, not today. She moves a hand behind her back to massage a pulled muscle at the base of her spine, still tight from that last panicked night at Tooley Farm.

The thought creeps up with the pain, then waves at her, fully formed. *I'm too old for this shit.* But what shit in particular? This is the question. Rescue duty, intense recovery ops. Pulling bodies out of wreckage. She has new clarity on all that. No more.

So what is it she's mourning now, craving to duplicate? Not so much the immensity of the task, nor the unexpected satisfaction of being truly in charge for a while. What she will miss, rather, is the thrill of the little things, the many mundane restitutions she and her staff provided to those thousands of displaced, bereft of the only homes they knew. A basketball hoop here, a kind word there, even a hokey cooking demo by a celebrity chef.

The magazine lies open to a spread on tiny rooms. One of them reminds her of a platform tent. The recognition kicks at something. Maybe Butch was right about what this mission meant to their charges, the men, the women, the children at their game. All those souls they rehomed and kept safe, if only for a little while—

But no. Not all of them. Not even close.

An image of Bembe Calel comes to mind, a loose-limbed kid running around in those knee-high socks, bouncing between tents like a pinball. His big sister, Luz, with her observant way, catlike and wise. Their parents could still be anywhere. Detained, deported. Dead. And here she is fretting about missing a sunrise.

Attention passengers in the gate area. With apologies for the slight delay, we are now ready to begin our preboarding process for Delta Flight 435 with service to Dallas . . .

Rain stops listening, and the magazine falls to the carpet, and despite the alluring pulse of home she knows what's next, what she has to do. DHS is a sprawling bureaucracy of a quarter million employees, with petty rivalries and budgetary sandboxing up and down the org chart. ICE doesn't mess around. Calls will be made. Angry ones. To her superiors. And yet.

She can almost hear Butch on the horn, snipping through the red tape by disguising his scissors as a bouquet of dahlias. The arc of bureaucracy bends toward—what, exactly? She's about to find out.

In Atlanta a neighbor has been watering her plants. A quick text extends the caretaking another week as Rain strides away from the gate, a plan already crystallizing in her mind. On the way back to the terminal she makes the first call.

THE GREAT DISPLACEMENT
A DIGITAL CHRONICLE OF THE LUNA MIGRATION

Itineraries

The narrative maps gathered here re-create the routes taken by displaced individuals and families through the stories and information they chose to share with our team. Clicking on the points of arrival and departure in each map will bring up a variety of resources—photographs, artworks, documents, oral testimonials, and others—speaking to experiences of dislocation and resettlement across the Luna diaspora.

24. The Calels: Flood, Flight, and the Politics of Family Separation

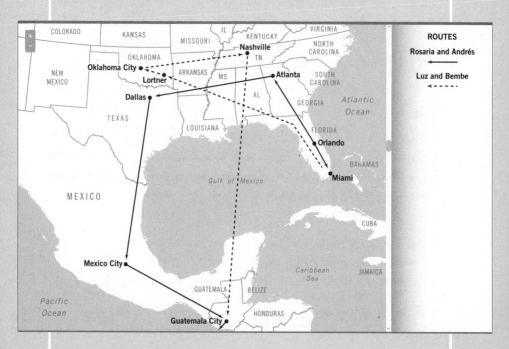

THE GREAT DISPLACEMENT
A DIGITAL CHRONICLE OF THE LUNA MIGRATION

▶ LUZ CALEL, STUDENT

In a hot kitchen in Amatitlán, Guatemala, Rosaria Calel chaperones my exchange with her daughter. While Luz and her brother were evacuated to Tooley Farm in Oklahoma, Rosaria and her husband endured the catastrophic failure of the massive dike system around Lake Okeechobee. Rather than tell her own story, here Luz relates what happened to her parents, who survived the floods only to be detained by GreyCorp mercenaries at the SeaBrite stadium megashelter in Tampa, site of the notorious Black Box incident. Luz was twelve years old when Luna made landfall.

Play audio file:

Transcript:

Bembe still has nightmares about the attic even though he wasn't there. We heard about it from our cousin because Papá and Mamá never told us all that happened. But Mamá won't know the difference because she can't hear anymore and she sucks at reading lips.

Our parents were working a berry farm called Harlsanson's down near Okeelanta. The day before Luna came we were all supposed to leave on three buses. We waited all night, and the buses didn't come, and they didn't come again the next morning. So they loaded two of the mothers and all the kids under sixteen into the farm truck. My tía Aldina was one of the mothers. She had all the phone numbers and drove the truck. Everybody else stayed behind in the main dormitory but it flooded a few hours after the rain started. So they all ran over to the mess building and climbed up to the small dorm on the second floor. They were there for a few hours but then that started flooding, too, because of the lake. So they went up a ladder into the attic.

The attic was really bad, my cousin said. There was only one window but it was small and dirty and you couldn't see out. You had to go in a bucket and by the third day they all started making jokes about eating each other. That's the part that always wakes Bembe up, the idea of eating somebody, or somebody eating him.

But they knew there was a kitchen full of food down on the first floor if they could just get to it. Mamá was the only swimmer so she volunteered. She held her breath and swam down to the kitchen to grab cans and bottles. She had to swim down the ladder and then down a few stairs before she touched the kitchen ceiling and found a food shelf. She made ten trips in three days and brought up four cans of food at a time. Someone had a pocket knife with an attachment so they were able to open the cans.

That's what gave them the idea of how to get out. The waters weren't going down and there wasn't a boat and they couldn't get out of the building so the roof was the only way. But there weren't any tools in the attic. Someone thought of using a knife but the pocket knife was too small. So Mamá swam down again and brought up two big butcher knives from the kitchen. It took her eight separate trips to find them. After the third trip her ears stopped working. She didn't tell Papá she was deaf until the next day.

The men took turns gouging through the wood of the roof. My cousin said the plywood was like cement. It took a whole day but finally they made a hole the size of a fist, then widened it so my cousin could get out because he was the skinniest. He took the longest piss of his life off the roof and saw bodies floating by.

People took turns going up there to wave shirts for when helicopters came, which one finally did on the sixth day. Boats came and got everybody, then they went on prison buses to SeaBrite. The stadium was filled with rescued farmworkers from all over South Florida. Hardly anybody had phones that worked so nobody's parents could get in touch with my tía to tell us they weren't dead.

And it wasn't like Tooley Farm. There weren't pavs or meal times or computers. No one emptied the toilets and there wasn't anything like a band. For food they had to eat powdered rations from the soldiers' supply and there was never enough.

One day a helicopter dropped a big pallet of water bottles and crackers on the field. My cousin, he swore they did it on purpose. For fun, like they were expecting everybody to rush the field and start killing each other like *The Hunger Games*. But instead these Honduran guys took over and handed out the water and the food, first to kids and old and sick people, then to everybody else.

Our parents and my cousin were all in there for five weeks until they finally got taken to a detention center in Georgia. Me and Bembe were at a center in Oklahoma until the lady from Tooley Farm got us out in time for Christmas. She put us all on a plane and flew with us down to Guatemala City. But we didn't see our parents again until April.

Now Papá works in Puerto Quetzal, at Szeto-Zhou Solar. Mamá starts there next month. It's a humongous new Chinese factory down by the port. They built a whole city there with housing for the workers, and the government is giving them

all this land to put panels up in the mountains. Bembe and
me are moving to Szeto-Zhou, too, once they build the school.
They need translators and my English is already fluent and
they're saying I can take Chinese.

Papá says we won't go north ever again because the better
jobs are here now and Szeto-Zhou gives health care. Nobody
wants to be a United Statesian anymore.

THE GREAT DISPLACEMENT

A DIGITAL CHRONICAL OF THE LUNA MIGRATION

The Arts of Displacement: A Virtual Exhibit

The Arts of Displacement captures something of the variety of artistic responses to Luna and its aftermath. The resource combines video, sound, and graphic overlays that allow users to "visit" dozens of works of public and environmental art, from the transformed shoreline of Galveston, Texas, to a sculpture garden in Dubuque, Iowa. By hovering over one of the art bubbles below, users can navigate to each work in turn and explore the range of visual and aesthetic approaches to displacement.

DECO

DEEP ECOLOGICAL
CONTRARIAN ORGANISM

MIAMI BEACH, FLORIDA

▶ **DAPHNE LARSEN, ENVIRONMENTAL ARTIST**

She walks the shore explaining the immense work of self-consuming environmental art she and her collaborators have created at the former site of the Art Deco district of Miami Beach. After spending several months with her family at a FEMA/Red Cross megashelter in rural Oklahoma, she returned to South Florida and now works for a local nonprofit devoted to community activism and urban resilience. Daphne's "living sculpture," *DECO* (for *Deep Ecological Contrarian Organism*), has garnered international praise for its imaginative approach to environmental aesthetics and reclamation. Daphne was forty-two when Luna made landfall.

Play audio file:

I never thought I'd come back. After the evacuation and the
shelter, Florida was the last place I wanted to see again.
We spent those first months in Sarasota but I guess our
curiosity got the better of us. Eventually, once we were
settled, my older son talked me into driving down to see
what we could see. By the time we got to Coral Gables—what
used to be Coral Gables—they were already reclaiming the
coast, piling up the new dunes. There were lots of places
you still couldn't go but we rented a boat and figured out
the GPS and got ourselves pretty much exactly over the site
of our old neighborhood.

Amazing how quickly it all washes away. We had snorkeling gear and did a couple of ventures off the boat. I fantasized about finding some of my pieces but the only thing I recognized was a neighbor's car filled with sand. At least I think it was theirs, it had a Wellesley decal on the rear window. The entire city was becoming an archaeological site before our eyes, like Atlantis.

And that's what sparked the idea for *DECO*, though it took me a few years to wrap my head around the concept. I was waiting tables during the garbage strike and suddenly these mounds of bags started collapsing in on themselves.

You think of the great pieces of public art, the works that have transformed how we think about space, landscape, the environment. Like *The Gates* in Central Park. Or Tyree Guyton's Heidelberg Project in Detroit, where entire city blocks are transformed into new ways of visualizing siding and junk, trees and shrubs. I love the things Krajcberg did in Brazil. The guy spends fifty years living in caves, trees, deploying his art against environmental destruction. It's art that fights back.

Miami Beach is a lot of things that it didn't used to be. It's truly an archipelago now, a part of the Caribbean. Lots of buildings are gone or just rubble, but so many are still standing, in whole or in part. It's illegal to squat here, but the enforcement isn't what it was even a year ago.

For me, though, Miami Beach is above all a canvas, a medium, as if I'm sculpting from the ruins of a dead city. But I'm also wrestling with the popularity the piece has found. Gavin—that's my older son—he likes to tease me about it. He teaches fifth grade up in Saint Pete and got special permission to bring his class down here for an overnight field trip because his mom's the kooky environmental artist behind this thing.

It does unsettle me, all the attention *DECO* has been getting from a certain set. People are starting to come out here on their yachts for canapés and cocktails at sunset, you know, Kip and Bunny sailing down the coast from Vero Beach to gawk at what we've been doing with the remains. I'm being asked to speak at fundraisers, conventions, academic conferences. I've even agreed to give a TED Talk next year. I do worry a lot about the spectacularization of the piece, that its ecological message will be overshadowed by its trendiness.

Because this project is a proposal, too, an argument about our immediate future. The hybrid animals you see to the south, down there by the hotel? They're consumers, at the apex of this new food chain we've created. The idea is they're turning every shingle, every piece of glass, every deck chair, every grain of contaminated sand into these objects of mastication. And their waste is the whole new archipelago as it now exists, this finger of land being shoved back down our throats. A kind of artistic regurgitation of everything we've done, to the earth and air and ocean, to other species, to coral reefs, above all to ourselves.

Because humans? At least as *DECO* imagines the ecosphere, we're at the base of the chain, or we will be soon. Doesn't matter where you live, how rich you are, how invulnerable you imagine yourself to be. This whole thing, it's coming for us.

Afterword

When historians look back . . . .

A phrase we both cling to and mistrust. What confidence do we have that there will even be historians a century from now? How can we know there will be universities left to employ them, or archives left for them to study, or publishers around to disseminate their knowledge? H. G. Wells may have been correct that history is a "race between education and catastrophe." But too much education about climate change seems a dangerous thing indeed. Overwhelming, stupefying, an invisible poison in the air.

The word *resilience* comes from the Latin *resilere*, a verb usually translated as "to bounce back" or "to spring up." Popular symbols of resilience reinforce this sense of the word. The resilient are those who rise from the rubble, dust themselves off, and get right back to work. Plucky Londoners after the Blitz; first responders in the wake of 9/11. Resilience is courage, adaptability, engagement in the world no matter the circumstances.

Yet the verb also translates as "to retract" or "to recoil." A turtle withdrawing its head into its shell, a caterpillar spinning itself into a chrysalis. Resilience isn't simply about bouncing back. It's also about self-protection, about pulling into your shell for a while and keeping up your guard.

One form of resilience, then, is the taking of shelter. In order to survive, we must sometimes go inward, recuperate, strengthen ourselves against what is to come. This is the passive resilience of the burned forest, perhaps, or the suspended resilience of the refugee. Think of the coronavirus pandemic, those years of lockdown and quarantine. Resilience as provisional retreat, as needful pause.

I witnessed this mode of resilience at a megashelter in Oklahoma, where my mother, Lorraine "Rain" Holton, served as director of the joint Red Cross–FEMA facility at Tooley Farm, a great American shantytown if there ever was one. I have come to understand only belatedly all she and her staff did to provide thousands of displaced persons with serviceable shelter, dependable food, and adequate sanitation. When I think of resilience now I think of the children of Tooley Farm, inventing new games to pass the empty time, forming new affiliations that taught them important lessons about others and about themselves.

A powerful source of resilience lies in the stories of others, stories that our team has recorded and transcribed by the hundreds in the years since Luna struck. These stories demonstrate how people from numerous walks of life have coped with displacement and its consequences. They also showcase some of the darker forces pushing against our solutions and even our survival: prejudice, conspiracy, propaganda and untruth, the unending extraction of fossil fuel.

How to account for this variety, these differences? The Middle Ages gave us the notion of the *florilegium*, a collection of written extracts—literally a "gathering of flowers"—that may be perused, enjoyed, admired, or ignored at the reader's pleasure. This botanical metaphor is appropriate for a genre such as a digital chronicle, with its many voices unbound by a single dominant narrative. Or think of this project as a huge tree. Every leaf is someone's unique story, every stem and twig connected to the stories of others, and ultimately to the one great story that we're all living together. Those involved in creating this project had to choose which leaves and petals to feature and which branches to prune.

But the project also encourages accretion and revision. Readers may graft their own stories to redress the oversights inevitable in a digital chronicle such as this: selective, partial, incomplete, riddled with the biases and blind spots of those who do the telling and the compiling. As the cultural experience of climate displacement grows in breadth and depth in the coming years, our species will continue to generate uncountable stories of uprootedness and resilience. The collective story of Hurricane Luna is but one.

When historians look back . . .

There is a profound optimism in this phrase, for it implies that our catastrophic era will be remembered and recorded just as we remember bygone cataclysms: as things of the past, as former threats no longer active. We prefer a more accurate, more conditional conjunction.

If.

If historians look back on our small segment of the Anthropocene, they will know us in large part through the stories we leave behind. They will know the story of how we confronted civilization's greatest threat, and they will know how we found it within ourselves to alter our relentlessly apocalyptic narrative from within. In our stories, they will hear the echoes of our hope, and learn how we survived (or less grandly, as my mother would say, how we managed).

Vanessa Holton
Principal Investigator

74.

So apparently the one thing his dad didn't fuck up is the car insurance. By some miracle the family minivan was never boosted from the side of the road, nor chopped up for parts. His stepmom makes the call from Oklahoma City and locates the Odyssey in a suburb of Tampa where thousands of abandoned cars were hauled after the evacuation. She uses up most of Grandma Flo's FEMA-supplied debit card to get the shattered window replaced and the van cleaned at a body shop near the lot. On the sixth morning after evacuating Tooley Farm, the family crams into a rented sedan and gets on the road.

They drive thirteen hours the first day to a Motel 6 outside Macon, Georgia, where Daphne splurges on two rooms. Mia bunks with Grandma Flo and Oliver sleeps with Daphne, meaning Gavin gets his own bona fide bed for the first time since August. Insane how much you miss the light bounce of a mattress, the cool slide of your skin between industrially laundered sheets.

His brother dozes off while Daphne thumbs her phone and Gavin flicks on CNN. The big news is that the president has approved a new geoengineering scheme to take to the UN. The idea, much discussed in the months since Luna hit, is to spray millions of pounds of sulfate particles from tanker planes into the stratosphere. They want to dim the sun, just maybe keep Greenland from going the way of Glacier National Park. The commentary is all about unintended consequences and butterfly effects. Very desperate. Very last-ditch.

When Mia wakes him up the next morning it's just after eight. They eat breakfast at a Waffle House. Over pancakes he exchanges a déjà vu look with Daphne. Raised eyebrows, nervous smiles.

A morning's drive brings them to Tampa. They drop Daphne at the repair place and return the rental car at the airport, where she meets them at the Budget lot. She hands Gavin the key, then they all climb in the minivan and now here they are, basically right where they started twelve weeks ago. The interior has a mildew smell, from the broken windows and the rain, Daphne explains, though the Odyssey still runs fine, and there's a full tank of gas.

"This is weird," says Oliver, as everyone buckles in.

"I know, right?" says Mia.

"What now?" Oliver puts into words what the rest of them are thinking.

"You'll see," Daphne says cryptically. They have to be in Sarasota tonight but there's a mysterious errand she needs to run on the way. She enters an address on the navigation screen, and a few hours later they're cruising along the coastal highway through the middle of Panacea, Florida.

The town doesn't quite deserve its name, Gavin thinks. Paint store, RV park, a Popeyes with a long line at the drive-through. A mini-mall and a stand selling steamed crawfish. On the last turn he makes a slow bank onto a tree-lined street arched by oak, pine, and palm. Through the bare trunks beyond the modest houses the Gulf waters glint. Gavin pulls to a stop at the curb.

They all climb from the van and stand looking at the house. A low-slung ranch, painted a mustard yellow with aquamarine trim, red highlights on the window shutters, lavender trim over a concrete porch. An ugly kind of beautiful.

"Is this our new house?" Mia asks.

Daphne says, "We're just here for a few minutes."

A waist-high fence runs along the front of the yard. The pickets and rails have been crafted of plastic bottles fused and twisted into three-foot lengths around which blossomed vines tangle and climb. Butter-flies dance among the flowers, bees hover and hum. Two brightly colored birds flap around a feeder. Gavin thinks of a coral reef.

"Why are we at this fairy house, Mom?" Oliver asks.

The front door opens and a dog comes out and stops at the lintel between the tattooed legs of the owner: Roberta Grimes, the same inked-up chick who drove them from Florida to Oklahoma.

"Cricket!" Oliver shouts.

"Cricket! Cricket! Cricket!" Mia screams.

His siblings burst through the gate and Cricket responds with a leap and a howl that sounds like pain. She sprints across the yard, runs through their legs and figure eights everybody, snuffles and licks and jumps. Gavin grabs her sleek body and takes in great heaving gulps of her smell, her perfect rotten breath.

"I see we got a love connection," Roberta jokes. She left Miami-Dade and is now looking for work in the area, so far without success, she tells them in the yard. "Managed to scrape up enough to buy this heap once I knew it was over for me down south. Everything by the water's going cheap these days. To look at me you'd think I was a cat lady but I love birds too much so now it's been dogs, dogs, dogs all the way down. Adopted five from rescue after the evacuation and their owners all came back for 'em. Now it's just me and her." A pause. "Cricket was my favorite, I gotta say."

She has made them a late lunch, Roberta's Famous Six Can Salad. Can of corn, can of garbanzos, can of peas, can of diced tomatoes, can of kidneys, can of green beans, throw some parsley and chopped onions and olive oil in there and you're golden, she says. They eat it with homemade sauerkraut fermented in her garden shed. Roberta's made brownies for dessert, served with a scoop of homemade nondairy ice cream studded with frozen cranberries that gunk up everyone's teeth.

Mom and Grandma Flo feed Roberta polite questions, get her talking about what things have been like in the area. The population has swelled in the months since Luna, but the employment situation is as bad here as anywhere else.

"But there's new jobs coming up around Tallahassee," Roberta tells them. "They're foresting this whole area so I hear there may be ag work. Our little experiment in carbon capture."

A tad optimistic maybe, but Gavin likes the way she says *our*.

"And the dogs have kept me company." Roberta scratches Cricket between the ears, and the dog leans into her thigh. "Swear to God, times coming like they are, we're all going to need a pack."

"We'll muddle through, I suppose," Grandma Flo says.

They've been sitting for less than an hour when Daphne flattens her hands on the table and pushes her chair back. "Well, kids, we should probably get going," she says, businesslike and prissy, as if they've all got orthodontist appointments in Coral Gables. "We need to be in Sarasota by dinnertime to get the keys. Roberta, thank you so much for taking care of Cricket. We've missed her."

Their hostess waves a hand. "Hey, she's a sweet thing, but this is a happy ending for me, you know? Getting these fellas back with their proper families, that's what it's all about."

She says it with a lot of bravado but Gavin notices how her face sags, how swiftly her eyes are blinking, how hard she's trying to keep her shit together in front of the big family that has come to take her last dog.

They process out to the porch, where Roberta insists on hugs all around, and when they reach the van Oliver pulls the handle on the sliding door and calls for Cricket while Daphne pats her thigh. Up on the porch, Cricket circles Roberta's legs, sits on her feet. Circles again, sits.

"Offer her a treat," Roberta suggests. "That'll get her over there. I'll just get a hunk of turkey jerky." She starts to go inside.

"Wait," Gavin says; then, despite almost everything he wants and feels: "Why don't you keep her?"

No one speaks. Roberta sticks her head back out the door.

"Gavin, we can't," Daphne finally says. "Roberta's taken care of Cricket and other dogs for months. She doesn't want our little mutt to be a permanent responsibility." She turns toward the porch. "Do you?" she asks rhetorically, but Gavin hears the doubt in her question, and his heart quails.

Roberta's eyes go wide, she looks almost dazzled by the question, as if someone has told her she won the lottery. "I mean, sure, I love the girl to death, but she's y'all's dog. Shouldn't she go with you?"

Shouldn't she? They rescued her from the kennel, after all, raised her from a puppy, moved her halfway across the country. But then they left her, and who knows if they'll have to do it again. But Roberta won't abandon Cricket no matter what. Hurricane, tornado, earthquake, nuke—Roberta will be there for her, always. Gavin knows it, they all know it, including Roberta.

"Let Cricket decide," Oliver says.

Gavin looks over at his little brother, blown away by the wisdom in that sunburned face. He turns back to the porch and Daphne takes his hand, already forgiving him, again. Together they wait.

The front gate shrinks in the rearview. Part of Gavin expects the dog to come leaping over the fence for a reunion scene, Cricket chasing after the van with her tongue flapping in the wind, Gavin pulling to a stop, Mia and Oliver leaping out, everything in slow motion until they meet in the middle and there's a gauzy ball of kid and fur on somebody's emerald lawn as Daphne and Grandma Flo gaze on approvingly.

Why look! Even the surly college dropout-slash-latterly reformed opi-oid dealer joins in. Swell of violins, sunbeams glinting off hair.

But the gate never opens, and they turn the first corner, and Ro-berta's house is gone. Mia and Oliver cry in the back, tucked under their grandmother's arms.

Gavin lifts his gaze to the scattered clouds, swallowing hard. Techni-cally hurricane season doesn't end for another week. There's still time for another big one to creep up the Panhandle and rip the place to shreds. Or maybe the sky will drop some locusts to chew up all this green.

The crawdad shack appears. Up ahead a Volvo sits on the shoulder, a newish electric sedan with a flattened tire. A man about his father's age stands at the open trunk talking into a phone while a teenage girl kicks gravel out into the road. Strewn unused behind the car: a jack, a wrench, a spare tire. Gavin pulls over twenty yards ahead of them.

"What are you doing?" Daphne says, shaken out of her stupor. He puts the Odyssey in park and gets out. "Gavin—" Slams the door, walks back toward the Volvo. The man has turned away from the car, sputtering at someone on the other end of the line.

"Can't you send the truck now? I've been sitting here for over an hour with my daughter and I—no, that's unacceptable." He gripes on, unaware of Gavin's presence.

The girl gives Gavin a once-over, then gestures with open hands toward the array of equipment on the ground. "Be my guest," she says, sounding bored. A gold spike pierces her septum and her hair is dyed coal black, a frizzed flop on one side, a buzz cut on the other. She looks about fourteen.

Gavin glances at the flattened wheel. He points down at the lug wrench. "You can use that to loosen the bolts."

She wrinkles her nose. "Um, what?"

"You put the socket on the bolt and step on it. Like this." He dem-onstrates with the first one. "You want to do the others?"

She looks over at her father, still ranting and oblivious. She's pretty small so it takes her a minute to get enough force on the kick. But she manages to loosen the other bolts, and Gavin shows her how the jack works to lift the car. By the time her dad's call ends she has the flat off and the spare on and the Volvo lowered back to the pavement. On her own she figures out how to retighten the bolts with the lug wrench.

Her father strides up. "How about that, Mollie," he says with a grating, self-conscious laugh. "We'll make a mechanic of you yet."

Gavin can't even look at the prick. When Mollie's done she stands with her wrists at her hips and the jack handle dangling from her left hand, chin in the air.

"You want to show him?" Gavin asks.

Her mouth twists in a lopsided grin. She reaches for the wrench.

"Actually we need to get back on the road," says her father. "But thanks for your help, young man. Can I give you a tip?" The guy actually pulls out his wallet. Gavin ignores him as Mollie attacks the bolts.

The minivan's doors open and Daphne steps out, followed by his grandmother, then Oliver and Mia. They all walk back to the Volvo, where the father stammers through an embarrassed greeting while Mollie works the flat. Gavin hunches down in the grit, his senses suddenly alive to the clang of a wrench on asphalt, the mineral smell of hot rubber, the greasy spin of a well-oiled bolt and the squeaky turns of the jack, sensations that stir something in what his philosophy prof might have called his soul, though what he's feeling isn't optimism, exactly, let alone hope, but it's a long way up from despair.

He tests this quavering flame inside him and remembers what his grandmother said earlier, at Roberta's. *We'll muddle through.* Nobody gets a medal for just dealing. For coping, managing, getting by. Emerson never wrote an essay about muddling through, and Gavin's father would have sneered at the feebleness of the sentiment. For his dad it was always about achieving, winning, getting promoted and kicking ass, and even when you weren't, pretending you were.

Maybe muddling through is underrated. Because that's basically what the future is now, Gavin sees, a near future of muddling through with your people close around you before that other future arrives from over the charred horizon, an era not so distant now and for many already here, this sharp new way of life.

To the south, a shimmer disturbs the air. Gavin blinks away a flash from above the tree line. A small plane has taken off from a nearby airfield, banking north. Its path parallels the road at first, the fuselage dazzled with light, though soon enough it begins to lift and veer west for the Gulf, heading straight for the scorching yolk.

The older ones are prattling on about potholes, the sorry state of the infrastructure. But Mollie looks up from the lowering tire, Gavin and his siblings crane their necks, too, and together they follow the craft's steady ascent until the glare is too much and the wings vanish, drowning in the sun.

ACKNOWLEDGMENTS

I am deeply grateful to friends, colleagues, and family members who read early drafts and provided invaluable feedback. They include Jabeen Akhtar, Steve Arata, Adrienne Ghaly, Anna Holsinger, Carol Holsinger, Allie Larkin, John Parker, Jim Seitz, Andy Stauffer, and Samantha Wallace.

Brian McNoldy and Dave Nolan of the Department of Atmospheric Sciences at the University of Miami answered numerous questions about hurricane strength, storm surge, wind speed, and the vulnerability of coastal megalopolises in this age of climate collapse; the harrowing scenarios they conjured surpassed even this novelist's tendency toward hyperbole. I am deeply grateful to Kirsten Gelsdorf and others in the disaster relief community for their corrections and guidance. Enormous gratitude as well to Erin Olds and her readers at Salt & Sage for their wisdom, sensitivity, and critical eyes. Alex Gil Fuentes and Beth Mitchell brainstormed with me about the digital humanities project glimpsed at various points throughout the novel. Beth helped conceive the visual designs, while Alex read the entire manuscript with intellectual generosity and a sharp eye for detail. Deep gratitude as well to Sophie Gibson at City Clay for the ceramics lessons, and to Anna Caritj for demonstrating the fine points of the potter's wheel.

A special thanks to Sarah McGrath, Delia Taylor, Alison Fairbrother, Jynne Dilling Martin, Shailyn Tavella, Geoffrey Kloske, and everyone else at Riverhead for making the process of publishing collaborative, transparent, and truly joyful. As always, I am indebted to Helen Heller, my tireless agent, for making it all possible.

I am more grateful than I can say to Campbell and Malcolm, for their humor, honesty, and eternally fresh perspectives on the world; to Anna, for the secret sauce of her ideas, edits, and inspirations; and finally to the beloved Daisy, a rescue beagle who spent thousands of early morning hours curled at my side, who often fought my laptop for attention, and who graced us with her own for the better part of nine years, sweet pup.